Not For Me

Jade Young

To anyone who wishes their man would just *listen*.

I think Harley Wingrove might be the fictional man
you've been searching for.

Contents

IMPORTANT

To anybody who decides to read my story, please keep in mind that while the majority of this story is a lighthearted, rom-com, there are topics that can be triggering for some.

These topics include:

Emotional Heartbreak / Cheating (not between the MC's), Body Image and Weight Loss, Alcohol Use, Life Altering Injury, Sex Intercourse / Foreplay.

If you choose to continue reading my book, I hope you find enjoyment in Cassandra and Harley's story.

Love, Jade.

Playlist

1. Small Things – Jojo

2. All Too Well (10 minute version) (Taylor's Version) – Taylor Swift

3. Tenerife Sea – Ed Sheeran

4. Traitor – Olivia Rodrigo

5. No Scrubs – TLC

6. Fifteen (Taylors Version) – Taylor Swift

7. thank u, next – Ariana Grande

8. September Song – JP Cooper

9. I Was Made For Loving You – Tori Kelly ft Ed Sheeran

10. I'm Yours – Alessia Cara

11. Cheerleader – JP Cooper

12. Latch (Acoustic) – Sam Smith

One

Cassandra

THERE'S SOMETHING SO DEFEATING about spending the eve of a milestone birthday alone, yet, that's exactly what I'm doing. It's nearing midnight on May nineteenth, and I'm curled up on the couch with a spoon and an almost empty tub of choc-fudge brownie ice cream, watching Friends reruns. All the while, feeling sorry for myself. I guess that's what happens when you have a gaping hole inside of your chest. You feel nothing.

You're forced to just...be.

Every year on the weekend that followed May twenty, we celebrated my birthday. Whether we had a gigantic party with our friends and families, or a dinner with just the two of us, we still celebrated. He still wanted to celebrate me.

This year was different, though. This year, we no longer coexisted in the same place that we always had.

Because he left. He took everything I had to give, and he left me behind. It fucking stung.

No one ever talks about what it's like to mourn a relationship. Everyone expects you to get on with life because it's "just a breakup". But you've just lost the person closest to you. Your best friend.

I've had no choice but to come to terms with the fact that I no longer made him happy, and it's inevitable that he's going to move on with somebody else.

I hate it.

How do you live knowing somebody else is someday going to replace you?

You don't.

At least, I don't think anyone would tell me I've been living over the last three weeks. I would call it surviving, and even that's a stretch.

I've been going through the motions since we broke-up and he moved out. My routine now consists of going to work and coming straight home to feel sorry for myself. Some days, I survive on coffee alone. Dinner doesn't even cross my mind unless my best friend, Jenna, forces me to be social. But even then, I'd move my food around on my plate to give the illusion that it at least looks eaten.

I mostly sit and go through photos on my phone, cry into my pillow, or drink an entire bottle of wine until I pass out in bed and the sun rises, ready for me to repeat my day exactly like the last.

He offered to come back and help me pack my things when our apartment eventually sold, but I told him I didn't need or want his help.

I shouldn't be mad at him. He didn't hurt me on purpose, and I know that. But I can't stand the thought of being alone in a room with him for hours, while we pack away everything that once tied us together.

Fourteen years, gone.

Just like that.

Scanning my eyes across our apartment, a hollow feeling washes over me, and I swallow the lump in my throat. All I see is open, empty boxes, ready and waiting to be filled with all of my belongings, and I keep putting it off.

I can't stay in this apartment.

It was our home; the first we shared together. Every corner of this place reminds me of him in some way. Like that photo of us that still sits on the counter, only now, it's face down with the glass shattered.

Heaving my body off the couch, I discard my now-empty ice cream container and I stare at the back of the frame. My fingers find their way to the white wooden edges, and even though I've spent years memorizing the picture, I still turn it over to see his face.

It was a selfie taken at our college graduation, both of us beaming at the camera with our blue caps and gowns on. I used to love this picture.

The color of our gowns made his royal blue eyes all the more intense, but in the best way.

I loved it until I found the frame laying down on the counter, face up, with the glass shattered and a small piece of paper folded beside it.

I can't do this anymore, Cassie. I'm so sorry.

He ended our fourteen-year relationship by writing nine words on a stupid piece of paper. I should have thrown the photo away when I threw out the note. But for some reason, I kept it.

I guess I like to torture myself for some messed up reason.

Wiping away a single tear, I take a deep breath, and throw the photo in the trash, head to the couch, and lay back down.

The constant vibration from my phone next to me tells me it's ticked over to midnight.

I'm officially thirty.

Fantastic.

I can already guess who's calling without looking at the screen, so I don't bother. Sitting up, I turn the volume down on the television and accept the call from my mom.

"Mom, hey." Clearing my throat, I realize those two words are the first words I've spoken since I got home from work this afternoon. I've avoided conversations at work unless they were absolutely essential.

"Hi, honey. Happy birthday," she says with a bright, but soft, voice. She doesn't ever miss a midnight birthday call. She's as cheerful as she is every year, always the first to remind me I'm another year older.

I've never really missed home. That is, until recently. I think part of it is because my mom has done everything in her power to convince me to come back, but there just isn't a lot that Grangewood Creek has to offer me.

My life is here.

My work is here.

I have so many brides depending on me to turn their dream wedding into a reality. I can't just leave them at the most exciting and stressful time of their life. But, as each agonizing day passes, the more tempted I am to say *"fuck it"* and load up a truck with all my belongings and never look back.

Go home, to where my life began, and start again.

"Did I wake you?" she asks, noting my croaky voice, and I clear my throat uncomfortably.

"No, I'm just watching Friends," I respond as I throw a blanket over my bare legs. Roxanne Herring has never appreciated my love for this show. She would much prefer me watch something that sets realistic expectations for how life should be, but considering the very first episode shows Rachel's long-term relationship come to an end, I think it's pretty fitting.

Only, I don't burst through the cafe doors in my wedding dress.

"I hoped you'd be out celebrating." I can hear a hint of something in her voice that I can't quite pinpoint. Sadness is my guess, and going by the sniffle she tries to hide, she all but confirms that I'm right.

"Come on, Mom. Don't do that." She always feels the things my sisters and I do. Sometimes, even deeper. I'm not surprised that my breakup with Austin is hitting her hard, too, but that doesn't mean I need to be guilted or made to feel worse for something out of my control. If it were up to me, he and I would be planning *our* wedding, riding off into the sunset, living happily ever after.

But it's not up to me.

I just wish everyone would let me heal in my own way.

"I'm sorry, honey. I really hate knowing you're all alone while you're going through such a hard time." She sniffles again, but it sounds clearer this time.

"Jenna's trying to convince me to go out. I'm not up for it, though." I shrug, even though she can't see me.

"You should consider it. Getting out of the house might do you some good. Hang out with your friends."

"I am with friends, Mom," I joke, but not even a hint of a smile appears on my face.

"Friends that aren't on a television screen, *Cassandra*," she says, matching my sarcasm out of spite, and we both know it's time to end the call here. "Go get some sleep. And please, will you think about coming home? Even just for a few days. I think you need a change of scenery," she says. Her voice is soft. I can tell she doesn't want to pester me, but she definitely feels that she knows best.

Obviously.

"I will, thanks Mom. Love you."

"Love you too." Taking my phone away from my ear, I check my notifications, but there's nothing from him, and disappointment crashes over me, knocking down any wall I'd temporarily built.

He beat my mom to it once in the last fourteen years, and he reminded her of it the whole day.

I beat you, Roxy. Fair and square. Get used to it.

He bragged about it so much. Mom would roll her eyes and smirk at me as she nudged my shoulder with hers but that was the first and the last time.

My phone pings multiple times in a row, and I see my younger twin sisters' names light up the screen.

> **Lizzie**: Happy birthday, bitch face. Love you. Come home soon.

> **Olive:** Happy birthday, Cass. Miss you. Wish we could celebrate with you.

> **Lizzie:** Maybe you can celebrate by getting under someone else.

> **Lizzie:** Some new dick could do you some good.

> **Olive:** Lizzie! Shut it, will you? Seriously though, Cass, when you're up for it, will you let me write about your breakup? My note-

books are itching to be filled with heart-break songs.

Lizzie: Stop being so boring, Ol. Get your own heart broken, and write about that. Love you, Cass.

Olive: Love you, Cass.

Me: Ha ha, very funny. Sure, go ahead, Ol. But I'm with Lizzie. Get your own heart broken if you want something juicy to write about. Love you both.

Olive: Hard no from me. Thanks though.

Chuckling to myself —a real chuckle— I somehow find the courage to peel my body off the couch, force myself to go to bed, close my eyes, and let sleep take me away.

For the first time in three weeks, I don't sob myself to sleep.

That's progress, I think.

***

The sound of banging on my apartment door shoots through my ears, forcing me upright, leaving me frazzled, confused, and pissed.

"What the hell?"

Groaning, I rip off my eye mask and blink away the blur. There's only one person in their right mind who would knock like a damn mad woman at nine in the morning.

On a Saturday, none the less.

Grunting, I throw my feet over the side of the bed, shoving my white, fluffy slippers on one by one, before making my way to my front door. The banging continues, but it doesn't quicken my steps.

"Hurry up, you old bitch," I hear Jenna's voice shout from the other side of the door. It blends with the sound of her fist pounding against it, and I've never longed for silence more in my entire life.

"What a pleasant surprise," I say sarcastically and I rip the door open and away from her invading knuckles. Rolling my eyes, I cross my arms over my chest and glare at my best friend. She looks a lot more put together than I do.

Her long, blonde hair is down in waves, while my brown hair is in a messy bun. Her soft, blue eyes pop, thanks to her oversized black t-shirt and light blue jeans that hug her thick thighs, while my hazel eyes are no doubt puffy and bright red, and my grey t-shirt is covered in wine and ice cream stains.

"Here. I got you this," she says, handing me a large cup of coffee as she shoves my body out of the way to make herself comfortable in my home. I guess I don't mind that she's here. Apparently, I craved coffee and company today, even though I'd never admit it.

"I've bought enough to make us your birthday breakfast," she says, slamming grocery bags down on my counter tops as I slowly make my way to join her.

"Thanks," I mumble in between sips of the magical cup of liquid gold that I cling to for dear life.

"Why are you here?" I ask.

I know *why* she's here.

But I don't understand *why she's here*.

"It's your birthday, silly. Of course, I'm here. I have big plans for you today, *Miss Herring.* " She winks at me while emptying the contents of her shopping trip all over my countertops.

"I'll only agree if it involves my couch, bed, TV, or wine."

"You've done nothing but watch bad TV on your couch, or in bed, for the last three weeks, Cassandra. Give me one day to celebrate you. Once your birthday is over, you can go back to feeling sorry for yourself. I'll even buy you a wine subscription box."

She's annoyed at me, and I get it.

She wants what's best for me.

I just wish she thought the couch and a tub of ice cream were what I'd needed.

But if I know Jennifer Rogers like I know I do, this day is going to be large, and I have no choice but to go along with it.

So, instead of putting up a fight, I roll my eyes and help her unpack enough food to feed a family of six as she prepares the feast.

Two
Cassandra

"I KNOW YOU DIDN'T want to leave the house today, but for what it's worth, I'm glad you did. I really wanted to spoil my best friend," Jenna says.

I hear the sincerity in her voice before I see it written all over her face, and it makes me feel guilty. I don't want to be here, and I think we both know it, but it doesn't stop her from trying.

"You spoiled me enough today already with your beautiful gift," I reply, bringing my hand up to my collarbone to touch my new necklace. It's a simple, gold chain, with a cursive *C* and a small, but visible, emerald stone attached to it.

My birth stone, and my favorite color.

"Not to mention, the feast you prepared for us this morning, too." I sigh. Even though I couldn't possibly fit any more food in, my mouth is still salivating as I remember the pancakes, the bacon, the eggs (fried, scrambled, and poached), the waffles, and the smoothies she blended, too. I hadn't eaten a proper meal in weeks until this morning.

I feel like I've gained back some of the weight I've no doubt lost in the last few weeks.

We had spent what felt like hours walking through Manor Mall, and even though I'm in sneakers, my feet are starting to burn. Jenna convinced me that we both needed a massage, so that was our first stop this morning.

I hate to admit it, but she was right.

We've been in about six different dress stores, too, and nothing has caught Jenna's eye.

"Oooh, let's see if there's anything in here," she says, clasping my hand in hers, pulling me into a store called Minko.

It looks expensive and way out of my budget, I won't deny it. But It doesn't stop my eyes from wandering, even though I have no events coming up that would even warrant a gown like these.

"This dress would look fucking incredible on you, C." Jenna's voice catches my attention from the other side of the store. The dress she holds out for me is floor length, deep, royal blue in color, and the softest looking velvet I've ever seen, with spaghetti straps and a hanging neckline to complete the dress.

"You never know when you're going to need a dress like this." She wiggles her eyebrows at me, and I can't help but grin.

"I have no events coming up." I shrug as I take it off her to hang back on the rack.

"Come *on*, C, just try it on. Humor me," she insists, and so I do.

Once I close the curtain to the change room, I shimmy out of my light blue jeans, pull my white singlet over my head, and slip the dress on.

It's too big, practically swimming on me.

"Can you pass me a smaller size, Jen? The sizing in this store is way off," I shout over the curtain.

Lie.

The sizing is right. I've just lost a lot more weight than I care to admit, especially out loud.

I haven't allowed myself to look in a mirror since he left. I didn't want to see a shell of myself looking back.

So rather than feel the weight of my own shame, I stopped looking in mirrors all together.

Out of sight, out of mind and all that.

Growing up, I was the tomboy of the family. I wasn't on the cheer team or dance team like Lizzie, and I didn't care for music the way Olive does. I rarely wore makeup or dresses. I preferred to be outside with my dad, getting my hands dirty.

Doing things like shopping for elegant dresses, buying expensive makeup, and getting my nails done were all things I'd only done as I'd gotten older.

Jewelry isn't something I loved to wear, either. I still forget most days, even now. Though, when I do, I try to keep it simple.

"You should wear the dress to Megan's wedding," Jenna says as she hands me a deep, emerald green version of the dress in a smaller size.

"I'm not going as a guest anymore, remember? I'm only going to be there because it's my job as her wedding planner," I reply, doing up the zip on the side of the dress.

Megan is Austin's sister, and we were really close while he and I were together. But now it just feels...weird. She seems a little distant, and I get it.

She and I decided together that I would only be in attendance as the wedding planner and not a guest.

Don't get me wrong, I'm happy that she's getting her happily ever after. I just don't think I could sit in the same room with Austin and come out of it alive.

"I'll buy both the green and the blue," I say to my best friend as she waits patiently for me to put my clothes back on.

"Yay!" she squeals, taking the dresses off the hook, heading straight to the counter.

"Is there anything you would like to do today?" Jenna asks as we walk mindlessly through the mall.

"Yes, actually. Can you squeeze me in for an appointment? I want to go back to my original color." Jenna is a hair stylist. One of the best in California. I have appointments with her every six weeks because Austin liked my hair lighter, so it needed to be constantly maintained. But now that he no longer has a say, I want my natural color back.

"Hmm, we don't have time for that, I'm afraid," she says, her voice oozing with sarcasm.

"Well then, what's next on your to-do list? Please tell me it includes going back home to bed?"

"Just a couple more things, then we can go back to your apartment and have a quick nap."

"Coffee first?"

"Absolutely."

As promised, she buys my now third coffee of the morning, takes me back home and we both pass out on my bed.

***

BARP BARP BARP BARP

Why do I keep getting rudely awoken today by loud noises?

And what the hell is that noise?

Groaning, I slide off my eye mask to see Jenna fumbling frantically as she searches for her phone on my bedside table to shut up the horrendous sound of the foghorn blaring through the speakers.

"Why is that the sound of your alarm?" I cover my ears to soften the blow, scrunch up my nose, and squeeze my eyes shut.

"Because I'm a heavy sleeper. No other sound wakes me," she croaks as she rests her back against the headboard of my bed while we both appreciate the silence that now fills the room.

"Why do you have an alarm set?" Forcing myself upright, I lean against the headboard and rest my head on her shoulder, stifling a yawn behind my hand.

"Less questions, more movement. In the shower, Herring. Chop chop, let's go."

She's awfully cheery as she rips my body off the bed while attempting to shove me into my bathroom, but my feet remain firmly planted on the ground. "I can get there myself. Relax, will you?" I shake her arms off me, watching as she raises her hands up in defeat.

Before heading to the shower, I make a pit stop at my underwear drawer in search of a clean matching set, while she hisses from behind me. "I'm going, I'm going," I mumble under my breath as I slam the door shut to give myself some privacy, and this time, I force my eyes to the mirror.

I stare at myself, longer than I did in the change-room at Minko, and tears pool in my eyes.

I don't think my collarbone has ever been as prominent as it is in this moment.

I hadn't noticed the extent of my regrowth earlier, either.

My brown roots are more visible under the natural light that my bathroom gives off, compared to the lights in Manor Mall. My hazel eyes have the darkest circles I've ever seen; I'm surprised Jenna let me be seen next to her.

I look like a malnourished zombie.

I put my health on the back burner, forgetting to make sure I wasn't burning out.

Whoever this person is staring back at me, I don't like her.

I don't even *know* her.

I hope she doesn't stick around.

Running my hand through my matted hair, I step into the shower, and let the scorching water spill over my entire body, relaxing under the stream.

"C, the girls from the salon are here. As usual, Tahnee will do your makeup while Margot does your hair."

Her voice is loud and commanding like the boss she is, as she helps her colleagues set up their products and equipment.

Everything is beginning to make sense.

Of course, she had this planned for me. I should have known.

Jenna owns her own salon, which means she has employees at her disposal for every occasion.

She is the stylist in California that everyone wants. Celebrities are lining up out the door, but her pre-booked clients always take precedence.

Reluctantly, I sit and smile while allowing the girls to work their magic, hoping they can restore me to my former self, even if it's temporary. I'll take even the slightest resemblance.

"What's all this for, anyway?" My eyes remain closed as Tahnee applies my makeup and Margot fiddles with my hair from behind me. They've given me strict instructions to not move a muscle and I oblige, as usual.

Jenna's team has done my hair and makeup for countless events, so I am well-versed in the rules.

Their movements stop in sync as the words come out of my mouth, and Jenna clears her throat before she answers my question.

If I didn't already know Jenna was up to something, I do now.

"I figured we could use a night out on the town. It just *happens* to be your birthday." I can hear the smile in her voice when she drags out her sentence.

To be fair, all Jenna has been trying to do over the last few weeks is distract, distract, distract. Like any best friend would do after your fiancé dumps you with a note. But I haven't really let her. I wanted to wallow in self-pity, and my kind of misery doesn't like company, so I didn't let her even try. I shut down any attempt by giving her excuse after excuse.

I think she got over asking, because eventually she just...stopped.

Until today.

Scanning my appearance in the mirror, Tahnee has done an amazing job hiding the dark circles under my eyes, and Margot has not only de-matted my hair, but she sprayed it temporarily back to my original shade, leaving me with fresh, bouncy waves that sit perfectly below my shoulders.

Giving myself a soft smile, I make my way toward my bedroom to find that Jenna has already laid out one of the two gowns that I'd bought earlier today. She chose the royal blue option.

The color of Austin's eyes.

Cursing my subconscious, I put the dress back on its hanger, swap it for the emerald green one, and let out a sigh of relief.

I clasp my new, gold chain around my neck, so it doesn't look bare, and my left hand feels suddenly empty. My stomach is in knots.

My eyes flick to the black, velvet jewelry box that's lived on my vanity for the last few weeks. A ring I wore every day with pride, but took off the day he left.

Opening the box, my heart thunders against my ribcage as I stare at a thick, silver band paired with a clear, teardrop cut diamond.

Simple, but elegant.

Gold had always been my go-to whenever I bought myself jewelry. I felt it always suited my skin tone nicer than silver. But I wore my engagement ring every single day because of what it meant to me, and who it came from.

But now... now I couldn't think of anything worse than being engaged ever again. The thought alone makes me cringe.

I remember the moment Austin proposed to me so vividly. Despite my wish for a private proposal, he made a grand, romantic gesture in front of our families on Christmas day. He always did whatever he wanted. I guess I should have expected him to do things his own way when he proposed to me.

"Are you ready?" Jenna's voice snaps me out of my trip down memory lane, forcing me back to reality. I slam the box shut and quickly place it back down on my vanity. Blinking rapidly, I stop the tears that threaten to ruin my makeup before I turn to face her.

"Ready," I say, forcing a smile.

"You chose the green?" She raises a brow, conveying her disappointment, but she quickly recovers.

"The blue reminded me of..." I don't have to finish my sentence for her to know exactly what I was going to say.

"You look beautiful either way."

"Thanks. So do you." My smile turns genuine as I admire her.

A high, wavy ponytail holds her blonde hair up, while her lips are coated with a deep, red lipstick and the perfect jet-black, large wing to make her soft, blue eyes pop. Huge silver hoops standout against her tight, black dress.

It compliments her curves perfectly.

Jenna has an hourglass figure—the type rich people pay for. But she's hated it for as long as I'd known her.

I, however, think she looks incredible.

"I've booked that new Spanish restaurant in town. Once we finish dinner, we'll go for drinks," Jenna says, closing my apartment door behind us as we head out of my apartment building.

The sun is still setting as we walk hand in hand down the busy streets of L. A, and I slow down our pace to take in the beauty.

This place has been my home for all of my adult life, and I've never really appreciated it for all that it is.

Returning to my hometown would have to be temporary. I couldn't trade in my window view of the ocean for small town living, where the closest bed of water is a dirty creek, could I?

No, I don't think I could.

Though, it hasn't stopped mom's pleas from constantly ringing in my head.

Do I really want to leave a job I love, for a job I could hate?

Or no job at all?

Would I seriously consider leaving my best friend behind to go back to a place where the only people I have left are my parents and sisters? I don't think I could.

Sabrosa, the new Spanish restaurant on the main strip, is just a few blocks from my apartment.

Austin and I would walk past it often, and I would always beg for us to go together, but he was always busy with work or complained that he didn't like Spanish food.

I could guarantee he had never actually tried it before, but he liked to argue with me, so I learned to stop asking.

A dark-haired girl wearing a white blouse and black pants greets us at the door of the restaurant.

"Reservation for two, under Jenna," my best friend says to Isabel, our hostess, while my eyes wander around the room, taking in its beautiful decor. The walls are a deep red with soft, yellow accents. The chairs are velvet red to match. I feel like I've stepped into luxury.

"Right this way."

She leads us through the busy crowd of people enjoying their drinks and food, until the sound of conversation quiets down and we're walking down a hallway. My stomach falls to my feet as we approach red, double doors, suddenly completely devoid of people eating.

Why aren't we being seated with everyone else?

Where exactly are we going?

The dress, the hair, the makeup.

Before I can even question her, she murmurs four words, "Please don't hate me," right as the crowd shouts one:

"Surprise!"

Three
Cassandra

THE SOUND IS EAR-SPLITTING.

And overwhelming.

Yet, I try my absolute hardest to appear fine.

Slapping a smile across my face, I step into the room, thanking anyone who approaches me to wish me a happy birthday with the most high-pitched voice I can will my vocal chords to do.

Everyone is here.

My parents traveled from Grangewood Creek, along with my two sisters, Lizzie and Olive, even though my mom made me feel guilty about spending the day alone.

My co-workers, Janelle and Frankie, are here, too, and the way this party is styled tells me they had everything to do with the planning.

Cousins from both sides of the family, uncles, aunties, and even some old friends from college dot the room as well.

I only really stayed in touch with Jenna from my college days, but it's nice to see their faces.

I don't expect anyone from high school to be here, so I'm not surprised when I don't see them. My eyes involuntarily scan the room for the one person who's been with me through it all, even though I know I won't find him.

Of course, he's not here.

Why would he be?

I'm nothing to him anymore, and if that wasn't already abundantly clear, it is now.

Fourteen years together, and I can't even get a simple text that says *"Happy Birthday, Cassandra"*.

Some guests are worried about my well-being, constantly asking how I'm doing, while others don't bother to even greet me and head straight for the open bar.

Hell, even I'm here for the open bar.

The room is stunning, and the canapé's look mouth-watering. I may not get to eat my body weight in Spanish food, my stomach will be satisfied, and that's all I could ask for.

If people weren't aware that this was a surprise party for a party planner, they would assume I planned it myself.

The decorations are in my signature white and gold. There's big three and zero balloons paired next to each other, along with a collage of photos from the last thirty years of my life.

I guess my colleagues know me well.

The photo collage covers an entire wall. Photos of me as a baby and a toddler with my parents. Photos with my younger sisters. Photos of my high school best friend, Bea, and I, even a photo of myself, Bea, and Harley, which surprises me the most.

Austin is noticeably absent from that photo. From all the photos, actually.

Even the photos I know he's in, he's been cut out of.

Finding Jenna amongst the crowd, I pull her into a corner to get her alone.

"Are you having fun?" she yells over the loud bass vibrating through every inch of the venue.

"Would you believe me if I said yes?" My voice remaining monotone. She shakes her head in response.

"I'm sorry. I'm trying," I assure her. "How did you pull this off, anyway?" It's my turn to speak over the music. My poor ears are going to be ringing tomorrow.

"I had nothing to do with it." She shrugs as she places the tip of a paper straw between her dark red lips.

"What are you talking about?"

"Don't be mad, C. Austin's been working on this for months. He planned everything with the help of Frankie and Janelle. He handed me the reins a couple of days ago with instructions on getting you here on time, but that's all."

He did this.

"Is he coming?" I ask, hopeful, but I know my hope is wasted when she shakes her head in response.

"He wanted to, but I told him no. It's too soon, and I didn't think it was a good idea. Please don't hate me." She squeezes my forearm as an apology.

She only wants what's best for me, and I know she has nothing but good intentions. I also know she made the right call, but it doesn't make it sting any less.

I don't want to dwell on something I can't change.

I chug the rest of my drink in the hopes it numbs the pain.

"Hey honey," my mom's sister says as she pulls me in for an embrace.

"Hi, Aunt Elly," I say as I reciprocate the hug.

"Happy birthday. Are you enjoying yourself?" Her face softens as she reaches for my hand, and I know she's concerned about me, but she doesn't want to pry. I want to respond with, "tonight fucking sucks, and I wish I never left my bedroom", but I don't.

I choose to smile and nod while taking a sip of my drink and decide not to linger, excusing myself while I head to the restroom for a breather.

Resting my hands on the sink in front of me, I close my eyes and will myself to take deep breaths.

It's how I've gotten through the last three weeks whenever I'm in an unwanted public setting.

Inhale, hold for three seconds, and exhale for three seconds.

I'm only able to repeat the words to myself twice before a voice to my right interrupts. "You look like you're having a rough night," he says. His voice is deep, and it startles me.

"You could say that," I reply, because my mom raised me to be polite, but I don't turn to face him. I keep my eyes closed and try to not give him any attention.

Drawing one last breath, I run my hands down the front of my dress to smoothen it out.

"This might be forward, but do you want to get out of here?" And now he has all of my attention, which is precisely what he wanted.

"Excuse me?"

Do I seem like the type to go home with a random guy from a bar? Because I'm not.

I've only ever been with one man in my life.

I'm a relationship kind of girl, not a one-night stand kind of girl.

That isn't about to change just because I met a very, very hot, random stranger in a public bathroom.

Is it?

No, Cassandra.

He's tall, probably just hitting six feet. His hair and eyes are dark, eyelids hooded while he wears a devious smirk, making him appear broody, yet mischievous.

He's wearing a navy-blue button-up shirt with rolled-up sleeves, showing off his drool-worthy forearms.

They're covered in tattoos, but even the tattoos aren't enough to hide the veins.

Maybe I can be the one-night stand type of girl, just once.

But I can't just leave my birthday party, can I?

No, Cassandra.

"I'll be out here if you change your mind." He winks and closes the door behind him.

Taking one final, deep breath, I find the courage to head back to the party, where I make my way straight for the bar.

"Two shots of vodka, please," I say to the bartender.

At that moment, I make a promise to enjoy myself. Because the people here deserve the best version of me.

I won't be a negative nelly.

Not tonight.

I accept every drink handed to me, dance until my feet hurt, and take pictures until I'm too intoxicated to walk and my poor father has to carry me home.

Four
Cassandra

THIS LAST MONTH HAS been absolute chaos. I haven't had a chance to even scratch my head.

Somehow, I've planned three bridal teas, four engagement parties, and two weddings. Including the wedding of my ex-sister-in-law, Megan. And the day is finally upon us.

Has it been easy?

God, *no*.

But I made it work.

I've avoided thinking about my ex-boyfriend or even saying his name. When he needed to be mentioned during the final touches of wedding planning, Megan would refer to him as 'my brother,' and his mom, Angela, would say 'my son.'

I appreciated it.

He's a groomsman, so I expected to hear about him in some capacity.

"Is there anything left to do for tomorrow?" my colleague, Janelle, asks, poking her head through my open office door.

Her jet-black hair is slicked back in a tight ponytail, and her dark eyes appear as exhausted as I feel.

"I don't think so."

The vendors Megan had chosen were ones we used regularly. They're top choices for most of our clients, so we're accustomed to each other's expectations. It made the show easier to run.

"There is something I need your help with tomorrow, though," I whisper as I usher her into my office, closing the door behind her.

"Whatever you need."

Janelle and I have been friends and colleagues for the last few years, so I know I can trust her with the last minute...*task*.

"I need you to be on Austin watch. This stupid engagement ring is burning a hole in my vanity, and tomorrow is my last chance to give it back to him."

"Do you want me to be the one to give it to him? I can be stealthy." She wiggles her eyebrows, my grin genuine.

I know Janelle. She's never shied away from confrontation, and I know she's been itching to confront Austin and ask him what the fuck he was thinking—her exact words—so I know better than to let her at him.

"No, I got it," I say, running through the rest of my fool proof plan with her.

Turning everything off in my office, I head home for the night to emotionally prepare to see Austin in less than twenty-four hours.

I'm a nervous wreck, but he won't get the best of me.

Once I showered and brushed my teeth, I curled up into bed and allowed my mind to play through every potential scenario.

Will he want to get back together? *No.*

Will he get on his hands and knees and beg for forgiveness, telling me he made a mistake? He's never been one to admit that he's wrong, so also no.

Will I end the night inconsolable? *Probably*.

Will I let him see my tears? *Hell no.*

***

"The only thing left to do is make sure the men are dressed and the rings are secure. Did you want me to do that?" Janelle asks, knowing that the last place I want to be is with the Groom and his men, so I nod, and she takes off to do what I'm not brave enough to.

Megan asked me this morning if I still felt comfortable running the show, or if Janelle was going to take over. She assured me she didn't mind. She almost pushed for it. But I've always kept my personal life and professional life separate, and that's what I intended to do today.

Plus, I had an ulterior motive to being here, too.

Taking the black, velvet box out of my purse, I admire the ring just one more time.

"Austin, what are you doing?" Shaking hands, I force a smile on my face, feeling the weight of every pair of eyes on us.

The Christmas lights are shining; presents galore under the tree. It's the most wonderful time of the year, and I suddenly don't feel so wonderful. I feel sick.

Of course, I knew I wanted to marry him, but I had always hinted that if he were to propose, it should just be the two of us. It would mean more to me that way. I've never been one to enjoy attention from crowds.

"What do you say, Cassandra Herring? Will you marry me?" His royal blue eyes were sparkling as he looked up at me. I couldn't tell if he had tears in them or if it was just the reflection of the lights.

"I-yes! Of course, I will marry you." Planting a soft kiss on his lips, I kneel at his level before he takes the beautiful, silver band with the teardrop diamond out from the box and slides it down my ring finger.

"I love you, Cassandra," he whispers, turning our kiss slightly deeper, before the eruption of cheers rips us back to reality.

Snapping the lid shut, I blink hard to force any leftover tears to fall and shove the box back in my purse.

"It's go time," Janelle says before we head toward the Bride and her bridesmaids as they step out of their limo.

The sight of Megan sends a rush through me, and I can't tell if it's jealousy or excitement. Either way, I push it to the side and focus on my job.

"How are you feeling?" I ask as she fiddles with the ribbon around her bouquet of all white roses.

"Excited." She smiles so bright, it takes over her entire face.

Her appearance is strikingly similar to her brother's, though her eyes are dark green, like their fathers, whereas Austin gets his blue eyes from their mom.

Her chestnut hair sits in a low bun at the nape of her neck. Thick straps from her plain, ivory, silk dress, sits on her shoulders, dress hugging her body like a second skin, with the train pooling at her feet, hiding her hot pink, open-toe shoes.

"Let me give your hair one quick spray and you're ready to go," Jenna insists, giving her work its final touch up.

"Remember. Shoulders back, bouquet low, back straight, and eyes on Elliot," I remind Megan one last time as she takes a deep breath and her bottom lip trembles.

"Eyes on Elliot. Got it," she repeats, smiling at me through her teary eyes. I pull her veil over her face, while Jenna ensures the clip doesn't move.

Megan and Elliot have been together for four years, so I've known their relationship from the beginning. They're polar opposite, yet couldn't be more perfect for each other. She's loud and the life of the party. He's socially awkward and quiet, but his whole face lights up whenever she's in the room.

She brings him out of his shell, and he brings her back down to Earth. The perfect dynamic.

Lining her bridesmaids up in order, I signal to Janelle, who starts Megan's chosen song while the girls prepare to walk down the aisle.

Ed Sheeran's Tenerife Sea plays, and I keep my composure while watching Megan hug her father, Max, one last time before she becomes Mrs. Elliot O'Neil.

Every guest rises from their seat, watching as the Bride slowly makes her way down the aisle. Elliot doesn't even attempt to hide his emotion as his tears slide freely down his cheeks for everyone to see.

They spoke their vows with clarity and certainty, as they cling to each other. Love, joy, and admiration written all over their faces when the celebrant pronounces them husband and wife, allowing Elliot to kiss his now bride.

Standing on the sidelines, I watch as they make their way back down the aisle, while their bridal party follows. I can feel Austin's eyes on me as he walks past, but I don't look in his direction.

Heading toward the reception venue, I make sure everything is ready for the celebration, while Janelle takes care of the group photos and making sure everyone knows where to go.

Guests arrive and take their seats seamlessly, while I have a ball in the pit of my stomach growing heavier by the second.

Tonight is my last chance to get rid of this ring, once and for all.

Even though I'll miss his family, I hope to never see an Anderson again.

It's better that way.

Formalities are almost done, and I'm nearly off the clock.

Which means it's officially Abort Ring time.

Janelle alerts me that speeches are ending, and the wedding is about to get loud. The first dance is about to follow, and I have instructed the entire bridal party to join the Bride and Groom for the final chorus.

With my nerves settling in, I sneak off to the bathroom for a final pep talk, black box in tow.

"Are you okay?" I hear from an unfamiliar voice as she washes her hands in the vanity beside me.

She's beautiful. A petite redhead, wearing a tight, grey, sequined dress, with a small, barely visible pregnancy bump displayed.

"Just hoping to avoid a confrontation with my ex." I nod and chuckle at how pathetic I sound.

"I know what that's like. I'm so glad I've found my person." She smiles while rubbing her belly and I'm hit with a wave of jealousy.

He changed his mind, so he set me free.

"How far along are you?" I ask to distract myself.

"I'm only fourteen weeks. My boyfriend hopes it's twin boys, even though all of our scans have shown one healthy baby." Her hand never leaves her stomach as she speaks. "He told me he wants a house full of boys so we can have our own football team. He doesn't even play the damn sport anymore." She chuckles and rolls her eyes playfully.

"How did you know he was your person?" I ask, watching her intently. She hesitates, but only briefly, before answering my question with complete confidence.

"He listens. He pays attention to the little things. He asks me about my day and always puts me, and now our baby, first. Even after three years, I still get butterflies when he walks in the room." She pauses to reapply her nude lipstick before placing it back in her purse.

"We did long distance for a while. I lived in Charlotte up until about two months ago, but now we live together and it's everything." Her cheeks a soft shade of pink as she gushes about the life she's created for herself.

"Are you engaged?" I ask, feeling the weight of the velvet box in my hand.

"Not yet. Soon, I hope. Anyway, I'm going to find him to dance with me before my feet swell up. Good luck avoiding confrontation," she says, drying her hands on a paper towel, and I watch as the door swings shut behind her.

Am I making a mistake?

Should I give the ring back?

Snap out of it, Cassandra.

In my ear, I can hear Janelle's voice telling me it's go time.

It's now or never.

Megan and Elliot are dancing to *Get Low*, with the rest of the wedding following suit, and I spot Austin alone at the bar.

It's time to make my move.

Head down, I speed walk as discreetly as possible, making my way to the bridal table where Austin's suit jacket hangs over the back of his chair. Slipping the black box into the pocket on the inside, I sigh with relief, knowing I've successfully achieved what I set out to do.

I attempt to walk away, but I don't quite make it when I feel the familiar warmth of his hand on my shoulder.

"Cass?" His word slurs, and my knees buckle. I haven't seen him since the night before I found the stupid note on our countertop. He looks different. Tired, maybe, but just as handsome as ever.

His light brown hair is longer than usual; it makes him look kind of rugged, but it suits him.

His blue eyes are red rimmed, no doubt from his alcohol consumption, but he seems happy.

And his lips.

God, those perfect, kissable lips.

"Austin. Hi." I clear my throat. "I was just, uh, returning something," I say quickly, desperately searching the room for my savior in the shape of Janelle, but she's nowhere to be seen.

"Returning what?" he questions, but before I can answer, I see a hand around his waist.

"Baby, come and dance with me. My feet are starting to hurt, and I want to dance with my baby daddy while I still can," a soft voice says, and my ex-fiancè's body stiffens.

All the blood draining from his face.

What?

"Uh, Cass. This is Alison. My...girlfriend. Alison, this is—" He struggles to find the right word to describe me and our connection, so I do it for him.

"The wedding planner," I say.

She's none the wiser.

Alison, the pregnant redhead from the bathroom, who told me all about her incredible boyfriend, who she'd been with for the last *three fucking years*?

"Oh, hi! We met in the toilets just now. Still trying to avoid your ex-boyfriend?" She smiles, wiggling her brows at me, wrapping herself in Austin's arms, oblivious to the tension thick in the air.

"Something like that. Now, if you'll excuse me, I have a plane to catch." The words sprint through the gates of my mouth before I can stop them, and I rush toward the double doors to the foyer of the venue.

I'm getting the hell out of here.

Running down the hallway, I burst through my office door, collecting my purse from my office. I message Janelle to tell her I've left while I hurry back to my car.

The quicker I leave, the better.

"Cass." His voice stops me in my tracks, just five steps away from my car.

Five.

Tiny.

Steps.

"Cass, would you wait a minute? Let me explain," he pleads.

"Explain what, Austin?" I step closer to him. "That you've had a whole fucking girlfriend for the last three years? A girlfriend who is fucking pregnant with your child? You proposed to me with that stupid ring, while fucking someone else?" His face burns with guilt and embarrassment.

"God, I'm so fucking stupid." I take a deep breath. "I don't need an explanation or your bullshit excuses, Austin. I just need you to be gone from my life."

Frantically, I search my purse for my keys and open my car door, but he holds it firm before I can slam it shut.

"I didn't mean for this to happen, Cassandra. Please, you have to believe me." His voice cracks as he speaks.

"Fuck you, Austin."

How could I not see it?

He knew I would see her tonight at his sister's wedding, so why would he even consider bringing her? Megan wouldn't allow him to bring a stranger to her wedding, unless...

"Your family. How long have they known?" His expression blank, before dipping his head between his shoulders, releasing my car door from his grip.

No wonder Megan tried to push for me to let Janelle take over.

They fucking *know* her.

I feel sick.

I saw the Anderson family as my own for the last fourteen years, and now, they're all nothing to me.

"Goodbye, Austin. I hope she makes you happy," I say as Alison walks out, wearing the same jacket I just disposed of my engagement ring in.

"Alison, check the pocket on the inside. I think there might be a gift for you. Sorry to ruin your surprise, Austin." I give the best fake smile I can, feeling extra petty as I cackle to myself. Hopping in my car, leaving Austin Anderson and his elated new fiancé in my rear-view mirror.

I pull out my phone out as I open my front door to send Jenna an S.O.S., and within thirty minutes, she's beating the door down.

Her signature move.

Five
Cassandra Age 21

"WHAT'S THIS?" I ASK Austin when he slides a blue box across the table. We've just finished eating lunch at Frenchies diner to kill time before our afternoon classes start.

Graduation is coming up, and we've been with each other every step of the way. Knowing that it's all ending feels so surreal.

"Open it," he insists, nudging it across the table. His blue eyes are gleaming with mischief, his smile like an excited kid on Christmas morning.

Hands shaking, I slowly reach for the box in front of me, hoping that it's not what I think it is. Butterflies swarm my stomach, and not the good kind.

The box is small. Small enough to house an engagement ring. After all, it is Tiffany blue, so it's not as though I have no reason to assume the box's contents.

I want to marry this man someday. It's the one thing I'm sure of. But the thought of there being an engagement ring inside this box makes me want to fake an emergency and run out the door.

"What are you waiting for?" His voice sounds mildly irritated, growing impatient with me taking my time, his fingers drumming on the table.

Opening the box, I see a silver, thin, chain necklace with an infinity symbol and a matching ring to complete the set.

"This is beautiful, Austin," I say, trying to pretend I'm not jumping for joy internally. Removing the ring from the box, he slides it down the ring finger on my right hand before standing from his side of the booth to stand behind me.

He hovers for a moment, tracing his fingertips down the curve of my neck before clasping my new silver necklace onto its new home.

"What's the occasion?" I gush as he sits back down in front of me while I trace the infinity symbol as it rests on my collarbone.

"So you remember that this," he gestures between us, "is forever," he says, giving me his best boyish grin.

He's never been one for big, romantic gestures, so whenever he does things like this, or buys me flowers, or even compliments me, it makes me feel slightly uneasy.

It's almost like he's doing it for a reason.

"I love it. And I love you." I smile.

My heart has never been so full and conflicted. I'm so ready for what the future has in store for us.

"You ready to get out of here?" He offers his hand, and I take it with a spring in my step, pushing away any negative thoughts that decided to rule my mind temporarily.

We haven't even been inside his apartment for a minute before he drags me past his roommate, Monty, without so much as a hello, and we head straight for his bedroom.

So, this is why he bought me jewelry.

Sex.

He doesn't need to buy my love. I'm not with him for his family's money and he knows that.

They have a lot of it. His father, Max Anderson, is still the biggest name to come out of the NFL, and he hasn't played in decades. Yet sometimes, Austin likes to show me—remind me—that we will be taken care of for life.

No matter what.

His bedroom door slams behind us and he nudges me onto the bed, where I land on my back.

Watching as he quickly unzips his jeans, they pool around his feet and he practically leaps, landing on top of me.

Pressing his lips onto mine, he kisses me once, twice, three times while he slides the condom down the length of him, lathers himself up with lube, and slides inside of me.

It doesn't take him long before he's out of breath, pulling the condom off himself and disposing of it in the bin next to his bed.

"I'm going to play video games with the boys. You can stay, but I won't be able to hear you," he says as he stands, placing a headset over his ears.

I no longer have an ounce of his attention.

This is the price I pay for accepting expensive, unwanted gifts, I guess.

Six

Cassandra

"THERE'S A FLIGHT BACK to Grangewood first thing in the morning. I'll arrange for the movers to come and collect everything from the apartment as soon as I can."

Jenna's been typing and scrolling frantically on her laptop since the second she got here, while I've spent every second filling the biggest suitcase I could find.

She and I met when I was in college. She was looking for a housemate and I didn't want to live in the dorms, so I responded to her ad. We've been inseparable since. I would be completely lost without her friendship.

"Have you packed enough clothes to get you by?" she says, slamming her laptop shut, eyeing me cautiously.

Going by her current outfit, you can tell she jumped straight out of bed and rushed right over to my apartment the moment she got my text.

A black, fluffy robe tied up around her waist, her black, old lady slippers hugging her feet, and her hair is in a messy bun on top of her head.

"I've packed my whole wardrobe and the entire contents of my bathroom," I say breathlessly, rummaging through my belongings to see if there's anything else I need.

But there isn't.

The apartment sold two weeks ago, and the settlement is next month.

The moment I accepted the offer, Jenna came over and helped me pack my life away into boxes, with the intention of putting everything into storage. We decided I would live with her, like old times, until I found myself a new place to live. But after tonight, California is the last place I want to be.

Everything I am, and everything I have, is about to be shipped and heading to a new place to call home—the very first place I ever lived.

Grangewood Creek.

"I don't think I want to come back," I accidentally say out loud, instantly regretting it. Not because I didn't mean the words that I said, but because I didn't want to see how Jenna would react to hearing them.

I expected her to be angry. Sad, even. But instead, she reaches her hand out to mine and squeezes it, giving me a reassuring smile.

Sometimes I feel like I've found my soulmate in this lifetime, and she is it. She knows I can't be here anymore and need time to just...figure out my life.

Start again.

She doesn't fight me on it. She doesn't beg for me to stay or try to change my mind, because she knows how important it is that I leave.

"I'll be back for your birthday party, though. Hell, I'll be back whenever you need me. Just say the word, and I'm on the first flight over," I say, and she chuckles, wiping a tear away from her makeup-free face.

I need distance from this place. It holds way too many memories for me to just forget and move on.

"You know, I would understand if you couldn't come to my birthday. I sent invites while you and Austin were together. There's a chance he'll show up, even though I'm going to tell him to not bother," she says.

"If he knows what's best for everyone, he wouldn't even consider it." I shrug.

He's clearly moved on. Way earlier than I'd even realized. It's time for me to do the same. I'm just glad I found out about it before it was too late.

Before I was the one carrying his child, forced to be stuck with him forever.

***

It's been a while since I've travelled back home. I'd forgotten how long the journey took.

When I'd fly back, I'd usually have company and it would flash by.

But this time, I was alone.

Thankfully, I loaded up my Kindle and kept my mind preoccupied with fictional men and love stories destined to end in a happily ever after.

My phone has been on aeroplane mode for the last four hours, so the second it's switched back on, the vibrating is non-stop.

I have text messages from Jenna telling me that my belongings will all be arriving within the week; texts from my parents, telling me they're at the baggage claim waiting for me; and texts from my sisters, telling me to be ready for wine.

I had four text messages from Austin too, but I deleted those without reading them and blocked his number.

"Hey, Mom. Hi, Dad," I say, as they pull me in for a tight hug.

God, I needed this. A hug from my parents always felt like a warm cup of hot chocolate on a Christmas morning.

Fucking *Christmas.*

"I have one rule while I'm here," I say to my parents as we load the car with my luggage.

"Hit us," dad replies, slamming the trunk shut.

"No one is to mention that man's name. He is ancient history, and I'm here to focus on myself. If any of you know any suitable candidates to take me on dates, I'm ready and willing." I'm partly joking, but the other part of me wants to eventually try dating.

Are there any eligible bachelors in Grangewood?

Will anyone here be able to sweep me off my feet?

Doubtful.

I've never even been on a real date before.

The type where you're not officially dating, but still getting to know each other.

The type where you ponder what to wear, nervous about what he'll think.

Where he picks you up at your front door and knocks instead of texting "*here*".

Where butterflies swarm your stomach the moment you lock eyes over the dinner table.

I want to go on a date *like that.*

Or, you know, any type of date will do.

I refuse to let my story end with my heart in a million pieces.

Am I ready to fall in love again?

Absolutely not.

I haven't fallen out of it yet.

Just thinking about it makes me feel violently ill. But getting back out there may not be the worst thing.

"You know, they've turned the old Maxwell farm into a winery estate. It's been completely knocked down and rebuilt from the ground up. They kept the old barn and turned it into a lovely space for weddings. Mrs. Bishop says they're on the lookout for a new event planner. Maybe you should pop in there and pay them a visit," mom says casually, looking out her window, as we drive through the quiet suburban streets.

Of course, Mrs. Bishop, the town's self-proclaimed gossip queen, has already informed my mom of a potential job.

Finding a new job isn't a priority at the moment.

I called my boss, Frankie, on the way home from Megan's wedding, told her about everything that had happened, and that I would be quitting immediately. She didn't take it well, and I understood why.

As my friend, she was supportive and knew I was doing what I had to do, but as my boss, she wasn't thrilled to be losing the best event planner in L. A.

As my parents' car pulls into the driveway, I'm met with a 'Welcome Home' sign displayed in the front windows, making my insides feel all warm and fuzzy. Our house I grew up in is your typical, small town, family home, and I love that there aren't any traces of change.

My mom still has her rose garden out the front, and the light blue swing is still in the same spot it always had been on the white wrap-around porch.

Dad's beat-up red truck still sits in the driveway, even though it doesn't start. He claims it's his 'next project', but I don't even think he has a current project that he's working on.

Stepping out of the car, I breathe in an unparalleled freshness that California air just doesn't have. It smells like freshly cut grass and blooming flowers, with no hint of an ocean breeze anywhere.

Opening the front door, mom has obviously spent all morning baking when the smell of fresh, chocolate chip cookies smothers my senses.

The one smell that always reminds me of home.

That, and the smell of the same vanilla coconut candle that she has burning all year round.

The old, blue and white checked couches sit across from each other with a worn, ragged, white throw blanket on top.

The burnt out, electric stove top and oven that somehow still works, and miraculously hasn't set the house on fire, is no doubt still warm from the cookies.

"I'm going to put my bags away and get dressed before the girls get here," I tell my parents as I head for the stairs.

Our yearly school photos hang up on the wall attached to the staircase, with each photo getting older the higher up the steps you get.

Lizzie and Olive's bedrooms are across from each other's, while mine is further down the hall.

Walking past their rooms, I'm hit with flashbacks of what feels like a past life. A life I'd all but forgotten about.

We all loved our own space, but we weren't lucky enough to have our own bathrooms, and we fought over the one we did have like crazy. Come nightfall, we were always bunking in each other's rooms, having slumber parties.

Mom always found us curled up in one of our three bedrooms. Two on the bed and one on the floor, just how we liked it.

We alternated rooms every single night, though, so the same person wasn't on the floor each time. It was the only way to avoid arguments.

Reaching my bedroom, I step inside and close the door behind me, dropping my bags to the floor.

Changing out of my comfy travel clothes, I opt for a casual black t-shirt dress that bunches up at the waist, with a pair of black sandals.

It's about as fancy as you can get in Grangewood Creek. I might even be a little overdressed.

Nothing about my bedroom has changed.

I've been back home a handful of times since I left for college, but we mostly stayed at the Anderson mansion because it was bigger. Austin's family could afford an NFL salary-type home, and he refused to stay anywhere else. He was used to living in luxury.

Today is the first time I'm really able to sit in my room and just take it all in.

Cautiously, I approach my study desk to see photos taped to every blank surface. Photos of myself with my high school friends; ex-boyfriend included. Most of the pictures are of my then-best friend, Bea, and I, but a lot have Austin and his best friend, Harley, too.

Well, his ex-best friend.

Bea and I, posing the night before our first ever hangover, on the bleachers while we watched Austin and Harley play football.

The four of us, smiling after they'd won an important game.

Harley was *hot* when we were younger. He had wavy, golden hair that he kept short on the sides, with emerald green eyes, a razor sharp jaw, and naturally pink, plump lips that I used to daydream about.

My stomach would always swarm with butterflies whenever he was nearby. Almost as if my body could sense whenever he was close, before my eyes even spotted him.

I used to paint the number *one* on my cheek, because my crush on Harley was major when I was fifteen, and Bea painted the number ten, so Austin wouldn't feel left out.

Austin wanted to wear the number one—regardless of the rules—because he claimed to be the best, but their coach assigned that jersey to Harley, because he was the quarterback.

Much to Austin's disapproval.

He would constantly pull the "do you know who my father is?" card, but Coach Gerard didn't care.

He cared about stats and facts.

And Harley's stats spoke for themselves. He was the best player on the team, and everyone knew it.

Even Max Anderson would come to games just to watch Harley, because he was so damn impressive. Especially for a high-school kid. But Austin didn't care enough to try harder, even though it was in his blood.

He refused to be like his dad.

When Austin asked me to prom, I hesitated before saying yes. I wanted Harley to ask me, but he was so focused on football that he showed no genuine interest in me, or anyone, so I agreed to go with Austin instead.

The pair were inseparable for years, but their relationship went from best friends to enemies in the blink of an eye, and because I was Austin's girlfriend, I automatically gravitated toward him and lost touch with Harley, too.

I don't think me and Harley spoke a single word to each other the whole of senior year.

Rummaging through my drawers, I find a pair of scissors and cut Austin out of any photos that I managed to find. If I'm planning on moving on and forgetting about him, I don't need to see his smug face everywhere I turn, and that includes photos of our teenage selves.

I keep the ones of Bea and Harley, though, and make a mental note to somehow find out what they're up to.

"Cass?" I hear my sisters calling my name in unison from downstairs. In a hurry, I bolt down to meet their open arms.

Lizzie is wearing a pastel blue, knee-high dress with her long, brown hair half-up, half-down, while Olive is sporting a white, floral, maxi dress, with her short, brown hair sitting dead straight, just above her shoulders.

Although we didn't always get along, I've felt overly protective of my baby sisters for their whole lives. They're only three years younger than me, but I'll always be the one they turn to.

Once we all finished high school and matured, we grew closer, no matter the distance.

Sure, we shared rooms as kids, but that's because at night time, all our problems vanished. We were each others safety nets.

The moment we woke up, though, it was like World War III, and those mornings made old man Hank wish he had three sons instead.

Do we still fight? *Absolutely.*

Do we apologize if we need to? Not always, but we get over it and move on.

There is nothing I wouldn't do for Olive and Lizzie. Nothing they wouldn't do for me, either.

"Get your purse," Lizzie insists before our hug has even finished.

"Where are we going?" I don't know why I ask, given the text I received earlier. I knew they were planning on getting me drunk, and there's only one place in town where everyone goes to do exactly that.

"Bridie's!" they both shout, each pulling at an arm, dragging me out of the house.

Seven

Cassandra

My sisters both moved away for college, and came back home once they'd graduated. Now, they share a small apartment across town, closer to their work.

Even though they're twins, they couldn't be more different if they tried.

While they both teach at the school here in town, Olive teaches English and music to high school students, and Lizzie teaches kindergarteners.

She's loud and carefree, with a lot of energy, and Olive is quiet and reserved.

Physically, though, we all have dark brown hair and hazel eyes, and used to get mistaken for triplets when we were younger. It didn't help that our parents dressed us alike.

Bridie's has been Grangewood's only pub for forever. It's, apparently, under new management, but from the outside, it still looks the same, with the giant, neon orange B still flashing like the wiring is somewhat faulty.

My friends and I used to come here after school all the time, so this place holds a lot of memories for me.

"Mom mentioned that the old Maxwell farm has been renovated. What's it like?" I ask as we pull into the gravel parking lot of the pub. I have enough savings to get me by, thanks to the sale of the apartment in California, but ideally, I would prefer to add to it rather than drain it.

While I don't need a job, I wouldn't say no if the job was the right fit.

Especially at a winery. Could you imagine the wedding photos that would be captured at a place like that?

"Oh, it's stunning. The new owner did an amazing job with all the renovations. Actually, I think you went to school with the guy who bought it. He's super rich now, and spared no expense. They kept the old barn and flipped it completely, so now it's a huge, rustic ball room. I haven't been to see it yet, but the photos online look beautiful," Olive says casually as she turns off the ignition to her hatchback.

"You forgot to say super rich and *super hot*." Lizzie giggles to herself, reapplying her clear lip gloss in the sun visor mirror.

"Mom said they need a new event planner. You'd be perfect for it," Olive continues, encouraging me, while simultaneously ignoring her twin.

We're both used to Lizzie's crude comments, so none of us bat an eyelid.

Mom must've gotten ahead of herself and told the girls that I'm here to stay. And while I might be, nothing is guaranteed. I only came here to get away from California and to catch my breath.

To find out who I am outside of being Austin Anderson's girl-friend.

If I find what I'm looking for in Grangewood Creek, great. If I don't, I'm sure my family will survive.

"Slow down, guys. I don't even know if I'm here to stay," I remind them as we walk into Bridie's, in search of an empty booth, finding one in front of the dart board.

"Didn't you have your whole life packed up into a moving truck with Mom and Dad's house as its final destination? Seems pretty permanent to me." Lizzie queries, raising a brow as the three of us slouch into our seats.

"Lizzie!" Olive gasps, nudging her twin in the ribs with her elbow.

"What? Mom never said we couldn't talk about that. She just said we couldn't say his name," Lizzie replies as she shrugs and picks up the menu.

She's right.

Jenna helped me pack my life away and had it shipped back to my childhood home.

I can't believe I packed up my entire life without a second thought. Heartbreak really does mess you up and make you do questionable things. I guess I have no choice but to face the consequences of my irrational decisions.

Looking around the pub, it hasn't changed at all, and I'm hit with flashbacks upon flashbacks.

The dart board directly in front of us, where Austin and Harley sulked like sore losers after being beaten by Bea and me, still hung in the same spot it had fourteen years ago.

The pool table we used to play on every Sunday afternoon still had the same scuff marks on the legs and rips in the pockets. I bet the booth across from us still had A+C carved in the bottom left corner of the table, too.

Whenever Austin and I would come back home to visit, we stayed at the Anderson home, and the only time we left his house was to visit my parents. We never really ventured into town. We had no real reason to, so this is the first time I've been back here since high school.

"First round is on me. What do you both want?" I ask my sisters before I head to the bar.

"White wine for me and water for Olive," Lizzie requests. You would assume it's because Olive is our designated driver, but I don't think she's touched any alcohol since her twenty-first birthday. She claims it's 'not good for her voice' or something.

Whatever that even means.

As I head toward the bar, a familiar pair of dark brown eyes finds mine, and my stomach turns with excitement and nerves all at once.

Bea.

She and I haven't seen each other since graduation, when we went our separate ways.

While we were the best of friends in school, we lost touch after graduation. I guess life just got in the way and the distance played a huge part. We lost contact, but none of us really tried to keep in touch. I feel mostly to blame.

"Cass?" she asks, her voice softer than I remember.

She stares at me in disbelief from behind the bar, cleaning up some spillage.

"Bea. Oh, my goodness, it's been, what?" I say excitedly as I leap over the bar to pull my first best friend in for a hug.

"Oh, about twelve years, give or take?" She chuckles.

Pulling away from her, I pull out a bar stool and take a seat.

She hasn't changed a bit, apart from a few visible tattoos down her arms and a piercing above her top lip.

Her soft blonde hair is in a neat bun, with her side fringe tucked behind her left ear. She's wearing black, high-waisted jeans, and a bright red crop-top.

Her style hasn't changed at all.

"Welcome to Bridie's," she says, waving her arms out as if doing a presentation.

"I've been to Bridie's before, you know that. I've been here with *you*." I look around the room for any signs of obvious change, but come up short.

"Ah, but you haven't been to *my* Bridie's." Her face beams with pride. Her smile taking over her entire face.

"You bought the place?" I ask, matching her excitement. She'd always wanted to own a bar, but I would never have picked that she'd own this exact one. Her goal after high school was to work as much as she could to pay for her mom's medical bills, hoping she could complete community college eventually and get her business degree.

"It's been mine for the past few years. It still needs a little work, and it's far from perfect, but it's mine." She smiles, resting her palms on the bench top. "The name held too much sentimental value for me to change, though."

She's right. Bridie's holds a special place in the hearts of everyone here in town.

"That's amazing. I'm so happy for you. How's your Mom?" I ask, as I pour myself a glass of water from the jug on the bar, getting comfortable to catch up with an old friend.

"She passed away eight years ago." Her expression changes from pride to pain, but she still manages a soft smile and I feel immediate guilt at the realization that I wasn't here to support my best friend at a time where she needed support the most.

"Oh Bea, I'm so sorry. I had no idea." I reach for her hand and she gives it a soft squeeze before she quickly changes the subject.

"How's Anderson? I hear you guys got engaged." Her eyes flutter to my left hand, then away.

"Well, let's see. He broke up with me almost two months ago by leaving a note on our kitchen counter, only for me to bump into him at his sister's wedding, where he introduced me to his pregnant girlfriend of the last three years." My lips form a straight line, creating the fakest smile I can muster.

"Oh, and the best part is, his entire family knew about it the whole time." I laugh so loud, I'm certain the entire bar heard it.

"I never liked that asshole. That whole family always seemed like pretentious jerks," she says while pouring me a shot of vodka.

"Wait, I just need two glasses of wine and a glass of water," I say quickly, hoping to stop her mid-pour, but she brings out a second shot glass and fills that up, too.

"I think you're going to need something stronger than wine." She chuckles as she slides my shot glass in front of me, keeping the other for herself.

"Cheers," she says, clinking our glasses together before we throw them back, each of us wincing as we embrace the burn.

"How long are you in town for? If you're here for a while, we should catch up properly," Bea says, pouring the three drinks for my sisters and me.

"I would love that. If I can find a job as an event planner, I might be here for good. If not, a few weeks at most," I say while standing, trying not to spill the drinks.

"You should check out the old Maxwell farm. It's a winery now, and I think they need a new event planner. I have a feeling the new owner would love to see you." She smirks and I nod, noting her cheeks turning a dusty shade of pink before I turn my back to her and approach my sisters.

I've been back home for less than two hours, and so far, my mom, sisters, and now Bea have all mentioned that I should check out the winery. It's piqued my curiosity.

Placing our drinks carefully down on the oak table, I take my seat.

"Who owns the winery?"

Eight

Cassandra

"IT'S JUST UP HERE on our left," Lizzie nods as we pull up in front of Wingrove Estates, like I'd forgotten where the old Maxwell farm was.

It's changed a lot in the last twelve years, and Olive was right. The owner spared no expense on renovations. It's completely redone and is absolutely breathtaking.

It just looks...luxurious.

The iron gates at the entrance display a huge W. E. on the front, catching my attention immediately.

My mouth hangs open as we drive up the gravel pathway, slightly uphill, passing the vineyard on both our left and right, with the view of the whole town behind it.

Matty Maxwell had hosted a campfire for our graduating class a week before graduation. We all had some drinks and spoke about our favorite memories throughout high school, while simultaneously overlooking our hometown.

I chose to sit next to Bea that night, knowing it would probably be our last night together for a long time. We laughed, we cried, and promised we'd stay in touch, and not following through with that promise will forever be one of my biggest regrets.

Driving further ahead, we find a parking lot in front of the old barn, which is now a stunning, functional space and looks brand new.

Right next door is an elegant, dimly-lit restaurant with a bar attached, and a wine cellar out front for you to hand select your own bottle from their collection on your way home.

This place is every wine lover's dream.

Disneyland for adults.

Heavenly.

"This is incredible," I whisper under my breath, but I know they can hear me.

"You can picture yourself working here, can't you?" Olive asks.

"More like she can picture herself getting married here," Lizzie corrects our sister, but I ignore them both.

The vineyards offer endless photo opportunities, and considering there's a restaurant next to the barn, I would assume they prepare all the food in house for the weddings that they host.

I can even see a little chapel up ahead.

"You guys don't mind coming back to get me in an hour? I want to look around and see if I can get a meeting about the potential job position," I say, trying to sound confident, but on the inside, I'm slightly freaking out.

"Sure, a *job* position. Say hi to your new boss for me." Lizzie winks, but Olive just nods in response.

"Get your mind out of the gutter, Lizzie. And thanks, Ol. See you guys in an hour," I shout over the engine, slamming the door shut, watching my sisters drive away.

Wiping my clammy hands down my thighs, I check myself in the reflection of one of the bar windows before I attempt to find the reception.

The place is enormous, but thankfully, they've installed street-like signs, pointing you in the direction of where you need to go.

Finding the sign I'm after, I follow it until I'm face to face with a girl named Ariana, who's staring at me like I don't belong.

I knew I should have gone home to change.

"Hi," I say, clearing my throat. "I'm here to see Mr. Wingrove." I smile politely at Ariana as she raises a brow as if to say, '*and who might you be?*'

"And you are?" she asks, looking me up and down. I hope she can't smell the alcohol on my breath.

"Cassandra Herring. I'm an old friend," I say, interlocking my fingers on her desk, and I swear she hasn't blinked once.

"I'm sorry, *Cassandra*, but Mr. Wingrove has a lot of...women, coming in here, claiming to be an old friend." Her mouth quirks at the corners. "Anyway, you need an appointment to see Mr. Wingrove, and unfortunately, he's not in today," she finally says, and I don't know why she didn't say that to begin with instead of assuming I was some sort of groupie.

"Thank you," I nod anyway, pushing away the anxious feeling I had about seeing him again, admitting defeat.

"Look who it is," a deep, almost recognizable voice says, stopping me as I'm about to give up for the day and head back to my parents' place.

Now that I hear his voice, I don't know if what I'm feeling in the pit of my stomach was nerves, or if my body could sense he was nearby, setting free the butterflies that had been lying dormant for the last fourteen years.

"Harley Wingrove," I say, breathlessly, because apparently, the sight of him snatches the air straight out of my lungs.

"Herring." He smirks, as if he knows the effect he just had on me, and I can't stop my eyes from drinking him in entirely.

He's taller than he used to be, well over six feet. The muscles in his long legs strain against his dark grey trousers as he stands, towering over me. His white, button-up shirt rolled up at the sleeves. His shoulders are broad, and his chest looks like it would feel so firm. My fingers would break with a simple graze.

What I would do to just...glide my fingers down his bare torso; feel the firmness and the warmth of his body beneath my hand. His chiseled jaw is sharp, ticking as he clenches it.

His lips are still pink and plump and so kissable.

And those *eyes*.

A deep, emerald green, twinkling with mischief as he—

"Herring," he says again, clearing his throat, and my mouth is suddenly so dry. I just checked this man out for a solid minute, in the most slow-motion, movie-esq, mouth-watering way possible, and he looks amused. Like he knew every inappropriate thought that was running through my mind.

"Harley," I repeat myself with a smile, hoping he hasn't realized that I just pictured him doing R-rated things to me. "Whenever I thought about you over the years, I never pictured you looking like...this."

Why am I allowed to speak?

"You've thought about me, Herring?" he asks, tilting his head with a smirk, revealing the lone dimple on his right cheek that I'd forgotten about.

Closing the gap between us, he pulls me in for a hug, and I'm embarrassed to admit that I'm the reason it dragged on for longer than it should have. My heart is beating erratically in my chest, and I hope more than anything that he can't feel it against his.

He laughs, releasing me from his arms, and I already miss the smell of sandalwood and vanilla that radiated through me.

How is he even hotter than I remember?

"What brings you home?" he asks, gesturing for me to walk alongside him, and I do exactly that while doing my best to keep up with his long strides.

He's aged like fine wine, looking hot as hell in his business suit.

Meanwhile, I'm dressed like I just came from a bar. At least I changed out of my travel clothes, I guess.

Silver linings.

Running my hands down my hair to smooth out any fly aways, I wonder where to start.

"I heard there was a new owner in town. I had to come and see for myself," I say with a smile. I don't want to seem too forward about wanting a job, so I decide to not mention it.

"I have about forty minutes until my next meeting. Have you eaten?" He doesn't slow his pace as he leads us toward the restaurant I walked past earlier.

"I have, but I guess I could pick at a bowl of fries." I know we're old friends catching up, and are both fully grown adults, but I'm nervous. I don't think I've ever even seen someone as hot as Harley Wingrove in real life, let alone had lunch with them, and it's doing all kinds of things to my lady bits.

The restaurant is beautiful. He's done a wonderful job with the interior and exterior of this place.

It's daylight outside, but you could never tell.

The restaurant windows are tinted so dark, that they block out any hint of natural light. The hanging light pendants slightly glow, creating a breathtaking, romantic setting. It'd be the perfect place for a date. No matter the time of day.

This isn't a date, Cassandra. It's strictly business. You're here for a job.

"How have you been?" he asks as he pulls my chair out for me before he sits in his own.

Such a gentleman.

Setting our menus to the side, he pours us both a glass of water, but his eyes never break contact with mine.

How do I say, "the last two months have been the worst two months of my life, so I packed up everything I own into a truck and moved back in with my parents because I found out my boyfriend of fourteen years, your ex-best-friend, had been having an affair and got another girl pregnant, so I'm not doing all that great," without actually telling him any of that?

I'm not here to talk about my personal life. I'm here for a job. If my brain could send that message to my body, that would be great. Otherwise, I'll never get what I came for.

Instead of going into detail, I keep it simple with, "I've been great."

Placing my paper straw in between my lips, I take a sip of water and I don't miss the way his eyes linger on my mouth, either.

Clenching his jaw, he nods, shifting in his chair slightly before opening his menu.

"How about you? I never picked you to be a wine guy," I say, opening my menu, too, even though I already know what I'm getting.

"To be fair, you knew me as a sixteen-year-old hormonal jock." He raises a brow, closing his menu gently, placing it down on the dining table, leaning back in his chair.

"I've been good," he continues. "I took over this place when I retired, about seven years ago. It's finally at the place where I want it to be, but things are constantly changing." He takes another sip.

There's something about him that just oozes confidence, but not arrogance. Like he knows that women check him out every time he enters a room, but he isn't an asshole about it.

"Retire from what, exactly? Aren't you a little young to retire?" There's a silence between us as the server, Morgan, comes to take our order.

"I'll have the steak special, and I believe Cassandra here will have a bowl of fries?" he asks, smiling at me, and I nod to confirm.

"That'll be all. Thanks, Morgan." He smiles at her, and she blushes, taking our orders back to the kitchen.

I wonder if he knows all of his staff by name, or if he paid attention to her name tag.

I would typically hate it if a man ordered for me. If this were a date, it would be a huge red flag.

But this isn't a date, and he isn't just any man.

Austin used to do it constantly by assuming he knew what I wanted, and I hated it. Half the time, he got it wrong, but I ate it anyway because I hated disappointing him.

I told Harley what I wanted one time, and he actually listened and confirmed it was what I wanted before ordering it for me.

"I retired from the NFL seven years ago after a shoulder injury." He shrugs like it's not that big of a deal. I didn't know he made it to the NFL, but I know it was always his goal. An injury to his shoulder, of all places, must have killed him. I guess that's the life of a professional athlete.

I never really followed sports. Austin stopped playing football the moment high school finished, so I didn't have any reason to follow a team.

"I'm sorry, I didn't know. Austin never—" I start, but he waves his hand in the air to stop me.

"Don't worry about it. It's in the past. I never expected you to keep tabs on me, Herring," he replies, and I know he's being genuine, but it doesn't make me feel less guilty.

"I should have, though. We may not have stayed friends, but we were friends, once upon a time," I say shyly.

I abandoned most of my friendships at the request of Austin, because I was sixteen and thought he was my forever, but I should have known better, at sixteen, that dating the boy on the football team wouldn't be a love that would last a lifetime.

"I don't think your fiancé would be happy to hear that you considered me a friend." He takes a sip of his water before changing the subject, but I don't miss how the word 'fiancé' sounded bitter on his lips.

"What have you been up to, anyway? How long are you in town for?" His unwavering eye contact and eager tone tell me he's asking because he's actually interested, not just trying to force conversation.

"Indefinitely," I admit. His face flashes with concern, but it quickly vanishes when Morgan brings over our food. "It's nothing bad," I try to recover. "I'm just here for a fresh start," I say, in hopes that the conversation on my personal life doesn't go any deeper. Picking at my nail beds on my thumb, I stare at my fries in silence, but he breaks it with a question I should have expected.

"Austin here with you?"

He mentioned my *fiancé* earlier, but I didn't acknowledge it. I didn't feel like delving into that part of my life. But I guess now I have to.

"Austin and I broke up a couple of months ago," I say, but Harley's facial expression doesn't waver. I expected a shocked reaction, maybe even amused, but his face remained the same.

I decided to stop hiding behind my failed relationship and start acknowledging that it's over. I guess I wouldn't be here if it weren't. But I realize that I don't feel sick to my stomach when I admit the words out-loud.

It feels more like... a relief.

A sense of freedom.

Like I can finally breathe.

"Actually, I'm here hoping you need an event planner," I say, letting out a deep breath.

If I'm being honest, I may as well go the whole way. We only have ten minutes left, and I've used none of the other thirty talking about the real reason I'm here.

"How'd you know?" he questions while digging into his meal.

"I bumped into Bea." I shrug, taking a handful of fries to dip in ketchup.

"Ah. Say no more."

The moment our forty minutes is up, I write my phone number on the back of an old receipt, slide it across the table, and let him know to contact me if he wants to discuss my experience or needs details for my references, because, after all, I met with him for a job, no matter how hard my body tries to convince me otherwise.

"Cassandra Herring, is that you?" I would recognise that voice anywhere, chills lacing my skin. Right as I'm about to open the car door to meet my sisters, too.

"Hi, Mrs. Bishop, it's nice to see you," I respond, smiling to be polite.

She and her husband used to own the diner in town, Katie's, before I was even born, so they're well known across town. But these days, she's known for being the gossip queen, not a business owner.

"We heard that you were back in town. Such a shame to hear about you and Austin," she remarks, giving me a soft smile.

"Yes. A real shame." My voice is sarcastic, my smile refusing to be genuine, but she can't see past the one-sided conversation she's having with herself.

"You must be proud of him for following his dream," she says, and I can only imagine the bullshit story Angela Anderson has spun to make her son not look like the bad guy.

Mrs. Bishop appears to really care, but it bothers me that people assume they know everything about your life, especially when they're so far from the truth.

I can't exactly tell her that I'm "so proud of him for lying to me, cheating on me, and getting another girl pregnant." It'll make me look like a vicious, lying, bitter ex. So, I say, "Whatever makes me happy."

"His parents were really sad to see you go. Angela said so herself. We had dinner with the Andersons last week. She'd said she wished things were different. Didn't she, honey?" She nudges her husband, but he stares mindlessly over my shoulder, clearly not paying attention to a single word that's been said.

"Yes, different. Sure, hon," he mumbles, searching his denim pant pockets for his keys.

"We best be off now, dear. But you take care of yourself. You're looking a little...*thin*." Smiling, she gives me a weak hug that I reciprocate before we both turn away from each other.

My tears don't wait for my door to slam shut.

They betray me and stain my cheeks the moment Mrs. Bishop can no longer see my face, and my sisters know better than to ask questions.

Of course, the Andersons are telling everyone that Austin broke up with me to focus on his career.

God forbid Grangewood Creek find out their Golden Boy's son was cheating on his long-term girlfriend. They couldn't have their son ruin his perfect image.

Max's reputation is the most important thing to their family, and they always did everything in their power to keep it safe, even if it meant betraying someone who was like a daughter to them.

Now, the whole town pities me for my broken heart. The girl who wasn't good enough for the career-driven man.

Oh, and thanks, Mrs. Bishop, for pointing out the fact that I've lost weight. Like I wasn't aware that my clothes were now swimming on me.

Frantically wiping the tears off my cheeks, Olive turns on the ignition, while Lizzie blasts *No Scrubs* by *TLC*, and we head back to my parents' house.

Nine

Harley

She was totally checking me out.

That much was fucking glaringly obvious. It was a dead giveaway that she and Austin had broken up, too.

Cassandra Herring would've never shown up in a place that I own, with the sole purpose of seeing me. Not if they were still together, anyway.

The guy was always attached to her hip, like some obsessive, untrusting puppy dog, who refused to let her out of his sight.

Regardless of all of that, it felt...good, to see her. I don't know how else to describe it. And I wasn't surprised that Bea was behind it.

Of course, she was.

It felt like a mini ambush, in a way. Best friends were supposed to support each other; not spring shit on them that could throw off their whole day.

Or week.

Or month.

Hell, it's probably going to change the trajectory of my whole life, and all we had, was one, measly conversation over lunch. Forty fucking minutes.

I could picture the look on Bea's face the moment Cassandra walked into Bridie's. Smug as fuck, with her plan already in motion.

She meddled immediately.

I guess she was just making up for lost time, considering she didn't get the chance to meddle in school. Very on brand for Bea.

While I'd admired Cassandra as she sat across from me, I didn't miss the sadness all over her face—which she tried to disguise with a smile—and the size of her tiny frame.

She spoke briefly about the work she'd done over the last few years, but I was too focused on trying to read her. Trying to figure out if she was okay. Trying to get her to tell me what happened with Austin without outright asking the question.

When she finally said the words, "Austin and I broke up," I could tell there was more to it, but I wasn't in a position to pry. We might have been friends years ago, but now we're practically strangers.

Plus, she would have told me if she wanted to.

I would've loved to just sit in her company, listening to her soft, husky voice as she spoke for hours, but my phone had other plans for me. It beeped three times to remind me that my next meeting was quickly approaching, so I had to watch her leave.

Again.

Only this time, I knew that her leaving would be temporary and I wouldn't have to wait years for her to come back.

When I was sixteen, I thought I knew what it meant to be in love. I thought Cassandra Herring hung the damn moon. She was so special to me, but my priority was always football and getting a scholarship to a good school, and I watched as Austin snuck in to get the girl.

When I went to college, I moved on.

I'd never fallen in love or had my heart broken. I never even came close. Because just like high school, football and getting drafted was my priority, and I don't regret it.

I achieved more than most, and my career was only just getting started.

I was the youngest person to ever win MVP and be submitted into the Hall of Fame, setting records upon records.

But now that Cassandra Herring is back in Grangewood, it almost feels like the universe is giving me a do-over, in a way.

Testing me to see what I would do now, given I'm more confident in myself, no longer focused on football, and don't have a giant road-block in my way by the name of Austin Anderson.

Even sitting with her for lunch was a test.

She had a way of making even the most mundane things sound interesting. She could have spent two hours detailing a park bench, and my attention never would have strayed.

Thankfully, she'd written her number down on the back of an old receipt, and I'd clutched it in the palm of my hand before copying it into my phone.

I saved her number under the name *Herring* and placed the receipt in my pocket.

Just in case.

Staring at my lock screen, I decide to text my best friend to thank her for my unannounced, but very welcome, visitor.

Me: Really, Bea?

Bea: Happy to help, stud. Shoot your shot, or whatever the kids say these days.

Bea is the only one who knows about my past, and my history with Cassandra. Or should I say, the history that I used to wish for?

And I guess Austin knew too.

But the moment we all moved away to go to college, I was in his rear-view mirror and forgotten about, once and for all, and he took her right along with him.

I figured that all of those feelings I once had, had finally disappeared, but now, I'm not so sure.

The universe loves to fuck with me. I know that now more than ever.

Scrubbing my hands down my face, I shove my phone back in my pocket, let out a deep breath, and make my way toward the only boardroom at Wingrove Estates to meet with our wine makers and creative marketing team for our quarterly catch up.

"Good afternoon, everyone." Pushing open the double doors, I admire the view immediately. The room overlooks the vineyard, with the town in the distance, and I never tire of seeing it. Even when I moved to Charlotte and had penthouse views, nothing could top this.

Taking a seat at the head of the table, we discuss multiple different wine flavorings for our winter launch, in time for Thanksgiving and Christmas, in five short months.

We settle on a smooth, Cabernet Merlot blend, fused with spiced fruit and blackberry characters, a lingering finish of oak.

"Have you hired someone to organize our stall at the Grangewood Carnival?" Simon, one of the marketing guys, asks, as we're all packing away our laptops and notepads.

The Grangewood Creek carnival is a yearly event, but I don't have the time to organize the Wingrove Estates stall this year. I have too many properties in development all over the country, all that require my attention. Cassandra's showing up looking for a job couldn't have come at a better time.

"No, not officially. I have someone in mind. I just interviewed her, actually. If all goes well, she'll have plenty of time to take care of everything."

All nodding, clearly pleased with my response, they rise from their seats and clear out from the room. Pulling my phone back out of my pocket, I stare at her name for what feels like an hour before I suck it up and type out a text.

> **Me:** Hey, Herring, it's Harley. If you're free tomorrow, would you like to meet in my office to formally discuss the position? How does 1pm sound?

> **Herring:** Great, I'll be there.

I tell her we're going to discuss the position, but the job is already hers if she wants it.

I just kind of want to see her squirm in front of me.

Now that I've finished my meetings for the day and I'm off the clock, I call Bea, because her text response was typical—way too vague and not good enough.

"Hey, stud," she says with a chuckle, and I roll my eyes, even though she can't see me.

"Don't 'stud' me. What are you playing at?" I huff, sounding more frustrated than I intended, but she knows me well enough to know when I'm actually pissed, and right now is not one of those times.

"You always wondered what you'd do if you ever got the chance to see her again. I thought I'd let her show up on your doorstep so we could find out." She doesn't sound apologetic in the slightest. She does, however, sound pleased with herself.

"You didn't think to give me a heads up?" I mutter through a clenched jaw, closing my office door to make our conversation more private.

"Would you have said yes if I gave you a heads up or asked your permission?"

I must've been silent for too long, because she speaks again before I do.

"Exactly. But hey, Wingrove?" The seriousness in her tone flicks my frustration to concern.

"Yeah?"

"Something tells me she's looking for a friend right now. It's not my place to say anything, but her breakup with Austin was..." she hesitates.

"Was what?"

"Brutal," she finally says. Bea is typically a sarcastic person down to the bone. The fact that she switched from sarcasm to serious so quickly tells me everything I need to know, and it leaves me feeling more protective of Cassandra than I have of anybody in a long time.

"What did he do to her?" I sit in my chair, running my hands against my day old stubble, furious over someone I haven't thought about in almost a decade.

"Chill, boy toy. I'm sure she'll tell you when she's ready."

Before I can object to yet another stupid nickname, she hangs up the phone.

Crossing that line with Cassandra Herring was something I thought about doing a lot when I was a teenager, and I'd be lying if

I said the thought hadn't popped into my mind once or twice over lunch. But I refuse to get involved with her while she's broken hearted and on the rebound.

So, if friendship is what she needs, friendship is what she will get.

Ten

Harley Age 16

"Go long," I shout as my best friend runs down the football field to catch the ball that I've thrown his way.

In typical Austin fashion, he fumbles the ball and blames himself. He's not wrong to do so; it was an easy catch. I just hate that he's so hard on himself all the time.

He's a decent football player—it's in his blood to be—but unless he focuses more on the game and less on his social calendar, he won't improve.

I don't think he cares, though. Not the way I do.

Football is my life, and I don't have a backup plan. I live and breathe the damn sport.

I've always had the same goal in life.

Earn a full ride scholarship to Ohio State, earn my business degree that I'll hopefully never have to use, and be drafted to play for the Charlotte Eagles.

A guy could dream, right?

Go big or go home, or whatever that saying is.

And if my dream doesn't become my reality, at least I have a safety net in the shape of a degree.

Austin, on the other hand, is a trust fund kid. He got everything he ever wanted, whenever he wanted it, knowing no matter what he chose to do in life, he would still live like a king.

The Andersons are the richest family in Grangewood Creek, by a long shot, so the guy knows he doesn't have to work hard to get what he wants.

But he doesn't want a name for himself in football. He wants to step out of the Anderson name and create his own legacy.

I respect it.

He'll never decline his weekly allowance, though.

"Sorry, man. I should have caught that one," Austin admits as he picks the ball up from the ground and runs it back to me.

"I don't know why I always drop it. It's like my hand-eye coordination just isn't where it should be." He shrugs. "Dad will be so pissed if I play like this on game day." He winces at the thought while running his hand through his damp, light brown hair, taking a large gulp of water.

Austin's father, Max, is tough on him. You'd think the fact that his son wants to step away from football and create a life for himself would make him proud. But he keeps trying to force Austin to focus more on the game than school. Thankfully, his mom, Angela, knows her son well enough to know that the game isn't his passion.

She doesn't force something on him if he doesn't want it.

The weight of his father's football legacy is a lot for him. Hell, it would be a lot for anyone. I think I'd be able to handle it, though.

I'd look at it as a challenge.

"Don't beat yourself up, man. You know, you don't have to be on the football team just because it's what your old man wants, right?" I remind him, but he barks out a laugh in response.

"Yeah right." He scoffs. "Do you even know who my dad is?" His laughter continues. "Max Anderson, former star QB of the Eagles, with a son who can't even catch a fucking ball." His voice booms like a commentator, his hands cupped around his mouth, voice echoing through the empty football field.

"What an embarrassment to the Anderson name I would be if I quit the team," he says bitterly before taking another long drink of water, but I don't respond.

He goes on these tangents often. I know it's best if I just nod in agreement and go along with whatever he wants me to do. It's easier than dealing with an inevitable tantrum.

"Go again." Throwing his water bottle onto the ground, he gears up for my next pass down the field.

So, we do exactly that.

Over, and over, and over again.

We finished practice an hour ago, but we don't stop until he's had enough, throws a fit, and tosses his water bottle into the bleachers.

Collecting the ball and his face towel, he rushes off to the change rooms with me hot on his heels.

"What are you up to tonight?" I ask, trying to diffuse the situation as I prepare to rinse myself in the showers before heading home.

"Matty Maxwell is throwing that party at the farm, remember? His parents are out of town for his dad's treatments," he replies. The Maxwells owned the only dairy farm in town, but Mr. Maxwell's cancer is progressing rapidly, and he can no longer take care of the animals while undergoing his chemo treatment, meaning the farm is no longer functioning. "You wanna go?"

"Who's going to be there?"

There's only one name I want to hear.

"I think Bea and Cass will be there too," he finally says, after listing the entire student body.

"Sounds good. Mom finishes work at eight, so I'll come past your place once she gets home." I try to seem casual about the fact that tonight might be the night I finally work up the courage to tell Cassandra Herring that I think she's pretty, or whatever.

Yeah, let's go with whatever.

"See you then."

Throwing his gym bag over his shoulder, he staunches out of the locker room with the party on his mind, seemingly forgetting all about his inability to catch a ball.

***

"Mom, can I take the car out tonight?" I ask the second she drags her heavy, blistered feet through the front door after her double shift at Katie's Diner.

Sliding her shoes off one by one, she winces at the instant relief.

Her golden brown hair is in a tight bun at the nape of her neck, fly aways looking like a crown on top of her head. Her brown eyes look exhausted, bounded by dark circles, and her blue and white striped uniform is splashed with coffee and food stains.

"Sure, honey. Just don't be too late."

Walking past, she gives me a kiss on the cheek before heading up to the shower and turning in for the night.

All my life, my mom is all I've ever known. My father abandoned her during pregnancy, so I never met him.

She's played the role of both parents since day one, and there's not a day where her hard work goes unnoticed by me.

It's another reason I've set such high—almost unreachable—goals for myself. I need to give her back everything she's given me; give her the life she deserves.

But, knowing her, she probably won't accept a penny from me, even if I was as rich as Bill Gates.

She's too stubborn. I'll figure out a way, though. She didn't raise a quitter.

Once I'm showered and ready, I pick up the keys off the counter and head out the door.

Arriving at the front of Austin's house, I pull out my phone to text him.

Me: Out front.

Austin: k

Slamming the door shut, he already reeks of booze, which is no surprise. It's why I offered to drive him. He's a loose cannon and a complete fucking wild card.

I couldn't have him drunk and wanting to drive himself home, or drunk and stranded out near the Maxwell farm. Neither of those were safe, nor were they practical options. Plus, I'm not a drinker, so it makes the most sense for me to be the one to drive us whenever there's a party.

"I ran into Bea and Cass after our training session. They asked if it would be alright if they could hitch a ride. I said yes. That cool?" He buckles himself in, and I feel myself swallow hard at the thought of Cassandra being in my car.

Luckily, mom cleaned it this morning before her shift.

"All good." I nod, gripping the steering wheel so tight, my knuckles nearly turn white.

I have even less time to hype myself up to face the girl of my dreams before I tell her I'm crushing on her.

Pulling up to the front of her house where the girls are waiting, I feel my stomach drop as I stare, unable to form a sentence.

Not even a simple hello.

Great, she probably thinks I'm a fucking loser.

"Thank you so much for picking us up," she says with her soft, husky voice, as they both barrel into the backseat of the car.

"It's no worries," Austin answers before I get the chance to. I nod in agreement as she looks at me, smiling in the rear-view mirror. I feel it directly in my chest.

She's wearing tight, blue, high-waisted jeans, a fitted, white crop-top that shows the slightest bit of skin on her stomach, and an open, red and black plaid shirt, paired with black combat boots.

"Nice outfit," I say to her, smirking as I notice mine is nearly identical. Only, my jeans aren't tight, or high-waisted, and my t-shirt isn't cropped or fitted.

"Twins!" She giggles and her smile spreads across her entire face, making my chest tighten and my stomach flutter. As terrified as I am to let her know how I feel, I can't fucking wait to hopefully be able to call her mine.

The moment we pull up to the party, we each go our separate ways. They've gone to get drunk, and I find myself alone in an empty field, trying to be my own hype-man.

"Just fucking tell her. Stop being a pussy," I mutter to myself as I pace back and forth, almost certain I'm stepping in cow shit, frustrated by my lack of confidence. I'm a confident guy, usually, but the fear of being rejected by the girl I've been crushing on since pre-k is a lot to deal with.

"I think you're really pretty and I want to know if you want to go out sometime? See! It's not that hard. Fuck, why do I sound like such a fucking loser?" I sigh. After repeating that same sentence so many times, it sounds repetitive, losing its meaning somewhere along the way.

"Yeah, it's not that hard," I hear a familiar voice say from behind me, stopping me dead in my tracks, and I feel all the blood drain from my face. "You should totally tell her how you feel." Bea smirks.

She's wearing a short, black, leather skirt, a tight, white singlet and her blonde hair is held up by a red and black bandana.

"Tell who?" I ask, claiming ignorance.

"Oh, come on, Wingrove. It's so obvious." She laughs, standing next to me, both of us resting our elbows on the edge of the waist-high fence.

"It is?" Oh God, of course it is, who am I kidding? I haven't exactly tried to hide it. But I haven't shoved it in her face, either.

"I think I've known about your crush on my best friend before you even knew about it," she says as we both push away from the fence. She links her arm through mine.

"Does she know?"

Do I even want to hear her response?

"No." She shakes her head. "She thinks you're too wrapped up in football to know any female exists, let alone her." She rolls her eyes and nudges her shoulder into mine, and I involuntarily groan.

Of course, I know she exists. How could I not? She's the prettiest girl I've ever seen.

I think I've had a crush on her since the first moment I saw her, when I was like, four, getting out of her dad's beat-up red truck.

"What should I do?" I ask as I run a hand through my hair.

Turning to face the direction of the party, I confide in the person who knows Cassandra better than anyone, hopeful that she can give me some sort of insight into how to win over her best friend.

"Let's go tell her right now," she chirps, picking up the pace in her strides.

"Just like that?"

"Just like that."

Eleven
Cassandra

"UGH, HE'S SO HOT," Lizzie says, fanning her face with her hands.

The three of us are sweaty and hungry from the gym, but I need to prepare for my meeting with Harley. My sisters are holding me accountable, making sure I eat (and eat well), and stay active, adamant to get me back to my old self.

"Please tell me you're going to hit that. I mean, come *on*. Olive, look at this photo." She shoves her phone in her twin sister's face.

She's clearly done a search of him online, finding God knows what.

"I wonder what happened to him here?" Olive asks, her voice woven with concern and curiosity.

"What photo?" My curiosity piques, and I peer over their shoulders, revealing a shirtless, very ripped Harley. Aside from his defined abs, tone arms, and golden skin, I notice the sling around his right shoulder and a slight black eye.

"The caption says *'Feeling positive about my recovery so far. Thanks for all the love and support - H.W.'* He's so...edible," my sister gushes.

"He mentioned his shoulder was the reason he retired." I shrug it off, ignoring the way my body betrays me, tingling in places I wish she wouldn't.

He didn't really talk about his injury, and I can't imagine it's his favorite topic of conversation.

"Can you guys please stop swooning over my potential boss?" I say, pulling the conversation from the phone back to me. Ignoring the jealously floating through my entire nervous system at my sisters eyeing off the first guy I ever felt anything for.

I have no right to feel that way.

I have to see him soon for our meeting today about a *job*. I don't need the image of him shirtless on my mind. Otherwise, it's all I'll see, and I don't need to sit uncomfortably in front of him, imagining him half naked.

"It's a business meeting," I remind them while reminding myself.

Austin hadn't given me butterflies or made my lady bits tingle since we were in college, so feeling those things for Harley caught me completely off guard.

Besides, I haven't even been single for that long. Why is my body craving what my mind isn't ready for?

"I wish I could have a business meeting with Mr. Wingrove," Lizzie purrs while putting the back of her hand on her forehead, pretending to faint onto my bed. Why she never took up theatre, I'll never understand.

"I don't think the vineyard is on the lookout for kindergarten teachers, but I'll ask for you," I joke, squinting at her over my shoulder, filtering through my freshly hung wardrobe, in search of the perfect outfit for our meeting today.

I've been back home for less than twenty-four hours, bumped into two old friends, and have a potential new job at the hottest wedding spot in town.

This move might be good for me after all.

Giddy with excitement, I pull out a white silk blouse and what once was a tight black skirt, somehow making it work.

Putting on the outfit, I stand in front of the mirror, flattening my skirt with the palms of my hands and satisfied with how far I've come in such a short amount of time.

"What do we think?" I ask my sisters as I turn to face them.

"Needs more cleavage," Lizzie says while Olive, surprisingly, nods in agreement.

I chuckle and jokingly roll my eyes before turning back to the mirror for one last outfit check.

"You're meant to be on my side, Ol. Can you both be serious for once, please? This is important to me," I say, reaching for the final details of my look: crimson red lipstick and a black, strapless heel.

"If that outfit doesn't make him want to fuck you, just undo a button and he'll be on his knees before you know it. Or maybe you'll be on yours." Lizzie cackles to herself as I turn my back on my sisters, storm out of my bedroom, and give them the finger before slamming my door shut, drowning out the sound of hysterical laughter.

That's the last thing I need. I don't want to be obsessing over the crush I had when I was sixteen, and I certainly don't need to imagine his head between my legs, or mine between his.

I've arrived at Wingrove Estates a little earlier than intended, but I was too on edge to be in my parents' house for much longer.

From the moment I stepped out of my mom's Prius, I found myself immediately in awe of what Harley has turned this space into. Taking a quick landscape photo, I send it to Jenna, and video call my sisters to gush about how beautiful it is here.

"Guys, this place is stunning. If I ever got married, which I won't, because to get married you need to be engaged, and I never want to be engaged ever again; I would want to get married here." I go on a tangent while Lizzie giggles and Olive gags.

Olive doesn't believe that love even exists, yet Lizzie is happy to kiss every single frog until she finds her Prince Charming.

"I can picture it already. Walking down a white carpet in the gardens, while my faceless groom stands under a rustic, wooden arch with a subtle splash of flowers in the corner—"

"Faceless groom? That's a weird way to pronounce Harley Wingrove, but okay," Lizzie cuts me off, and I continue as if she never said a word.

"You guys and Jenna are all wearing gold, silk gowns while standing across from my *faceless groom*, waiting for me as I walk arm in arm with dad down the aisle. Our reception would be in the barn with an enormous dance floor, because my future husband and *faceless groom* would join me and want to be the life of the party, while all of our guests dance beside us."

It's like I'm talking to a brick wall. Neither of my sisters utters a single word, but I need to tell someone about how beautiful this place is, and Jenna is at work, so they'll have to do.

"The rounded tables would be decorated with white tablecloths and gold chairs to match your dresses, with candles and white orchids as the centerpieces. I want fairy lights hanging from the ceiling, too." I finally finish rambling.

"Wow, for someone who never wants to be married, you've sure thought a lot about how this day would play out," Olive says.

"You forget that I'm a party planner, Ol. Of *course*, I've put a lot of thought into it. Besides, I never said I didn't want to be married. I just don't want to waste fourteen more years of my life on someone who doesn't know for sure if they want to be with me. I want to be with someone who tells me that I'm their person forever. Who knows, maybe I'll meet someone who wants to skip an engagement all together, and we can simply just... get married."

I didn't use to be anti-anything, but my proposal, engagement, and overall relationship with Austin left a sour taste in my mouth. I don't want to put myself in a position that leaves me wide open for heartbreak.

But it's hard.

My relationship with Austin was all that I knew. I have nothing to compare it to. I hoped to be a wife one day; to live happily in a house that we worked to make a home.

Maybe even a kid or two running around. But I think I've accepted that my reality might look a little different these days, and I'll learn to be ok with it.

"Got it. Faceless groom. Wingrove Estate. White and rustic with splashes of gold. Can we hang up yet?"

Rolling my eyes, I hang up before they get the chance and make my way inside.

Knocking on Harley's office door, I take a deep breath and allow myself a moment to be a little nervous.

To accept the fact that things have changed, but to remind myself that sometimes, change is a good thing.

"It's open," his deep voice booms and now my heart is beating like I've just ran a marathon, mouth as dry as cinnamon.

"Hi, Mr. Wingrove," I say as he stands from his seat to greet me, one hand on stomach to keep his tie in place, the other gesturing to the empty seat on the other side of his desk.

It sounded weird the moment '*Mr. Wingrove*' rolled off my tongue, but it was the only thing that felt appropriate given he could be my new boss, and I panicked.

Frankie and I weren't on a first name basis for the first six months.

"That's my grandfather's name." He chuckles as he runs his hand down his tie as he takes his seat.

"Sorry, I guess I'm nervous," I reply as I take mine.

"We're old friends, Herring. The job is yours already, if you want it," he says, while skimming his thumb over his plump bottom lip, leaning back in his chair.

Now his lips are all I can see.

"It is?" I ask, and he nods, my attention refocussing on his face.

"If you want it," he repeats. His expression is firm, and I know he doesn't take who he hires lightly.

After all, he worked really hard, turning this business into what it is today.

"Did you even call my reference?" I ask jokingly, because I know I didn't give him Frankie's number.

"Sure, let's pretend that I did. He gave you raving reviews."

"She." I smirk and let out a sigh of relief.

The job is mine if I want it.

And I want it.

We spend the next hour talking about what is expected of me as the Events Manager at Wingrove Estates, from arranging weddings, to elaborate baby showers, bridal teas, and corporate events, and we're now on the topic of the annual Grangewood Creek Carnival.

"It's in two weeks, and I haven't had time to arrange anything for it. I'm going to need your help to organize, well... everything. The wine selection, the food samples, the décor, the works. I need you to pull out all the stops. I want the restaurant to be booked out weeks in advance," Harley says.

Yesterday at lunch, I saw the relaxed, cheeky, and flirtatious Harley. But today he's all about business. I admire how he's able to switch it off and on seamlessly. He asks me about any ideas off the top of my head for the carnival, and I described my vision to him, which he was thrilled with.

I also told him all about the quarterly Bridal Expo that happens in California and asked if he would be interested in showcasing Wingrove Estates. He tasked me with finding out as much as I could, like pricing and booth requirements, and told me that if we had no weddings or events booked in the barn that weekend, he would accompany me to California for the duration of the expo.

"What's good to do around here these days?" I ask, looking around the room, glad to no longer feel the tension in the air that I'd caused myself.

His office is...minimalistic.

A single desk sits directly in the middle, one computer screen perched on it, with his laptop sitting below, a filing cabinet and some shelves, a drinks cart with a few bottles of whisky, a jug of water, and five clean, empty glasses, and a something out of character that piques my interest.

A lone, white, fake orchid.

My favorite flower.

That's all.

No photos, no certificates. No sign of personality or who Harley is, outside of these four walls.

"The kids still jump off the cliff rocks into the creek," he says, eyeing me suspiciously, knowing I never bit the bullet and jumped off.

Heights are my number one enemy.

"The cinema is still open, though, hanging by a thread. It's only still open because of the arcade. Katie's Diner is still as busy as it always has been, but their milkshakes have improved drastically. Bea and I go every week for our fix, and Bridie's, as you know, is more popular than ever." He gives a cheeky grin, and the Harley from yesterday is slowly peeking through.

"Does your Mom still work at Katie's?" I ask, and he shakes his head while pouring us both a glass of water from the jug on his drink cart.

"No, she actually runs this place for me. I'm hardly ever here, if I'm honest. You caught me on one of the few days I'm actually in the office," he replies, taking a sip, and I remember the receptionist mentioning something about that.

"What do you do when you're not here?" My eyes involuntarily flick to his left hand, noticing no ring in sight. No tan line, either.

"I own a property development business with my good friend, Robbie Crossland. We flip houses, apartment buildings or empty lots we come across, and sell them. It keeps me really busy. When I'm not here, I'm at one of my other job sites or dealing with paperwork. But otherwise, I kind of just do whatever I want. I used to be hands-on, doing the renovations myself, but the company is at the point now where I can hire people to do it for me." His cheeks turn a soft shade of pink as he humbly brags about his success.

"My shoulder can't handle heavy lifting these days, either." He reaches his left hand across to his right shoulder, squeezing it gently before I steer the topic away from his injury and back toward real estate.

"Do you know anyone looking to sell their apartment? I have a job now, so it looks like I'm in Grangewood for a while. Plus, I can't stay with my parents forever." I sigh.

"I know just the place. Let me contact the owner and get back to you. Leave it with me."

***

"How did it go?" my mom asks as I clear the table after dinner.

"Good, the job is mine if I want it."

Turning on the tap, I get started on the dishes while she stands beside me, towel in hand, ready to dry them.

"Do you want it?" she asks.

"I do. I think it would be good for me. My belongings arrive this week, too. So, timing wise, everything is lining up perfectly. Once they get here, I'll be out of your hair. Harley even offered to help me look for an apartment," I say, my attempts to stay on task wavering, feeling my mom's eyes burning a hole into the side of my head.

Even though I love being back home, I'm thirty and I refuse to go backward. The longer I stay here, the harder it will be to start my new life; to create a new routine for myself.

Thanks to the sale of my apartment in California, I have enough savings to secure myself a place to live, and now that I'm starting a new job, I'll be able to afford the payments without my savings taking too big of a hit.

My independence is key, and being independent means having a space of my own to call home.

"What's the rush? It's nice having you here," Mom says, and I know she's saying it because she thinks it's what I want to hear, but it's not. I won't apologize for wanting to move out, but I am grateful that I would have a roof over my head, regardless.

I know many people don't have that luxury.

"I'm thirty, mom. If I move back home, I'm at a standstill. I need my space and privacy, and I don't need a curfew and I would like my bedroom door to remain firmly on its hinges," I joke, flinching at the memory of my teenage self without privacy, while she nudges me with her shoulder.

Taking a deep, shaky breath before she speaks, I sense her hesitation, and I smile to encourage her to say what's on her mind. "Are you doing okay, honey?" Turning off the tap, I take my time to reflect on her question.

Am I okay?

The short answer is *yes*.

If you had asked me last week, before Megan's wedding and the whole incident, my answer would have immediately been no. If he left me because he just didn't see a future with me anymore, that'd be a harder pill for me to swallow. Harder for me to just forget about him and move on.

But I went from feeling heartbroken to feeling instantly angry as soon as I learned about his three-year affair.

My anger surpassed any love I'd ever felt for him.

"I'm doing really great, mom," I tell her honestly. "It helps to be back home. Our relationship may have started here, but our life together didn't. Sure, this place is full of memories, but they're mostly at the high school, Katie's Diner and Bridie's. We were just kids. I'm glad I made the move back home." I can feel her cheeks swelling from her smile against the side of my head as she pulls me in for a hug.

"I'm so glad to hear it."

"I'm going to shower and get some sleep." I turn to head for the stairs.

"Cassandra?" she calls my name and I pivot back to face her. "You don't know how much love you have to give until you meet the person you're meant to give all of your love to," she whispers.

"Love you, mom," I whisper back, careful not to let my voice crack as I wipe away the tears that are running down my cheeks.

Taking the stairs two at a time, I push my bedroom door shut, leaning against it to compose myself when I feel my phone vibrating in my pocket. I can't help the smile that spreads across my face when I see his name, and I don't feel guilty that his name alone brightened my mood instantly.

> **Harley:** Herring. What are you up to?

> **Me:** Not a lot, Wingrove. Just had dinner, about to shower and head to bed. You?

> **Harley:** Up for a late-night milkshake with Bea and me?

I spend more time than needed staring at my phone before replying.

My mind instantly goes to Austin. My working for Harley and spending time with him off the clock would infuriate him.

But as quickly as that thought arrives in my head, I push it away with the reminder that he made his own bed. I don't live my life to please him anymore, and I sure as hell won't be worrying if he approves of my rekindled friendships.

> **Me:** Didn't get enough of seeing me today, huh?

> **Harley:** Enough of Cassandra Herring? Never.

Me: You're making me blush. Where should I meet you guys?

Harley: Katies. 30 mins?

Me: See you then :)

Thirty minutes is plenty of time to have a quick shower and make myself look semi-presentable, but not like I'm trying too hard.

I don't want to come across as too eager, so I settle on a bit of mascara to thicken up my naturally long lashes, some lip balm, blue jeans, and a black, knitted sweater with my signature black boots before I head out the door to have a milkshake with my very first best friend and my very first non-celebrity crush.

Twelve

Harley

I TEXTED BEA, LETTING her know that I'm out the front of her house the moment I put my car in park. Tapping my fingers on the steering wheel, her words play on repeat in my head.

"Something tells me she's looking for a friend right now."

I don't want to be more than friends with anyone right now, so I can be just friends with Cassandra Herring.

After all, it's all I know how to be.

In high school, I thought there were moments of sparks and chemistry between us, but I realised quickly how in my head it all was when she started dating Austin. Everything I'd felt for her was all one-sided.

Instead of letting a girl consume me, I spent the rest of high school focusing on football and trying to avoid Austin's spiteful comments toward me.

Once we'd graduated, I refused to let his name ever cross my mind or come out of my mouth.

He wasn't worth it to me.

Cassandra, though? I thought about her often.

I mostly wondered how she was and hoped that she was happy. I accepted the fact that if I were to ever see her again, it would be a complete accident and would be from afar.

Especially while Austin was in the picture.

While I had accepted that they were together a long time ago, a tiny piece of me shattered when the news spread about their engagement earlier this year. Maybe that same piece was holding onto hope that there was still a chance for Cassandra Herring and me, but that dream was one of a teenager.

When Bea had told me to just be friends with her, I told her I would, and I meant it.

Sure, she still has the most beautiful eyes that have ever looked my way, and plump lips that I never got the chance to kiss, but that doesn't mean I'm going to jeopardize the friendship we could have.

No matter how often the big guy below begs and aches for her.

Pulling my passenger side door open, Bea slams it shut like she does every time she gets in or out of my Range Rover. She's not gentle with anything she touches, and I flinch in anticipation.

"Is Laney sure she doesn't want to come?" I ask. Bea's wife is one of the best people I know. The three of us hang out constantly, but it's not uncommon for her to not want to join us.

"She likes her own company. She asked if you could keep me forever." She rolls her eyes playfully as she rolls down the window before pulling her seatbelt over her shoulder, clicking it in.

They've been married for three years, and I was the man of honor, standing by Bea's side. I made her a promise that she would be my best maid if I ever got married.

Looking me up and down, she sizes up my outfit and a shit-eating grin forms across her lips, and I shift uncomfortably in my seat. Following her gaze to my black sweater, I check for stains or anything out of the ordinary, but nothing stands out.

"What?" I ask, confused.

"You and I go to Katie's for a milkshake weekly, and you only ever wear sweats unless you're in a suit from a long day at work, but today, you're in a knitted sweater and jeans?" she asks, raising a brow and puffing out her cheeks. "You could have told me we were trying to impress her. I would've dressed for the occasion," she teases, pulling at the fabric of her maroon, hooded jumper, and running her hands down her black tights, while her short, blonde hair is down, embracing her natural wave.

"Whatever."

Piling into the old beige booth at the back of the diner, we wait for Cassandra to arrive before we order anything.

"So, you hired her, huh?"

"She needed a job, and we needed someone to fill the position. She was the right fit, and I wanted to help out a friend."

"Make sure it stays that way, Wingrove."

Her voice remains firm, reminding me for what feels like the hundredth time.

"Just friends," I say, maintaining innocence.

Hearing the bell above the door chime, I glance up, only to do a double take as I notice Cassandra walking toward us with a bright smile spread right across her face. My eyes wander down her petite body, beginning at the messy bun on top of her head. Her eyelashes, looking extra thick and making her hazel eyes pop and sparkle under the terribly old lights of the diner, and her smooth, naturally pink lips that I don't let myself linger on for too long.

Just friends.

Ripping my attention from her lips, I take in the rest of her outfit.

She's paired her black knitted sweater with tight blue jeans and black combat boots. Bea's snort breaks my concentration, and I fling my eyes to my laughing best friend beside me, not bothering to hide her amusement.

"What the fuck are you laughing at?" I ask as I flick her bicep with my finger that's hidden under my folded arm.

"What did I miss?" Cassandra asks as she sits down, placing her phone, keys, and wallet down on the table. Her usual chirpy self is none the wiser that Bea has created some sort of inside joke with herself.

There used to be four of us sitting in these booths, eating fries and chasing them with milkshakes, but I think I speak for everyone at this table when I say that I'm glad four has officially become three.

"You mean, you guys didn't plan this?" Bea's body shakes as laughter continues, pointing her finger back and forth between Cassandra and me.

"Plan what?" I ask, just as confused as I was a minute ago, but Cassandra is giggling as she sits across from us, picking up her menu.

"Stand up, both of you," Bea insists, taking deep breaths to steady her laughter while Cassandra does as she's told, no questions asked.

Glaring at my best friend, I groan while I stand, walking toward Cassandra until we're side by side, and that's when I notice what Bea found so comical.

It's happened again.

Looking down at my outfit and back at Cassandra's, I wish I opted for my usual attire of sweats and a hooded sweater.

Instead, I chose to not look like a slob and wore a black jumper, blue jeans, and black combat boots, identical to the girl standing beside me.

You'd think we'd coordinated this, but nope.

It seems some things don't ever change.

"Twins!" Cassandra exclaims with a giggle, looking at us both up and down, and God damnit if my chest doesn't squeeze at the flashback of this happening in my mom's old truck, fourteen years ago.

"You guys are like one of those lame couples who plan to match whenever they leave the house." Bea pretends to gag as she opens up the menu, even though she orders exactly the same thing weekly.

The waitress, Luna, takes our order, where Bea orders a salted caramel shake with fries for the three of us to share, Cassandra orders a chocolate shake and I order an Oreo one.

The next hour flies by so quickly, it's easy to forget that it's been years since we've done this. We've laughed so much my cheeks are on fire, tears streaming down both girls' cheeks.

"Do you guys remember the party at Matty Maxwell's farm?" Cassandra asks as we reminisce about high school, while she dips her final fry into her shake.

"I was the designated driver while you guys got wasted. Of course, I remember." I scoff, pretending to be annoyed at the memory.

"Do you remember much from that night?" Bea asks Cassandra, and I kick her foot under the table, causing her to wince slightly as she smirks for only me to see.

I know exactly where she's going with this.

"I don't remember a thing aside from getting there and spending the next day throwing up. My dad punished me by taking away my bedroom door for a week."

We all erupt with laughter, and Bea's milkshake comes out of her nose before she says, "I remember that!" while wiping her face clean with a napkin.

Who takes their teenage daughter's bedroom door away because she was hungover? Take away her social privileges, or her phone. Not her privacy.

"I do vaguely remember having a conversation with you, Harley, but I also know that conversation was rudely interrupted because someone threw up on someone else's shoes." She shakes her head and chuckles in disbelief. "I'm so sorry about that, again," she says shyly, visibly blushing. Her fingers picking at the nail-bed on her thumb.

That's not quite what happened, but I'll let her believe it.

"I drove you all home in my underwear and threw those pants in the trash the second I walked through my front door," I say as laughter erupts from the table once more.

"It's getting late. I should head home," Cassandra says after a moment of silence.

The three of us have been far too comfortable in this very uncomfortable booth for two hours.

My body is too large to be stuffed in such a confined space for so long. Every part of me hurts.

"Living back at home sucks. Hopefully, I can find a place soon. Once I'm settled, I would love to have you both over for dinner sometime. Laney too," she says, smiling at the both of us as she rises from her side of the booth, collecting her belongings.

"Text me when you get home safe." The words leave my mouth so quickly, Bea registers that I've said them before I do, but it's just a habit of mine.

She nods, leaning in to give Bea and me a hug, before she heads toward the door, and I let out a breath of relief as I slouch back into the worn-out, almost non-existent padding of the booth.

"Wingrove," Bea hisses as she whispers my name.

"What?" I whisper shout back.

"Look."

Following her gaze, we both try to hide the fact that we're staring at a very uncomfortable Cassandra and a very persistent Angela Anderson. She and her husband, Max, have stopped Cassandra for what I bet is a very unwanted conversation, where Angela looks to have a hold on Cassandra's wrist, but she rips her arm free quickly.

Reluctantly, we peel our eyes away from the scene and wait until they've finished talking and the bell chimes before we get up and attempt to sneak out of Katie's, unseen.

"Harley, it's good to see you, son," Max Anderson says, ruining our cover.

He stands from his booth, placing his hand out for me to shake, and I do.

"Hi, Mr. Anderson, Mrs. Anderson," I respond, acknowledging his wife, who barely nods in return. Ever since my falling out with her son, she's always been cold toward me, but Max has always shown me nothing but respect, so he'll always have mine.

"Good to see you both," Bea says politely, placing her hand in mine and dragging me out the door.

"I don't imagine that was a pleasant conversation," she says, letting go of my hand while I reach in my pocket for my car keys.

"Herring hasn't told me what happened between her and Austin." I shrug, unlocking the door with the key fob. "For all I know, she and Austin ended on good terms and are still in contact," I say, but I know it's not the case.

She wouldn't be here if it were.

"They didn't," is all Bea says, slamming the door shut, forcing my mind to automatically assume the worst.

If Austin is anything like he was back in school, I don't have a shred of doubt that he hurt her in some way.

It might not have been physical, but it doesn't make her pain any less valid.

Pulling up in the parking lot under my apartment complex, I stare at my phone as I wait and wait for a text message from Cassandra to let me know that she's home.

But I wait and wait for a text message that never comes.

Thirteen
Cassandra

"WHAT DID THEY SAY?" Jenna's eyes widen in disbelief the moment she answers the phone.

I sent her a quick text rundown when I got to my car and told her I would video call her when I got home to explain in full detail.

"They caught me as I was leaving," I say in a whisper as I rush up the stairs, closing my bedroom door behind me as quietly as possible. "I had such a nice time catching up with Bea and Harley, too. Knowing they saw me standing there awkwardly with my ex-in-laws while Angela tried to talk to me, somehow makes it all seem worse," I say, my voice still hushed as I shimmy out of my jeans and sweater, slipping on something warm and comfortable for me to sleep in.

"Why would it make it worse? The way that family behaves is in no way a reflection of you. You were just caught in the crossfire of their shitty antics," she tells me.

She's right, but I don't want my friends to think that I'm still entertaining the idea of being friendly with people from my past, especially knowing they betrayed me. I don't want them thinking it was anything more than a one-sided conversation.

Adjusting my pillows on my bed, I wrap myself in my duvet as I prepare to give Jenna the complete rundown of the conversation the Andersons decided to have with me.

I pranced toward the door of Katie's Diner with a smile spread wide across my face. I'd scored a new job earlier today and ended it by catching up with two old friends. It had probably been the best day I'd had in two months, and I'd thought nothing could've wiped the smile off my face.

Yet, hearing Angela Anderson call my name wiped the smile clean off and sent a chill straight down my spine, just as I was about to walk out the door.

I'd been so close to leaving the diner.

So close.

I could've pretended like I hadn't heard her and ran straight out the exit, but my mom raised me to be respectful, and right now, I'd cursed her for it.

Damn you, Roxanne Herring.

It took every ounce of my willpower to turn around and face her.

"Angela. Max," I'd said as I turned to see their faces. Max's looked slightly guilty, but Angela's looked...smug. Like she wanted to rub it in that I would no longer be a part of their family.

I didn't smile at them, though. I couldn't even pretend to be happy to see them. I just didn't have it in me.

"What can I help you with?" I'd asked them, trying to remain as calm as I could.

"We just wanted to see how you're doing," she'd probed me, reaching out to grab my hand, but I ripped it away, crossing my arms over my chest.

She turned to look at the direction in which I'd just walked away from, clearly able to see that I'd just been at a table with their son's number one enemy.

"I'm great," I'd said, refusing to return the question. Nodding, she sighed before speaking again.

"Look. We just wanted to apologize. Although we knew about the Alison situation, we said nothing because it wasn't our place," Angela said, while her husband remained quiet, his silent refusal to make eye contact with me blatantly obvious.

"No worries. Have a good night," I'd replied.

I'd given the fakest smile I could muster, not wanting to hear anything else they had to say. I wanted to tell them to shove their apologies where the sun doesn't shine, but I didn't have the energy. I didn't want to cause a scene.

I refused to dwell on the past anymore.

The moment I'd decided I was done with Austin Anderson, I'd decided I was done with every single person from the Anderson family, and I meant it.

"Be careful with the company you keep, Cassandra," she said as I opened the diner door and let it close behind me.

"I'm so fucking proud of you," Jenna said, listening intently to every word I just told her.

"Thanks. I used to hold them at the same level I held my parents, you know? But now...now, I don't hold a place for them at all," I admit. The truth feels so freeing.

"Rich of her to tell you to be careful of the company you keep. What a bitch," she said, pouring herself a glass of water.

"I hope you never see that family again."

"The day I do will be a day too soon."

"Good riddance, I say."

Good fucking riddance, indeed.

Fourteen
Cassandra

"Hello?" I answer my phone on the third ring after frantically searching my purse for it. I'm heading out the door after my first successful week at Wingrove Estates.

I've completed the final touches on the stall at the Grangewood Creek Carnival and am really looking forward to experiencing my first one since I was a teenager.

Work has been quieter than what I'm used to, though. I'm used to planning everything from the venue to the caterers, florists, photographers, and celebrants. I've even had to arrange for fake groomsmen in the past.

But here at Wingrove Estates, I need to do less than half of that.

I welcomed the change of pace, though, and it feels like a breath of fresh air. Something I so desperately needed.

"Hey, Herring," Harley's deep voice drawls through the phone, and I can't help but smile as I hop into my mom's car. I haven't seen him since the diner because he's been working out of town on one of his other projects, so he hasn't been at the winery at all.

"I'm going to text you an address. Meet me there on your way home from work," he says, and I agree before the call ends.

Pulling into the parking lot of an apartment building, it looks like something out of an architectural magazine, and completely out of place here in Grangewood, but in a good way.

"Where are we?" I call through my open passenger window as I see Harley step out of his Range Rover, approaching my now-parked car.

"Well, hopefully, your new place." He smiles at me as he opens my door for me, holding his hand out for me to take, and I do.

More eagerly than I expected to, but I shake it off and step out of the car, my hand still clutched in his.

"The current owners are clients of mine. They want to sell it at a cheap price and want it gone as soon as possible," he responds as he closes my car door gently, bringing me in for a hug hello.

Sandalwood and vanilla.

He's dressed a lot less business and a lot more casual today. Sporting a black, backward baseball cap, replaced his slacks and button-up with dark blue jeans, and a gray t-shirt that hugs his biceps and chest in a way that I force myself to appreciate from afar.

"If you want it, you could be in it as early as next week," he says, leading us toward the foyer, where an elevator door is already open, waiting for us to ride up.

Pushing the button for the twelfth floor, we spend our journey up in silence, the air cracking around us, elevator music muffled somewhere in the clouds, nowhere to be heard.

My stomach has been swarming with those damn butterflies since I left work. I can almost feel his body warmth radiating from beside me.

His hands hang by his sides, so close to mine, but he reaches for the keys in his pocket before our fingers can touch, and we've reached our destination, leaving a feeling of emptiness slicing through me.

Pull yourself together, Cassandra.

"What do you think?" He beams, pushing the double doors open to my potential new home, giving me full access to view the wide-open space.

The apartment is enormous, almost twice the size of my old space in California, and my first thought automatically goes to how much of a pain it would be to keep it clean.

"How many bedrooms does this place have?" I ask. My mouth is hanging wide open, my eyes popping out of my head. I've never seen a place like this before, and I've only seen the hallway so far.

"Four," he pauses but quickly continues so I can't interject. "You could have a spare room for your friends. Or for your sisters when you need a girls' night. You could even use the space for a home office, if you wanted one." He smiles and I have to look away before I melt into a puddle and damage the hardwood floors.

Harley has taken into consideration all things I never would have dreamed about, but this place is still too big for me. Not to mention, probably way out of my budget.

"Before you make your decision, at least see the whole place first," he insists, sensing my hesitation. Gesturing me down the hallway, he leads me to the rest of the house.

"On your right is the full laundry with a mudroom attached," he says, and I get excited instantly, knowing I won't have to use the communal washer and dryer with everyone else from the building.

As we walk, I'm creating a pros and cons list in my head, with laundry slotting directly onto the pro list, the sheer size of the apartment, cons.

Continuing to walk down the hall, we're met with the most beautiful kitchen I've ever seen.

"This room is pretty self-explanatory," he says casually as he drags his fingertips along the stone countertops and I mimic his actions, settling when my fingertips connect with the cool, yet warm, stone.

The nearest beach to Grangewood Creek is half a day's drive away, yet this kitchen screams costal. The countertops are white, and the cabinets are light oak with gold furnishings.

I'm a sucker for anything gold.

"This kitchen alone is bigger than my old apartment in Cali," I admit. "I could never afford it," I accidentally blurt the words out loud, but his response comforts me in a way I never would have expected.

"This is Grangewood, Herring. Not California. Things are cheaper here." He reaches his hand out for me to take for the second time since we arrived here, and I haven't hesitated to take it either time.

I like the feeling it gives me.

He leads the way to show me the master bedroom and ensuite, the three spare bedrooms, and the spare bathroom, which has more white and gold to match the kitchen.

"So, what do you think?" he asks once we're standing back in the kitchen, and I realize my hand is still very much in his.

I don't let go, but he does, and I try really hard to not take it personally.

Try being the key word.

"I love it. But like I said, I couldn't afford it."

"I thought you'd say that," he says, pulling a folded yellow envelope from his back pocket.

"What's this?" I stare at it, fighting every urge to not rip it open and find out for myself.

"It's the contract and the asking price from the owner. Open it when you get home. Think about it and let me know."

***

Throwing myself on my bed, I hold the envelope in my hand that I opened the moment I walked into my bedroom.

My decision is obvious.

Of course, I need to snatch up this apartment for the price written on the contract.

I'd be stupid not to.

I could buy it outright, be mortgage free.

I would need to buy new furniture too, considering everything I currently own has memories attached to them. If I'm getting a fresh start, it needs to be done properly.

Sure, my savings would be well and truly drained, but it's about damn time I do something just for myself.

There has to be a catch.

Maybe it's a typo?

Or maybe the apartment is insect infested, or termites were the last residents.

If something seems too good to be true, usually it is, right?

Either way, I pull out my phone to text Harley just to make sure.

Me: Are you sure this isn't a typo?! It seems too good to be true.

Harley: haha, not a typo. It's yours if you want it. I know the owner and he just wants it gone. It's been sitting empty for too long.

Me: I'll take it. How can I thank you? Can I have you over for dinner like I promised?

Me: And Bea and Laney too, of course.

Harley hasn't given me any reason to think he wants anything romantic with me, but I had to send that last text just to make sure he didn't think dinner would be anything more than it was.

A thank you.

Waiting for his reply, I anxiously bite my nails in anticipation, staring at the little grey dots that appear on my screen.

Harley: I think it's time you jump into the creek, Herring.

Harley: But I'll take you up on your dinner offer, too.

Me: It turns out I don't need the apartment after all!! Tell the owner I said thank you, but no thank you.

Harley: I'll be there to catch you.

I pause. To really consider what he's asking me to do.

I never could jump off the rock cliff into the creek. It's always been my biggest fear.

Could Harley Wingrove really be the one to help me face it and...take the leap?

Me: Promise?

Harley: Promise.

Regret.

Regret.

Regret.

Why did I just agree to do the Grangewood Creek infamous cliff jump?

Do I have a fucking death wish?

I don't reply because I'm not actually going to follow through with this silly idea of his, and I hope that if I ignore him, he'll forget and it'll just magically go away.

Dinner is much more my style. Something that I genuinely want to do to show my gratitude toward him. It'll be a nice way to get to know Laney, too. Jumping into the creek was so far off my radar, it never even crossed my mind that he would have suggested it.

But I should have known.

Austin, Bea, and Harley would do the jump into the water every weekend in the summer.

They'd flip, dive, or bomb so seamlessly, while I stayed with our belongings. My feet rarely even touched the water.

I was the only kid in school who never made the leap.

It was almost like a rite of passage here in Grangewood, yet, I never found the courage.

"Come on, babe. You can do it," Bea shouts, cheering me on from down below.

"I don't think I can," I yell back to her and Austin, who were both waiting, treading water.

Bea's patient. Austin is the furthest thing from it.

"Don't be a wimp, Cass. Hurry up about it. My balls are shrinking down here," he said, no sign of embarrassment, loud enough for me and everyone else to hear. I could sense the frustration in his voice, but it didn't encourage me to jump. It put me more on edge than I already was.

I don't know what Austin's problem is with me, but he always seems so cold toward me. Almost like he only hangs around Bea and me because he feels like he has to. But no one is holding him hostage. He's free to leave if he wants.

And right now, I kind of want him to.

Bea thinks he has the 'treat her mean, keep her keen' mindset because he has a crush on me, but I don't believe that for a second. He's shown no interest in me, and I doubt he ever will.

Feeling a familiar warmth approach, I hear his soft, deep voice from behind me, and I close my eyes to take a deep breath.

"You don't need to jump if you're not ready, Herring." Harley's voice is only slightly more than a whisper, reassuring me, and I feel instantly at ease. shivers coating my skin. "But if you decide to jump, I'll hold your hand on the way down." His words get my attention, my gaze to flick to our hands as his knuckles graze mine ever so slightly.

I feel my body heat from the temptation.

"I don't think I can do it." I can't tell If I'm talking to him or if I'm talking to myself, but I know he hears me, and for that, I'm glad.

"Well, then, maybe I'll wait down there to catch you when you decide to jump."

His voice is still low, arms shaking by his sides, preparing to launch himself off the cliff.

"Do you promise?" I match his tone, hiding the quiver in my voice, making sure no one else can hear me.

"I promise." He nods as he smiles at me, revealing his lone dimple, throwing himself off the cliff while he lets out a loud "woo".

I can't believe I'm agreeing to this. All for a damn roof over my head.

At least it's a pretty roof, I tell myself.

> **Me**: Ugh, let's get it over with.

> **Harley**: I'm on my way to your house. Be there in 5.

"Your house isn't five minutes away from here. Were you already on your way over?" I ask as I hop into the passenger side of his Range Rover, and it hits me that I haven't been in a car with Harley since we were sixteen.

He drives a much more expensive car now than he did then.

"I was hopeful," he says. His voice woven with humor, he keeps his eyes firmly on the road.

"I can't believe I'm doing this." I cross my arms over my chest, sinking further into the leather seats to get comfortable for the drive.

"You better believe it, baby," he replies casually, as if he calls every-one baby, but it's the first time those words have left his mouth directed toward me. The realistic part of me knows it's just a figure of speech, but I kind of want to hear it again.

Get a grip, Cassandra.

"I can't do it," I shout below me as I see Harley's figure floating in the dark, murky water below. "How do I know a giant eel or anaconda isn't going to swallow me whole the second my body hits the water?" I ask, biding myself more time.

Did I mention I hate open water?

It's dark out, with the only light shining on us being the natural light from the moon, and while it's enough to show me the outline of Harley waiting for me, it's not enough for me to spot any potential threats.

"Herring. I promise, I'm the only one in this creek waiting for you."

It's cold. I'm shivering, knowing I'm about to voluntarily throw myself into a bed of water with god knows what waiting for me, that I forget all about my nipples and how they're poking through my pastel blue bikini. I cross my arms over my chest to hide them, hoping Harley can't see my body clear enough from where he is.

"I can't!" I shout back, my right foot taking a small step forward.

"Yes, you can!" he yells back for the tenth time, yet he sounds just as encouraging as he did the first time he said those words to me.

The wind is picking up. The leaves in the trees rustling to the beat of my thumping heart in my throat, in my ears and in my fingertips.

"Could you come up here and push me? I need a little nudge." I opt for sarcasm, but part of me thinks the only way I'm getting in that water is if I'm pushed or if I somehow slip and fall.

"I would never push you, Herring. Do you want me to come hold your hand?" He offers, trying to help, but I shake my head.

I need to do this alone, but I feel safe knowing he's ready and waiting below.

"I'll be right here waiting. I have all night."

Patient.

"My feet are turning into prunes though, Herring. So maybe I'll get out until you're actually ready so my toes don't fall off." He laughs, clearly amusing himself. I roll my eyes.

Sarcasm is not what I need right now, even if I'm the one who started it.

"Okay. Okay! I'm going to jump. Can you count me down from ten?" I ask, taking a deep breath to calm my nerves, running my hands down my arms to keep me warm.

"I will count down from ten."

Silence fills the air, but only for a moment, and then the countdown begins. My legs feel like jelly.

"Ten. Nine. Eight—" he starts, my stomach churns.

Please don't be sick.

"Seven. Six. Five—"

"Do you promise to catch me?" I interrupt his countdown, hovering over the edge.

"I promise. Four. Three. Two—" And before he can get to one, I leap off the rock, letting out a not-so-subtle scream, his voice cheering me on from below.

I did it.

As my body crashes against the ice cold water, his arm grips around my waist, pulling me up for air.

"I knew you could do it," his excited voice sounds over the crashing waves my body caused, and I don't miss the pride in it.

To steady myself and catch my breath, I wrap my arms around his neck and my legs follow suit instinctively, wrapping around his waist. The moment they do, I regret it.

I'm taken aback by what I can feel.

I know I'm not imagining this.

I'm not imagining the sensation of his cock growing harder against me. My body shudders at the simple touch, swimsuit fabric the only thing separating us.

We remain completely still, knowing how it'll end if either of us even moves slightly. If we were naked, it would be so easy to just slide down and have him fill me up and right now, I'm craving nothing more.

But I'm not ready.

My breathing quickens. I close my eyes, resting my forehead against his before I place a soft, almost missable kiss on his lips before quickly pulling away, knowing we can't go back if we cross that line.

Knowing such a simple movement can ruin everything we've built in such a short amount of time.

Unwrapping my legs from around his waist, I use his hard chest as leverage to push myself away, swimming to the edge of the water and climbing out.

"I'm sorry about that," he whispers, drying himself off with a towel.

"You have nothing to be sorry for", I whisper back. We're alone here. No one can hear us, but it feels wrong to have this conversation in any other way. "I'm not ready for—" I begin, but he cuts me off before I can finish my sentence.

"I know. Just friends, I get it."

His jaw ticks as he looks away from me, probably to hide the frustration in his face, but I can hear it in his voice. Only, I don't know if he's frustrated with himself, or if he's frustrated in the words that I attempted to say.

"It's not my fault." I shrug. "I could feel your giant erection getting bigger by the second. It was hard...to miss. Pun intended." I need to lighten the mood, and hearing him chuckle is like music to my ears.

"You think it's giant, hey?" he jokes, using his towel to dry his hair one last time before using it to pretend to whip my ass, making me squeal and giggle, using my hands as a shield.

"Jerk." I pretend to scoff.

I'm glad it's dark out, because my cheeks would be a dead giveaway that he makes me so nervous.

Right now, more than ever.

"Hey, Harley," I say as he starts his car, my hair still dripping wet on his leather seats.

"I'm not saying no to *you*. I'm just saying no to *right now.*"

I really hope he understands.

I need him to.

I can barely see his face in the dark, but while I do see his head nod, he remains laser focused on the road and getting me home.

I meant what I said. I'm not ready to be with anyone else, physically or emotionally. I'm not clinging to hope that Austin and I will get back together, because I meant it when I said he was in my past.

But I am clinging on to the hope that I can be my own person without being attached to someone else.

But after tonight, I don't know how much longer I'll be able to resist Harley Wingrove.

Does he feel the attraction, too?

Or does he want to be just friends?

Fifteen
Harley

Fuck being, *just friends*.

Sorry, Bea.

Sixteen

Cassandra

I'D REALLY ENJOYED MYSELF over the last few days at the Grangewood Carnival. The whole town had come out to support all the local businesses, while eating their body weight in cotton candy, popcorn, and all the fried food you could imagine.

Parents were losing their hard-earned money trying to win stuffed toys for their kids, while those same kids were having the time of their lives.

It'd been a hit for us, too.

The wine and food samples had sold out each night, and the restaurant is fully booked for the next few weeks, according to Harley.

I think it's safe to say that the carnival has been a success in gaining the attention that we'd hoped for.

He'd been gone for the last few days, traveling with his business partner, Robbie, while the two of them looked at new potential business opportunities. Which meant he hadn't had the chance to see and enjoy the carnival yet.

He'll be here soon, though.

We haven't seen each other since the *incident* at the creek, and I'd be lying if I said I wasn't at all nervous about seeing him.

I'm nervous as hell, actually.

We'd spoken throughout the week, but mostly to do with work, so there are clearly unspoken feelings. I just didn't know what the feelings were and if I'm the only one who feels them.

I don't want to feel them, and I've tried to tell them to shoo, but it doesn't seem to be working.

I've barely been single for three months, yet my body is screaming for whatever he wants to give me. I'm just glad I'm mentally strong enough to resist. How much longer I'll be able to resist, though? That remains to be seen.

Snow globe lights dangle between each booth, lighting up the signs, the food and drinks, the games, and all the stuffed toys you could imagine.

Right in the center, stands a Ferris wheel, giving you the most incredible view of the quiet, but lit up Grangewood Creek.

The entire town has come out for the last night of the Carnival.

Nothing beats the feeling of a small town coming together to support its community, and I didn't realize how much I'd missed it. I even overheard Mrs. Bishop talking about something that didn't involve Austin or me, and it was pure bliss.

"Are you sure you don't need me anymore?" Bea shouts over the noisy crowd. She's been helping me out over the last few days to make sure everything ran smoothly, and it has, largely thanks to her.

"I'm sure." I nod. "Find Laney, and enjoy yourselves. Harley and his Mom will be here soon. Tell your beautiful wife I said hi," I say, smiling at her. She leans in to give me a hug. "Thank you for all of your help," I call out to her as she runs to find her wife, waving her hand in the air to say goodbye.

"This booth sure is something." A chillingly familiar voice snatches my attention almost instantly, but I'm reluctant to turn and face her.

I feel her eyes burning into the back of my head from behind me and I can't help but roll my eyes as I take a deep breath to calm myself before I turn in her direction.

"Angela. What can I get you?" I attempt my best customer service voice, even though we both know she doesn't deserve it.

"You can't seriously be working for that man. You really think I want to spend my hard-earned money on something from his business? You're as delusional as I thought. No wonder Austin cheated on you," she spits, crossing her arms over her chest, blue eyes rimmed red.

Her piercing stare makes me uneasy while she attempts to hurt me with her words, but I don't let her. I'm all too accustomed to the venom that spews out of her mouth.

"Why are you here then, Angela? Why are you wasting my time if you don't plan on spending your *husband's* hard-earned money?" I meet her gaze head on and match her energy.

I can't help it.

Mom may have raised me to be polite, but she also taught me to stand up to bullies. Angela Anderson is the biggest bully in town, and everyone is afraid of her. I used to cower when she was around, using her son as a shield, but not anymore.

I no longer have a reason to be kind to her.

"I just had to see if the rumors were true. That you are working for that...that family." The word family sounds so forbidden on her tongue, like she's never known the true meaning of it. "It's just like that man to take things that belong to my son." Bitterness is the only face Angela Anderson wears well.

"Firstly, Angela, Harley has taken nothing from your son and we both know it," I start before I'm cut off and unable to continue.

"Second, it is none of your business who my son hires to work for the business that he worked hard to build, let-alone, who my son has relationships with, professional or otherwise." Joanna Wingrove's voice is the one I hear over my shoulder, and I can't help but smirk at the instant change in Angela Anderson's face.

Almost like she's seen a ghost.

"Third, there is absolutely nothing that I want that your son currently has." Harley's eyes briefly flick to me before they return to Angela.

He's here.

"Now, if you don't leave this area, I'll have security escort you off the entire grounds, considering I own the land where the carnival is currently being held. If you don't want the whole town to see you dragged away, kicking and screaming like the toddler you're trying to be, I suggest you walk away. Willingly."

Angela Anderson is a proud person. She's arrogant and incredibly rude, and I put up with it for fourteen years.

But I don't have to do that anymore.

Harley putting her in her place is the hottest thing I've ever seen.

"Come on, honey, let's go."

Max Anderson appears from her side, gripping her wrist before forcing her to walk away, but I don't miss the apologetic smile he briefly flashes Harley and Joanna before turning his back.

"I had her handled," I said, because I did. I had so much more that I wanted to say to her now that I finally found the courage.

"I know you did, but that woman has always hated me. I'm not a kid anymore. I had to put her in her place."

"Why doesn't she like you?" I ask, looking between Harley and Joanna, who is busying herself with replenishing the empty wine shelves, pouring a glass for the three of us.

"Beats me. When Austin decided to hate me, she did too. No skin off my back." He shrugs as we both accept the glass of wine his mom offers us.

"She's not worth it, Harley," Joanna says reassuringly, while resting her hand on his shoulder.

"No one in that family is."

Seventeen
Cassandra

IT'S WILD TO THINK that I've been back home for almost a month. I already have a new job that I love so much, and as of today, my very own apartment.

They gave me the keys two weeks ago, but I'd been too preoccupied with the carnival to focus on moving in. But the day had finally come. I haven't lived by myself in my thirty years of life, so this is going to be a change for me. A challenge, even. But it's one I'm looking forward to.

I've taken so many steps in bettering myself since being back in Grangewood Creek, but buying my own place has to be the cherry on top. I'm hoping to keep the friendships that I've rekindled, too, which is why I'd invited Bea, Laney, and Harley over for dinner tonight.

I missed out on a lot over the last decade, and I only had myself to blame.

Living with my parents has been brief, but I've overstayed my welcome. Their constant berating and hovering are getting to me, too. It's suffocating, and I just needed to catch my breath.

"Have you spoken to Austin?"

"Do you think you'll move back to California, or are you happy here?"

"What's Angela's issue?"

"Are you going to date your new boss?"

It's all just...too much.

My sisters are insistent that tonight with Harley, Bea and Laney is a double date, no matter how many times I've told them that Harley and I are just friends.

I told Lizzie that I would consider creating an account for *one* dating app once I got settled into my apartment, even though I don't actually plan on it. I just needed to shut her up.

"Getting on a dating app will prove to me that you don't want to fuck your hot boss. Download it, create an account, and I'll get off your case. Don't download it, and I will hound you until you let Harley pound you. The choice is yours," she had said, followed by a manic, evil laugh, like she was the wicked witch of Grangewood.

Watching as my father and Harley unload the last few boxes out of the truck, I don't miss how he winces and rubs his shoulder once he places the box down onto the ground. I tried to read about his injury online, but I couldn't find anything of importance, so I gave up pretty quickly.

He and I still haven't spoken about the night at the creek, either, but it plays on my mind a lot. We've seen each other at work and gone for more milkshakes with Bea, but we've never been alone. I don't exactly want to talk about it in front of anyone, so I've ignored it all together.

While the kiss at the creek was brief, it still happened, and it left me wanting and craving more.

More of Harley Wingrove.

More of what I've been fighting so hard to stay away from. But I couldn't admit that to anyone. I could barely even admit it to myself.

I've hardly been single for four months. And even though I know my feelings for Austin have well and truly vanished, I still need to get to know myself again. And I don't know how long that's going to take. Which is another reason I invited Bea and Laney to dinner. Who know's what I'll do...or allow *him* to do, given the chance.

I'm not ready to find out.

Today has been long.

The move itself is finished, but I still need to unbox and find new homes for everything, all while entertaining guests.

Who arranges a dinner on move in day?

I guess I just assumed there would be less pressure on everyone if the vibe was more casual. Eating pizza, drinking beer, attempting to distract myself by slowly unpacking boxes.

"Are you sure you want us to stay?" Bea asks as she and Laney wipe down surfaces in my new kitchen to prepare for all of my brand-new appliances.

"You guys have been a huge help to me today. The least I can do is buy you pizza and beer as a thank you." I smile, and they nod, making their way to my new couch, getting themselves comfortable.

I realized earlier today that I've had someone by my side with every decision I've made my entire life. It's been really easy, focusing on things that I want, not having to factor in anyone else's opinions.

I picked out my dream couch in the color white. I bought a fridge that tells me the weather and reads out recipes to me as I cook. Just because I could.

I decided to turn one of the bedrooms into an office and a library for my ever-growing book collection. I even bought the biggest tv I could find so I could watch whatever I wanted *whenever* I wanted.

I made all of those decisions for myself.

"Thanks so much for all of your help today," I say to Harley as I watch him head for the fridge to grab himself a beer, already making himself comfortable.

I kind of liked that he already feels relaxed enough to make himself at home.

Okay, not kind of.

I *really* liked it.

"You know I'd help you with anything." He flashes me a smile, the amber beer bottle at his lips. Taking a sip, he grabs three extra beers from the fridge and four brand new coasters, placing them down on my new, glass, gold rimmed, coffee table.

"Who's ready for pizza?" I ask, clasping my hands together.

"I'm starving," Laney replies, her stomach grumbling right on cue.

Taking my phone out of my pocket, I order three large pizzas from *GC Pizzeria* for the four of us to enjoy over good company, alcohol, and even better conversation.

"So, you found out he cheated on you at his sister's wedding?" Laney gawks at me while chewing on a slice of pizza, and I nod while chugging the rest of my drink.

I guess Harley now knows about what happened between Austin and me, but he hasn't said a word to disrupt the conversation. It's not like I was hiding it from him. I just hate talking about it. But Laney asked, and I didn't want to lie.

"I can't believe you were actually engaged to that guy." She points her finger to her open mouth as if to gag, and I laugh.

"Me neither. Honestly, the entire situation makes me never want to be engaged ever again." I shiver at the thought, and I hate Austin for making me feel this way.

"Never?" Bea asks, and I shake my head while swallowing a bite of pepperoni pizza. "Not really. I don't see the point of wasting time, hoping one day my fiancé will decide he actually wants to marry me, you know? I got sick of begging him to pick a date. Trying to meet vendors with him. Trying to plan anything at all. It became more of a chore instead of an enjoyable experience." I shrug.

"That sucks," Bea says. "In school, you always used to talk about wanting to get married and be a Mom someday."

"Oh, I would still love both things. But if it were up to me, I would skip an engagement all together. Maybe my future husband will want to suddenly elope on the same day he proposes. With our families and friends." I chuckle. I don't miss the fact that Bea's watchful eyes float between me and Harley, who still hasn't even mumbled a single word.

What he has done, though, is shift uncomfortably in his seat on more than one occasion.

"Babe, I hate to break it to you, but that's not how you elope. An elopement is with, like, one witness." She smirks, and the conversation changes.

We talk about how I'm enjoying my new job, how Bridie's has been overwhelmingly busy, how Laney is getting client after client in her new yoga studio in town, and how Harley just negotiated and secured the old Mercury Hotel in town that he's hoping to turn into an apartment building.

My friends are all thriving, and it made my heart swell.

"So, what's the story here?" Laney asks, changing the subject, closing the lid of the last pizza box. "She told me not to ask about it," Laney says, gesturing to her wife, "but the sexual tension is *thick* in here tonight." She whistles. "Something tells me that *you* want to rail her." She points from Harley back to me. "And you want *him* to fuck you senseless," she says, finishing with her eyes locked on mine.

"Wow, you really don't sugar coat shit, do you?" Harley laughs, placing his empty beer bottle down on his coaster, but doesn't address her comment.

One thing I've learned about Laney in the short time I've known her is that she has no filter. She's a lot like Jenna, and I guess that's why I like her so much.

"Another beer, anyone?" Bea asks, trying to fill the silence by changing the subject, but I beat her to it by instantly replying with "I'll get it," before heading to grab another round for everyone.

You want him to fuck you senseless.

Laney's words screech like a broken record, going round and round in my head.

Is it that fucking obvious?

"I'm right, aren't I?" Her voice startles me, and I realize I'm staring into the fridge, not even looking in the direction of the beer.

"I don't know what you're talking about," I lie as I turn to face her, beers finally in hand.

I see why Bea likes her. Not only is she funny and brutally honest, but she's also stunning, too. Her long, slender, athletic legs are almost always shown off, thanks to the different-colored activewear she sports daily. Her subtle abs are on display tonight as she wears a soft yellow crop that hovers above her belly button, and I have to fight myself to stop staring.

Her hair is long and dark, with tight curls; her skin is naturally tanned from her Argentinian heritage, and her eyes are dark brown. She's also slightly taller than me.

"Don't play dumb with me, *Herring*." She chuckles, mimicking the nickname that only Harley calls me.

"Have I fantasized about being..." I trail off, too uncomfortable to finish the sentence, but I should have known she would finish it for me.

"...fucked senseless by Harley?"

"Fucked senseless by Harley," I repeat reluctantly, clearing my throat. "Maybe once or twice," I lie.

I've had the same recurring fantasy since the second I saw him at Wingrove Estates.

"But I would never act on it." I sigh, placing four beer bottles on the countertop, reaching for the bottle opener in my top drawer.

"Why?"

"Because it's too soon."

"Too soon for who? Who decides if it's too soon?"

I don't answer right away, because I don't know how. Who's the person that gets to decide how much time is enough time to move on? How long is long enough for you to let yourself stop wallowing in self-pity and allow yourself to actually be happy?

How long is long enough for you to open your heart back up, knowing full well it could get crushed again all the same?

"I just don't think I'm ready for that yet," I finally say, and she's quiet for a while before she responds.

"Just don't let yourself miss out on something good because society tells you that you need to wait to move on. There is no right or wrong time, Cassandra. You have nothing to prove to anyone. He's an incredible guy and if I were straight, I would have let him fuck me senseless a long time ago," she jokes to lighten the mood, clinking her beer bottle with mine.

"Just don't close that book yet, okay?"

"Okay."

***

My three visitors stayed later than any of us expected, but Jenna was still up and waiting for my FaceTime call, regardless that it was nearing midnight.

"Jenna, hey," I say, trying to sound excited to speak to her, but my exhaustion is winning out.

I love my best friend, but I hope our conversation is brief.

"Hey C, I miss you. Can you come home?" she asks, her voice has an unmistakable sadness attached to it.

"I *am* home, Jen," I say with a sigh. I know she misses me. I miss her just as much.

"I know." She draws a breath. "I just miss my best friend, that's all." My chest tightens at her admission. The only thing she needs from me is reassurance, so that's what I give her.

"No matter where we are, you're always going to be my number one. And I'm seeing you in five days," I say excitedly, reminding her that her birthday party is fast approaching.

I planned the whole thing.

Even while I've been away from California, I've still organized it all remotely for her, because I would do absolutely anything for my best friend.

"I can't wait!"

"Is it okay if I bring Harley and Bea?" I ask, knowing she wants to meet them as much as they want to meet her.

I've talked about them to each other nonstop over the last month. It feels like I have a huge circle of friends, but they don't know each other at all.

"The more the merrier. Plus, I want to meet the man who has my best friend feeling all kinds of naughty things." She chuckles. "I haven't heard from your ex, by the way, so I assume he won't come. But if I do, I'll tell him to fuck off." She rolls her eyes.

"Honestly, Jen, don't even worry about it. If he shows up, he shows up. I'll be fine. Being home has really put things into perspective for me. I don't miss him like I thought I would," I say, and it's completely the truth.

"I'll always care about him and a part of me will always have love for him, but I stopped being in love with him a little while ago." I shrug and Jenna lets out a sigh of relief.

"You don't know how happy I am to hear you say that. I'm proud of you, C."

"Me too."

The quick call I hoped for was a bust, and we spent the next hour gossiping about everything and anything while I unpack boxes and put some things away.

Who knew a gossip session was all I needed to be productive after a long night?

***

"Hello?" I knock on his office, but there's no answer.

Needing to place these documents on his desk for this weekend's wedding, I barge in without permission, stopping in my tracks at the sight before me.

His perfectly sculpted, bare back faces me, his belt lies on the floor in front of my feet, his light blue button-up shirt beside it.

His trousers are noticeably unzipped, while his pants sit lower around his waist, and I can't help but admire the curves of each muscle, the dimples on his lower back, forgetting to take in the fact that he has a woman pinned up against the wall in his office, with her legs linked around his waist.

I want to back away without being noticed or heard, but I can't bring myself to look away. I'm watching as he fucks someone else right in front of me, while a pang of jealousy knocks me off my feet.

"I've wanted this for so long," his deep voice grumbles, his breathing staggered.

"Me too," the female voice responds, and I pull my attention away from him, to her.

Me.

I'm watching myself have sex with Harley up against the wall in his office.

Edging closer to the scene in front of me, I stare as our mouths collide and a moan slips from my throat.

Raising my fingers to my lips, it's almost like I can feel and taste him there.

Trailing my eyes down our bodies, I watch as he thrusts in and out of me at a rapid pace, and I hear the sound of my own orgasm vibrating through the walls.

"You feel better around my cock than I ever thought possible," he whispers into my ear. "God, you're perfect, Herring."

Even though I can see that it's me he was fucking, hearing my name leave his mouth in such a way makes my toes curl. Makes me feel things I never expected to feel.

He peppers kisses along my jawline, down my neck, my back arching against the wall.

"Come for me again," he demands her—me.

As she does what he says, I envy myself and the fact she gets to fuck Harley Wingrove and I haven't even come close to doing anything of the sort.

Scurrying out of the office, I slam the door behind me—

Jolting awake, I'm drowning in sweat as my hands grip onto the blanket to steady myself, underwear completely soaked.

What the fuck was that?

Eighteen
Cassandra Age 16

My phone buzzing next to me is one way to wake me up, but the sound of my dad's fists banging on the door?

That's something else entirely.

Pair those two together with my first ever hangover, and you have yourself a recipe for disaster.

My father, Hank, has always been a loud man. He never really does anything peacefully. He even yawns and sneezes so loudly, I'm convinced the entire neighborhood knows when he's tired or sick.

"Get up," his angry voice roars from behind my door, while his fist continues to shake the four walls that hold my bedroom together. For how much longer, I'm not sure.

Clearly, the word has spread that I have my very first hangover, and old man Hank has no sympathy for me. He's obviously and understandably pissed that his sixteen-year-old daughter, and role model to his two youngest daughters, got drunk out of her mind last night.

If he didn't already have a full head of grey hair, he definitely would now.

"I'm up," I groan, just loud enough for him to hear me, hoping it's enough to make the banging stop.

Please let the banging stop.

My head feels like there's a bowling ball rolling around inside it, crashing into my skull with every move I make.

Dragging one leg over the side of my bed at a time, I slide each foot into my slippers before lugging my heavy body into my bathroom.

I put it off as long as possible, because I know the sight of the toilet is going to make me be sick, but I can smell the alcohol seeping through my pores.

A shower is a must.

"Having. Shower," I try to shout, but my voice screeches like nails on a chalkboard. Putting full sentences together is painful and nearly impossible, but I do the best I can.

Reaching for my phone before I stand up from my bed, I see five missed calls from Bea and a text message from Harley reading, "I hope you're feeling okay."

Smiling through the aches surging through my body, I call Bea back quietly, so the caveman outside my door can't hear me.

"Cass!" she says with a shout, and I instinctively pull the phone away from my ear. Her voice is so fucking loud.

"What do you need?" I hiss.

"Did you have a good night last night?" she asks.

Racking my brain, I try to remember anything at all, but I come up short. Aside from the car ride there with Austin and Harley, where Harley and I wore basically the same outfit, everything else is blank.

That particular memory makes my heart smile and my stomach flutter.

Or am I just nauseous?

"I remember nothing, apart from getting there."

Sighing, I reach for the tap in the shower to let the water run, hopefully drowning out the sound of my voice from Hank, the eavesdropper.

"Nothing else?" Is she always this pushy or am I too hungover to deal with anything or anyone today?

"No. Why? What happened?" I try so hard to not be frustrated, but it's nearly impossible, given the self-inflicted pain I feel.

She's silent for what feels like an entire minute before responding.

"Nothing. Hey, do you think Harley is cute?" I could've sworn that Bea was a lesbian, so hearing her talk about a guy this way catches me off guard.

"Uh, yes, you know I do."

"Okay, gotta go. Bye!"

I'm not even going to attempt to dissect that conversation.

I just know I need a cold shower and mouthwash to remove the taste of vodka, mixed with vomit, from my mouth.

I have no memory of actually puking, but I text Bea to find out for sure.

> **Me**: Did I puke last night?

> **Bea**: Yep.

> **Me**: Did you hold my hair back?

> **Bea**: Not me, but I know someone didn't make it out vomit free hahaha

Me: What do you mean? Please tell me I didn't vomit on anyone.

Bea: K then I won't tell you.

Me: Who do I need to apologize to?

Bea: Wingrove.

Shit.

Nineteen
Cassandra

Knocking on Harley's office door, I get an immediate sense of déjà vu and I almost back away entirely. Even though it's been a whole four days since my sex dream, I can't avoid him forever.

And unfortunately, today is one of the two days in the month that he's actually in the office. That, and we're traveling to California tonight for Jenna's birthday party tomorrow, so it's inevitable that I see him.

Hearing a muffled "come in", I open the door quickly, making eye contact with a topless Harley, where he looks at me like a deer in the headlights.

Surely, I'm dreaming again.

I *know* a shirtless Harley isn't standing directly in front of me.

I should peel my eyes away, but I can't seem to do it.

I don't *want* to do it.

In my mind, I'd pictured his body almost identical to this. I wish I was close enough to touch him, just to make sure I wasn't dreaming again.

His pants sit higher around his waist with his belt well and truly done up, unlike it was in my dream. My eyes flick quickly past his perfectly sculpted torso, skimming past his eight-pack, noticing a subtle scar near the right side of his collarbone, before finding his eyes as they search my face.

For what, I'm not sure.

"Oh, I'm so sorry—" I mumble, bringing my hand up to cover my eyes, but it doesn't completely block my view. I can still see the silhouette of him, and oh God, what is happening?

"Close the door," he says, his voice firm, and I do just that, accidentally locking myself in the room with him.

"Shit."

Realizing my mistake, I use my free hand to fumble for the door handle, slightly opening it, while the other hand remains firmly over my eyes.

"Herring. Stop panicking and close the door. I spilled my coffee on my shirt as you knocked." He sighs once I've closed the door for the second time, hoping no one else can hear or see us.

"Can you please pass me the spare that I have hanging behind my door?" It's more of a request than a question, but I do it anyway, eyes remaining firmly shut.

"Cassandra. Open your eyes."

Oh shit, he first named me.

He's serious.

I don't even know why I'm panicking like a teenage girl. Like I've never seen his bare chest before. Like we didn't just go swimming in the creek, where I practically dry humped him.

Wait, we were in the water.

Wet humped?

I don't even know.

Plus, the memory of him half-naked is probably going to be burned into my brain forever.

It's a beautiful sight, and I could think of worse things to be etched into my memory forever, but it still doesn't make me feel any less...awkward.

Peeling my eyes open one at a time, the look on his face rips the air straight out of my lungs.

His clenched jaw ticks, his piercing, emerald eyes stare into mine and, damnit, here are those butterflies again.

He's your friend, you agreed on friends.

You. Told. Him. Friends.

No matter how many times I remind myself, it doesn't lessen the attraction I feel toward him.

But it's totally normal to have hot friends that you're attracted to, right?

Right?

I don't know what it feels like to even have male friends. I wasn't really allowed to have any. I spent most of my time in college studying, at home with Jenna, or with Austin and his friends.

Jenna and I snuck out to a frat party once, and Austin gave me the silent treatment for almost a week.

The guy was a walking red flag, but I knew nothing different. I thought he wanted me like no one else did, and I was blinded by that.

"I'm just here to make sure you're ready for our flight this afternoon." I scramble, trying not to stutter, all the while refusing to break eye contact with him as he buttons up his crisp, new white shirt.

"All packed and ready to go." He nods to his black duffle bag in the corner of his office while adjusting his collar before wrapping his tie around his neck.

"Could you help me with this?" he asks after his third attempt. I've been watching him try to do it, but he seems kind of clueless.

"Uh-yes sure." Clearing my throat, I close the gap between us quickly, wiping my clammy hands on my skirt before I begin focusing on the task at hand.

I do what's asked of me, but realize when I'm done that my hands are lingering, resting comfortably on his chest. He's so much taller than me, his chest feels so firm under my palms.

His deep, emerald eyes look into my hazel ones and my pulse quickens while my knees quiver, and suddenly Laney's words replay in my head.

"There is no right or wrong time to move on," she'd said to me, and every moment I spend with Harley, the more and more I want to give in.

To take whatever he's offering me and just run with it.

Live in it.

Let myself be free in it, but be free with *him*.

He smirks on the right side of his face, revealing his single dimple that I used to obsess over as a teenager, cocking one brow as if he just read my thoughts, and I can feel all my blood rush to my cheeks.

His confused and amused expression doesn't deter me, despite our past conversation by the creek.

Where I told him that I wasn't ready.

That I just wanted to be friends.

Yet, my feet refuse to move, no matter how hard I try to force them.

Dropping his forehead to mine, I watch as his eyes close and he inhales deeply. I can feel the rise and fall of his chest beneath my palms as he attempts to steady his breathing. His hands slowly gripping onto my waist.

I know the ball is in my court.

I know I just have to say the word, and he'll give me whatever I want.

Walk away, I try to convince myself, but nothing happens.

My feet are betraying me by tip toeing against my will, edging my lips closer to his, and he doesn't back away.

He's letting it happen.

Closing my eyes, I try to pretend that it isn't.

Out of sight, out of mind.

But it doesn't work, because I want him, and I've never been surer of anything.

His breathing gets heavier and heavier, closer and closer to my skin. He's gone ninety. I just need to go ten.

"Knock knock." The words startle me, and I leap out of his arms.

Of course, just when I'd decided to go for it, the universe sends his mother as a roadblock.

"Hi, Ms. Wingrove." Smiling at Joanna, I flatten my hair with my palms, trying to hide hints of sexual *anything*.

"Cassandra." She smirks the same smirk as her son, while clearly enjoying the sight of me being uncomfortable.

"I'll leave you both to it. I'll see you at the airport," I say, closing the door behind me, hurrying back to my office, where I can hopefully dig a hole big enough for my body to hide in forever.

Twenty
Cassandra

"ARE YOU SURE JENNA doesn't mind that we're here?" Bea asks, as we head up the stairs of The Velvetine, the current hotspot for celebrities in California. Given that my best friend is the hottest hair stylist in Los Angeles, I thought the venue suited her perfectly.

"Of course, it's okay. She's excited to meet you both."

Linking my arm through hers, Harley shortens his strides as he walks beside us like the third wheel he claims to be. If I thought I couldn't get our kiss from the creek out of my head, I'm even more confused after what nearly happened in his office.

I felt grateful to his mom at that moment for her interruption, but I spent the whole flight to California in the middle seat, with my hand an inch away from his, thinking about it. Wanting so badly to intertwine our fingers, just to know what it felt like.

Once we got back to our accommodation, Bea could sense there was something off, but we were both adamant that everything was fine. When we all went to our respective bedrooms, I hovered out the front of his door with my fist up, ready to knock, but I couldn't bring myself to do it.

I chickened out.

It's probably better that way.

Making our way to the top of the stairs, we step foot inside the venue, my two friends wide-eyed, mouths hanging open, oohing and ahhing at all the little details I'd put together for the party.

The rustic ceiling is barely visible anymore, with hanging black roses covering almost every inch, and fairy lights filling the gaps. There's a stop motion photo booth in the corner, where most guests are lining up, waiting for their turn. Black silk drapes over every wall, and I'd had rose gold, floating candles strategically placed in the middle of each cocktail table for a small splash of color.

Even though I couldn't be here to help set everything up, I trusted Janelle and Frankie to execute my vision, and they nailed it.

"What's this?" I hear Harley's voice ask the server as she holds a tray of canapés in front of him.

"Chicken Liver Parfait with an onion glaze," the server says, a flirty smile on her face, batting her eyelashes at him.

Shrugging his shoulders, he takes two off the tray, none the wiser of the young girl's flirtatious gaze, and shovels them into his mouth.

"How are they?" I left the food choices to Jenna, so this is the first time I'm seeing any of it.

"They taste expensive," he replies with a mouthful of food, before bringing a napkin to his lips.

"Says the rich guy," Bea teases.

"Exactly, so I know what expensive tastes like." He gives her a cheeky smile.

"Let's find Jenna."

Everybody is dressed to impress, including Bea and Harley.

Bea has borrowed the blue dress I'd bought unknowingly for my birthday but never wore, after I determined it looked way better on her than it ever did me. It somehow made her brown eyes look lighter.

Her short, blonde hair is dead straight, sitting on her shoulders, without a kink in sight.

She's paired it with a neutral smoky eye and a bold cat wing, and nude lips.

Harley is wearing black chinos that he had tailored to fit him this morning, slightly rolled up at the ankle. His black button-up shirt has the top button undone, and I wonder what he would do if I just...*no, Cassandra*.

His hair has been freshly cut, too, and his face is cleanly shaven, leaving his dimple visible for me to enjoy.

Not that he knows I like it.

"Cassandra," Jenna calls my name from the other side of the bar, and I run toward her as fast as my heels allow. She and I have spoken every single day since I'd been gone, but it's just not the same as seeing her whenever I wanted. Before I moved back to Grangewood, we lived three song lengths away. Every Thursday night would be our night.

No matter what.

The distance between us is now two and a half movie lengths by plane, but we still FaceTime each other every Thursday night with a glass of wine and our dinner already made, ready to dissect the last week.

We call and text each other daily, too, and it helps fill the void that my departure created.

"God, I've missed you."

She squeezes me so tight it's almost hard to breathe.

"I'm so glad you came." She pats away tears that formed in the corner of her eyes, careful to not ruin her makeup as she pulls away from me and looks me up and down. "Miss Herring, you look fucking sexy," she purrs, whistling as she takes my hand in hers above our heads, forcing a twirl out of me. I opted for a short, tight, satin, dark red dress with a deep v for the neckline, showing just the right amount of cleavage. Just enough to make me feel sexy without making me uncomfortable.

My long, brown hair is in large waves, and even though I did my own makeup, Jenna nods in approval.

"Thank you." I blush. "This is Bea and Harley," I say, gesturing toward the two people standing beside me, waiting patiently for their introduction.

"It's so nice to meet you both." Jenna smiles, taking them in, one by one, for a hug, and I notice her hug with Harley lasts a little longer than her hug with Bea.

Knowing my best friend, it's absolutely intentional.

"This place looks incredible," Bea says as her eyes float around the room.

"We can thank our girl here for pulling it all off." Jenna nudges me, and I wave my hand as if to tell her to stop making a fuss.

I've been doing this job for so long, but I still get jittery when people brag about me and the work that I do. It's a nice feeling, though, I'm just not used to compliments.

"There's an open bar. Go grab a drink," she tells them, and they don't waste any time.

"Now, C. Tell me *everything*."

Giving her an overview, I skim past a few details because it's her birthday, and the last thing she needs is to hear about my sex dream. I do tell her about our near miss in his office this morning, though, and the minx hasn't been able to hide her devilish grin the entire time.

"Girl, how have you not hit that yet? You better do it soon, or someone else will."

I hate that she's right. The idea of Harley with anybody but me...it's not something I want to think about.

The music is so loud, and the vibe is immaculate. The dance floor hasn't been empty the whole night.

Everyone has a drink in their hands at all times, and it's now time for speeches before the cake.

"I would like to thank everyone for coming to celebrate our girl, Jenna," I begin, because what kind of best friend would I be if I didn't make a speech at her party?

"Jenna and I met when I was in college. I saw an ad for a roommate in the local diner, and gave the number a call," I say. I make jokes about how she could've been a serial killer or a creepy old guy who wanted rent money for drugs, and the whole crowd laughs before I reach over to grab her hand and continue my speech.

"She's the strongest, most passionate person I know, who would do anything for the people she loves. I remember in college, I got invited to a frat party, so the two of us went together without our then-boyfriends," I say with a shudder, but continue immediately.

"There was a guy who kept trying to get me to go up to his room, but I wasn't interested at all. Jenna caught sight of it in the corner of her eye, marched over to the guy, kicked him in the balls and said, 'no means no, asshole!' before grabbing my hand, leaving the frat guy curled up in a fetal position, crying on the ground." The entire crowd laughed and cheered, while I smiled and squeezed her hand as it stayed locked with mine.

"You've always been the biggest light in my life, Jen, and I'm so glad you never let anyone put out that spark. Nothing was handed to you on a silver platter. You've worked so hard for everything that you have in your life, and I had the privilege of being able to witness it first hand. I couldn't be prouder to call you my best friend and my soulmate." I look over at her and watch as she folds a napkin in half, using the corners to dry her eyes.

"So, on that note, I would like everyone to raise their glass."

With about seventy drinks raised in the air, I scan the room, smiling, until my stomach drops and my eyes lock onto a pair of royal blue eyes, staring back at me.

Shit.

"To Jenna," I finish, the crowd repeating the words back to me, clinking their glasses together.

"I'm going to get some fresh air," I whisper in Jenna's ear as I take her in for a tight hug.

None the wiser, she nods at me, thanking me for my speech, and I head for the staircase, with Austin Anderson hot on my heels.

Twenty-One
Harley

THE VELVETINE IS FUCKING fancy.

A lot fancier than most of the places back in Grangewood, but I think Wingrove Estates beats it—only just. I'm probably biased, though. According to Cassandra, this is the '*it*' place for these types of events, and her friend Jenna 'deserves the best'.

I'm having a good time tonight.

It's nice to get away and not focus on work for a change. It seems like Bea is enjoying herself, too. Though, I've been counting, and she's checked her phone twelve times in the last five minutes, so I assume she's waiting to hear from Laney.

"Do you want another drink?" I stand, noting her almost empty glass.

"I thought you'd never ask. Get me the strongest cocktail they have on the menu." She raises a brow to see if I'll protest, but I know better. She owns her own pub. Of course, she likes her booze strong.

As I make my way to the bar, my eyes instinctively search the room for Austin Anderson.

I hope like hell I don't see him.

I don't even know what I'd do if I did.

Enough time has passed for us to let bygones be bygones and start again. I'd be willing to leave the past in the past, but would he? Maybe seeing him tonight would be a good time to bury the hatchet. I don't need to know his reasons for hating me anymore. I just hate that I've had it hanging over my head for over a decade.

Shoving my hands in my pockets, I wait patiently for the bartender to serve me so I can take the drinks back to our table, where my best friend now sits on the phone, smiling ear to ear.

"I hope you're ordering a drink for me?" a low, seductive voice asks from behind me.

My body automatically tenses, my head turning in her direction.

I'm no stranger to being hit on in a bar, but tonight, a flirtatious conversation with a stranger isn't something I want to entertain.

I'm not blind.

She's fucking hot. She could easily pass as Megan Fox's twin. And I can't lie. My dick twitches in my chinos of its own volition at the sight of her.

Bright blue eyes, long, dark brown hair, a skin-tight, lime green dress, and tits pushed up, making them look double their size. I would love to consider the idea of another woman. It's been a long fucking time since I've been laid.

But I can't do it.

After the creek, and the kiss we almost shared, I knew right then that I wanted Cassandra.

Not as a rebound and not as a one-night stand.

I wanted to be with her.

Our lips might have grazed ever so slightly, and she might have considered it a kiss, but I didn't. Our first kiss needed to be...explosive. Not almost missable.

A kiss that made her never want to kiss anybody else again.

So, no. I don't want the Megan Fox wannabe.

I wouldn't even want the real thing if she showed up on my doorstop.

I just want Cassandra Herring, and I will patiently wait until she realizes that she wants me, too.

"How do you know the birthday girl?" she speaks again, purposely making her voice sound sultry.

"She's a friend of a friend." I only reply to be polite, but my focus stays locked on the bartender, watching as he pours our drinks.

"Playing hard to get, I see." She tries again, but her voice is now irritated, yet somehow, more eager than it was. This time, I give her an answer I know she wasn't expecting and isn't used to hearing from men in bars.

"I'm not playing hard to get. You're just not my type and I'm not interested. Sorry." I lie, because my mom might have told me that while lying was the coward's way out, sometimes it's easier and less painful than admitting the truth.

"I'm everyone's type." She pouts before nibbling on her bottom lip, and I clear my throat while I wait.

Come on, bartender.

"That's a shame. I've heard *huge* things about ex-QB Harley Wingrove. It would have been the best night of your life."

"I guess I'll never know."

"The strongest they had was a Long Island Iced Tea," I say to Bea, placing the tall glass down in front of her. She wastes no time taking her paper straw to mix all the alcohol together, but her eyes never leave my face.

"Why are you staring at me like you want to fuck me?" I tease, swirling my drink around in my glass before I take a sip.

"Gross." She gags, washing down her disgust with the first sip of her drink. "That girl was hitting on you at the bar, and you shut her down," she says. "She was hot as fuck, Wingrove. What the hell, man?" she asks, and I sigh.

"I can't be just friends with her, Bea. I can't. I tried, I really did; but too much has happened between us since she came back. I can't ignore my feelings for her anymore."

"Can't or won't?" she asks, and I shift uncomfortably in my seat.

"Both."

"What do you mean 'too much has happened'? What have you not told me?" Bea and I haven't had time alone to talk, so she doesn't know about the apartment, the creek, or my office.

"I don't even know where to start," I admit, dragging my hand down my face.

"The apartment. I assume that was the starting point for all that has happened," she says, staring at me impatiently.

"She needed a place to live. No one was renting it from me, so I figured I would help a friend. I told her the owner wanted it gone, and it was hers if she wanted it. I gave her an offer she couldn't refuse." I shrug as I take a sip, looking everywhere but at her.

"So, you sold her an apartment in the apartment building you own?"

I can't tell if she's confused, pissed off, or impressed by what I did, but I also know she isn't the least bit surprised.

"Yes. It was practically a spare."

"A *spare*?"

I don't know why I said that. It's not a tire or a damn key, but it was sitting there empty.

I saw a solution and helped a friend in the meantime.

"Okay. So, what happened after the apartment?"

I tell her I convinced Cassandra to jump off the rock into the creek and that she accidentally walked in on me shirtless in my office. I didn't, however, tell her that if it weren't for a measly piece of fabric, we probably would have fucked in the creek, or that things almost went a little too far in my office.

She doesn't need to know any of that.

"Harley fucking Wingrove. You better not have fucked her," she seethes.

She's pissed, I get why. I don't feel guilty about it, though.

"No, of course not. And frankly, I'm mad that you would even think I would do such a thing. You know I'm celibate," I joke, trying to ease the tension, but it's just making it worse. "I helped her find an apartment, and she wanted to thank me. So, I suggested she make the jump. It's not a big deal." I try to play it off, but I don't think it's working.

"I thought that's what the pizza and beer were for," she yells over the music. Thankfully, everyone at the party is too focused on having a good time and not listening to our conversation.

"It was," I say, unconvincingly.

"Oh God. She just came back into our lives and you're going to fuck it all up." She groans before chugging back the rest of her drink. "And you've only been celibate since she came back to Grangewood, so don't pull that shit with me, Wingrove." She rolls her eyes. "I can't believe you convinced her to jump. She's fucking terrified of heights, Harley."

"It took a lot of persuading, but I promised I'd catch her once she hit the water." I sip my drink to swallow my discomfort.

"Just like you promised her when you were sixteen."

"How did you know about that?"

"Sixteen-year-old girls don't keep secrets from their best friends." She smiles. "What happened after she jumped?"

"I pulled her out of the water by her hips. She wrapped her arms around my neck and her legs around my waist because she panicked. That was it. She pulled away before anything else could happen." The lies tonight are just toppling out of my mouth, but there are some things that don't need to be shared with the class.

"Oh, brother. This is a recipe for disaster," she says, pinching the bridge of her nose. "Okay, and now your office? Why were you half-naked? You didn't fuck her in there, did you?"

"I haven't fucked her at all, period." My frustration grows each time she accuses me of doing something I told her I wouldn't do. "She barged into my office when I yelled 'don't come in,' but she mustn't have heard the word 'don't' and came in anyway."

"Why were you half-naked?" she asks again.

"I wasn't half-naked. I spilled my coffee when she knocked, and it went all over my shirt. I was in the process of taking it off as she barged in. There was nothing more to it, Beatrice. Can we drop it?"

"Wow. My full name, huh?" She knows she's hit a nerve.

"You know me, Bea. You know how I felt when everything went down with Austin. But he's not in the picture anymore. Why can't I see where this goes?"

"I've never told you this." She leans forward, tucking her short, blonde hair behind her ear. "Cass had a giant crush on you from the moment she saw you. She kept obsessing about the color of your eyes and the dimple on the right side of your cheek." She pretends to swoon as she chuckles, holding her glass up to her lips, knowing she's stirring up trouble.

"I don't want to know that." I groan.

I don't want to know that I had a chance in high school and blew it.

That I watched as my best friend coaxed her into liking him instead. Even though he knew.

He knew about it all, and he laughed at me.

"Why would you want to waste your time on a girl like her?" Austin had said to me, but I knew that she was special, even back then.

She still is.

"What do I do now?" I ask.

"If you're serious about it, just tell her," she says firmly, emphasizing the word *serious*. I'm getting flashbacks of the night of Matty Maxwell's party. Only this time, I don't think I should listen to her advice.

Not again.

"I can't just tell her. That didn't work out so well when the last time I tried," I say, wincing at the memory of a drunken Cassandra, nearly passed out on my shoulder after I'd confessed my feelings for her.

I had told her I had a crush on her. Told her she was the most beautiful girl I'd ever seen. That she was kind and smart. She'd looked up at me with her big, hazel eyes, smiled and said, "You're so funny, Wingrove," before throwing up all over my jeans.

I never got the chance to tell her again.

"I haven't seen her since her speech," Bea says, pulling me back from memory lane as she pushes her chair away from the table.

The last I saw of Cassandra, she was hugging Jenna and heading out the doors of The Velvetine.

"I think she went outside. Should we find her?" Bea is up on her feet, slurping the rest of her cocktail through her paper straw, and I'm not far behind.

Walking down the stairs and out the exit, the smell of the beach and a slightly cool breeze hits me right away. The weather in Los Angeles is mostly always beautiful, and tonight is no different.

The streets are packed full of people, celebrating whatever their occasion may be. The sound of the waves crashing in the distance is only slightly louder than the music coming from each venue. Drunk men and women are everywhere, including a couple pressed against a brick wall, with her hand down his pants, while they shove their tongues down each other's throats. It's almost like a mother bird regurgitating food for her chick, and I can't help but chuckle and be grossed out at the same time.

It looks messy, but sometimes drunk, sloppy hook-ups are the most fun.

"Fuck." Bea's voice filled with urgency, gaining my attention right away. I follow her line of sight, only for it to land on a visibly upset Cassandra Herring, and an angry Austin Anderson. My vision goes from clear to a cloudy, red sky in a matter of seconds.

Without hesitation, I lunge forward, but Bea grabs my arm, holding me in place.

"Don't. This is not your fight," she orders firmly, strengthening her grip around my bicep, but I just want to rip it free.

To protect her.

Help her.

Save her.

Instead, I'm forced to stand in place and watch from a distance as Austin berates her even more.

We can't hear a word between the two of them. They're too far away. But we can see Cassandra's visible discomfort. Her arms are wrapped around her body while it shakes uncontrollably, crying, as Austin's body towers over her to intimidate her. She attempts to turn and walk away, but he doesn't let her. He grabs her by the arm, turning her back to face him. She lets out a blaring yell, and Bea flinches beside me.

This conversation between them should be private and we shouldn't interfere, but I can't just stand here and watch.

"Let go of me, Austin," she pleads, this time loud enough for us to hear. We can hear her cries in the distance, but he doesn't do as she asks, so she yanks her wrist free of his grip. It only makes him angrier.

He continues to tower over her, stepping closer as she backs away. His jaw is clenched, shoulders squared, and he's pointing his fingers in her face while her body continues to shake violently through tears.

He takes another step closer to her, cupping her face with his hand, and that's when it happens.

That's when I snap.

My blood boils.

This time, Bea doesn't even attempt to stop me as I storm in their direction.

She drops my arm, giving me permission to do what I have to do.

I'm sauntering my way toward them, but neither of them realize until it's too late and my hands firmly wrapped around Austin's throat.

"She told you to leave her alone," I spit through gritted teeth. My voice quietly filled with rage.

"Harley, it's fine." Cassandra's voice is shaky, and I can feel Bea's arms trying to tug me away by my shoulder, but it's no use.

Austin has all of my attention.

"Yeah, *Harley*. She's a big girl. She can handle me." He winks at me like my hand isn't holding his throat hostage. Like his ability to breathe doesn't rely solely on me.

He's acting like a smug asshole, as if this is all a big fucking joke to him and it's taking everything in me to not knock this arrogant son of a bitch on his ass.

"Please, Harley. Take me home," she begs, and I slightly loosen my grip, listening to her.

Sixteen-year-old Harley really wants to make him suffer for all the shit he put me through back then, and thirty-year-old Harley really wants to make him suffer for all the shit he's put her through over the last few months.

But I don't.

I let go of him completely, take her hand in mine, and walk away. But Austin Anderson always has to have the last word.

"Yeah, Harley. Take the slut home. But when you fuck her, just know I fucked her first. She's still isn't worth it, Wingrove. Don't waste your time on her."

What the fuck did he just call her?

I've never been a fighter.

I always walked away if I could. Sometimes, I wasn't so lucky.

But tonight, Austin would be the unlucky one.

One, two, three strides, and I'm back, face to face with my old best friend.

Close enough for my arm to swing and connect my fist to his jaw.

Close enough to hear the crack as my fist collides with it.

Close enough to watch as he drops to his ass and whimpers in pain, clutching the side of his face.

"You deserve way worse, Anderson. Consider yourself lucky." I spit on the ground next to him as I stand over his body, watching as he cowers in pain, conscious.

My words cause a reaction out of him I don't expect.

Fear.

I don't care to prove him right or wrong.

The scene unfolding beneath me triggers a tidal wave of memories, bringing out old trauma that I've worked so hard to grow from.

Rather than doing more damage like I could easily do, I close my eyes, take a deep breath, and walk away, leaving Austin below me.

My only priority is making sure Cassandra is okay and taking her wherever she wants to go.

Twenty-Two
Harley

I KNOW CASSANDRA IS going to be pissed at me and my fist is going to hurt for a few days, but fuck, it was worth it.

The asshole had it coming, and I will die on that hill.

The moment we got back upstairs and joined the party, she put on her poker face, drank as much alcohol as she could, danced with Jenna, and pretended there was nothing wrong, no matter how many times Bea insisted we leave.

When the Uber picked us up, she stumbled out the door of the venue, climbed into the back seat with Bea, and that's when she let her tears fall, staining her make-up covered cheeks.

The car ride back to the apartment was silent, sniffles appearing even more obvious. I don't think she was even attempting to hide them.

My heart broke for her, but I knew she had Bea's shoulder to lean on, and her hand to hold. I hope it helped to be consoled by her childhood best friend, even if there were no words exchanged.

The three of us had pre-booked an apartment with three separate bedrooms to stay at while we're in California for Jenna's birthday, but I kind of wish I'd booked something separate from the girls, so I could collect my thoughts and replay tonight over and over, and Cassandra could confide in Bea. So they could talk about how much of an idiot I was for turning to violence, and Bea would have told her that Austin deserved it.

I'd be lying if I said I was looking forward to being in Cassandra's company right now.

She refused to even look in my direction once we made it back to the party. I know, because my eyes tracked her every move.

My urge to protect her took over and I won't apologize for that. She can be mad at me all she wants, but I'll never regret it.

Reaching into my pocket for the key to the apartment, I hold the door open for the two girls to enter before me.

"I'm going to bed." Bea burps, taking her heels off as she walks toward her room, waving her hand in the air, leaving Cassandra and I alone for the first time in weeks.

The creek.

My office.

All the things we should discuss but have both been avoiding, and now we need to add Jenna's party to the list. I guess there's no time like the present.

Great.

Emptying the contents of my pockets, I place my phone, wallet, and keys on the kitchen counter, wincing in pain at the pressure of my chinos against my knuckle.

"Does it hurt?" Cassandra asks, words slurring while her big hazel eyes stare at my hand.

She's drunk, but she's trying her hardest to appear sober, using the dining table to keep herself from losing balance.

"It's fine," I say, opening and closing my fist to assess the damage, noting the bruising and swelling that have already appeared.

Her eyes are red and puffy.

If that wasn't a dead giveaway that she'd been crying tonight, the black marks under her eyes from her mascara definitely are. I hate knowing I played a part in hurting her.

Watching as she slides one shoe off at a time, my eyes involuntarily trail up her bronzed, toned legs, stopping at the hem of her red dress above her knee before she clears her throat, snapping her fingers, forcing my attention back to her face.

"My eyes are up here, Wingrove." She squints her puffy eyes at me before turning her back toward me, heading toward the kitchen.

I understand that she's mad at me, but a cranky Cassandra is cute as hell. I can't help but chuckle to myself.

Following behind her, I get myself a glass of water, hoping she's about to do the same, but she heads straight for the freezer instead.

"Ah-huh!" she says, sounding victorious as she turns to face me, holding an ice pack in the air like it's some sort of trophy. "Come here," she commands, propping herself onto the granite countertop, spreading her legs slightly, with just enough room for me to stand in between them.

We're both drunk, but she's drunker, so even though I'll be in between her legs, I won't be taking advantage of the position we're in.

I need a fully coherent Cassandra Herring.

I need her to be completely sober when she invites me between her legs.

When she begs me to fuck her.

It's inevitable.

I'm just waiting for her to be ready.

"Give me your hand." I take a deep, shaky breath as I step closer to her, bridging the gap between us, standing between her thighs before giving her my right hand.

Slowly, she places it on her bare thigh. I don't miss the way she shudders at my touch.

The way goosebumps cover her skin.

The way my thumb grazes her thigh involuntarily, causing me to flinch in pain, thanks to one simple movement.

Noticing my physical discomfort, she gently places the ice pack on top of my knuckle, and I close my eyes at the sweet, sweet relief the ice cold brings.

"Does that feel okay?" she whispers as I open my eyes to search hers. Redness slowly fading, replaced by speckles of gold.

I've never been close enough to Cassandra Herring to study her in this way.

Subtle freckles cover her nose.

She has dimples on the sides of her face, but not on her cheeks; they're only visible if her hair is up or tucked over her shoulders, like it is now.

I would kill to be able to read her mind. To be able to hear what she's thinking right now.

"I had a crush on you in high school," she blurts out, as if knowing exactly what I was thinking in this very moment.

"Trust me when I tell you that I would *love* to hear all about this, but I think we both need to get some sleep. It's been a big night." It nearly kills me to not hear her tell me I was who she wanted, but I'm not an idiot.

I want her to remember telling me.

Not while drunk out of her mind and emotional about seeing her shitty ex.

"I don't feel so good," she quickly changes the subject, her face losing any trace of color, and just like that, the conversation has gone from something I desperately wanted to hear, to something no one wants to hear from someone who consumed their bodyweight in alcohol.

Frantically searching the kitchen for a bucket, I find one under the sink, but either I don't make it in time, or she has terrible aim, because before I know it, my shirt and chinos are covered in vomit.

All thanks to Cassandra Herring.

I wish I could say this was the first time, but fuck me, I certainly hope it's the last.

Twenty-Three
Cassandra

Oh God.

This can't be real.

I can't have just thrown up on Harley Wingrove.

Again.

Before embarrassment can drown me, he strips down to just his boxer briefs and I've lost the will to speak.

Not a single word wants to come out of my mouth, no matter how hard I try.

His golden skin looks darker under the dim kitchen light, creases in his chest more defined. His green eyes are glimmering with mischief, no doubt watching my eyes bore into his bare, sculpted torso. He's so close, I could touch him with the slightest movement from any part of me.

So close that I could taste him.

So close that I could... "Did you hear me?" Startled, my gaping mouth snaps shut, eyes blinking rapidly as he brings me back down to Earth and out of the mouth watering trance I'd entered.

"Huh? I-oh *god*. I'm so sorry."

Leaping off the counter, I scoop his puke covered clothes off the ground and run to the sink to rinse and soak them, so they're ready to be properly washed in the machine.

"It's okay." His voice is calm as he stands, leaning against the counter, rubbing a hand over his freshly shaven jaw, watching as I frantically try to undo whatever damage I may have caused to his probably very expensive outfit.

And get rid of the smell of vomit. It feels like it's surrounding me.

I'm still nauseous, the smell is like a trigger.

"I said, you have vomit in your hair, Herring."

That explains the smell.

How do I always get it in my hair?

Ripping my dress over my head, I stand in front of him in matching black lingerie, and it's impossible to not notice how his body reacts to seeing mine. "I didn't even pack pajamas," I mutter to myself quietly, irritated at my forgetfulness.

Using his hands to cover his growing erection, he repeats himself for a third and final time.

"I said you have it in your *hair*, Herring. Not your dress." He barks out a laugh, my cheeks setting on fire.

Groaning, I run toward the bathroom, slamming the door shut behind me, the sound of his continuous laughter echoing behind it. I quickly turn on the shower.

Tonight is a fucking disaster.

"Are you okay in there?" He knocks, his deep voice turned soft and genuine, no amusement in sight, calming me instantly.

"Fine. Thanks," is all I say as I glare at the mess of myself in the mirror. Streaks of my bare skin showing from where my tears had fallen down my cheeks, mascara blending in with the bags under my eyes.

He's covered in vomit. He needs a shower just as much—if not more—than I do.

My body wants so badly for him to join me.

It's telling me to invite him in, but my brain is telling me it's a bad idea.

But he needs a shower too.

Hovering my hand over the doorknob, I yank it open to find him sitting on the floor, with his bare back leaning against the door. Quickly, he stands to face me.

"Uh, I was just wanting to see if you wanted to, um, join me in the shower? To save water." It was the first excuse I could come up with, and I want to kick myself.

Looking away, I'm suddenly nervous, feeling his eyes burning into every part of my body, drinking in every inch like I do his.

Resting his arm on the doorframe, he dips his head so his lips are at my ear, lifting my chin with his finger before he whispers, "When we shower together, we're both going to be completely sober. It's going to be after I've fucked you, then tasted you, then fucked you again. But tonight is not that night. Goodnight, Herring," he says, before kissing me on the cheek and heading to his bedroom.

What?

***

To say my mind is foggy this morning would be the understatement of the year.

I check my phone for the time; we need to check out of the apartment in an hour to catch our flight.

Sliding my feet into my slippers one by one, I throw my still damp hair into a bun on top of my head and make my way out to the kitchen, where Bea and Harley are seated, drinking a coffee in silence.

"There's some on the bench for you," Bea says, sensing my desire for some.

"Thank you." I smile weakly as I head toward the kitchen to pour myself a fresh cup. I barely have a voice left. It hurts to speak.

I briefly remember screaming my lungs out to *'Say My Name'* while knocking back shots of tequila.

I guess the song spoke to me.

"Nice shirt." She cocks a brow as she holds her coffee mug to her lips to cover her smirk.

I've never seen this shirt in my life, and definitely have zero recollection of putting it on before bed. But the black t-shirt has W. E embroidered over my left breast, telling me who the shirt belongs to.

It sits just above my knees, the scent of sandalwood and vanilla overriding my senses.

"Oh God, did we—"

"No. I left it on your bed while you were in the shower because you said you forgot your pajamas," he says casually before taking another sip of his coffee.

"Thank God."

I don't mean to say it out loud, but I do before I can stop myself. Harley's face flashes with an unmissable look of confusion and hurt, while Bea's eyes widen as they wander between us.

"Trust me, *Cassandra*," he says as he clears his throat. "If we had sex, you would remember it."

He called me by my first name.

He's pissed.

I can hear it in his voice and see it in the way he stalks toward the sink to pour out his cup. But I don't reply.

I don't trust myself to say something that I won't regret, even though I know it's already too late for that.

I'm too mortified with every single event that took place last night, so I zip my lips together and throw away the damn key.

***

The journey back to Grangewood Creek was... quiet.

Not only were we all hungover, me probably more so than the other two, but I was torn with how I felt about Harley and how everything transpired last night. I wasn't sure how I could feel mad, guilty, and turned on, all at the same time.

He didn't need to turn to violence, but coming to my rescue like that was something I had never experienced before, and it made my lady bits tingle, even though I begged them to just...*chill*.

I can't count the number of times I had been in a compromising position in college and Austin just sat back and ignored it because his roommate Monty 'wasn't a threat'. Yet, he continued to make me uncomfortable every time I visited their apartment.

Harley didn't even need to hear the entire conversation before he jumped to my defense. He saw Austin lay a hand on me, and that was all the motive he needed.

I don't condone that behavior, but I think Harley had been waiting a long time to be able to put Austin in his place.

Also, I'm pretty sure Harley told me he wanted to fuck me. But that also could have been a dream or part of my drunken haze, even though I accidentally shut it down this morning.

Do I want to sleep with Harley?

Probably more than I need oxygen to survive.

But so many things keep getting in the way, and I feel like it's a sign from the universe to not cross that line.

What I remember with one hundred percent clarity, though, is that I threw up on him and my drunken apology wasn't enough.

I needed to apologize to him properly. I just had to figure out how.

***

We got back to Grangewood Creek a week ago, and Jenna and I are only now catching up.

She's been overwhelmingly busy with work, and I've been busy trying to not fuck up anything else.

"So, what happened?" she asked over our FaceTime call, while I'm finally curled up in my bed after a long, harrowing week back at work. A long week of avoiding Harley to the best of my ability.

"I'm so sorry. I hope it didn't ruin your night," I say, feeling even more guilty about the interaction with the man I hoped to never see again.

"Nope. We're not doing that. You didn't expect to see him. You took the conversation outside before the argument even began, because you didn't want to cause a scene and take the attention away from me. The only person at fault is him. Besides, I had no idea that anything had even happened until you left. Tahnee waited until then to tell me she saw Harley punch Austin in the face." She chuckles while tying her long, blonde hair into a bun at the nape of her neck before washing the day's make up off her face. "Super hot of him to come to your defense like that, by the way. Your knight in shining armor." She swoons. "Now, tell me what happened. Don't skip any details."

Racing down the stairs, I feel Austin right behind me with heavy footsteps.

"For fuck's sake, Cass. Just wait," he said, putting his hand on my shoulder, turning my body, forcing me to face him.

"Not here," I spit, shaking his hand off me, leading him as far away from the party as possible.

Once we're an acceptable distance away from The Velvetine, I stop in my tracks, turning to see his face, and stare at the royal blue eyes I once adored, and now despise.

"Speak," I demand.

He takes a while to think about what he wants to say. It's like I'm watching him try to come up with an excuse or a lie that he thinks I'll believe, though we both know he isn't capable.

"You have some nerve coming here with him."

Really? That's where he wants to start this conversation? This is all about Harley?

"That's what this is about?" I ask, rolling my eyes, placing my hands on my hips.

"I came here to win you back, Cass. To explain myself," he says, and the laugh that escapes my throat is the most obnoxious sound I've ever heard.

"I don't think there's anything you can do or say that could make me want you back, Austin. I know enough. I don't need you to explain anything, and I don't need closure. I don't want you. It's that simple," I reply. I couldn't be more honest if I tried.

He eyes me warily in disbelief, like he's waiting for me to admit I'm joking, and I'll ride off into the sunset with him and live happily ever after. Be the Cassandra he once knew, who would always pick him over anybody. But that girl is long gone.

"But you love me. I know you do. You don't just stop loving someone, Cassandra." I laugh again. Ironic, coming from him.

"That's funny, considering that's exactly what happened between us. You *stopped loving* me *first, remember? And let's not forget, you fucked someone else for three years and now have a baby on the way." I'm even angrier now. He's given me no other choice than to throw his actions back in his face.*

"I never stopped loving you. I made a mistake. I couldn't abandon her once I found out she was pregnant. I just couldn't," he whispers through his teeth.

"I don't need to hear this, Austin. I've moved on. You forced my hand. I don't want this anymore. I don't want you. You made your bed, so fucking lie in it." I can't stop the tears from falling down my face. They're not sad tears, though. They're tears of relief and frustration, all wrapped up in one.

Hugging my arms around my torso to keep myself warm and calm myself down, he sees my tears as a sign of weakness.

A sign that I'm about to crumble.

An invitation for him to continue.

"Don't fucking lie to me, Cassandra. You love me. *You are* mine. *I will not let you be with anyone else, especially him." He's seething.*

Spoiled boy, Austin Anderson, is used to getting his way.

"Tell me, Austin. Would you be as furious if I were here with someone else? Or are you just jealous because I brought Harley as my date?" I don't know why I said that. He's here as my friend, but I guess part of me wanted to enrage Austin more.

He's silent, staring at me in shock, like he never expected me to bite back. Like he expected me to smile and nod and forget about everything, because *that's the girl I used to be.*

But I know I'm right.

I could be here with literally anybody else and he wouldn't bat an eyelid, but the fact that I'm here with his old best friend, his enemy, is the only reason he wants to 'win me back'.

"You know that's not the case, Cass." He sighs. He's forgotten that I know him better than anyone else in the world, which means I know when he's being truthful and when he's lying.

And right now, he's lying through his teeth.

"Okay, let me ask you another question." I'm feeling brave. Because the more lies he tells me, the more truth I know. "Do you love her?"

Silence.

The busy streets of L. A. are packed full of people and cars tooting their horns, but the silence coming from the man in front of me is so loud, it's deafening.

Running both hands through his light brown hair, it's obvious he's frustrated that things aren't going his way. Loosening the tie around his neck, he tries to catch his breath. He doesn't need to say his answer out loud for me to know it. But I still need it said. "Yes." His eyes glaze over, tears refusing to spill as he draws a staggered breath.

"Then go be with her."

But he doesn't move. His face remains stern, jaw clenched tight. I can tell he still feels like he owns me, that I'm his property, and if he can't have me, then no one else can.

"You're making a mistake, being here with him. He's nothing, but a broken, washed up wannabe. But I guess that's what whores are drawn to, aren't they? Was he the first man to show you attention since I decided

I could do better? Did he promise to bring you home to his family? Oh wait, he doesn't even have one of those."

"I don't have time for this, Austin. Go back to your fiancé," I say, ignoring him as I turn to walk away, but he doesn't let me. He grabs my wrist, holding me in place. "Let go of me," I demand, ripping my arm out of his grip, but he doesn't. He strengthens his hold on me, and this time, I struggle to pull myself free.

Hearing the sound of footsteps behind me, I turn to see a red faced, rage-filled Harley approaching and my stomach drops at the confrontation that is inevitable.

"She told you to leave her alone," he says while gripping Austin's throat. His voice is angry. There's no denying that. His rage is under control. But I can see in his eyes that he's close to the tipping point. He just needs one more thing out of Austin, and that will send him over the edge.

"Harley, it's fine," I say, attempting to keep my voice steady.

"Yeah, Harley. She's a big girl. She can handle me," Austin says as he winks at Harley, and I shudder as Bea pulls me closer to her.

"Please, Harley. Take me home," I beg, because right now that's all I want to do. Go home.

Taking my hand, relief crashes into me like a tsunami as I drag him to walk away, and he does, reluctantly. But the relief vanishes quickly when Austin decides to have the final say.

"Yeah, Harley. Take the slut home. But when you fuck her, just know I fucked her first. She's still isn't worth it, Wingrove. Don't waste your time on her." The words that leave his mouth are venom, and I know they've angered Harley in the worst way. They're what he needed to tip him over the edge, free falling into complete darkness.

Before I can stop him, he drops my hand, turns to face his old best friend, and I watch as his fist connects with Austin's face.

"And then what happened?" Jenna gasps as she asks.

"I stormed back inside, had a few shots of tequila, danced until I could no longer stand straight, then went back to our apartment and threw up on his clothes. That's not even the worst part." I groan, reliving my embarrassment all over again.

"What could be worse than that?" She teases.

"I invited him to have a shower with me, to which he politely declined, even though he told me he wants to fuck me. Then when I woke up in his t-shirt this morning, I panicked thinking that we'd had sex, and said, 'thank god' out loud when he told me we didn't." I finish my ramble, letting out a deep breath.

I didn't mean it in that way at all.

I just meant that if we had sex, I wanted to be sober so I could remember it.

"Oh boy," is all Jenna says.

"I've barely spoken to him since, and it's been a week. We have that wedding expo coming up next month and now I don't think I want to go." I sink further into my bed.

"Girl, you're going to the expo because it means you get to see me. With the whole Harley situation, I say suck it up." Blankets cover the screen as she gets herself comfortable. "Maybe take him out to lunch. Thank him for defending you, but express your concerns, too. Tell him that while you appreciated it, you don't condone violence. Ask any burning questions you have and be open and honest with him about any questions he might have."

She's right.

Violence is something I would never tolerate, especially over me, knowing we could have all walked away without injury.

Sure, Austin said some vile things, but he would have had to deal with the consequences of that alone. But now Harley has to deal with the mental and physical consequences of hurting someone, too.

His old best friend.

The Harley I knew in school was never violent. Even during games, he would be the bigger man and walk away. No matter what.

"Okay."

"Worst case, just tell him you want to ride him into oblivion and figure the rest out later." I adore a sarcastic Jenna at the best of times, but not at times like this, where I need my best friend to be serious. "Start from the beginning, C. Start with the break-up. Tell him you weren't in a rush to move on, but the moment you saw him, you reconsidered every choice you ever made in your life." Finally, something logical. I mean, I won't say any of that, but he deserves honesty from me.

What's the worst that could happen?

"I'll text him," I say, pulling my phone away from my ear to text Harley, only to see that he's beaten me to it. "Wait, he's texted me." Anxious, I fumble my phone in my hands as I swipe to open the message.

"What does it say?" she squeals.

"It says 'Can we talk?' What should I say?" I stare at the phone in my hand, mind going blank.

"Just tell him yes," she replies.

"Okay, hang on," I say as I open the text to reply.

> **Me**: Sure, when?

> **Harley**: The barn at the winery, 20 minutes.

"Shit, he wants to meet tonight. In twenty minutes. I can't get ready in twenty minutes." Leaping out of my bed, I look at myself in the mirror and groan as I stare at his oversized t-shirt that I've worn every single night since we've been home.

"Yes, you can. Just take a breath, put some sweatpants on, and go hear what he has to say," she says, and I do exactly that.

Only, I opt for a cute, yellow, long sleeve dress and a denim jacket, because I can't have the hottest man on the planet see me in sweatpants and his t-shirt that I haven't washed in seven days.

Me: see you there.

Twenty-Four
Harley

FROM THE MOMENT WE stepped off the plane, my phone hasn't stopped.

Wingrove Estates has been booming. The restaurant is fully booked out weeks in advance. We'd had several weddings booked, too, which was a first for us.

Robbie and I had been on the phone more than usual, discussing potential new clients and the next steps for the Mercury Hotel. He'd called me during the week to let me know about a piece of land that had become vacant here in Grangewood Creek, but I didn't even know it had existed until this week.

He'd known for the longest time that I was on the lookout for land to build a place to call home, and that I'd wanted it here in Grangewood, but nothing felt right until now.

My apartment is great, but it's never been something I saw for myself long term. It's the penthouse of a twenty-story building that I own, and I occupy the entire top floor. But I never created that space with the intention of having it be my forever home.

I wanted something...secluded.

I want land for my future kids to run around on, and a swimming pool for them to splash in until the sunset, and me or their mom were letting them know that dinner was ready.

When Robbie told me that there was an empty piece of land for sale in town, I knew I had to at least check it out.

"The owner of the land is looking to sell. The price is a bit steep, but I figured money isn't an issue for you," Robbie said once I'd put my car into park in front of the giant, open, empty space. He was right. Money wasn't an issue, especially for something that I'd wanted ever since I could afford to want things. Then, when he told me how big the land was, and that it backed onto the far end of Wingrove Estates, I was sold.

No matter the price.

It was big enough that I could build my dream home and extend the winery without either interfering with the other.

Robbie had the paperwork drawn up and was ready for me to sign in less than twenty-four-hours, and once I'd had them signed, my architects were already on the job, putting all of my ideas onto paper.

I wasn't surprised that Robbie had found this for me. Aside from Bea, he knows me better than anyone.

He was with me at the time of my accident and never left my side for a second during my recovery. Even during my darkest days, he dragged me out of my slump and never once complained.

I'll forever be indebted to him.

I tried all week to busy myself, but I couldn't stop thinking about California. I needed to get what happened there off my chest. I needed to get Cassandra out of my head.

But it was proving impossible.

No matter what I did, the image of her was cemented in my mind.

The way she'd consoled herself while Austin had yelled at her. Her black-smeared eyes once we'd gotten back to the apartment.

But the image that refused to leave my mind was her standing in a matching lingerie set, asking me to join her in the shower.

And I'd said no.

I fucking said no.

I wanted her too badly to be just a drunken revenge fuck. But after what she'd said to Bea the next morning, I doubted I would ever be anything more.

I thought we were heading down a path of...*something*, but it seems friends are all we're going to be, and I have to learn to be okay with that.

I've got no choice.

I texted her tonight with the intention of not only coming clean about everything, but to apologize to her, too. She can choose to do whatever she wants with the information I give her, but it won't feel like I've done everything I can until she hears what I have to say.

My emotions have been all over the place since California, with anger at the forefront and guilt not far behind. I'm not an angry person. I never have been. But Austin just brings it out of me, and I can't explain why. He hated me because I was a better football player who his father favored, but I never understood how that was my fault.

While I liked the fact that my talent wasn't going unnoticed, especially by an ex-pro QB and my personal football hero, Austin was my *best* friend, and I always put him before everyone else. He was like a brother to me, but he showed his true colors before prom, and every day since.

This conversation I'm about to have with Cassandra is well overdue, and I'm not looking forward to it.

It's late, but it was my idea.

It's been a week, and I've avoided her as much as I know she's avoided me. It's been fucking hard. I wanted to knock on her apartment door, just to see her face, then head back home once I'd gotten my fix, but that wouldn't have helped mend what felt almost broken.

Putting distance between us is what we both needed, especially if I'm not who she wants. I need to move on, but I need to lay it all on the table before I do.

Collecting the pre-made picnic basket off my passenger seat, I head toward the barn at Wingrove Estates.

The air is cold tonight. Winter is slowly approaching, so I've opted for warmth and comfort over style, throwing on grey sweatpants, a white tee, and a light blue denim jacket with a hood.

Taking advantage of the big, open, empty space, I sit down the thick, grey and white plaid blanket, taking out a bottle of sparkling wine with two champagne flutes, when I hear the sound of the heavy, wooden barn doors being pushed open.

There she is, looking cute as hell while she cautiously walks toward me, fingers intertwined over her stomach, forcing her eyes to remain on mine.

She's wearing a long, yellow, flowy dress and a denim jacket (of course) with her hair down with a slight wave. She makes my heart stop, yet pound dangerously fast, every single time I see her, as though it's the first time, and she has no idea.

I really need to get my shit together.

She isn't going to make it easy to move on, but if I can't have her, I need to figure out a way to be okay with letting her go.

Again.

"I want to apologize," we both say in unison, sitting face to face on the blanket.

She's playing with her nail cuticles, visibly anxious, as I try to stop my heart from hammering against my ribcage, hoping like hell she can't hear it.

"What are you sorry for?" She smirks, taking a sip from her champagne flute, and I feel the tension in my chest ease, no longer rendering me anxious.

"A lot of things, actually, but mostly for punching Austin. I'm not a violent person, Herring, and you know that. Seeing him be aggressive toward you made me feel an overwhelming urge to protect you," I say, knowing she doesn't need my protection, but deserves my honesty.

"I can handle Austin," she replies, all but confirming my thoughts. "But he did deserve it." She sighs.

"Will you tell me what happened between you guys?" I ask, her body stiffening as she slowly places her glass down on the ground.

We briefly spoke about it over pizza with Bea and Laney, but I mostly heard that he'd cheated on her and she only found out at his sister Megan's wedding.

Taking a deep breath, she sits up a little straighter before going into detail about their relationship behind closed doors.

From college, where he was too preoccupied playing video games or getting drunk with his roommate—who she never really felt safe to be alone with—, Austin's poorly thought-out proposal, tainting her favorite holiday, right down to his three-year affair that resulted in a baby on the way, that his family knew all about before she did.

This guy really had Cassandra Herring wanting to spend her whole life with him, and he just threw it away.

"Wow, Herring. I'm so sorry," I say, briefly placing my hand on her leg before bringing it back into my lap, unsure what lines are safe to cross.

Shaking her head, she waves her hand in the air before picking up her almost-empty glass.

"Don't be. He did me a favor." She smiles softly. "But now it's my turn to ask." She pauses, tipping the last of her wine down the back of her throat, pouring herself a fresh glass, topping mine up.

"I'm an open book. Ask away," I say, and suddenly, I don't feel ready for whatever questions she's going to throw at me.

"What happened between you and Austin? You guys were best friends then, suddenly, enemies?" she says and yep, the one question I didn't know how to answer now lingers in the air.

"I racked my brain for such a long time, but always came up with nothing. I tried to get it out of him while we were in college, but all he told me was that you were the bad guy and that I needed to drop it." She scoffs, and I laugh out loud. "The irony, huh?" she remarks before taking another sip. I stare at her in awe, even if it's just for a moment.

The alcohol has made her cheeks a soft cherry color, the spray of freckles across nose and apples of her cheeks are even more obvious, with not an ounce of makeup to cover them, and her hazel eyes are so honed on mine, waiting patiently for me to spill my guts.

Having nothing left to lose, I decide to leave it all out on the table, recounting everything my memory will allow.

"Prom is coming up," I say to Austin as we head toward my car after training.

"You got a date yet?" he asks before slamming the passenger side door. He has a beamer in his driveway, yet still chooses to hitch a ride in my mom's old pickup truck daily.

"Not yet, but I want to ask Herring. I reckon I have a shot with her."

"But there are so many hotter girls you could pick from," he shouts over the sound of my engine roaring. "Literally anyone from the cheer team

is hotter. And guaranteed to put out." He licks his lips at the thought, no doubt wondering how many notches he can add to his bedpost.

"It's not about that for me, Anderson, and you know it." I've never been that guy. I don't do casual hook ups like every other guy on the team, and I was not about to start with Cassandra Herring.

Hell no.

Rolling his eyes, he grabs my shoulder and squeezes it tightly before shaking me. "You gotta lighten up, man. Not everything needs to be taken seriously all the time. It's prom, for fuck's sake. Get your dick wet and have a good time." He laughs as he squeezes my shoulder tighter while I drive.

"You don't get it. I don't want to take anyone else. I want to take Cassandra Herring because I like her, and I want to explore whatever she and I could potentially have." I say the words slowly and clearly, speaking to him like he's a toddler, because apparently, it's the only way he'll understand.

"Trust me, she's not worth it. Wait until she loses her virginity, then go for it. Hell, I might take it from her, then she's all yours," he jokes, but his humor doesn't sit well with me. "Prom isn't about going with the girl you think you love and hope she loves you back. It's about drinking spiked punch, losing and taking virginities, and waking up seedy in the morning. Lighten up, Wingrove. I'll find you good pussy for the night."

I know my best friend is an asshole, and I know he fucks around with different girls as often as he can. But considering Cassandra, Bea, Austin, and I are all friends, I thought he would have a bit more respect for her.

I guess not.

Gripping my hands around my steering wheel, I continue the drive toward his house in silence.

"Later, man." As he opens my passenger side door and slams it shut, his father, Max, comes out to greet me.

"Hi, Mr. Anderson," I say, calmly, ignoring the fact that my whole body stiffens, palms drip with sweat, losing grip around the wheel. I'm in the presence of a legend. No, a God. He's a big deal in the NFL world, so whenever he wants to talk to me, I'm all ears, taking in every single word.

"Hi, son. Listen," he says, looking over his shoulder at Austin, who is spinning a football in the palm of his hand. "I have some Ohio State recruiters coming to the game on Thursday and they are interested in you." My whole body heats.

"In me? How do they even know about me?" I ask, confused, considering I'm not even in my senior year yet.

"I put in a good word." He winks as he leans into the passenger side, resting his elbow on the window ledge.

"Fuck yeah. Ohio State is my top school," Austin exclaims from behind his father, reminding us that he's still there.

"They would be at the game for Harley," Max repeats himself to his son, but nods his head toward me. "If you impress them, they might offer you a verbal scholarship. It would obviously depend on your performance on and off the field for the rest of this season and the next, but I have faith in you." He smiles, tapping on the passenger side door, before taking a step back from my car.

"You're going to need to bring your A game, kid." His voice is a little louder now as he tries to speak over my engine and I feel my stomach fall to my feet.

I can bring my A game. I always do.

Nodding, I wave in his direction as a thank you and head to my house to come up with a master plan for my promposal with the help of Bea, while trying to not freak the fuck out about what just happened.

"She isn't a fan of enormous gestures. Whatever you do, keep it simple. Just the two of you," Bea instructs, giving me some much-needed advice, making damn sure I don't make a fool of myself.

"Her favorite flowers are white orchids, but real ones can be expensive, so try to find a fake one if you can. They last longer. And honestly, just be yourself."

Keep it private, be myself, and buy a fake orchid.

Got it.

"I listened to Bea's advice. I had the flower, and I had planned to come past your house the next night after school to ask you on your front porch. Just you and me." I shrug, taking another sip of my wine, thinking about the lone orchid that sits in my office that I've kept for fourteen years.

"But Austin beat you to it," she says with a whisper, eyes remaining firmly on mine.

"Austin beat me to it," I repeat, feeling the same sense of defeat I felt back then. "I think the conversation between his dad and I really tipped him over the edge," I admit.

"I know at the start, he was just trying to make me jealous and angry, probably to throw me off my game, maybe ruin my chances of getting scouted. In my head, he was using you to get to me because he knew how I felt about you. But you don't stay with someone for fourteen years if you don't love them," I say, hating that I had to admit any of that to her.

"I'm so sorry, Harley. I wish I'd known earlier." Reaching across the rug, she softly touches her hand with mine, tears forming in her eyes.

"Hey, it's okay. You have nothing to be sorry for. None of it was your fault," I reply, leaning forward to wipe the tears that have fallen down her cheeks. "You kind of knew, though." I chuckle, remembering my ruined jeans thanks to her drunken night.

"No, I didn't. I just thought you were too focused on football to even notice me. I had a major crush on you, but Austin acknowledged me in ways that you didn't, and I just went with it," she says with a shrug and soft laugh to mask her cry.

"I told you I had a crush on you the night of Matty Maxwell's party. And then you puked on my jeans afterward," I say, and we both burst out laughing.

"I'm so sorry about that, too. And your pants in California. What size are you? I'll buy you a new pair." She nibbles on her lower lip.

"I have plenty of pants." I smirk. "But you were right. I had absolutely no clue how to do anything but play football, so that's what I focused on," I reply, edging my way closer to her.

"I wish I'd remembered that you told me," she whispers.

"Why? It wouldn't have changed anything."

She's quiet for a moment, deep in thought, eyes roaming my face, lingering on my lips. I would do anything to know what's on her mind right now.

"I have something else to apologize for."

"What?"

"When I said, 'thank God' about us not having sex, I didn't mean it in the way you think."

"What did you mean, Herring? Because I'll be honest, I have whiplash. One minute you're almost riding my cock in the creek, nearly kissing me in my office, and inviting me to join you in the shower, and the next, you're avoiding in me like the plague, saying you're glad we didn't have sex," I say. "I'm sorry about the creek and my office, though. I was way out of line. You said you wanted to be friends, and I didn't respect your boundaries."

"I don't want to be...I want you to kiss me."

Twenty-Five
Cassandra

TURNING HIS BODY TO face mine, we both slowly gravitate to our knees. I stare at my favorite green eyes as they hood over, looking at me in a way he never has before.

Like I'm the only person he's ever seen.

Is he going to kiss me or will I have to beg?

"Are you sure?" His voice is soft and husky, like he hasn't spoken in days. "I need you to be sure, Herring. Because once I do this, there's no going back," he whispers, and suddenly, I feel it too. It's like everything finally makes sense.

I feel everything he feels, and I just. Want. *Him*.

"I didn't mean it when I said, 'thank God.' I meant that it would have been a mistake if we had sex while we were drunk, because I wanted to be able to remember everything about it. I want you, Harley. I want you to kiss me. I want you to touch me. I want everything with you, if everything is what you're willing to give me," I tell him, and the moment the words leave my lips, his arm hooks around my waist without a second thought, our bodies collide, and his lips come crashing down on mine.

The kiss starts slowly, with me following his lead, happy to just be in the moment. His hand cups my cheek as his thumb grazes the side of my face and I loop my arms around his neck, giving in to the temptation that is, and always has been, Harley Wingrove.

Pulling away from the kiss, he stares into my eyes, his own deep green ones sparkling with mischief and desire. Our mouths collide again, only this time, there's a sense of urgency behind it.

It's explosive.

Passionate.

Almost as if he's afraid I'll change my mind, and he's taking everything I have to offer.

But I don't think I ever will.

His tongue swipes across my bottom lip, teasing, drawing me closer, and I give him full access to my mouth and full access to me. My fingers intertwine with each other, my arms remain firmly around his neck. His grip around my waist tightening and I pull his body on top of mine, laying us both down on the blanket beneath us.

Pulling away from our kiss, he rests on his knees in between my legs, chest rising and falling heavily as he stares at me, eyes trailing slowly from my legs back to my eyes.

"What's wrong?" I ask, steadying my breathing, propping myself up onto my elbows, appreciating every inch of his face as it glows beneath the natural light of the moon.

"I just wanted to make sure I wasn't imagining this," Harley replies, hiking my dress up slightly, resting his palm on my thigh to give it a soft squeeze. I feel it all over my body and I shudder beneath his touch.

Reaching for the hem of his t-shirt, I tug at it, urging him to take it off. I need to see all of him.

He pulls at the sleeves of his denim jacket first, sliding each one down the length of his arms. His t-shirt next, pulling it over his head in one tug.

My breath hitches in my throat, his eyes remain glued on mine.

The room is dark, illuminated only just, but it's enough to highlight every curve in his torso; every muscle and every vein that tattoos his skin, glowing, making him look golden, yet somehow pearlescent, too.

I've been lucky enough to accidentally see Harley Wingrove half-naked so many times in the last few weeks, and each time, I'm in awe, but always force myself to look away.

This time, I allow myself to look.

Allow myself to look at him like *this*.

Allow myself to look at him and beg him to fuck me with my eyes.

Because that's exactly what I want, and I've never wanted anyone or anything more.

I see everything I need to see, even though the room is barely lit. A subtle amount of hair on his chest that I never noticed before, with a small birthmark right under his left peck.

A long, nearly faded scar sits slightly beneath his collarbone on the right side. His biceps and forearms are decorated with veins and his six-pack that I've dreamed about, leading to the most alluring V I've ever seen on a man.

There's only one body part of his that I haven't seen yet, and am so desperate to.

To touch.

To *taste*.

Feeling my underwear soak at the mere sight of him, I copy his movements, slipping off my denim jacket awkwardly, sleeve by sleeve, lifting my dress above my head, leaving me in nothing but a matching white lingerie set.

I didn't plan on having sex with him tonight, but I never leave the house in mismatched underwear.

Just in case.

Stopping mid movement, his eyes meet mine before they roam down my body again, but this time, I'm almost naked and more vulnerable, but I feel more confident than I ever have.

He makes me feel sexy and beautiful and everything in-between without even uttering a word. The look on his face tells me everything I need to know.

Slowly, his eyes wander back up to meet my gaze. "Why are you looking at me like that?" I ask, as his emerald eyes twinkle, full of hunger.

"Like what?" He smirks, hovering his body over mine.

"Like you haven't eaten in days, and I'm the only thing on the menu." I raise a brow as he licks his lips, his clenched jaw softening.

"Because, Herring, I've been fucking starving for fourteen years."

His lips fuse together with mine and we pick back up where we left off. Our mouths move in sync, like a choreographed routine that we've practiced together for years, until his lips move from mine, sprinkling kisses down my jaw, down the length of my neck.

One of his hands snakes its way up my back, gliding his fingertips up my spine softly before moving to unclip my bra and I shiver, excited to be on display for him.

Sliding my bra off my arms and away from my chest, his hand wanders, covering every inch of my stomach, cupping my breasts one at a time, his tongue finally finding my nipples, my hips involuntarily rocking beneath him.

"Are you sure you want to do this?" he whispers to me, his thumb dragging along my bottom lip.

'I've never been surer', is what I want to say, but the words refuse to leave my mouth, so I just nod frantically and, apparently, it's the only answer he needs.

"I've waited so long for this moment, Herring. I'm going to take my time with you," he says, but I shake my head at him.

"Take your time with me later. Or tomorrow. Or even the next day. I don't care when you do it or how long it takes. But right now, I just need to feel you inside me," I beg, not caring if I sound too desperate.

I'm past the point of no return.

I have all this pent-up sexual tension from the last few weeks, and he's the only one who can relieve it for me.

"I don't have a condom. I didn't expect any of this. I didn't come prepared," he says, panic filled gaze. We both pause, panting, as he dips his head to rest on my shoulder.

"I'm on the pill and I've always used protection," I say, reassuring both of us.

"I'm clean, too," he promises. "I've never not used a condom. And I get checked regularly."

And with those words, my mouth is on his, my hands at the button of his jeans. Wildly trying to break free what's hiding behind it; what I've been longing for.

Staring at his cock as it springs free, my whole body tenses at the reality of what's about to happen.

He's a lot bigger than I'm used to, and it terrifies and excites me all at once.

"We'll go slow." He chuckles, detecting my sudden fear.

"Okay. Slow." Nodding, he positions himself on top of me, teasing my entrance with the tip of his cock while kissing me softly. My body whimpers underneath him at the sensation.

"Please," I beg, unable to control myself any longer. My hunger for this man is something I never knew I could feel, and I'm growing more impatient as each second passes.

"I need to feel you." As soon as the words leave my mouth, he slides his cock inside me with one smooth movement, catching me off guard. Stealing the air from my lungs, my nails digging into his back.

"Are you okay?" he asks, steadying his body over mine, cock buried comfortably inside of me.

Relaxing my body into his, his slow thrusts grow deeper and deeper, turning the pain to pleasure. Moaning, my back arches against the ground beneath us, curving into his body as his hands trace my skin.

Landing on my sweet spot, his thumb moves in circular motions on my clit and if I was standing up, my knees would have buckled beneath me. I've never had pleasure cover every inch of my body, never felt the way he makes me feel.

Nothing's ever come close.

"You feel so good," he groans into my ear before taking my mouth with his, kissing me in ways I could only ever dream about. "Come for me," he commands, thrusting harder and harder, burying himself deeper and deeper.

As if it's that easy, my body gives in as he fucks me over the edge, his cock pulsing inside of me.

His heavy body collapses on top of mine, kissing me one last time before he lays next to me. Steadying his breathing, he takes my hand in his, intertwining our fingers.

Content.

That's what I feel at this very moment with a naked Harley Wingrove laying to the left of me.

But as I turn to look at him, I notice his signature cheeky, devilish grin, and I know this night is far from over.

Twenty-Six
Harley

SWINGING MY FRONT DOOR open, we storm inside my apartment as one, Cassandra's legs remaining firmly locked around my waist. Exactly where they have been from the moment we stepped out of my car and into the building elevator.

All while her mouth covered mine.

I never liked to kiss women for long because I never wanted them to get the wrong idea, but fuck, I never wanted to stop kissing her. I wanted every single idea of the possibility of us to be floating around in her head.

Being over six feet, my strides are long, so we made it to my front door in record time, but it felt like a God damn eternity. I told her I wanted to take my time with her earlier tonight, but she wouldn't let me. She wanted me to fuck her hard and fast because she wanted to feel me inside her.

So I did exactly what she asked.

Who am I to deny her?

But now, it's my turn to have my way with her and I can't wait to savor her slowly, explore every last inch of her body with my hands and tongue, until she can't handle it anymore and she *begs* me to fuck her.

Kissing her softly and slowly, I stumble blindly toward my master suite, the front door of my apartment slamming shut behind us.

I won't rush this.

I need to remember every single detail.

Once we enter my bedroom, I throw her body onto the bed and watch as she eagerly strips off her dress and props herself on her elbows, licking and nibbling on her bottom lip. My cock strains against my sweatpants.

Her body is breathtaking.

It's the only word I can use to describe her.

She didn't bother to put her underwear back on when we left the barn. She knew it would be a waste of time. Which meant that the car ride to my apartment was agonizing, knowing my dream girl was beside me, dripping wet, wearing nothing beneath her dress.

With a flick of the switch, the lamp on my bedside table illuminates the room. Only just.

Her eyes search mine, wide with lust, wondering what my next move could be.

"You can't just stand there fully clothed while you stare at me." She snickers, drinking me in, but that's exactly what I plan to do.

"I'm going to take my time with you, remember?" I say, and as much as I'm in a hurry to taste her, I want to appreciate her in every way, too.

"I told you in California that I was going to fuck you, then taste you, then fuck you again. And I plan on doing it exactly in that order until you're begging for it. Begging to feel my cock inside you. And since I've already fucked you, it's time for me to taste you, Herring." She groans, eagerly trying to reach for the waistband of my pants, but I shove her hand away.

This is going to be fun.

"Spread your legs." She does as she's told, without any hesitation. "That's my perfect girl," I say, attempting to stifle a groan that forces its way out, rumbling through my chest.

Settling on my knees right in front of her, I make sure I have the best seat in the house.

"Show me what you would do if you were alone. Tell me what you think about while you fuck yourself with your fingers," I say to her, and she slowly glides her hand down her stomach, hovering over her pussy before I nod, as if to give her permission.

"You," she whispers, her fingers reaching for her clit. Letting out a deep breath with a soft moan, her fingers move in slow, perfect circles and my cock aches at the sight in front me of, begging to take part, knowing I'm the reason she is the way she is.

"Good girl." I don't even try to hide my arousal as I see her pretty, pink pussy spread wide for me, glistening in the light.

So fucking wet.

"How does it feel?"

"So good," she whispers, her breathing staggered while she continues pleasing herself.

As one finger slowly slides inside of her, her back curving off the mattress, I watch as she unravels right in front of my eyes.

Rising only just, I grip my hands around the sides of her hips, pulling her body closer to the edge of the bed, spreading her legs even further apart, giving me better access to the place I can't wait to taste. Kissing up her inner thigh slowly, she shudders, goosebumps inking her skin. Her stomach and legs tense beneath my touch.

When I arrive at my long awaited destination, it's even better than I could have imagined.

So pink.

So wet.

So ready for me.

I could do this for hours, and it'll never be enough.

Softly and slowly, I lick her clit. An animalistic growl escapes my throat, and I feel as her body relaxes at my touch, both of her hands gripping my bed sheets.

"Fuck. You taste so good, Herring. So sweet," I say, hearing her breathing quicken as my tongue does, and I know I'm right where she needs me to be.

"Right there, please don't stop," she begs me, like I ever had any intention of doing so.

Sliding one finger inside her, she gasps as she releases the bed sheet with one hand to grab a fist full of my hair, making sure my tongue doesn't break contact with her clit. Torn on if I want to fuck her with my tongue or my hand, I decide to stay put so I can taste her on my tongue as she comes.

Her hips buck as she thrusts against my face and I can tell that she's on the brink. She's so close to tipping over the edge for the second time tonight, and a heavy, guttural moan escapes her.

"Please." I know she's begging for my cock, and I chuckle.

"Not yet."

Not until you come.

Watching her through her spread legs, I pick up the pace, reaching my hand up to cup her breasts, pinching the firm peaks of her nipples, heart beat pounding under my fingertips.

Her breathing stops when her clit beats under my tongue, and her pussy strains around my fingers. Screaming my name, she grips my hair tighter.

"Fuck me, Harley," she begs one more time, her voice huskier than before as she pleads for me.

"Fine, but only because you asked so nicely." I give in, but not before I make her come against my tongue once, twice, three more times, so the sweetness of her pussy can linger.

My cock's impatience is palpable; it's as though he's been held in captivity for fourteen fucking years and is ready to be unleashed.

Taking it in my right hand, I glide up and down my length to ready him for what's about to come.

"Up," is all I have to say for her to do as she's told, while I lay down in place of her on my bed. "I want to watch as you ride me."

She straddles me with a hunger that's impossible to ignore, her pussy sliding down my shaft with ease. She takes a second to adjust to my size before taking control, fucking me how she begged me to fuck her.

Hard and fast.

Gripping her hips firmly, she bounces up and down on top of me, her tits moving in perfect rhythm.

Flipping her body over, she softly moans, and I take advantage of the leverage I have on her hips. With her ass up and her face buried in the duvet, her sounds muffled as I moved inside her.

"Please. Don't. Stop. I need to come again." Her pussy drips, quivering around me, but I don't stop.

I can't.

I need to know that I've done everything in my power to please her.

"Fuck, you feel so good," I say through gritted teeth as I continue to fuck her from behind, tucking my hand underneath her to find her clit with my fingers.

She's fucking dripping wet.

"I'm going to come," I warn her, unable to hold it any longer.

Just as the last words leave my mouth, I feel the tightness of her around my cock and I completely lose myself inside of her, taking us both over the edge at the same time.

Rapidly panting, I collapse on top of her back. She kisses my arm that's now draped over her shoulder, both of us breathing in unison before I roll off her back, getting comfortable on the bed. She moves to rest her head on my chest.

When those hazel eyes look at me, for a brief moment, I forget where we are.

I want to stay right here, in this bubble, forever.

"I wish I didn't have to go," she whispers, bringing my black sheet over her bare chest.

Tracing my torso with her fingers, she runs them across the scar that's had seven years to heal, yet I still wince as if the pain is raw, and I hope she doesn't ask about it.

"So don't."

I've let her go once before, and I won't do it again.

She's it for me.

But I won't tell her that.

Not yet, anyway.

"I don't have any clothes," she protests, biting her lip with a mischievous, knowing smirk on her face.

Standing up from the bed, still naked, I head toward my wardrobe and find a plain black t-shirt for her to sleep in, and no doubt add to her new collection.

"Sleep in this." I throw it onto the bed at her feet and make my way to my ensuite. Pulling open the second drawer, I pull out a bright blue toothbrush, still in its packet. "You can have this one to keep here." I place it on the marble, black, stone countertop in the bathroom before I head back into the bedroom, where she now sits on the edge of the bed. Sheet wrapped firmly around her while she clutches her new pajamas.

Smile burnished across her face.

"And as for underwear," I say with a smirk. "You won't be needing any. But for when you do, I will have these washed, dried, and ready for you whenever you decide to go home," I say while picking up her white lace matching set from the ground and heading toward the laundry. "Until then, this house is an underwear free zone," I shout over my shoulder without looking back.

Her chuckle fades behind me, drowned out by the sound of my shower water running, and I know she's given in.

She's decided to stay.

It feels like I've just won MVP for the second time.

Leaning against the doorframe of my bathroom, I watch as she stands with her back to me, hair sitting at the top of her head as she lets the water drape over her body, over her perfectly round ass.

"Would you like to join me?" she says without turning to face me, and I get flashbacks of having to turn down this exact request a week ago.

Thanks, alcohol.

It was the hardest '*thank you, but no thank you*' of my fucking life, but I don't regret it.

This moment, right here, is what I hoped for. Way better than any drunken revenge fuck.

"I thought you would never ask."

Standing behind her with my cock pressed up against her back, she leans her body into mine as I dip my chin into the crook of her neck and wrap my arms around her waist.

"Are you okay?" I ask.

"Are you sure this is what you want?" she whispers her reply.

"I told you before that once we do this, there's no going back, and I meant it. Now even more so," I reply. Turning her to face me, I lift her chin up with my finger, placing a soft kiss on her lips.

"Good. Because your bed is so comfy, I don't think I'm ready to give it up yet." She giggles as she places a gentle kiss on the scar below my collarbone.

"Just my bed?" I gently tickle under her ribcage to hear her laughter roar again.

"I guess the sex isn't too bad." She pokes her tongue out at me before turning once more, so we're chest to back and my hands trace her stomach.

"It isn't too bad?" I scoff, pretending to be offended. "Baby, no man is ever going to come even close to me. You're never going to want anyone else," I tease. My tone is light, but I mean every word that comes out of my mouth.

There's no going back.

We didn't sleep the rest of the night.

I spent it memorizing and worshipping every inch of her body so I would never forget how it felt to be with the woman my body has longed for since I was sixteen.

My lips dotted kisses along every inch of her skin so I would never forget how she tasted, and I planned on doing it every single night for as long as she'd let me.

Twenty-Seven
Cassandra

With work being so busy lately and Jenna having client after client, we haven't properly spoken since last week, aside from brief check in texts to let each other know we're alive. Given that tonight is Thursday, we've saved it for each other like we always do.

A plate of food and a glass of wine on my dining table, I finally sit down, ready to unload the last seven days to my best friend.

"I'm going to need you to repeat all of that, but slower." Jenna squeals as I recount every detail of playing house with Harley.

So, I do.

I tell her how we both opened up completely. How he told me about his hope to ask me to prom, but Austin asked first. I tell her how my mind suddenly filled with clarity, and I knew I was where I was supposed to be.

All the while, heaping spoonfuls of spaghetti into my mouth.

"I'm so fucking jealous." She rolls her eyes playfully, and I can't wipe the smile off my face.

"We only left his bedroom for food." I scrunch up my face nervously at her through the phone as she fake gags in envy.

After leaving his place on Sunday, I went straight home to pack a duffle bag full of clothes and toiletries for the work week ahead, and went straight back to his apartment.

He wasn't supposed to be at Wingrove Estates this week, but he made his way in every single day so we could (secretly) have lunch together. I finally got to meet his friend Robbie, too.

He swung by Harley's apartment while I was there to deliver a contract that needed to be signed. He gave me the 'what are your intentions with my friend?' speech, but aside from that, he seemed nice.

Harley assured me he was just protective, but I didn't mind it. It's nice knowing he has good people in his corner.

Today is my first night back at home, because it's Thursday. And Thursday is Jenna's night, no matter what.

It does, however, suck that I'll be sleeping alone for the first time in a week. I've gotten used to waking up next to Harley or with his head between my legs. It's been utter bliss.

"Wipe that smug grin off your face," my best friend says jokingly, but it's impossible for me to do.

We spend the next hour talking about her job and how she could potentially be working on a movie set in the new year, and how no guy she meets is able to 'satisfy her'.

"Trust me, C. I've had my fair share of dick, and nothing is as good as my trusty friend in my top drawer." She cackles to herself, and I almost spit out my wine. "On that note, it's getting late," she says, changing the subject, and I realize we've been talking for over two hours. It's well and truly time for us to call it a night.

"Love you."

"Love you, too."

Hanging up my phone, I see an unread message lit up on my screen, and I know who it's from without even opening it.

Harley: My bed is so empty without you.

Me: Well, maybe you shouldn't have bought such an enormous bed.

Harley: Or, you could just come and sleep in it.

Me: Since when did you get so needy? ;)

Harley: You take that back. You love it when I'm needy.

Me: You're so right.

Harley: Goodnight, princess.

Me: Princess? I almost threw up in my mouth.

Harley: Ok, I'll just stick to calling you Herring. Goodnight, Herring.

Me: Better. Goodnight, Wingrove.

***

"How's the new place treating you?" mom asks as she puts five plates down around the dining table.

"It's going way better than I expected," I say, avoiding all eye contact as I place cutlery around the table, keeping the reason why to myself.

She can read me like a book and I don't exactly want to tell her that I'm spending all of my free time at Harley's apartment.

"And you're still exercising?" she asks and I nod.

It isn't completely a lie. I *am* doing a lot of cardio. But the cardio I'm doing isn't the kind you discuss with your mother while setting the table.

Or at all.

Harley and I have kept, whatever this is, under wraps. Until we know for sure, anyway.

If it were up to him, everyone would know about us. But it's me who wants to keep things a secret for now and he respects that. Not because I'm ashamed or embarrassed. It's the opposite, actually.

I'm just sick of having everyone involved in my business, and I don't want anyone or anything to ruin what we have.

"I'm happy for you, honey. You look really healthy. You have this..." she pauses to smile and touch my hand. "Glow about you. You're beginning to look more like your old self. The happiness is back in your eyes," she says before heading into the kitchen to check on the food in the oven.

I know she means well; I do. But the words are like a knife to the gut and a warm, fuzzy hug around my heart. Knowing that I'd lost myself so badly that it became visible to everyone in my life, apart from me.

But I know I'm getting that girl back with each day that passes.

"Thanks. Olive and Lizzie have been keeping me on a super balanced diet, so it must be that," I lie again, partly. Because my sisters have been holding me accountable, but my mood and '*glow*' lately has nothing to do with the food I'm consuming, and more about the man who consumes me.

"Speaking of your sisters, they'll be here soon. Go freshen up." She ushers me out of the kitchen, and if I wasn't on such a high, I would tell her off for being bossy.

My phone vibrates in my pocket and I smile when I see his name light up on my screen.

"Hey," I say, blushing as I dry my hands on the hand towel in the bathroom next door to my old bedroom.

"Hi, sexy. What are you wearing?" he jokes, knowing it'll make me uncomfortable with my parents in ear shot.

"Stop it," I hiss, while nibbling the side of my cheek, smiling like a love sick teenager.

"What are you doing after dinner?" he asks as I head back down the stairs.

"You, I hope." Giggling to myself, I don't know when I became this sex-crazed maniac, but I don't think Harley has any complaints. He's all I think about, and I know the feeling is mutual. He never fails to tell me when I'm on his mind.

My sex life used to be very vanilla. Get the job done and go to sleep. I would be lucky if it happened twice a month. Orgasms for me weren't even an option. I had to sort myself out in the shower.

But now, I can't count on both hands the amount he's given me in such a short amount of time, and still, he's all that I crave.

"Okay, let me rephrase that." He chuckles. "I want to take you out on a proper date tonight. How do you feel about ice cream?" he asks, and I say yes without a second thought. He could take me fishing and make me put the bait on myself, and I would still say yes.

"Text me when you get home and I'll come and get you."

When he hangs up, I bring my phone to my chest and steady my breathing before emerging back into the kitchen.

"Why are you blushing?" Lizzie asks without so much as a 'hello', and I instinctively touch my cheeks to cover them, feeling the warmth of them under my fingertips.

"I'm not blushing." I frown, clenching my jaw while nudging her as if to say 'Shut. Up.', but, in typical Lizzie fashion, it goes right over her head.

"Seriously. You're like a tomato," she continues, and I want to throw myself against a wall.

"Yeah, Cass, what's up with that?" Now it's Olive's turn to call me out.

Fan-fucking-tastic.

"Your sisters are right. You do look a little flustered, honey," mom chimes in, and I've never wanted our weekly family dinner to be over so soon, just so I could throw myself in the trash and be done with this god forsaken moment.

"What's new in your world, girls?" dad asks as we all sit quietly, enjoying mom's casserole.

"I have that wedding expo in California coming up," I say. I wipe my mouth with my napkin before placing it back down on the table, excited to get away for a few days.

Not only do I get to see Jenna, Janelle, and Frankie, but Harley is coming with me. It's a work event, but we decided to treat it like a personal getaway for us, too. Grangewood Creek is a tiny town, and word spreads fast. The moment we're spotted together hand in hand, everyone will know about it in less than twelve hours, with Mrs. Bishop at the reins.

Being in California, we won't have to worry about being spotted and becoming the talk of the town.

We can hold hands in public.

We can go on dates to busy places.

He can kiss me whenever he feels like it, like no one's watching, even though we'll be surrounded by people.

"I submitted one of my songs to be featured in a film," Olive says casually in between mouthfuls of food. The entire table stops eating and mom drops her cutlery.

"What?" Lizzie screeches, nearly jumping out of her seat at the dinner table, tears prickling on her waterline.

"Relax, will you? I probably won't even get chosen," Olive bites back, urging her twin to sit back down with a simple look.

She's always been her biggest critic, but the four other people at this table have always been her biggest fans. She's ridiculously talented, and we have no idea where it comes from. The rest of us are completely tone deaf and can't hold a tune, but Olive? She's destined to be a star.

"When will you find out?" Old man Hank's face is as straight as ever, with no hint of emotion anywhere in sight.

We never know what he's thinking or how he's feeling, but I know he's proud of his youngest daughter right now.

"In a couple months, I guess. Can we drop it?" She shrugs her shoulders like it's no big deal, while the rest of us are still staring at her in disbelief.

"And I thought one of my students wanting to marry me was exciting," Lizzie says about one of her kindergarteners. "Now all the kids in class are in on it and call me Mrs. Beckett while he walks around proudly." She rolls her eyes and smirks, causing the entire table to erupt. Olive's body relaxes.

Lizzie always knows when her twin is in need, and even though the conversation is with her family, sometimes Olive still needed saving. Lizzie was always her knight.

I'm so happy to be home.

***

I haven't even walked through my door when I text Harley to let him know that I'm home. I somehow had enough time to change into some warmer clothes, opting for black jeans and a cream-colored knitted sweater with ankle boots.

Grangewood Creek is known for its ice cold winters, and this is just the beginning.

You'd think I'd be used to it, given that I grew up here, but considering I spent more than a decade in California, my body adjusted to the temperature there, so these cold nights are going to take some time to get used to.

Most people might think ice cream on a night like tonight isn't the smartest idea, but it's one of my favorite things to do.

Popsicles in summer and ice cream in winter.

It's always been my thing.

Hearing a knock at my door, I practically run to open it and my heart nearly tips over itself as my eyes meet his emerald ones.

"Hi." I'm breathless at the mere sight of him. He's wearing a plain black hooded sweater, dark blue jeans, and all black sneakers.

"Hi," he says back, chuckling as we stand in my open doorway.

"Should we get going?" I ask before I have time to change my mind and drag the both of us inside my apartment and lock the door for the night.

Or week.

"In a minute," he whispers, as he presses my back up against the side of the door frame. His body towering over mine, resting one hand at the top of the frame above us, while the other tips my chin up so my lips can meet his.

Kissing him back briefly, trying to ignore the butterflies in my stomach and the excitement down below, I reluctantly push his chest away from mine, causing our lips to part, and pull my front door closed behind us. His laughter echoing through the hallway of my apartment building.

"Where are we going?" I ask as we buckle up and he turns the ignition on for his car.

"You'll see." He smirks, flashing me that dimple that I adore.

Reaching his arm across my lap, he takes my hand in his, bringing the back of it to his lips before placing both of our hands in his lap.

As we drive through town, I realize that since being back, I've mostly stuck to places in my comfort zone.

Mostly.

I have absolutely zero plans to jump off the cliff again, but at least now I can say I've done it.

Harley, Bea, and I frequent Katie's for milkshakes, and I've been to Bridie's with my sisters a handful of times, too. But otherwise, the rest of my time is spent at work, my family home, or split between Harley's apartment and mine.

I have no intention of changing any of that anytime soon.

It's getting late out, which means everything in Grangewood is closed or closing, so it's basically a ghost town. But as I look around our surroundings as we drive, I realize that not a lot has changed.

There are a few new clothing stores to help the town keep up with the latest fashion trends, and Laney's yoga studio, but aside from that, most things are exactly how they used to be, and it makes me happy.

Change isn't always necessary.

"I thought we were going to eat ice cream?" I try to hide my slight disappointment as we drive past the only ice cream parlor in town, watching as it closes its doors for the night.

"We are." He grins as he reaches into the back seat, patting the freezer bag that occupies the space. My disappointment is instantly replaced with an overwhelming feeling that I can't quite place, but I don't want to question it. I'm not ready to.

He *planned* this.

He put in effort.

A real date.

My very first one.

"How do you know that you got a flavor that I like?" I tease, raising a brow as I look in his direction. Realistically, I'm not picky with ice cream, but he doesn't need to know that.

"I have a good memory. Salted caramel crunch, with cookie dough and sour worms," he says, scrunching up his nose. I haven't had that combination since high school.

"How did you—" I begin, but he kisses my hand again.

"I told you. Good memory," he says while tapping his temple with his finger. Keeping his eyes firmly locked on the road, I note the turn he takes, and it hits me where we're going.

"Our high school?" I ask, confused, as he parks his car in the dark, empty parking lot. Racing around to the passenger side of his Range Rover, he opens my door for me as I take his hand and step out.

It's barely changed since graduation.

The brick sign that reads '*Grangewood High - Home of the Panthers*' still has signatures from every student who's ever graduated.

My parents were the graduating class who created the tradition.

Squealing, I run toward it and immediately find my own, right next to Bea's, with Austin's not far off.

"Where's yours?" I ask, but he just shrugs.

"I don't think I ever signed it," he admits, and I don't know why, but I feel sad for a sixteen-year-old Harley, that he didn't get to do something that all of his peers got to. "I didn't even know it was a thing. I was way too focused on football. You were right about that." He chuckles uncomfortably, reaching for my hand, but I don't take it.

I can't help but wonder if that's actually the case or if he's just trying to spare my feelings.

Did he really not know, or had Austin isolated Harley so much that he felt as though he had no right?

He attempts to take my hand again, but I shake my head in response, feet remaining firmly on the ground. "Wait," I tell him. Rummaging through my bag, I know I have a black marker in there somewhere, and it doesn't take me long to find it. "Here. Sign it." My voice is firm as I hand him the pen, foot tapping on the ground.

I demand he do what he should have done years ago with the rest of the graduating class.

"You're so bossy." He groans sarcastically, taking the marker from my finger tips to sign his name right next to mine, where it should have been all along.

"Much better," I say, and he blushes.

I feel like I've created a core memory for him, only twelve years late.

Better late than never, I suppose.

"Now you can take me." I giggle as he puffs air into his cheeks, and I place my hand back in his, and we make our way toward the only place I expect Harley Wingrove to take me.

The football field.

Twenty-Eight
Harley Age 16

"ARE YOU GOING TO get ready for prom, honey?" mom asks as she pokes her head into my bedroom, my eyes staying glued to the comic in my hands. "You're going to be late." She pushes, trying to encourage me to stop reading and to pick up the pace, but there's no part of me that actually wants to go.

"I told you, I'm not going," I remind her for the fifth time this week.

Rising from my bed, I head toward the bathroom for a quick shower before I turn in for the night. Prom is the last place I want to be, and my mom's constant harping only makes me want to skip it even more, but I'm mentally preparing for the mom guilt trip that's bound to come my way.

"Why not?" She raises a brow, marching behind me, hot on my heels. Standing in the open doorway of the bathroom, she crosses her arms over her chest, waiting for me to say anything, but I don't have an answer for her.

Not one she would be happy with hearing, anyway.

It's not like I can say, 'Austin asked the girl I like even though he knew I liked her,' because that sounds childish and petty as fuck. She knows he and I had a falling out, but she doesn't know the reason behind it, so she's left to speculate and fill in the blanks on her own.

Hell, I'm still trying to figure it out myself.

Mom keeps telling me that things have a way of working themselves out, but I won't hold my breath.

After hearing Austin had asked Cassandra to prom, I was annoyed about it, but not annoyed enough to stop talking to my best friend. When I got to his place to pick him up for school the next morning, his mom told me that I wasn't welcome in her home, but his dad apologized about his wife and son's behavior, and said Austin had already left for the day.

When I got to school, his arm was draped over Cassandra's shoulder while he refused to acknowledge my existence at all. She gave me a brief smile that I would have missed if I weren't paying attention. But Austin was paying attention too, and her smile faded while he dragged her away.

He stopped training alongside me and worked with the second-string quarterback instead. He insisted it would be better for his game, whatever that meant.

Coach wasn't happy about it, but he was so deep in Mr. Anderson's pockets that he went along with it.

Thankfully, I still had Bea.

She treated me the same as she always did, and we'd grown closer over the last few weeks, because while I'd lost my best friend completely, hers was distracted and distancing herself slowly.

We stuck by each other.

"I just don't feel like going." I try to keep my voice calm, because I hate being annoyed with my mom. I've never even been big on dances anyway, so I didn't see the point of going.

I don't know why she bothers to guilt me into things she knows I don't want to do.

Right now, football is my priority and going to the prom wouldn't benefit it at all.

"Honey, I worked really hard to save money for your suit."

Here we go.

Groaning, I drag a hand down my face while I stare at the navy suit that she's hung on the hook behind the bathroom door, coming to terms with the fact that the decision has been made for me.

Like always.

Fuck it.

"I'll go for an hour, and nothing more."

"Better than nothing, Harley. Please, try to enjoy yourself. It wouldn't kill you to let everything go for the night." Fat chance of that happening, but I nod and shrug instead of protesting, ripping the suit off the hanger.

Slamming the car door shut, I slowly lug my heavy body into the school gym.

Mom helped me do up my tie, but the moment I closed my front door, I loosened it around my neck because I felt too restricted.

I just want to fucking *breathe*.

"Hey, stud." Bea smiles as she approaches me, linking her arm through mine. "Let me fix your tie." She tries, but I nudge her hand away.

"Can we just get this over with?" I ask. I'd called her on my way, and she said she would meet me out front and we could go in together.

People would probably get the wrong idea and talk, because gossip was the hottest hobby in Grangewood, but I didn't care. She and I knew we were just friends, and it's no-one else's business.

Bea's wearing a black princess cut ball gown. Her long, blonde hair is dead straight, half-up, half-down. She's rocking black lips like its nobody's business, and bright red shoes slightly peek out the bottom. The only pop of color in sight.

I know absolutely nothing about fashion, but I know a pretty girl when I see one, and Bea looks immaculate.

"Are we doing this?" she asks with a deep, steady breath. She wants to be here about as much as I do, but she didn't want to let her dress go to waste.

"One hour," I remind her before we step foot into the school gym.

"One hour." She nods, gets on her tiptoes to plant a kiss on my cheek that I wipe away, and into the gym we go.

'So What' by PINK! Is blasting through the speakers as the crowd jumps around, dancing and shouting the words like a bunch of drunk morons, and I already know to stay away from the punch. It's at that moment that I decide to find a place in the gym's corner to occupy myself for the remaining fifty-five minutes I have left.

Not that I'm counting.

Someone caught Bea's eye the moment we pushed through the doors, and I haven't seen her since we arrived.

"Hey, Harley," a soft, husky voice says from over my shoulder. My breath lodges in my throat, my heart skipping an entire beat. I would recognize that voice anywhere.

"Hey, Herring," I say, looking at her up and down, indulging in her for as long as I can. Her dress is long, sparkly, and deep green, hugging her body like a second skin.

The sleeves hang off her shoulders and a slight v exposes just the right amount of cleavage, with a slit on the right side, cutting almost high enough to see her underwear.

Almost.

"You look beautiful," I say, clearing my throat. She blushes instantly. It's true.

I have no reason to lie to her and now that she's dating my best friend, I have nothing to lose.

"Save a dance for me? I've requested my favorite song with the DJ," she says, knowing Austin will never allow it, but I nod anyway.

His hands glide around her waist from behind, snaking up to her cheek, turning her to face him.

Her body stiffens at his touch.

"Here you are." His voice is gruff as he forces a kiss on her lips that she's clearly too polite to decline.

Her cheeks turn a different shade of pink, and I can tell it's not because she's nervous to kiss him.

It's because she's too shy to kiss him in front of anyone.

In front of *me*.

"Come on, let's get away from *him*." Austin's words slur, nodding in my direction as he pulls her away from me. He's clearly drunk, and she's visibly uncomfortable, but she goes with him anyway, most likely to prevent a scene that would inevitably occur if she chose to linger.

Looking back over her shoulder, she mouths the word *'sorry'*, and I shrug in response.

She has nothing to be sorry for. She has no idea how I felt about her.

How I still feel about her.

Checking my phone, my hour is almost up, and I hear *'Make you feel my love'* by *Adele* playing over the speakers.

It's Cassandra's favorite song, and the one that I want to dance with her to.

Leaving the gym for silence, I dial mom's number.

"Hey Mom. Just letting you know I'll stay for one more song, then I'm heading home."

"Are you sure, honey?"

"Positive."

The line goes silent, and I slide my phone back into the pocket of my navy suit pants, let out a deep breath, opening the doors for the gym.

I don't have to search the room for long before I spot Cassandra.

She's impossible to miss, even amongst a crowd of people.

But I wish I hadn't spotted her.

Her arms are wrapped tightly around Austin's neck, while his arms are around her waist.

Her head rests comfortably on his chest with her eyes closed, and that's when I admit defeat.

When I realize that whatever chance I might've had no longer exists.

Hurrying back to my table, I take my jacket off the backrest of my seat, text Bea to tell her I'm leaving, and I don't look back.

***

"Great game, son," Mr. Anderson says as he slaps his palm on my back.

The team is heading back to our locker room after another win. "Thanks, sir. I appreciate the pointers before the game tonight," I respond, smiling, before sipping some water.

I tried to not look for him or the recruiters in the crowd tonight. I wanted to focus solely on my game. Hearing Mr. Anderson say I played a good game puts me instantly on cloud nine. This was the third set of recruiters he'd invited to watch me play, and I've had verbal offers from each school so far, with Ohio State being my top choice.

"You made me proud." He grips my shoulder, and damn, hearing that from him makes my confidence grow.

It's nice to have someone be proud of me.

Having Max Anderson around the last few years has worked wonders for my game, and I think he's the reason I got to be the player that I am. But now that Austin and I spend no time together, I don't see his father as often as I used to, so he has my full attention whenever he's in the room.

"That's rich," Austin's voice seethes from behind us as his father quickly removes his hand from my shoulder. "Pathetic. Just because your daddy didn't stick around, it doesn't give you free rein to mine." His words cut deep, but I don't let him see it.

"Watch it, boy," Mr. Anderson warns his son, but Austin hasn't been intimidated by his father in a long time.

"Whatever, Max," he mutters before shoving his gear into his bag and rushing out the door.

Rolling my eyes, I take my time. I refuse to match his energy. If he's so happy to lose ten years of friendship over a girl, then so be it.

But she's not just any girl, is she?

"See you, Coach," I say over my shoulder, preparing to the leave the locker room.

"You played well today, kid. Don't let that boy get in your head."

"I won't," I assure him as I make my way toward my mom's old, rusty car.

"Harley, please wait." I hear Cassandra's voice from behind me.

My steps falter, but I don't stop.

I don't want to hear what she has to say. I don't need to hear all about her prom night with Austin.

How she's happy with him.

I just wish it was me she was happy with.

Twenty-Nine
Harley

"Why are we here?" Cassandra asks with a smile on her face as she stares up at the bleachers.

Picnic blanket and cooler bag in tow, I place the bag with ice cream on the ground and shake out the blanket while she grabs two corners to help flatten it before we sit.

"It was my favorite place growing up. Where I used to come to think. Pre-game, post-game, weekends. Even holidays," I reply while digging into the freezer bag for my mint chocolate chip ice cream, and Cassandra's weird as fuck combination.

I remember when we were sixteen, the four of us went to get ice cream and Bea casually let me know what her best friend's favorite ice cream combination was, in case I ever needed it.

I guess I never forgot what it was.

I even ordered it once and regretted it after the first bite. The worms were frozen solid.

"I was standing right over there when I passed Austin what would have been the championship winning ball. If only he'd caught it." I nod to the left of the field and chuckle to myself at the memory. We lost the title of champs in our senior year because he fumbled the ball under pressure, yet he blamed me for a bad throw. Somehow, he convinced everyone we lost because of me.

The scouts didn't think so, though. And to me, that was the most important.

"His dad was furious at him for missing such an easy catch," she says, recounting her version of events. She and Austin had been together for a year at that point, so I assume she knew Austin and Max's relationship well.

"He was so hard on him all the time, but over the years, I learned that Max Anderson was just... not a good guy." She shudders.

Obviously, she knew their family dynamic better than anyone, so she saw what Max Anderson was like behind closed doors.

"He visited me in college right before I was drafted," I mumble through a mouthful of ice cream, but surprisingly, she can make out what I'm saying.

"Didn't your parents ever teach you to not speak with your mouth full, Wingrove?" she asks through a giggle, leaning across the blanket, using her thumb to swipe the excess ice cream off my lips.

"Mom was too busy working to teach me anything," I tease as I reach for a napkin to clean off the parts she missed.

"What about your dad?" Her question catches me off guard, and I realize she doesn't know a lot about my upbringing, because in high school, we only really ever hung out in group settings and never got the chance to hang out one on one.

"I've never actually met him. He took off when Mom was pregnant with me, and she always changed the subject whenever I tried to bring him up." I shrug it off.

It doesn't affect me anymore.

"Even now?"

"I stopped asking about him once I'd reached high school. I guess I got used to having only my mom. I saw a photo of him once. He was cradling my mom's bump. The back of the photo said *'Don and I - Pregnant with Harley - 1993.'* She used to keep it in her drawer." I give her a weak smile before heaping another spoonful of ice cream into my mouth.

Mom took on both parental roles, so I never felt the need to mention the photo. She alone was enough for me. Sure, she could barely make it to any of my high school games or even take me to practice when I was young, but she was working so hard to provide for us, making sure we always had food on the table, and a roof over our heads.

I was taught at a young age that if I wanted something in life, I had to work hard for it.

And that's exactly what I did.

"She doesn't need to work anymore. I retired her years ago." My chest swells with pride, knowing I was able to change the course of our lives by living out my dream.

But she refused to accept it.

She needed to work to keep herself busy.

"How come she's working at Wingrove Estate?" She raises a brow before eating her first mouthful of ice cream.

Apparently, she was too focused on our conversation to think about her tub of frozen... worms.

"She's too proud of a woman. She didn't want anything from me. She wouldn't let me buy her a new car or buy her a new house. She wanted me to make her work for it, so that's why she runs the winery. She loves it and does a better job than I would. I just oversee everything from behind the scenes. She's the real boss." Looking up from my tub, I realize that her eyes haven't left me.

"Do I have something else on my face?" I ask, but she shakes her head.

"No. It's just nice hearing you talk about your Mom and your upbringing. Nice getting to know you." She smiles.

It's nice opening up to someone who genuinely wants to know me for me. Someone who doesn't care about the money or the fame and status that I used to have. Any girl I'd met in the past was based purely on physical connection or hoped I would provide them with a luxury life.

There was never any real emotional connection. And while Cassandra and I do spend a lot of time in the bedroom, I love that we're comfortable enough to talk about whatever we want, without judgement.

"Do you ever think about finding him or wonder if you have any siblings?" she asks, veering the conversation back to my father, but I shake my head in response.

Swallowing the last of my ice cream, I put the tub back in the freezer bag.

"He knows about me. If he wants to find me, he can, but I have no intention of knowing him. I'm not a kid anymore. There's nothing left for him to teach me." I'm fulfilled with my life, and I truly mean that. If he came into my life now, it'd be thirty years too late.

Laying down on the blanket beneath us, I pull her down to join me so her head can rest comfortably on my chest as we both stare at the clear night sky.

"Hey, Harley?"

"Yeh?"

"I like us," she whispers.

"Me too."

***

"Are we all good for the expo tomorrow?" I ask Cassandra as she sits in the chair at my desk.

It's been just over a month since we started seeing each other, but we're not quite ready to tell anybody about it just yet. We decided that once we get back from the bridal expo, we'll tell our families.

I'm too wrapped up in our little bubble to care.

"We're all set. I have photos, brochures, lists of suppliers we use, food and wine options, posters, and signage. Tables are provided, so we just need to supply as much information as we can about what services we're able to offer for future couples."

I wouldn't usually go to anything like this, but because the barn space at Wingrove Estates is a relatively new addition, it could use the exposure.

Plus, I couldn't let Cassandra go to California and stay in a big hotel bed all by herself.

She would miss me too much.

Okay, I would miss her.

Potayto, potahto.

Hearing a knock at my office door, she cuts our conversation short, saying, "I will meet you at the airport at six this evening, Mr. Wingrove."

She sticks to keeping our interactions as professional as possible whenever anyone else is around. The only people who know about us are Jenna, Robbie, and Bea, and we intend to keep it that way.

I'm just happy to spend some time alone with her, away from Mrs. Bishop's prying eyes and her gossip train.

My colleague, Simon, cuts right to the chase at our meeting.

I'm trying to focus, but my phone beeps five times on my desk, making it really difficult to do so.

"Someone's popular," he says, raising a brow while my eyes glance at my lit-up phone screen.

"Sorry about that. What were you saying?" I ask, flipping my phone face down, but it beeps two more times.

"You should get that. It could be important," he insists.

Seven text messages from Cassandra, and panic overwhelms me... until I read the messages.

Herring: Can't wait

Herring: To be in Cali

Herring: Curled up next to you

Herring: Naked

Herring: While stroking your thick, hard cock

Herring: Before I taste you

Herring: Wow, what just happened? I blacked out and when I came to, I was day-

dreaming about…never mind. What I meant
was, pick me up at six. See you later ;)

I've gone from panic, to relief, to discomfort with a raging hard-on while my employee sits in the chair across from me, to super fucking horny and ready to fuck my girl into oblivion, all in the span of a millisecond.

She did it knowing I was in a meeting.

Making a mental note to give her payback, I turn all of my attention to Simon for the last hour of my work day.

I arrive at Cassandra's apartment a little earlier than I told her I would be, but she left me so riled up during my meeting, I couldn't stay away any longer.

"Coming," I hear her breathy voice say from behind the door.

Yes, you will be, I think to myself. She has no idea what she's in for.

The second she opens the door, she doesn't even get the chance to say hello before I scoop her up with my hands on each ass cheek, wrap each leg around my waist, and crash my mouth to hers.

My tongue parts her lips, and I can feel her mouth turn into a wide smile and she chuckles.

"Harley, what are you doing?" she asks, her tone husky.

"Just giving you what you daydream about, sweetheart."

Thrusting my cock against her as I walk her to her bedroom, she moans into my mouth, making me want to fuck her even harder.

"Harley," she says my name again when our lips briefly break apart. "We're going to be late." I ignore her and kiss her deeper.

"Then we better make this one quick. On your knees," I say as I place her feet firmly back on the ground in her bedroom.

"What—"

"You said you wanted to taste me, Herring. On. Your. Knees." I refuse to repeat myself for the third time and she does what she's told.

Looking up at me with her hazel eyes, she licks and nibbles on her bottom lip.

"It's been a..." she pauses. "What if I'm bad at it?" she asks innocently, batting her eyelashes.

"Impossible." Hesitating, she strokes me with her hand before placing the tip on her tongue, and with that feeling alone, I know this is about to be the best blow job I've ever had.

Finding a fresh wave of confidence, she no longer second-guesses herself, taking my cock as deep as she can without breaking eye contact, her hazel eyes turning almost golden as they fill with desire.

Taking the base of my cock in her hand, she pumps back and forth while her mouth works the tip. "Fuck, fuck, *fuck*." My breath hitches in my throat. "Touch yourself," I say with a fistful of her hair, and she does.

Sliding her hand inside her underwear, I can hear her wetness as she circles her clit with her fingers.

"Up," I tell her, but she refuses.

"Uh-uh. You're so bossy," she says, before taking my cock deeper and deeper into her throat.

"Now, Herring. I want to be inside you." My teeth are clenched, my abs tensed.

I couldn't make myself more clear if I tried.

Finally, she slowly rises to her feet, slipping off her jeans and pink singlet, leaving herself in a red laced bra and matching thong.

Laying herself on the bed, I flip her around so her round, toned ass is up in the air and I get the perfect view. Needing to know how she tastes, I give her pussy one smooth, swift lick so I have her on my tongue, before I guide my cock toward her entrance and slam so hard into her that her bed shifts.

"Hold on to the headboard," I whisper in her ear as my body hovers over hers, watching as she grips it so tight, her knuckles turn white.

"Good girl."

Groaning into her neck, her body quivers underneath mine while my thrusting continues.

"Fuck me," she moans, tightening her grip. "*Harder.*" Her back shudders and her legs twitch, but I don't hold back.

"You feel so good inside me." She whimpers like she can hardly breathe, and it somehow fuels me even more.

"There's nowhere else I'd rather be. Come for me, baby."

With three more deep thrusts, I feel her pussy pulse around my cock, causing me to chase my own release, and sending us both over the edge, together.

When we both catch our breath, she quickly checks the time before jumping off the bed.

"We're going to miss our flight."

Thirty
Cassandra

THE WEDDING EXPO HAS been packed full of excited brides and defeated grooms, who realize their life savings are about to be wasted on one day, and the last day is no different.

"It's just an expensive party. Why can't we just elope?" one over-ly-disgruntled groom said, while his fiancée walked past every booth, collecting as many samples and brochures as her arms would allow.

Jenna's salon booth is directly across from ours, so we've seen each other constantly and it's been so nice.

I've seen Janelle and Frankie too, and formally introduced them to my new boss. Janelle couldn't peel her eyes away from him, while Frankie spent the entire time talking his ear off about football, and how her husband would be so jealous that she got to meet his favorite QB.

They briefly met him at Jenna's birthday party, but they'd been too busy actually working the event to talk to him or say more than a polite *'hello'*.

"He's so good for you," Jenna said to me when we had lunch by ourselves the day we arrived. "You have this glow about you I don't think I've ever seen." She sounded like my mom.

"Probably all the sex," I said jokingly while I shifted uncomfortably in the chair I'd sat in as we drank our coffees.

Jenna was finally being serious, and I was the one to throw the sarcastic curve ball. I just wasn't ready to admit that the reason for my glow is undeniably the way he makes me feel, day in, day out, and I definitely wasn't ready to admit how fast I'm falling for him.

"Seriously, Cass, you look incredible." She reached for my hand across the coffee table, and I'd taken it. "Whatever you're doing, keep doing it." My heart ached with how much I'd missed her, but I knew I made the right choice in going back home.

The first two days at the expo were a hit.

We booked two weddings, and arranged five separate venue tours with potential couples, all of them more than happy to travel.

"Where is your winery located?" a stunning, soon to be bride asks as she approaches our booth. Her long, dark hair is straight and draped over her shoulder, and her face is bare of any makeup, showing off a single freckle under her left eye. Her dark doe eyes stand out against her pale complexion.

"It's a four-hour flight from here, in a small town called Grangewood Creek. I'm Cassandra, it's nice to meet you." I smile, handing her a brochure full of information.

"I'm Chloe." She smiles back, taking it from my hand before she picks up one of our displayed bottles of wine. "I've had your wine before," she exclaims, her voice enthusiastic. "I had no idea you were located in Grangewood."

"Have you been?"

"Once, when my fiancé and I first got together. He wanted to show me where he grew up." She nods over her shoulder toward him as he approaches. "You might know him. His name is Matthew Maxwell."

She blushes, watching as a man with a familiar face approaches behind her, planting a kiss on her temple.

"Well, isn't this is a pleasant surprise," he says as he brings me in for a hug.

"Hi, Matty." I beam, excited to see an old friend, accepting his embrace. His dark hair is long, tied up at the nape of his neck. He's obviously growing out his facial hair, too, and his dark eyes glaze over the moment he finds his girl.

Wrapping her tiny frame in his, I can feel the love oozing out of them.

"It's good to see you, Cass."

"You too, Maxwell. I'm here with someone you might know, actually," I say, looking over my shoulder to see Jenna and Harley, deep in conversation.

"Harley," I shout, stealing his attention, not surprised he could hear my voice over the chattering crowd of excited women.

Apologizing to Jenna, he rushes over when he sees who I'm standing with.

"Maxwell." Clapping his hand on his arm, he brings him in for a side hug, while Matty introduces him to Chloe.

"Man, I was sorry to hear about your shoulder. I followed your career so closely, even went to a few games. How did it even happen? There was next to no publicity on it, and I never understood why." Matty cuts right to the chase, gaze zeroed in on Harley, and while Harley's face doesn't change, I feel his body slightly stiffen beside me.

Every time his retirement comes up in conversation, the topic changes quickly, so I've never bought it up myself.

I've seen and felt his scars, but haven't been brave enough to ask.

"It's all good, man. Injuries are always a risk, pro or not. It's part of the game," Harley answers casually, giving his old friend a soft smile.

"Anderson told me you guys broke up. I'm sorry to hear." Matty's face softens as he squeezes my forearm. I didn't realize they still kept in contact.

"Don't be. I, for one, am glad I'm not with a man who was having a three-year long affair and a baby on the way." I shrug. "But that's just me, I guess." Maxwell's eyes bulge out of his head. Clearly, Austin left out a few minor details.

"There's someone at our booth. I'll go talk to her," Harley says to me, saved by the bell. "It was good to see you, man. Nice to meet you, Chloe. Good luck with the wedding planning," he says before turning his attention to the future bride waiting at our booth.

"How long are you guys in California for?" Matty asks.

"We're just here for the expo. Harley heads back tomorrow, but I'm here for a couple of days to spend some time with my best friend," I say as I nod toward Jenna, whose booth looks overwhelmingly busy.

Harley took time away from work to be here these last few days. He's heading back for meeting upon meeting with Robbie, while I get some much-needed girl time with Jenna.

"Well then, it looks like we will have to come and tour the place." Chloe claps her hands together, a grin spread wide across her face.

"Something tells me Matthew here will know exactly where to find it." I smile back as he chuckles before pulling me in for a goodbye hug.

"It was good to see you, Herring."

"You too, Maxwell."

"I'm glad Wingrove grew some balls and finally got the girl," he whispers in my ear, and my cheeks heat.

I don't confirm or deny his assumption, but I do chuckle and watch as they move on to the next booth.

The crowd is dying down.

My feet ache from being on them for three days straight, and I can't wait to get back to our hotel and spend some quality time with Harley before he heads back home.

Turning to face him, my stomach drops when I see who he's been talking to for the last few minutes.

"Herring, come over here," he calls out, realizing I'm no longer busy and able to join him in conversation.

My feet move on their own, even though my brain is screaming *no*, and I head toward my ex-fiancé's new fiancée, while she talks to my new...*boyfriend*?

God, what a mess.

"Cassandra, this is—" Harley tries to introduce us, but I cut him off, not needing to be introduced to the woman who fucked my fiancé. Her hair is down in what I assume is her natural curls, and her makeup is minimal, yet she's absolutely glowing.

She's wearing a long, white, polka dot dress that hugs her growing bump, and God, I don't want to like her.

"Alison." My voice is firm, and he nods while looking in my direction, confusion written all over his face. "Austin's fiancée," I say to them both, each taking my words differently. Alison smiles proudly at the title, but Harley's green eyes widen.

"Oh, Cassandra, hi. It's so good to see you again."

It's good to see me?

What?

"Listen," she begins, and it takes everything in me to not roll my eyes and tell her to find a different venue, but the other part of me wants to hear what she has to say. "Austin filled me in. There are no hard feelings on my part." She sighs with a soft smile, and I don't think I'm quite understanding what she's trying to say to me.

"No hard feelings? Sorry, what do you mean?" I ask as I look down at her left hand as it rests on her baby bump, noting the familiar engagement ring sparkling on her ring finger.

"Oh, Austin explained that you two dated in the past, which is why bumping into you at his sister's wedding was a little awkward. He said his sister, Megan, refused to use anybody else to plan her wedding and didn't care how it would make him feel. He wasn't too happy about it, but he let it slide for his baby sister. You know how he is with her." She winces as she rubs her belly. "Sorry, baby Anderson is active today." It feels like a brick wall has collapsed right on top of me.

She has no idea the role she played in ending a fourteen-year relationship.

Turning my focus on Harley, I attempt to say, *'what the fuck do I do?'* with my mind, but it doesn't work.

He just stares at me, dumfounded.

Men.

I'm not jealous about the fact that Austin is still with her, or that they're actually getting married and having a baby together.

I've moved on.

But does she really not know?

Can I let this girl marry a man who was lying to her and cheating on her, too? Who proposed to her with the same ring he proposed to me with while they were together?

Does girl code even exist in these types of situations?

Fuck, I don't even know.

"Sorry, I just need to step away for a moment." I'm as polite as I can be, squeezing Harley's hand as he calmly takes over, going through our gallery and menu with our new potential bride, while I power walk toward Jenna, who's staring at me with a look of horror on her face.

"Is that who I think it is?" she asks, her mouth making the perfect '*o*' shape, and I nod.

Jenna wasn't there for the end of Megan's wedding, so she didn't get to see what Alison looked like, but a little social media stalking can go a long way, and Jennifer Rogers is like the damn FBI.

"What the fuck do I do?" I hiss through a clenched jaw, trying to not draw attention as my hands anxiously move from my sides, across my chest, to my back pockets until Jenna holds them still.

"Are they engaged?" she whispers back.

Nodding, I say, "She's wearing my old ring, too." I shrug and Jenna barks out a laugh so loud I swear the entire expo can hear her. I feel terrible for Alison. He couldn't even buy her a new ring, but I guess that's partly my fault.

"What do I do?" I ask again, agitated, because I genuinely don't know if I should be a good person and save this girl from any future heartache and embarrassment, or do I let her suffer like I did, hoping she figures it out on her own?

"You tell her," she urges me. I know she's right. I just don't know how I'm supposed to break that sort of news to someone.

"How am I supposed to tell her that her person isn't who she thinks he is?" I sigh, picturing how this is going to go. "Oh my God, what if I stress her out and she goes into early labor?" Now I'm completely terrified at the thought of potentially being the reason that this woman has her baby prematurely.

"Cassandra Herring. Take a deep breath." Jenna lets go of my hands and snaps her fingers in my face before giving me a play-by-play on how this is going to go.

"You are going to ask to take her for a coffee, and you are going to tell her the truth. Because you would rather her find out before they get married and before the baby is born. She's already going to be stuck with him forever because that poor, innocent baby has that man for a father, but she doesn't have to be tied to him through marriage on top of it."

Ah, Jenna, the wise one.

I heard her clearly, but my mind is constantly repeating, *'please don't go into labor, please don't go into labor'.*

"Who knows? Maybe she knew about you all along and being the other woman is like...a kink of hers, or something." She wiggles her brows, lightening the mood, and I tap the back of my palm against her chest to get her to stop joking around.

"Okay. I can do this," I tell myself, straightening my back, puffing air into my cheeks.

"Atta girl. Go get 'em, tiger," my best friend says, slapping me on my ass and sending me on my way.

"Sorry about that." My voice shakes as I hide my hands in my pockets to disguise that they're doing the same.

I'm about to potentially ruin this girl's life, and she doesn't deserve it.

"Alison, I was hoping you were free right now for a coffee?" Her red, curly hair bounces as she turns her attention to me, blue eyes wide, like she misheard what I'd said.

"Uh, sure." She nods reluctantly, looking back at Harley for some sort of reassurance, but his expression is blank. His emerald eyes are less enthusiastic than they were. "It'll need to be decaf, though. I've hit my caffeine limit for today," she jokes, easing the tension, and I squeeze Harley's hand discreetly, letting him know that everything will be fine.

"I won't be too long. Call me if you need me," I whisper in his ear, planting a soft kiss on his cheek before walking away, with Alison right by my side.

Thirty-One
Cassandra

"I don't mean to be rude, but what's this all about?" Alison doesn't waste a lick of time, asking the burning question the instant we're seated in a booth at the back of the nearest cafe.

"I'm not sure where to start," I concede, her confused, but polite, smile turns to disbelief, her eyes filling with tears.

"I wanted to believe him so badly, you know? I wanted to believe every word that came out of his mouth. I wanted to trust him, but this whole time, there was this feeling in the pit of my stomach that he was too good to be true. My momma always told me to trust my gut, but I refused to let my gut be right this time." She blows out a shaky breath, blinking away her tears, attempting to dismiss them.

"An ex from years ago wouldn't be that...*upset*, unless it was still raw. I said that to Austin too, but he just told me you were crazy." She scoffs, bringing a tissue to wipe her nose.

Reaching my hand across the table, I take hers in mine, and we sit in complete silence. I don't know this woman sitting in front of me, but I know that Austin never deserved her. He never deserved either of us.

"How long?" she asks, killing the quiet while taking her first sip of her untouched decaf.

The cafe is empty, our voices remaining low enough for only us to hear.

"Fourteen years," I reply, and her brows crease.

"I'm confused. You mean *I* am the other woman?" She fiddles with the spoon she used to stir the sugar into her coffee, waiting for me to say something to make this all go away for her.

"He proposed to me with that exact ring last Christmas, almost a year ago." I point to her shaking left hand, giving her the best smile I can, knowing that no matter what I tell her, her heart will never be the same.

This is necessary, I remind myself, while allowing myself to ask any questions that come to mind, and to answer any questions that come to hers.

"I'm so sorry," I say, and while the tears are freely falling down her cheeks and her neck, her voice remains steady.

"You're sorry? I'm the one who unknowingly broke up your engagement." She leans back in her chair, her hands cradling her bump, as if protecting her innocent baby from all of this. I just want to leap over the table and hug her, tell her I'm lying, that this was all some sick joke, and I am just a crazy ex after all. Let her live her life with Austin and their baby as a happy family.

But I can't.

"I'm okay now. I've well and truly moved on and I know you'll be able to, too, if that's what you want."

"How?"

"You just do." I take a sip of my coffee. "When Austin and I first broke up, I became a shell of myself, and I hated it. After his sister's wedding, I was distraught, and I thought moving back home would fix everything. In part, I guess it did. When I came back, my Mom said to me, 'you don't know how much love you have to give, until you meet the person you're meant to give all of your love to'. The more I remember those words, the more I start to believe it. It reminded me that Austin Anderson wasn't my right person and that one day, my right person would eventually come along." I take a deep breath, keeping my eyes locked on hers.

"I spent fourteen years with him, and yet somehow, after him, I was able to find a happiness within myself that I hadn't known before, and that's what allowed me to accept the happiness that Harley makes me feel so effortlessly. What I have with him is something I never saw coming, but I refused to let myself miss out on something *so good* when I already wasted so much time on something that was the complete opposite," I say, noticing the twinkle in her eyes slowly returning.

She's going to be okay.

"When did the two of you meet?" I ask, because while I no longer care that he was unfaithful, Alison now means something to me and I think it will help her to get it off her chest, too.

"We actually met for the first time about seven years ago. He was at a bachelor party for his friend Chad or something." I remember the trip she's talking about. It was the end of February. 'Chad', aka Monty, was his roommate in college. That was the weekend before his almost wedding.

His fiancée, Shantel, called off the wedding the day before, because according to Austin, Chad stole money from her family, and is in prison now.

The guy always gave me the heebies. He would always try to hit on me when Austin wasn't around, so I avoided being near him, even though Austin told me I was being dramatic. And now, he sits behind bars.

Go figure.

Refilling my glass with water, I hear keys rattling in the door, telling me that Austin's home.

It's late, the apartment is dark, but his walk is different. His body seems stiff.

"Hey," he says, his voice quiet even though there's nobody here who could be disturbed by the volume in which we speak. Coming up behind me, he wraps his arms around my waist, nuzzling his head into my neck. "Mmm, I missed you." He breathes into my hair. The smell of alcohol and cigarette seeping out of every inch of him.

"I missed you, too."

It might be dark in the apartment, but he has a visible bruise on his cheekbone. His under eye is slightly discolored, but I know his face too well to miss it. The damage is minimal, but it's there.

"What happened?" I cup the side of his face with my palm, and he leans into it, letting out a shaky breath.

"Monty and I got into a fight. I called him out and told him he needed to come clean to Shantel, or I will, so he clocked me in the face." He pulls away from me, but I resist the urge to let go of his hands.

They're rougher than usual, callouses on his palms. Catching sight of them in the streetlights that shine through the gaps in our blinds, his knuckles are bruised and busted with dry blood, too.

He fought back.

"Let me get some bandages to patch you up." Kissing his knuckles, I make my way to our bathroom to rummage through the cabinets, finding the first aid kit filled with butterfly stitches and saline water. It's everything I need to clean and patch up his wounds, while he gets comfortable on the couch, turning on the TV.

"The eagles have no further comment," are the only words I hear from the television, before the screen turns black and Austin throws the remote to the other side of the couch.

"You should see the other guy." He smirks while raising a brow, trying to make light of the situation. Even as he winces in pain while I clean off the dry blood, he still finds humor in it all.

"Someone could have seriously gotten hurt, Austin. Monty is your friend. You should have let him sort it out." My focus is on his hands, but I can see him nod in my peripherals.

"We're not friends anymore."

"I take it nothing happened back then with the two of you?" I ask, and she pales.

"We slept together that night." Her confession turns her face beet red. It's as if someone has written 'guilty' all over her face with red lipstick.

That explains why our sex life had been so bland for the last seven years.

"He was upset. Apparently, he got into a huge disagreement with his brother or something. He told me he just needed some company. We reconnected three years ago and I've fallen more in love with him every day since."

"No, Monty, sorry, *Chad*, is his friend. He doesn't have a brother," I correct her, but she shakes her head.

"No, I'm positive he said brother. I haven't met him yet, and Austin says I never will. They don't get along." She shrugs. "Apparently, his dad had an affair years ago or something, so he and his brother have different moms, but are the same age." She takes the last sip of her coffee and slides her engagement ring off her finger.

"He doesn't have a brother," I repeat my words, this time harsher, almost accusatory, without intending to, but she's adamant about it.

"I've asked him a bunch of times why they don't speak, but he gets really heated when I bring it up."

"You're sure?" I need her to be *sure*. My mind is racing with possibilities. I just need it to be quiet for even a second so I can filter through the information.

"I'm one thousand percent sure. He said he found out about him after one of his football games or something. That's when everything changed for him." She blows her nose into a tissue.

One of his football games.

Austin hasn't played football since high school.

Reaching for my phone, I unblock Austin's number. I need to figure this out, stat.

> **Me**: I'm in Cali. We need to talk.

> **Austin**: ok.

While my body remains firmly seated in the same chair it's been in for the last hour, my mind has taken off. Running straight back to high school, trying to recall every interaction, every gesture, every look and smile.

Before Austin asked me to prom, he barely showed any care for me as more than a friend. And now when I think about it, he was hardly ever even kind to me. He only ever talked to me when Harley or Bea were around.

But the day he asked me to prom is the day it all changed for me, for him, for Harley.

He showed me a little too much attention, especially when Harley was around. He was too eager to let me know he liked me. Something changed in him back then, and now I know what it was.

Now, I hold on to information that could destroy a good man.

A *great* man.

And I don't know what I should do about it.

"I'm due on Christmas Day." Alison's words snap me back to reality, to our conversation, and as much as I try to find any interest in the topic, I can't, so I just smile and nod.

Christmas Day used to be my favorite day of the year.

But now, it's tainted.

Reminding me of my failed relationship and engagement and a poor, innocent, little baby who has a sorry excuse for a father. I guess the apple doesn't fall far from the tree after all.

So much for not wanting to be like his father.

Seeing my phone light up on the table with Harley's name, I apologize to Alison before standing up from the table, hesitating to answer his call.

"Hey, Herring," he says, and I can hear the smile on his face. Usually his soft, deep voice sends shivers down my spine, but now I just feel guilty.

"Hi." I try to sound calm and confident, hoping it's not obvious that my mind is elsewhere.

"It's getting quiet in here, so I've packed up our stall." He chuckles, and now I feel even worse that I wasn't there to help him.

"Great. That's...great."

What is wrong with me?

I know how to communicate with Harley.

I flirt with him every single chance I get, but now I can hardly form a sentence?

"Take your time at coffee. Don't rush back to the hotel. I know this is something you need to do, so do whatever you have to do, okay?"

He's so good to me.

He's good to his fucking core.

He doesn't deserve any of this.

"Okay."

Thirty-Two
Cassandra

AUSTIN CHOSE THE SPOT for us to meet, and I should have known it would be here.

At *our* spot.

The rooftop of our old apartment building, where we would come after a long day to wind down. If one of us were stressed, we always knew where to look, with a bottle of wine and a block of chocolate in hand.

Our relationship was just so...easy. It was all I knew for so long. I didn't know how to be anyone or anything other than Austin's girlfriend, and somewhere along the way, I lost myself and believed that Austin's girlfriend was all I was.

My entire identity.

The last few months have been a breath of fresh air for me. I got to figure out who I am and who I want to be in this life. Being back home, surrounded by my family and old friends, showed me how much more I deserved than a man who gave me less than the bare minimum.

To never settle.

Opening the heavy door, I expect to be left completely breathless just by looking at the man in front of me. For all the feelings I once felt to come rushing back.

But they don't.

I don't feel anything.

I expected my heart to race so fast that I could feel it in my ears.

I expected to be so nervous that it would cause me to shiver, but nope.

None of that.

I'm breathing steadily, albeit a little anxious, but more anxious about the potential confrontation and what Austin is capable of. The Austin I once knew wouldn't hurt me. Wouldn't hurt anyone. Or so I thought, anyway. But the last time I saw him, he was unhinged.

Drunk and angry.

I don't know what to expect going into this. I just know I'm the reason we're here. I'm the one with the questions and unfortunately for me, Austin is the only one with the answers.

I just hope he's not a coward and gives them to me.

His back is toward me as he looks out over the busy streets below, with his arms resting on the concrete ledge in front of him, still in his maroon suit from work.

"I miss it here," he says without turning to face me. My feet guide me to the vacant spot next to him.

"Me too." I take a deep breath, and stand with my arms crossed over my chest, taking in the view.

California winters aren't cold compared to Grangewood Creek, but the breeze tonight is especially icy. Still, the beach ahead of us is crowded, like it always is.

While I don't long for the memories attached to this place, I miss the view and being able to come up here when I need to escape from reality. But these days, I don't need or want an escape from the reality I'm living.

Slowly turning to face me, he searches my eyes that I hadn't realized were filled with tears, as one rolls down my cheek. "What's this all about?" he asks, and I force myself to look away.

I can feel him searching the side of my face for answers, but aside from the tears, my expression is blank. While his words are laced with confusion, his voice is softer than I expected, letting out a deep, shaky breath.

"I need you to be honest with me," I start. "But I have a feeling you're not going to like what I'm going to say."

"I'll tell you anything you want to know."

"I bumped into Alison today." The words fly out of my mouth, and I see his jaw clench, his shoulders tense. He closes his eyes, running his hands down his face.

"Cass, I'm—" he tries to talk, but I raise my hand to cut him off because it's my turn to speak, not his.

"I'm not here for an apology or explanation, Austin," I whisper. While the old me needed one—was desperate for one—the current me realizes that I never needed one to move on. "If you didn't cheat on me, I would have still been trying to fight for you. For us," I admit.

Especially after my birthday party, seeing everything he did for me. I thought for sure he still loved me. And maybe he did. But even if he loved me fully and never cheated on me, I believe our relationship would have run its course, and I would have found my way back to Harley.

No matter how long it took.

"But I know now that you're not the person I was supposed to end up with. And I think you knew it too. I think you figured it out seven years before I did." I raise a brow, watching as he pales, realizing I know about the very first time he cheated on me.

"Are you happy?" I ask before he can attempt an apology.

"I am." He doesn't need to make eye contact with me for me to know he's telling the truth. But given the fact that he's telling me he's happy, I'm going to guess that Alison hasn't had the chance to speak to him yet.

After the way she and I left things, I don't think he's going to have a home or a family to go back to.

"That's all I ever wanted for you. And for me," I say as I reach over to rest my hand on his forearm, squeezing it gently.

"Does Harley make you happy?" I can hear the anger bubbling inside him.

"Actually, Harley is the reason I'm here." His head snaps toward me, confused, anxious, and angry all in one.

"What did Alison tell you?" he asks, his hair looking more disheveled than it had when I arrived. He used to always look well put together. Smart and handsome.

But he doesn't look anything like the man I once knew.

Swallowing the lump that was sitting dormant in my throat, I finally build up the courage to ask the question that's been eating away at me for the last two hours.

"Is Harley your brother?"

Thirty-Three
Harley

Once the crowd at the expo dwindled down and I hadn't heard from Cassandra, I made the executive decision to pack up our stall.

We'd gotten more interest than I expected us to receive, considering guests would have to travel to Grangewood, but none of the couples seemed to mind.

It helped that our wine was sold in all fifty states and was growing rapidly in popularity.

"Have you heard from Cass?" Jenna asks as I take a seat next to her very busy, still open stall.

"Not since our phone call earlier. She sounded a bit distracted, so I guess she was in the thick of it with Alison." I shrug.

I'm glad that she's able to find out directly from Alison what her history is with Austin, but I also wish we never bumped into Alison at all. I just want to be able to move forward.

I'm a logical person, though. I know she isn't going to snap her fingers and magically forget about the man she was with for fourteen years. That shit takes time.

Things have happened quickly with us. We almost skipped being friends entirely and became whatever we are now, in only a matter of weeks.

We're still getting to know each other, and I'm not going to let anything fuck this up again.

Especially Austin.

I just hope she knows I'm not going anywhere while she figures this whole thing out.

"You seemed pretty busy today," I mention to Jenna, nodding at the crowd that still surrounds her stall.

"Incredibly," she replies, her wide smile taking over her entire face as she watches two of her workers busily talking to potential clients.

"I've booked eight brides over the course of the next six weeks. I don't know how I'm going to get it all done, on top of all my usual clients, but I'm sure I'll figure something out." She chuckles, nudging her shoulder into mine.

"Herring always talks about how brilliant you are. You'll definitely figure it out," I say, and she blushes.

"I don't know if C told you, but I was asked if my girls and I would do hair and makeup for a film production happening next year. I just met one of the executive producers, Laurel Jo. She's here today scoping out potential filming locations for the big wedding scene in the movie. I may have mentioned Wingrove Estates, so if she calls, you're welcome," she says jokingly.

"Thanks for letting Cass stay an extra few nights with me," she says to me before rising and approaching Tahnee, who has called out to her for assistance.

***

Throwing my body onto the hotel bed, I didn't realize how exhausted I was until I stepped foot in the hotel and sat down to take my shoes off.

Between the winery, the four properties we're currently renovating (including the old Mercury Hotel), and finalizing the design on the build of my new home, I haven't had time for much else.

Realistically, I shouldn't have spent the last few days here at the expo in California. Cassandra could have handled it all on her own, but I craved her and hated knowing we'd be apart for the length of the expo, plus the few extra nights she decided to stay with Jenna.

So instead of being away from her for six days, I opted for three.

I'm a sucker for that girl.

Robbie has taken the brunt of the workload for the renovations, so it gave me a little extra time to spend with her, but it's not enough. As greedy as it sounds, I don't think I'll ever have enough of Cassandra Herring.

The more of her I have, the more of her I want. I don't have an addictive personality, but I'm addicted to her.

She fuels me.

Excites me.

Makes me nervous as hell, in all the best ways. Even when I'm with her all day, I miss her like fucking crazy.

The next three days without her are going to fucking suck.

I haven't heard from her since our phone call a few hours ago, and I was hoping to take her to dinner for our last night here. But that would require messaging her or calling her to let her know and interrupting whatever it is she's doing right now.

It doesn't stop my mind from spiraling and expecting the worst, though.

Where is she?

Is she still with Alison?

Is she with Austin?

Fuck.

The last time she was with Austin, he was screaming at her, begging that she take him back. *Demanding* that she take him back.

She wouldn't go back to him, would she?

I know they haven't been broken up for that long, but I thought for sure she was done with him.

Is he her weakness?

Is he her addiction like she is mine?

Shaking my head at the thought, I know I'm overreacting.

I have to trust her.

I have to trust that she wouldn't lie to me.

I have to trust that she wouldn't do anything to hurt me.

At least, not on purpose.

So, I wait. And wait. And wait.

Minutes turn to hours when I finally hear the hotel door click at two in the morning.

"Herring?" I whisper, even though I know none of us are asleep.

"Sorry if I woke you." Her tone matching mine, while she uses her phone screen as a light to navigate around the hotel room, careful not to use her flashlight.

"I couldn't sleep," I confess as I move to sit on the edge of the bed in nothing but my boxer briefs, reaching my arms out to pull her body toward mine.

To make sure she knows she's safe with me.

To make sure she knows that whatever happened, everything will be okay.

"I missed you," I say, pressing my cheek to rest on her chest.

"Me too."

Letting out a shaky breath, she bends her head down so her lips can meet mine, filling my whole body with warmth I hadn't realized I was lacking. A warmth I was hoping to make her feel, but she gave to me instead.

"I'm going to take a shower," she whispers, pulling her body away from mine, forcing me to let her go.

I would confidently join her in the shower because I can't keep my hands off her. We've showered together every single night since we started this—whatever this is. But I know in my gut that me joining her right now is the last thing she wants me to do.

I know she needs space and time to process whatever happened tonight, and I know she needs to process it alone. Whenever she's willing, I'll be all ears, ready to listen to what she has to say, but I refuse to force her to tell me when she's not ready.

Crawling back into bed, her hair is wet and her body lightly trembles against the edge of it.

She's crying, and it takes everything in me to not beg her to tell me what's wrong.

"Are you okay?" I ask, inching myself closer to her, wrapping my arms around her body to cuddle her from behind.

Above everything, I just need to know she's not hurt. I don't need to know the little details right now. I just need to know she's okay. But she doesn't respond with words. She responds by nodding her head, a movement that I can feel against the pillow.

"Whatever it is, it's going to work out. I promise. It's going to work out," I say softly in her ear.

Finding her hand rested against her stomach, I lock my fingers through hers. I don't know who I'm reassuring, but I know we both need to hear those words.

So I repeat them every few minutes, until she finally falls asleep in my arms, and still, I refuse to let her go.

Thirty-Four
Harley Age 22

"THE DRAFT IS TOMORROW. You feelin' confident?" my roommate, Emerson, asks as he throws me a bottle of water from the fridge.

We both play college football for Ohio State University, but he has no intention of going pro, so he didn't offer his name up for the draft. I, on the other hand, have been looking forward to this day since the first time I threw a ball.

"Hell yeah, I'm confident," I reply, trying to keep my voice as steady as possible.

But I'm not confident.

I have a lot riding on this.

A lot to gain and even more to lose.

Sure, I have a backup plan. I'd be stupid if I didn't. But it's not where I pictured my life going. Football is the one thing I've wanted to do for as long as I can remember and I plan to do it for as long as my body will allow.

I say I'm confident, but I'm fucking terrified. I might have the best arm in college football, and everybody knows it, but that doesn't guarantee a damn thing. It's all a waiting game, and today feels like the longest day of my life.

"How do you find out?" Emerson asks as he opens the fridge again, this time in search of a snack.

"Coach said they'll call me." I bite into an apple while throwing myself down onto the couch, flicking the TV on for background noise.

"Well, I guess I better prepare for a rowdy afternoon tomorrow for when we celebrate." He chuckles, heading toward his bedroom, protein bar in hand, slamming the door shut behind him.

We've lived together since freshman year. Originally, we lived in a dorm, but eventually moved to an off-campus apartment with two of our other teammates, Carter and Angus.

Carter offered his name up for the draft, but Angus was a bit like Emerson. Football was a hobby, something to keep them out of trouble. Getting their degree was always more important, and I respected the hell out of it.

Our apartment has been tense the last few days, with Carter stressing about not getting called up while everyone hypes me up in front of him.

He's a defensive lineman, one of the best on our team. But there are a lot of good defensemen in the college league. It's not a sure thing for him, which is why he's on edge. I can't say I blame him. He wants to play for the New York Panthers, but I want to play for the Charlotte Eagles; the team I followed my whole life.

My dream is so close, I can almost taste it.

Feeling my phone vibrate from my pocket, I see Coach Benson's name on the screen and I automatically sit up straighter before I answer, knowing full well he can't see me.

"Wingrove." His voice is loud. It always sounds like he's shouting.

"Hey, coach. What's up?" I keep myself calm, repeating '*be cool, be cool, be cool*' in my head, but it's no use. He never calls me for no reason. There's always a motive, and it's usually never a good one.

"Get down to my office." He's still yelling, with his tone hard to decipher as I spring from the couch, as if someone lit a match under my ass.

Scrambling, I put on my shoes while my ear is pressed to my shoulder, and I head out the door.

"On my way."

I pace the front of Coach Benson's office for what feels like hours before he shouts my name, inviting me in.

"You wanted to see me?" I say to him as I knock on his door, wiping my clammy hands down the front of my dark blue jeans. I made it in record time, somehow out of breath, even though I drove here and parked directly in front of his office.

"Take a seat." He gestures to a seat across from him, and it's only then that I realize there's a man occupying the seat next to mine with his back to the door.

Shoving my shaking hands in my pockets, I take the empty spot next to the last person I expected to see.

"I believe you know my visitor," Coach says as he nods toward the man to my right. He sounded furious over the phone, which had me panicking, but I've played for him long enough to know when he's actually pissed off.

Today isn't one of those days. Though, I wish I realized it when he called me, or I wouldn't have spent my entire car ride here imagining worst-case scenarios.

I instantly recognize the man next to me. He has a face I would never, ever, forget. Retired sporting legend, all-star quarterback, and my football hero, Max Anderson.

"Mr. Anderson," I say, reaching my hand out to shake his, doing my best to keep the handshake firm, all while trying to mask the fear in my voice.

"Hi, son. It's been a long time," he replies with a smile.

Nodding, I turn my attention back to my coach.

"I'm a bit confused. Why am I here, exactly?" Squirming in my seat, I focus my attention solely on Coach, before Mr. Anderson requests it back on him.

"I'll take it away, Alec. If you don't mind?" He addresses my coach by his first name, making me even more anxious.

"Be my guest."

Taking a deep breath, Mr. Anderson turns in his chair to face me, my stomach feeling like it's about to drop out of my ass.

"I'll cut right to it." He pauses before smirking at me, enjoying watching me panic. "I've been asked to let you know that you're the number one draft pick. You're going to the Charlotte Eagles."

Silence.

Nothing but silence fills the room while he stares at me, an awkward smile on his face, waiting for any sort of response.

Instead, he gets fucking nothing.

"Uh-sorry. I think I've misheard you," I say, stunned. I just need him to repeat the words one more time.

"You're in the NFL, son." He clamps his hand down on my shoulder while I stare at him in disbelief.

"I-wow. Thank you, sir." I can't find any other words to express how I feel, no matter how hard I try.

The fucking *Eagles*?

The team I followed my whole life and dreamed about playing for? How is this real life?

For the next half an hour, he goes over the details.

He tells me how the Eagles are expecting big things from me next year, and that my offer is the highest package offered to a rookie that the league has ever seen.

He tells me that the current QB for the Eagles is about to retire, and they want me to step up to the plate right away.

They want me to take them to their next championship.

All things unheard of for a rookie, but things every rookie wants to hear.

Fuck. Yes.

"No offense, sir, but why were you the one to tell me? Coach said I would get a phone call tomorrow." Coming back down to reality, I'm dumbfounded.

I haven't seen this man since high school. Considering his son and I haven't been friends since we were teenagers, I expected to never see him again, yet he's the one to tell me the news that just changed my life?

"I have friends in high places, Harley." He smirks. "I told them you were like family to me," he says, a lot more serious this time, his voice softer.

As we both stand from our seats, he brings me in for a hug that lingered way longer than I care to admit, but I'm too overwhelmed to question or pull away.

A hug from my childhood hero after hearing the best news of my life?

It doesn't get much better than this.

"I'm proud of you, son."

I'm going to the NFL.

Thirty-Five
Cassandra

LAST NIGHT WAS LONG.

Probably the longest night of my life.

I ended up heading to the beach after my conversation with Austin, desperately needing the sound of crashing waves to help me find clarity, before slowly making my way back to the hotel where Harley was waiting up for me.

Harley.

He'd sat on the edge of the bed in nothing but his boxer briefs, pulling me in for a hug, and I'd welcomed it. Allowed myself to sink into him, even if just for a moment.

He didn't demand that I tell him why I was back so late.

He didn't demand to know what had happened.

He didn't demand to know who I was with, even though deep down I think he knew, but didn't want to say the words out loud.

Didn't want to hear me say it, and have it be...*real*.

Once I'd finally showered and crawled into bed, he let me cry without trying to pressure me into talking about it. Because talking about my night and everything I'd learned made me feel sick.

I wasn't ready to tell him.

I wasn't ready.

And Harley knew that.

He made sure to keep telling me that everything was going to be okay. And I'd hoped, with every fiber of my being, that he was right, even though something in the pit of my stomach told me he wasn't. Everything was about to change, and I couldn't stop it. I couldn't protect him, no matter how badly I wanted to.

I couldn't keep it from him.

Not this.

But I couldn't just blurt it out, either.

I needed to talk to Jenna. Because, through everything, she's my voice of reason. She's the only one who can help me see things clearly, dissecting every single word that came out of Austin's mouth. Maybe she'll help me see something I missed. She's the only one I trust enough to tell me what I need to do, no matter how badly it might hurt the man I love.

Love.

His heavy, steady breathing changes, laying in bed next to me, but he hasn't moved. He's awake, but his arm remains firmly gripped around my waist, where it was all night, his head remaining nuzzled into my neck.

"Good morning, Herring," he whispers, sending shivers down my spine. He's only ever referred to me as Herring.

My last name.

And it made my heart tingle every single time.

Ever since high school, he's never called me by my first name unless conversations were serious. Only then would he refer to me as Cassandra, but it was rare.

I have a feeling I'm going to be hearing it a lot, and I already know I'm going to hate the way it sounds on his lips.

"Did you sleep okay?" he asks, scattering soft kisses on my shoulders and the back of my neck.

"I did," I lie, fully aware that I probably slept an hour at most.

"Do you want to talk about it?" I can hear the concern in his voice, but I know he won't push me if I tell him 'no'.

Instead of replying, I turn to face him. I need to see his face and look into those emerald eyes. I need to see if there's even a glimmer of hope or forgiveness.

Both things I need so desperately, but unsure if they'll exist once he finds out the truth.

"Not right now. I need to speak to Jenna," I admit, and his face floods with defeat.

He's hurting, and it's because of me. I hate that I've caused him pain, but I just need *time*.

I need the facts.

Austin may have told me all about Harley's paternity, and how he found out about it, but he was only skimming the surface and not being completely honest. Like there was something on the tip of his tongue that he desperately wanted me to figure out, so he didn't have to confess it outright.

Harley doesn't utter another word.

He turns his body to get off the bed, and heads for the bathroom to run his usual morning shower.

How do I fix this mess that I had no part in creating, yet feel completely responsible for?

Sliding out from under the covers, I stand from the bed, willing one leg at a time to follow him to the bathroom. Watching as he stands underneath the water, I allow myself to take in the sight before me.

His wavy, wet hair is slicked over to one side. His golden skin glistens under the water, while my eyes find their way to his arms, decorated with veins, and I ache to drag my hands down them. His bare chest and abs are tense while he lathers himself with soap, and I let my eyes trail down his defined V until they land on his cock, still hard from his morning wood.

"You checking me out, Herring?" He chuckles, squinting one eye open, washing the shampoo out of his hair.

"I might be." I feel the blood rush to my cheeks as I lean against the door frame. He still makes me nervous.

"You can join me, but I can't promise I won't bite." He cocks a brow, stepping out from under the water, reaching his hand out for me to take.

I can't stop the smile that forces its way across my face as I pull his t-shirt over my head, slowly sliding my underwear down my legs, and I know his eyes never left my body.

"God, you're perfect." His voice is nearly a whisper, but he said it loud enough for me to hear.

Taking his hand in mine, I step into the ice-cold shower before I let out a scream.

"Why is the water so cold?" I gasp as I quickly reach for the tap to change the temperature.

"Because I don't like to feel like I'm showering in lava, Herring," he jokes, making fun of the fact that I need my showers to almost melt my skin off.

"You never complain when you join me in the shower, *Wingrove*." Wiggling my eyebrows at him, he wraps his arms around my waist, pulling my body closer to his, and I forget for a moment that things between us are about to change.

"That's because I know you like it. Who am I to change how you do things?" he says as he buries his face in the crook of my neck, breathing me in before pulling himself away.

"Are we okay?"

My breath hitches in my throat at his question, catching me off guard while his eyes search mine, desperate for answers. I can see the pain behind them. Like he needed to ask for clarity, but he doesn't know if he wants to hear the answer.

"What do you mean?" I ask, heart slamming against my ribs. I don't know how they don't break. I had a feeling he suspected my whereabouts last night, but I didn't think it would make him worry about us.

Of course, he's worried.

He thinks I spent the night with my ex-boyfriend.

How could I be so stupid?

"Did you decide to go back to him?" Fear is written all over his body, waiting for my response. I never told a soul that I was with Austin. Not even Jenna. But Harley didn't need to be told. He figured it out all on his own.

I hate that he thinks I would even consider going back to Austin.

That his trust in me has been questioned.

"Because if you've decided to go back to him, Cassandra, I need to know. Before I get too deep in this, and I can't find my way back to the surface." His hands drop by his sides, releasing me from his warm, comforting grip, leaving us both standing naked and vulnerable in the shower while he waits for my reply.

And there it is.

My first name.

I was right.

I hate it.

"Do you really think I would go back to him?" I ask, wrapping my arms across my chest to cover myself from something he's seen every single day for the last few weeks.

"I don't know what to think," he admits as he turns to turn off the water, leaving the space silent and now even colder than it was moments ago.

There isn't a hint of anger in his voice, but the pain is impossible to miss.

"I know you're not ready to tell me what happened and please know that I will never force you to, but I just need to know. Is this—" He gestures his hand between us. "Are we over?" he asks as his eyes glaze over.

My heart shatters seeing him so vulnerable. Even though the water is off, neither of us has moved even an inch. Our feet remain firmly planted, still at arm's length from each other, and goosebumps all over the both of us.

"No. We are far from over, Harley." I slowly bridge the gap between us, and he lets me. "I meant it when I said I was all in," I say, placing a kiss on the corner of his lips as he lets out a shaky breath.

"That's all I needed to hear."

Slamming his mouth down on mine, it feels like our first kiss all over again.

Right here, right now, I promise myself to live completely in this moment.

I refuse to think about the last twelve hours and how I'm holding onto information that will change everything.

Thirty-Six

Harley

REFUSING TO RESIST HER any longer, I glide my hands from her hips and up her back before grabbing a fist full of her hair. She tilts her head to the side, giving me better access to her neck, and her whole body shudders at the feeling.

"Mine," I whisper in her ear before I kiss her mouth again, down her jaw, trailing back down her neck. I make my way to her tits, showing them both equal attention, nipping and sucking at each peak as a subtle moan escapes from her throat.

Kissing and licking my way down her body, I kneel on the marble shower tiles beneath us, lifting one of her legs, perfectly perching it over my shoulder.

Giving me a full view of her pussy, she uses her hand to spread herself wide for me.

"I love the taste of you." My words are soft as I glide my tongue softly and slowly over her clit, causing her nails to dig into my shoulder with her free hand. "So sweet," I say, and boy, do I have a newfound sweet tooth for this woman.

"Right there, Harley. Don't stop," she begs me, speaking in between moans, her chest rising and falling, with her bare back pressed up against the cold surface behind us.

I slide one finger inside of her, circling my tongue on her clit as she throws her other leg over my shoulder, placing her entire weight on my body. I'm all but suffocated by her, and if I died right now, I couldn't think of a better way to go.

Her hands are pulling at my hair as she steadies herself.

"Fuck, your mouth feels so good on me," she says, legs tensing around my neck. Knowing how much she's enjoying this makes me want to do it forever.

"Don't stop. Please." I love when she begs for me. Her breathing intensifies, and I don't have to be told twice.

Her grasp on my hair tightens in one hand, while her other remains on my shoulder for leverage, nails sinking deeper and deeper. My cock is aching, eagerly wanting to replace my finger as it slides inside of her, but I can feel her swollen clit on my tongue and her pussy clench around my finger. I can't bring myself to stop.

"Come for me, baby," I say to her, briefly breaking contact, and right on cue, she unravels on top of me.

Unravels *for* me.

Her clit pulses on my tongue, her frame shivering on top of me. Her pussy wetter by the second, clenching around my finger.

Slowly steadying her legs back onto the ground one by one, my lips make their way back up her stomach toward her tits as my hands follow suit.

Our mouths fuse together, my hand resting comfortably, but firmly, around her throat.

"That's my pretty girl," I whisper, and she chuckles, nibbling at my lower lip.

Taking back what's mine, my mouth finds hers again, her hands gliding down my back.

"We're just getting started." I smirk as I watch the way her hazel eyes widen, searching mine for reassurance.

"I'll be gentle," I say, but only half of me wants to be gentle with her. The other half of me has animalistic tendencies that are eagerly wanting to take over and hope that she likes it.

"Don't be gentle with me, Harley. *Never* be gentle," she replies, and those words might be the most beautiful words ever spoken.

Wrapping her legs around my waist, my cock finds its way to her pussy, sliding past her lips, giving one hard thrust, coaxing a moan so loud I'm convinced the entire hotel can hear.

"Fuck me, Harley," she pleads.

Gripping her ass in my hands, I carry her back to the bedroom, throwing her body down onto the bed, and somehow manage to stay buried deep inside her.

"Tell me what you want." My voice is coarse. She refuses to break eye contact.

"I just want you," she says, but I need more.

Thrusting harder, she moans louder, her stomach tensing at the slightest touch, legs twitching as my hand grazes her now sensitive clit.

"Tell me *exactly* what you want," I echo, only slightly harsher than before. Her eyes flash away from me briefly, but I pull them back in my direction, noticing that they've softened, speckles of gold glimmering through them.

So innocent, and so sweet, yet, "I want you to fuck me, hard. I want you to make me come, then I want you to come in my mouth," she says, and I lied before.

Those words are the most beautiful words ever spoken. And at those words alone, I know I'm not going to last very long. My fingers grip firmly onto her hips before my cock makes its way back inside of her.

"So good," I groan as thrust into her, snatching the breath from her lungs, leaving her gasping for air.

"Right. There. Please don't stop. Never fucking stop, Harley."

I won't.

Her begging fuels me more. I grip her hips tighter, hoping I don't bruise her, but knowing it's probably already too late.

"I need you to come for me again, baby," I tell her, and her body convulses under my grip, pussy tightening around me.

Turning to face me, she drops to her knees, and a devilish grin wipes the innocence clean off her face. She places the tip of my rock-hard cock onto her tongue to tease me, gradually taking more and more of me inside her mouth, until she has to steady herself.

Licking and sucking me, she takes my length as far back as her throat will allow.

"Fuck. *Fuck*," I hiss.

I don't have any other words in my vocabulary.

I need to come inside of her, and I need to do it now. I need to feel the warmth of her pussy wrapped around my cock as I cross the finish line after her.

As soon as the thought crosses my mind, I act on it. Picking her body up off the ground, I throw her onto the bed, sliding inside of her before both of our bodies shudder in unison, coming together one last time.

Panting, she rolls onto her back as I lay next to her, bringing her head to rest onto my chest.

"I didn't realize you were so..."

"I guess you bring it out of me"" She shrugs, giggling beside me, grazing her fingertips across my scar.

"Well, I loved it." I laugh, kissing her lips one last time, and her cheeks flush a soft shade of pink.

"What time is your flight?" She quickly changes the subject, snatching her hand away from my chest, reaching for her phone.

I miss her touch already.

"I fly out at twelve." Disappointment briefly appears on her face, but she disguises it with a soft, genuine smile.

"I'll miss you when you're gone," she says sadly, and I reach my arms out for her to hold her tighter.

"Whatever you need to do, just know I'll be waiting for you when you get back," I reply, trying to reassure her.

Because no matter what, everything will be okay.

We will be okay.

"Do you promise?"

"I promise."

Placing a final kiss on my lips, she rolls over to get out of the bed, packing her suitcase while I pack mine, and we head our separate ways.

***

"Do we have any updates on the house?" I ask Robbie as he sits across from me in my office at Wingrove Estates, sipping on a glass of our newest blend.

"Beau and the guys are working on the final touches of the draft. I think you're going to be really happy with what they've created." He beams, knowing how important this project is to me.

My future home.

Beau is the lead architect for Beckett Designs, and we've used them for all of our work over the last two years.

They're working on the Mercury Hotel for us, too.

"How was California and the expo?" he asks, putting his glass down on the desk in front of him.

He's built like me, only I'm slightly taller by about two inches. His complexion is significantly paler than mine, with bright blue eyes and strawberry blonde hair.

"It was weird, man. Bumped into an old friend from school, which is always a good time, but we had a bride who was interested in having her wedding here." My stomach drops as I recall the look on Cassandra's face when she recognized who I was talking to.

Her usually tan skin suddenly pale, as if she'd seen a ghost. How I so badly wished I was a fly on the wall at the café.

"Isn't that a good thing?" He raised a brow, expression blank.

"In usual circumstances, yes. But this bride wasn't just a random bride off the street," I say. Robbie knows all about my past with Austin and all about my present with Cassandra, along with everything in between. But he doesn't know about their history, because it's not my story to tell.

It's not my place to be talking about her private life, so when the conversation ever came up, I changed the subject and Robbie had respected that.

"The heavily pregnant bride," I pause for effect, adding in the important detail. "Is Austin Anderson's fiancé."

Silence fills the room as I watch my friend in front of me, mouth gaped open while the wheels in his head turn, putting all the pieces together.

"Wait," he says, eyes bulging out of their sockets as he watches me in disbelief. "That mother fucker cheated on Cassandra?" While Robbie and Cassandra had only met briefly, he had nothing but good things to say about her.

Hell, if she and I weren't a thing, he probably would have tried to shoot his shot.

"He cheated on her for three years and knocked up his new girl-friend, now fiancé." I laugh out loud at his absolute stupidity. I've always stood by the fact that if you're unhappy in your relationship, end it. Don't cheat on them and make them suffer.

It makes you selfish and a coward.

Two words that perfectly describe Austin Anderson.

But that's just my opinion.

"What a fucking asshole," he finally says, running his hand across his face, staring at me wide-eyed.

"I would have chosen a different word, but that's only because I've known the fucker my whole life," I say, sinking back into my desk chair.

"Did you tell his new fiancé '*fuck no*?" He mimics my actions.

"No, I didn't. Actually, Cassandra took her for a coffee."

"She's a better person than I am," he replies, pinching the bridge of his nose before taking one last swig and slamming his now-empty wine glass onto the desk. "Hell, you both are. I would have dropped that mother fucker years ago, ran away with the girl, the football career he wasn't good enough for, and the superstar rich daddy he couldn't impress."

"How many glasses have you had?" I joke.

"Seriously, man. It just shows all good things take time. His lies caught up with him and now he has to suffer the consequences," he says, straightening himself in his chair.

"I don't know about that. Something happened after Cassandra's chat with his new fiancé that caused her to want to see him afterward."

A weird pang fills my chest. Even though she never told me she saw him, she didn't have to.

She had guilt written all over her face and she wouldn't feel guilty over just anything. But she assured me we were good, and I had to trust her.

"She hasn't told you what happened?" he asks, pouring himself another glass.

"No, she said she needed to talk to Jenna about it. Jenna knew them both together and separately, so she knew their relationship well. But her best friend is as brutally honest as they come. I know she'll tell her what she needs to hear, even if she doesn't want to hear it."

The thought of it even coming to that makes me feel squeamish, but I trust her.

I've got no choice.

"Is Jenna single?" he asks, giving me a lopsided smirk, trying to hide it behind his glass of red wine.

"Don't even think about it, asshole. Plus, she would eat you alive," I reply, shutting that shit down real quick. "Stay away from her sisters, too."

Prick.

Thirty-Seven
Cassandra

JENNA'S BEEN AT WORK all day, and I haven't stopped pacing her apartment, impatiently waiting for her to get home.

When Harley and I left the hotel, I rushed straight here, knowing she left a key out for me. The buzzer to her intercom has gone off more times than I care to admit. Each time, a different package has been delivered, thanks to her online shopping addiction, and each buzz has left me a little more on edge and defeated than the last.

The sound of her keys rattling from behind the door stops me in my tracks and I stare at it blankly, waiting to see her face.

When our eyes lock, her expression softens and my lips tremble until she says, "Oh, Cassandra," and I burst into tears. Tears that have been eagerly fighting to fall all day, but I haven't allowed.

Jenna's face, and those tiny two words, were all the permission I needed to crumble. And now they won't stop.

I've never been able to hide my emotions from my best friend.

"Oh boy, this is going to be a doozy."

Closing her front door, she drops her purse to the ground and ushers me to sit down on the couch that I'd forgotten existed until now.

My body melting into the cushions she's propped up behind me.

"Let me get into comfy clothes and wash this hair off me before you break it all down," she says, rushing to her bedroom to retrieve clothes, before turning on her shower.

She takes roughly eight minutes to have a quick shower, wash off all of her clients' hair clippings, and slip into a pair of black leggings that show her thick curves perfectly, paired with a grey, oversized t-shirt.

I know she wears oversized clothes because she's self-conscious, but I wish she saw herself the way I and so many others see her. I wished she put the same energy into loving herself as she puts into loving the people around her.

"Wine?" she asks, heading toward the kitchen that's attached to her lounge room. Her apartment is small, but she doesn't need much else for just her.

"Got anything stronger?" Tucking my legs underneath me, I know we're in for a long night and wine just won't cut it.

Not this time.

"Margaritas it is."

Moving around her kitchen in silence, she takes out the tequila, ice, lemon mix, and some salt for the rim while I lay down on her couch, staring at her ceiling.

Replaying the last twenty-four hours in my head over and over on a loop.

How could I have not seen it sooner?

Austin bears a strong resemblance to his mom, and Megan to their dad.

But Harley?

Harley has his dad's eyes.

Their dad's eyes.

My body shudders, my stomach is in knots.

It was right in front of my face this whole time. I obsessed over Harley's eyes.

"Here you go," Jenna says as she hands me our iced margarita while placing the jug of the remaining mix in front of us on the coffee table, and I sit up, taking a deep, shaky breath.

"From the beginning."

She turns to face me and squeezes my hand, encouraging me to let it all out. And that's exactly what I do.

I tell her that Alison didn't know who I was to Austin. That she thought I was an ex of his from before they got together. I tell her that Alison and Austin met seven years ago in Charlotte, and they had a one-night stand.

I tell her that according to Alison, Austin had seemed really down the night they met, and he needed some comfort.

"And he sought comfort from another woman's vagina? Man, fuck that guy. What a son of a bitch," she says with a hiss, before taking a sip.

"That's not all," I say, standing to continue pacing her apartment with my margarita clasped firmly in my hands.

"Surely nothing can beat the fact that he had an affair seven years ago, and he only broke it off with you because she fell pregnant. If she never did, how long would he have waited before he told you, if ever?" She sits up straighter on her couch, her ass on the edge of it, taking another sip.

"Alison said he was upset because he had an argument with his *brother*, Jenna. His brother." I stop dead in my tracks, staring directly into her soft blue eyes, hoping she understands what I'm trying to say.

"He doesn't have a brother," she replies, just as confused as I was when I first heard those words leave Alison's mouth.

"Brother."

"No fucking way."

Leaping off the couch, she brings her hands up to cover her mouth as it hangs open, somehow managing to not spill a drop from her glass.

"That can't be right. Does Harley not know his dad?" I shake my head.

"No, he said his dad took off when he found out his Mom was pregnant."

"What a scumbag," she spits, pacing alongside me, and I'm surprised we haven't damaged her wooden floors with all the back and forth.

"Do you know for sure?" she asks, scooping up her margarita glass from the table.

"I just kind of assumed at first, but decided to go to Austin to find out the truth. I was with him last night for hours."

"You were with Austin last night?" She puffs air into her cheeks. "I'm going to need to sit down for this," Jenna replies as we both scull the leftovers in our glass before pouring fresh ones.

Taking a seat beside my best friend on the couch, I relay everything to her.

"Is Harley your brother?" I repeated my words, because it seemed like he hadn't heard me the first time with the way his empty blue eyes had stared into mine.

Almost like there was no one home.

"Austin." I snapped my fingers in his face, bringing him out of his trance.

"Alison never knew his name," he confessed, clearly confused about how I'd figured it out. I'd spent fourteen years of my life with this man and had been spending all of my time lately with Harley.

I was able to put together the pieces from a single conversation with Alison.

"I figured it out," I said with caution, walking to the lone bench that the rooftop had, taking a seat.

"Is that why you hate him?" I asked, and he nodded, but didn't say a word. "Did you ever love me, Austin? Or was it all just some ploy to get back at Harley for something he had no idea about and no control over?" I don't know why I'd asked, but I had to get it off my chest.

I didn't need closure from him anymore, but I couldn't stop the words from spilling out of my mouth. I deserved to know if the last fourteen years of my life were a lie.

Letting out a long, shaky breath, he's embarrassed as he sits down beside me, eyes still locked ahead of us.

"At first, no."

His honesty catches me off guard and I won't lie. It hurt. I didn't love him in that way anymore, but to hear him tell me our relationship started out of spite was hard.

"In high school, sure, I thought you were cute, but I never really cared to pay much attention to you in that way." He shrugged it off like it was no big deal, and I knew he felt like he had nothing to lose, so he wanted to let it all out. Like he'd been holding onto the truth for too long.

"The night before I asked you to prom, I heard my parents arguing. Mom found photos and articles of a young Harley in his football gear hidden in the top drawer of my dad's office. Mom knew immediately. I guess she'd suspected it for a while, but she had no proof. Dad tried to deny it at first, but why else would he have kept articles of Harley's accomplishments and photos of him growing up?" He sighs while running a hand through his hair.

"That's when I heard dad admit that he'd slept with Joanna. That they were in love. But when she told him she was pregnant, he pan-

icked. He found out my Mom was pregnant with me not long after. My parents were already married. He thought he was doing the right thing by his family." He dipped his head between his shoulders, knowing defending his dad's actions was a lost cause.

The similarities of Austin and Max's lives were eerie.

Thankfully, I *wasn't pregnant too.*

"Mom gave him an ultimatum. Either he cuts ties with Harley and Joanna completely, or she'll tell the whole town that the Golden Boy didn't have such a clean image. He chose his image." It was like a knife to the gut.

His image was more important to him than knowing his son in the way that Harley deserved. And his wife was the one dangling it over his head.

I don't know which Anderson was worse.

There were so many things that I wanted to say, but I'd held my questions until the end. Until I knew he'd said what he needed to say.

"It didn't stop my dad from favoring him, though, and it fucking pissed me off. So, I went for the thing I knew he wanted the most. You." Tears streamed down my cheeks, but I didn't hide them, either. I just let them fall.

"By the time senior year had come around, you and I had spent all summer together. What I felt for you had only intensified. So, if you're asking if I really loved you, Cass? Of course, I did. I still do. I'm just a man who made a mistake." His voice was pleading for forgiveness, but I don't think I'd had it in me to give it to him.

"It was never Harley's fault, Austin. Shame on you for making him suffer." My voice almost a squeak. I was afraid to speak up, no longer knowing what he was capable of.

"I know," he said. *"But I couldn't control my hatred for him after that point and I don't know why. I knew what I was doing was wrong, but I*

also knew he was the son my dad always wanted, not me, the son he got. Even when Harley got to the pros, my dad followed his career so closely. He flew to Ohio to be the one to tell Harley he was the number one pick for the draft. He negotiated with the Eagles to make sure Harley was taken care of and got the best deal any rookie had ever seen. He even made sure Harley would be starting QB, which was unheard of for a rookie."

"Harley was an incredible player, Austin. Don't you dare dismiss his talent because he was better than you."

"You think I don't fucking know that, Cassandra? Of course, I know. He proved all the haters wrong and proved to the league why my dad vouched for him the way he did. Only, he had no clue my dad was behind it." His voice was raised now. He knew deep down his anger should have been aimed toward his father, but Harley was the easier target.

I could read Austin like a book. I knew he was mad at his own actions, but he was too stubborn to even consider admitting his wrong-doings or apologizing.

"What happened when you went to Charlotte for Monty's bachelor party, Austin? Seven years ago?" I asked him, hoping he'd be honest with me.

"What are you talking about?" He played dumb, acted like he didn't know what I was talking about. But his face turned so white, it was almost like there was no blood left inside of him to drain out.

"Alison told me," I shout at him as I stand from the bench, rage bubbling inside of me.

I don't care who can hear me anymore.

I owe nothing to Austin Anderson.

"Tell me the truth, Austin."

"It was a mistake, Cass, I swear. I regretted it the moment I got home and saw you." He's standing now, too, finally looking me in the eye and I feel hollow.

"How do you accidentally *do that? How can you call that a mistake?"* My typical non existent temper threatening to break free, my hands shaking by my sides.

You don't accidentally fuck someone else.

You don't just slip and fall and end up inside another fucking vagina.

"I was pissed off, Cass. His face was plastered on every TV in every sports bar across the damn country. They just won the fucking championships. The 'superstar quarterback *at age twenty-three'. The 'next* Max. Fucking. Anderson.'" *His voice grew louder, more aggressive with every word.*

"Then, when I saw him in the bar, my anger just took over. I saw red." The vein in the middle of his forehead bulging, face filled with fury.

"So, what? You saw your high school enemy, your brother, *at a pub and you decided to cheat on your fucking girlfriend? The same girlfriend who was waiting for you at the home you shared? You took your anger out on me? I didn't deserve that, Austin. I didn't deserve to be on the other side of your wrath and betrayal." His steps falter. His brows crease, head tilting. His face covered with raw confusion and guilt, but if I didn't know his face the way I did, I wouldn't have spotted it.*

"I...Cassandra, I'm—"

"You what? You were fucking angry, so you fucked someone else? And you kept it from me for seven fucking years? You proposed to me, knowing you were cheating on me? Fuck you, Austin."

Cheating isn't a fucking accident.

"I came up here with the intention of just hearing you out. Hoping to give you the benefit of the doubt. Thinking you could explain to me why. Why you cheated on me? Why you went from being best friends with Harley to hating him so passionately that you treated him horribly? But all I'm getting are fucking excuses and rage that should have been

directed at your father. You don't just fuck someone else accidentally, Austin. That shit is not an accident," I yelled as my finger poked at his chest with every point I made.

"Harley is a good man. No thanks to you or Max. And you led me right back to him, so thank you," I said, picking up my handbag up from the seat, and headed toward the door.

"Cassandra, please just wait. Please, you can't tell him."

"Alison deserves way better than you. We both do. I really hope for the sake of the baby growing inside her, your baby, that you're a better father than your dad was. She knows you were lying to her, by the way. Go home and try to salvage what's left of your family."

"Once I said that, I slammed the door behind me, and I haven't heard from him since. Although, to be fair, I blocked his number the second the door slammed shut," I say, chugging back my third margarita.

"Fucking hell, that's a lot to unpack. You are going to tell Harley, though, right? You have to." Jenna's voice cracks.

"Of course, I am. I just need to figure out how," I reply, pinching the bridge of my nose.

This shit is about to get messy.

"We're going to need more of this," my best friend says, trotting off to the kitchen to refill the empty margarita jug. "It sounds like there's more to the story than what he's admitted to," Jenna shouts over the sound of the blender, but I can hear her clearly.

"He's not. He's just mad that he got caught." I knew she would think that, because I thought it too. I knew it last night, but I cut him off before the conversation went that way. I didn't want to hear that he would be capable of that, but he was, wasn't he?

"Think about it, C. He said he was furious about seeing Harley's face plastered all over the news, that he was being set up to be the next Max Anderson. That would have been a blow for him to hear his estranged brother was more like their father than he was." She pours us a fresh glass.

"Then he said he saw Harley after they were crowned champions, and his rage took over." She takes a big gulp of the fresh batch, then re-fills her glass. Even though we're on our fourth cocktail, our conversation is making more and more sense as time goes on.

"It sounds to me like he was about to admit that they got into a fight, but you cut him off and forced him to admit that he fucked Alison instead." She's right. I didn't want to hear him admit it, but I refuse to defend him.

Not anymore.

"If my memory serves me right, I remember you telling me that Austin came back from a bachelor party a few years ago with busted knuckles." Damn this girl and her memory.

"You're right. He did. He said he and his friend Monty got into a fight. I brushed it off because he said Monty was a jerk and deserved it. Austin was in one piece, with only a few surface injuries, so I ignored it, hoping it was nothing." I shrug, feeling defeated, slouching into the back of the couch, head starting to spin.

"Do you remember the exact date?" she asks, walking back to the couch with our drinks, placing them down onto the coffee table in front of us. Pulling her laptop out from under her coffee table, she opens it up, waiting for my answer.

Shaking my head, I ask, "Why?"

"Because I want to see what Harley was up to around that time."

"February 2017, I think."

Over her shoulder I see her type into the search bar 'Harley Wingrove, Brawl in Charlotte', but the results are a dead end. 'Harley Wingrove fight', brings up countless videos of Harley getting into fights on the football field. *'Harley Wingrove February 2017',* are the last words typed into the search bar, and both of our eyes scan the results page.

After a moment of searching, I give up and sink back into the couch. "Wait, I think I've found something." She stalks to her kitchen, taking the laptop with her. Hurrying to my feet, I follow closely behind her, trying my hardest to focus on the blurry screen while she reads the article out loud.

"Superstar quarterback Harley Wingrove has been given career ending news today as an injury to his shoulder has been deemed irreparable. It's unclear how he obtained the injury, as his management and team have remained tight-lipped, declining to speak on the matter, but the team doctors have confirmed with the press that his promising career is well and truly over at the ripe age of twenty-three."

After reading the article, she doesn't take her eyes off the screen. She continues scrolling, typing and searching for more information about his injury, while I stand completely still, hearing her confirm what I didn't want to hear.

"There's more," she says, taking a seat next to me on the couch. "A video of Harley doing a press conference confirming his retirement."

She clears her throat before she presses play.

"I wonder why these articles didn't come up right away? They were on, like, page twelve of the search." Her brows pinch together. She rests her hand on my thigh before pressing play on the video.

"Unfortunately, I recently obtained a severe injury to my right shoulder, amongst other places. We sought first, second, and even third opinions, but it was eventually confirmed that the damage couldn't be fixed. I'll never be able to play professional football again."

He sighs, clenching his jaw, and my eyes slowly make my way to his emerald ones that stare right into the camera, and it feels like he's staring directly at me.

Talking directly to me.

He looks sad.

Broken, almost.

Not at all like the Harley I know.

My heart squeezes when I look at the young man on the laptop screen, who knows his lifelong dream has been cut short way too early at the hands of another person.

His right arm is wrapped in a sling, while his left wrist is bandaged up. There's evidence of a black eye, clearly covered up with makeup, crutches resting on the side of the table next to him.

"I just want to thank everyone for your support and love over the last few days. The next few weeks are crucial for my recovery, so please respect my privacy at this time." His smile is weak as he stands to limp out of the room, his crutches placed firmly under his left arm.

"The Eagles have no further comment." The familiar words ring out, buzzing in my head as it spins while I try to steady myself.

While they never confirmed the cause of his injury, they didn't need to.

It's obvious.

Just by looking at him, his injuries are the result of a fight. If Austin is responsible, he can't have done it alone. Harley is much bigger, much stronger than Austin. By himself, Austin wouldn't stand a chance, so it's hard for me to imagine Austin being capable of doing irreparable damage. But knowing Monty was there, too, it's written in black and white for me to see.

This was swept almost completely under the rug with next to no publicity on the fight itself. Only talk of Harley retiring, but not really the *why*. That alone tells me that the perpetrator had friends in high places and a lot of money. Or, in Austin's case, a rich, famous daddy.

Royalty in the NFL.

"I feel sick," I say, rushing to the toilet where all of today's alcohol makes its way back up.

Austin took *everything* from him.

All because of something he couldn't control. Something he still, to this day, has no idea about.

But if Austin is responsible for ruining Harley's career, why hasn't he told me?

Does he even know?

Thirty-Eight
Harley Age 23

"MY RIGHT HAND FEELS so heavy right now," Robbie jokes, flashing his championship ring toward a group of hot girls that pass us by. "We're the fucking champs, baby!" he screams as loud as he can, the word *'baby'* sung out, cars honking their horns with Eagles flags flapping around in the wind. The feeling is indescribable.

The entire team is still on a fucking high. It's been nearly a week since we were crowned the champions of the NFL, and the celebrations are nowhere near stopping.

I wouldn't usually allow myself to let go and just enjoy the feeling, but I think I have every right to celebrate.

Especially considering I'm the youngest player to ever win the Max Anderson award, aka Most Valuable Player, thank you very much. No rookie had ever won the award, but I did what the Eagles wanted me to do. What they signed me for.

Take them to the end and win the whole damn thing.

Every weekend, I was underestimated by the other team, and every weekend I showed them who was boss, ensuring the team went the entire season undefeated.

I deserved every bit of this.

Robbie and I decided to start the celebrations early tonight, with some of our teammates meeting up with us later. Even though we agreed we'd start low-key, he's not exactly hiding the fact that the 'champs are in town'.

His words, not mine.

The Globe is the first stop on our bar crawl tonight, and it's surprisingly busy for a Thursday, with a line almost halfway out the door. We bypass security with ease and, to my surprise, we're yet to be bombarded with excited fans wanting pictures, or chicks throwing their half-naked bodies at us, desperate for our attention. Desperate to screw a professional athlete.

I give it thirty seconds before we're noticed, tops.

Not that Robbie would mind, though. Hell, I've been single and celibate for so long, I don't think I would mind, either.

"The next round is on me," Robbie screams loud and clear for the entire bar to hear, causing the growing crowd to cheer with excitement. Right on cue, some barrel toward us for autographs and photos, some cheer their glasses with ours, or put their phone numbers into our back pockets, while the rest admire us from a distance.

I like those people the best.

"I don't think this week could get any better," Robbie mutters in my ear, two beautiful girls making themselves comfortable under each of his arms, while he holds onto a shot of vodka in his hands. Chuckling, I sip my beer and I sneak away from the drunk, rowdy crowd, heading to the pool table in the corner.

My face is plastered across every single television screen in this place. Even if I tried to be discreet, I doubt I'd be very successful. I guess that's what happens when you go into a sports bar the week after the biggest gaming event in American sporting history.

"Feel like a little competition?" a soft voice asks from behind me, instantly snatching my attention.

My eyes trail down, where a short, petite girl stands in front of me, a cocky smirk on her face, her right eyebrow raised.

Her blonde hair is short, tied half-up, half-down, with waves falling around her neck. She's cute, and I can already tell she's feisty. "Why not?" I reply, hiding my own smirk behind my beer glass, watching as she picks up a cue that's nearly taller than her.

"You can break. It'll give you a chance to, you know, sink a ball or two," she jokes, nodding her head toward the already racked table. "What are you doing alone in the corner?" the blonde asks. I can feel her brown eyes staring at the side of my face, probably trying to read my expression, but I know it's blank, giving her nothing.

"Hoping to go unnoticed," I say, nodding toward my face on every screen.

"No offense." She watches as I break and sink two balls. "But even if you weren't the man of the match, it'd be pretty hard to miss a six-foot-tall guy with broad shoulders and jaw that looks like it was sculpted by the genetic Gods." She laughs, leaning over the table, pushing her cleavage up directly in my line of sight.

"I'm six three, actually. And you're cheating," I tease, and she snickers in response before shrugging her shoulders, pushing her body off the table. "What are you doing out on a Thursday night?" I ask, making my way around the table to get a better angle for my next shot.

"I own the place."

"Nice." I'm doing my best to concentrate, but I can feel her body brushing up against mine now, and I miss all the balls completely.

"My turn." Lifting her cue, she steadies it over the side of the table before making her first shot, sinking her target with ease.

"You don't look like the type to own a sports bar," I say, hoping to distract her with conversation, but clearly, this isn't her first rodeo.

"And what does a sports bar owner typically look like, Mr. Wingrove?" She doesn't take her eyes off the ball while she talks, continuing to sink every ball she aims for.

Definitely not her first rodeo.

"Usually an old, sleazy guy with a beer belly." I sip my drink, knowing that's not at all true. But at the rate she's playing, the game is going to be over in a matter of seconds, and I'm liking the attention.

Sue me.

During football season, I never entertained the idea of dating or even hooking up with women. It's how I got to be the best of the best.

Give it all of my attention, get all the results I want.

"Another game?" I ask while emptying the pockets to collect the balls, centering them in the triangle.

"Not scared to lose again to a girl?" She winks, helping me.

"Do I look that fragile?" I scoff, pretending to be offended. She barks out a laugh.

"I'll break. You go get us drinks."

On my way to the bar, I bump into Robbie, who looks overly pleased with himself. "You scored yourself a little hottie," Robbie shouts over the music into my ear as he stands beside me, waiting for his drink.

"And you look like you've bagged yourself two." I nudge his shoulder with mine.

Clinking our glasses together in cheers, we both head back in the directions we came from, and I can see that not only did this little blonde break, but she sunk all of her balls, leaving the table covered with all of mine, the black ball and the white. "Ego bruised yet?" she says with her cue pressed up against the side of her.

It's obvious she waited for me to come back so I could watch her sink the black ball right in front of me, and she does exactly that without taking her eyes off of mine.

Her arrogance might annoy some, but I find it endearing.

"I told you, I'm not fragile. I'm impressed, more than anything." Smiling, I make my way over to her, handing her a fresh pint of beer.

"You know," she says after taking a sip, leaning her back against the wall. "I may be tiny, but I'm not fragile either." She nibbles at her bottom lip. I slowly close the gap between us, resting my arm on the wall behind her.

"Oh, yeah?" I whisper as my head dips so low, my lips graze against her ear.

"Why don't I take you upstairs and show you?" She intertwines our fingers, and I follow her without a second thought, both of us placing our fresh beers on the nearest table.

Letting her lead the way behind the bar, she drags us toward the stairs that lead up to her office, but not before an eerily familiar voice stops me in my tracks, body tensing.

A voice I haven't heard since high school. It's slightly deeper than it used to be, but I would recognize it anywhere.

"Are you sure you want to go up there with him?" he says, and I roll my eyes as I turn to face him.

"I see you're still not over your obsession with me, Anderson." I'm only half joking, but I know just the right thing to say to get under his skin. His laugh is loud and obnoxious. I've struck a nerve.

Good.

"I'm living the life you wanted, remember? I got the girl. I got the superstar dad," he reminds me, like I could forget. But in high school, he made it impossible. He always liked to remind me that my father abandoned me and that his dad not only stuck around, but he just happened to be my sporting hero, too.

The icing on the cake was when he hooked up with the first girl I'd ever been in love with. Actually, the only girl, still, to this day. But to me, it wasn't enough to lose our friendship. I would eventually get over losing her (I hope. Still waiting on that to happen), but he and I had been best friends all my life, so that loss hit me hard.

Bros before hoes, right?

Wrong.

He reminded me every chance he got that she was on his arm, and that his dad was in the stands watching *him* play and mine was nowhere to be seen. '*Where's your daddy, Wingrove?*' he would mock me, trying to make me lose focus as if we were on opposing teams, but it never worked.

I was too determined, and that aggravated him even more.

"Are you following me, Austin?" I ask, frustrated that he's trying to ruin my week of celebration, delaying the fact that I'm about to get laid for the first time in nine months.

"You wish." He scoffs, inching closer, his nose a hairline away from mine. "Enjoy the high you're on, superstar. It won't last," he whispers in my ear, shoving his way past me to head back to his group of friends.

"Are we heading up?" the blonde asks, and I realize I never found out her name.

Nodding, she grabs my hand again, leading me up the stairs and I follow behind her, even more desperate for the distraction.

I don't bother to take in my surroundings, and she seems more than happy with it as I scoop her tiny body up with ease, wrapping her legs around my waist.

I'm not a selfish lover under typical circumstances. If we had come up here without the interruption of Austin, I would have worshiped every inch of her body before fucking her like both of our lives depended on it. Maybe in a different universe, I would've gotten her name and taken my time with her. Right now, though, I just want to chase that release and hope she doesn't mind.

Her mouth slams down on mine, and I stop her before it gets too intimate. I don't want her to get the wrong idea. I don't want her to think that this is more than it is.

A one-night stand.

No strings attached.

She rips my t-shirt over my head and I'm thankful she's wearing a short, denim skirt that I can slide up and a white, spaghetti strap singlet that I easily pull down to reveal her tits, as it bunches with her skirt around her waist. Pulling a condom out of my back pocket, she unbuttons my jeans, reaching for my already-hard cock before I slide the condom down the length of my shaft.

Her eyes widen as she sees my size, and I wear a shit-eating grin across my face. "Are you sure you're not fragile, Blondie?"

I don't want to hurt her, so I ask to be sure. I may be arrogant, but I'm not an asshole. Taking one last glance down, she nods frantically, and that's all the permission I need before I finally slide inside of her.

I'm feeling selfish tonight and fuck, she feels so good wrapped around my cock, but I'm not selfish enough to be the only one who comes. Lucky for her, I know my way around a woman's body and know how to get them off quickly.

"Yes, right there," she moans into my ear as I pound hard inside her. Screaming out in pleasure, she begs me to fuck her harder, shaking the pictures that hang on the wall behind her. "Oh fuck, I'm going to come," she says and a heartbeat later, I feel her pussy pulse around me as I fill the condom, coming at the same time as her.

Leaning my head against the wall to catch my breath, I slowly slide out of her, placing both of her feet firmly back onto the ground before I head toward the bathroom in her office.

Emptying the contents of the condom in the toilet before discarding it in the trash, I do up my zipper before heading back out the bathroom door to meet my new friend.

"Did you just empty your come down the toilet?" She crosses her arms over her chest, nose scrunched up.

"The last thing I need is to be baby trapped, Blondie," I say as I check my appearance in the mirror before heading back downstairs.

"You don't trust me?" Her voice is sarcastic, clearly annoyed.

"Respectfully, I don't know you," I remind her without looking back.

"There you are," Robbie says, clapping his hand against my back. "Are you ready to head to the next bar? Jensen texted and said they were heading there now." His arm now rests over my shoulders and I'm even more in the mood to party than I was twenty minutes ago.

"Where are you hot shots going?" A drunk guy slurs from behind when our feet hit the pavement right outside The Globe. "The party's only just beginning." Turning, we're met with a group of five drunk men waiting for us, who don't look like they're wanting to celebrate.

One is sporting a black hoodie with his face completely on display, the rest are wearing balaclavas to hide theirs.

As a professional athlete, being approached in situations like this isn't new to me. Especially if we just beat their favorite team. And given we just won the championships, I'm going to say these guys are fans of the Jaguars and not the Eagles.

"We don't want any trouble," Robbie insists, putting his hand out for the man in front to shake, but he shoves it away.

"Well, that's too bad. I was really hoping to beat some Eagle ass," he says as he takes a step forward.

He's so close to me, I can smell the alcohol on his breath, and even though it's dark, I will remember this guy's face for the rest of my life.

"Get out of my face, asshole." I lightly shove him away, but he's a big dude. He barely budges.

"Is that a threat?" he says through a clenched jaw.

Rolling my eyes, I turn my back toward him. "I don't have time for this," I mutter as Robbie follows right behind me.

"Turn back to face me, you coward. I want to see your face while I fuck you up. I want to watch your blood as it runs all over the concrete."

"Oh, I'm so scared. Whatever will we do?" Robbie mocks, but before he can enjoy the moment, one of the masked men connects his fist with Robbie's jaw and he nearly drops to the ground after one hit.

It's officially five against two, and while we're outnumbered, we still put up a hell of a fight. Robbie knocks one guy totally unconscious, leaving four men standing as the only one brave enough to show his face gives mine blow after blow, my arms pinned behind my back by two others.

"Take out his shoulder," one of the masked men growls, holding me still, but Robbie knocks him to the ground, forcing him to let me go, right as the owner of the bar swings the doors open.

Not my fucking shoulder.

"Monty, go the fuck home. The cops are on their way," she says, addressing him by name, providing the distraction I need at the exact moment I need it.

I lunge on top of him with my fist closed, connecting it with the side of his face. Once, twice, three times, and the back of his head collides into the ground with the last hit, and only then do I stop.

When *his* blood is running all over the pavement.

My chest is heaving, trying to catch my breath while I kneel next to his limp, bloody body, more exhausted than I care to admit.

Not my fucking shoulder.

Thinking Robbie is the one to pull me off, I relax my body, falling from my knees to my ass, while I stare at the man named Monty. The man who threatened to take everything from me.

"Harley, behind you!" Robbie shouts from the left of me, and I have no time to defend myself. Forced down onto the concrete, my right arm pulled behind me, copping hit after hit with some kind of metal pole.

I can nearly feel and hear every bone in my shoulder shatter, and every muscle tear.

Not my fucking shoulder.

The pain is blinding. Like nothing I've ever felt before.

Slowly, I attempt to roll onto my back to ease the pressure, but it's no use. I'm screaming so loud, it seems silent. I cradle my shoulder with my left hand. Roaring about the pain, and for everything I know I've just lost.

Everything I worked so hard for.

I don't need a doctor to tell me the outcome.

I search for hope that this isn't the end of my football career, but the pain shooting down my arm and through every bone in my hand tells me otherwise.

My fucking shoulder.

As if the attackers hadn't done enough damage, one of the masked men hovers over me, crouching down to my level, the sound of the sirens growing louder and louder.

"You deserve nothing less," he whispers to me, spitting on me and stomping on my leg above my knee, then laying his boot into my head.

That's when everything turns black.

Thirty-Nine
Cassandra

A week.

I stayed in California for a week, hoping Jenna's apartment would swallow me whole.

I've been avoiding all contact with everyone from the outside world, trying to pretend that everything was blissful and not at all about to fall apart. But avoiding the world meant avoiding Harley, and I hated that I felt like I had to.

It felt like I was betraying him, but I guess I have been.

Time has been at a standstill.

At least, for me, it has been.

It felt like I was almost paralyzed by it, and the only person who could bring me back to life was the person who could take it all away again. I wouldn't even be able to blame him if he tried.

Austin and I have been broken up for six months now. Most people would tell you that six months isn't long enough to grieve and mourn a lost love and relationship. But when that person ends up being the wrong person for you, and the right one comes along? Moving on is effortless.

Falling in love again is pretty easy, and boy, have I fallen in love with Harley Wingrove.

It snuck up on me quicker than I expected it to, and now that I've accepted it, it's crushing me like a tidal wave, knowing he may not love me back. Or worse, knowing he does, but won't be able to forgive me for keeping this from him. But I'm not afraid of the feelings that I have.

Six months ago, I thought my heart was shattered beyond repair. I thought it would never be capable of beating the way it used to. It may be a little bruised and completely terrified right now, but it feels...different.

Stronger, almost.

Deep down in my heart of hearts, I know everything will happen the way it's supposed to.

How am I supposed to tell him? Do I just blurt it out? Do I start from my coffee with Alison? I don't fucking know.

But I do know that it's time to face the music, and that's exactly what I'm about to do.

It's getting late, the sun is setting, and I can see the lights on under the front door of his apartment, telling me he's home, and awake.

Taking a deep breath, I tap my fist on his door and wait until my eyes are met with the most incredible emerald one's staring back at me. His hair is messier than usual. He's still wearing his grey suit from the day, but his tie is hanging loosely around his neck. His sleeves are rolled up while he cradles a glass of scotch in one hand.

"Herring," he whispers, almost breathless. He wasn't expecting me home.

"Hi," I say back, pulling my eyes away from his, terrified to look in his direction, but he doesn't let me.

Dragging me by my hand, inside his apartment, he holds my body against his for a long, much-needed embrace, and I allow my whole body to sink into his, knowing it's temporary.

"I'm so glad you're here," he says, whispering in my ear, his hand scrunching my hair. My cheek is pressed firmly to his chest.

"Me too," I reply, trying to keep my tears hidden as I reluctantly pull away from him.

Sensing my hesitation, he eases his grip, letting me go, but I know he doesn't want to. I don't want him to let me go, either, but I don't think he's going to want to hold me after what I have to tell him.

"Are we okay?" he asks, with his voice still soft, but I can hear the doubt and reluctance in it, no matter how hard he tries to hide it.

"I hope so." Shrugging, I take his hand in mine, leading him to sit on the couch beside me.

I don't want to beat around the bush.

I want to cut to the chase and leave no stone unturned. But before I tell him everything I found out a week ago, I need to know what he knows about it.

"Tell me about your injury," I say to him, watching as his body stiffens. Reaching my arm out to hold his hand, to reassure him that it's okay to talk about.

"What do you want to know?" he asks.

"I know it wasn't caused during a game. I want to know if you know who did it to you," I say, taking a deep breath, eyes caged in on his.

Something flashes across his face.

Confusion, maybe?

But he shakes it away before finally opening up to me.

"We had just won the championships. Robbie and I had gone out to celebrate at a local sports bar and got attacked on our way out," he says, clenching his jaw at the memory. "I only knew the name of one offender, because the owner of the bar shouted it when she said she was calling the cops." His tone is steady as he rises from the couch to make himself another drink, only this time its water.

"What was the name you heard?" I press him for more.

"Monty, and I'm pretty sure he's in jail still," he says mindlessly as he turns off the tap.

"Chad Montgomery. Austin's college roommate." Hearing those two names together does something to Harley. His glass of water slips from his grip, shattering on the wooden floor at his feet. His once-golden face now pale, staring back at me in disbelief.

Instead of leaving him to wonder and try to fill in the blanks on his own, I tell him everything.

From my conversation with Alison at the cafe, to meeting up with Austin on the rooftop and piecing it all together with Jenna. All the while he stands silently, letting me finish, not interrupting me once.

Not a single word the entire time.

He broke eye contact with me a while ago, too.

"Harley?" I ask, hoping for something. Anything at all.

"I have to go," he finally says, collecting his keys, storming out the door.

Fumbling for my phone in my bag, I dial the one person who knows Harley better than he knows himself.

Bea.

"I need you to do something for me," I say, trying to remain calm as I shut Harley's apartment door, locking it behind me.

"What is it?" she asks.

"Go to Max Anderson's house. I think Harley is on his way there, and I have a feeling Max isn't going to like what he has to say."

"I'm on my way."

Forty
Harley

HAVE YOU EVER BEEN told news that left you feeling completely numb? Completely betrayed?

Because I have.

Growing up, all I had was my mom, and I liked it that way. She was all I knew. I'd asked her a few times about my dad, but that was mostly because the majority of the people at my school had one. It felt like I was missing out on a tiny piece of me that everybody else has.

Everybody but me.

I would overhear parents talking about my mom, and how brave she was raising a son without his father. How sad it was, because boys needed a man in their lives, and all I had was a mom who worked too much to raise me.

How else would I learn to change a tire?

How would I learn to fix things that were broken in a home?

Who would take me camping, help me catch my first fish?

My father was right in front of my face my whole life, and yet, my mother was the one who taught me all of those things.

If I was thinking with my head and not my heart, I would go straight to her house, demanding answers. But I'm not thinking rationally at all. I'm thinking about all the things I was robbed of and now I know who was to blame and why.

I didn't grow up with a father, so I don't know what it's like to have one.

But I did grow up playing football.

It was a constant in my life, and when that was taken away from me, I went to a dark place for a long time.

A long fucking time.

I went through months of physical therapy, and that wasn't just to repair the damage to my shoulder. I had injuries all over my body.

They had broken my right leg just above the knee, which required major surgery. My collarbone was so badly broken that it tore through my skin, needing three different surgeries over a two-week period.

I fractured my left eye socket, leaving my vision temporarily impaired.

And my shoulder.

My fucking shoulder.

My rotator cuff was torn completely, along with a shoulder displaced fracture. Doctors told me surgery could help, but there was no guarantee I would ever be able to throw a ball again, let alone at a professional level.

It required a lengthy, complex surgery. Even with rehab, the success rates were low.

I tried to remain hopeful. Robbie and Bea kept telling me I'd make a full recovery, and I wanted so badly to believe them. To show everyone what I was capable of.

But I didn't.

I couldn't.

No matter how hard I tried, or how long I spent in physical therapy, no team wanted me. I was damaged goods, forced to figure out a new life, a new normal, and it took me a long fucking time.

The person responsible was a person I once considered a brother.

My fucking brother.

I think a part of me had a gut feeling that it was him. It was too much of a coincidence that I'd seen him the night of the accident. The thought briefly crossed my mind, but I shook it off instantly, and hated myself for even *thinking* he could be capable. There was no way someone I valued so highly, no matter what, would do something like that.

Especially without reason.

And now I know the reason, and it was something beyond my control.

When he and I stopped being friends, I thought it was some petty high school shit. Not because we shared a father, forcing me to become enemy number one.

How could I not see it? He called me son more times than he called me anything else. He gave me pointers before, during, and after every single game. He was the one who arranged for college scouts to see me play, which turned into a full ride scholarship at my dream college. He was the one who traveled all the way from Grangewood Creek to Ohio to tell me I was the number one draft pick. He had no reason to do any of that.

Or so I thought.

If what Cassandra is saying is true, and Austin was behind my injury, did our father use his name to get him off with no consequences? Without so much as a slap on the wrist? It couldn't exactly come out that Max Anderson's son delivered the career-ending blow to the best quarterback the league has seen in years, so, of course, he paid them off.

It would have ruined his reputation.

The moment I arrive at the Anderson residence, I suck in a deep breath. Staring at the home in front of me, the life I could have had briefly flashes before my eyes. Weekends spent growing up with my siblings and bonding with my father.

Two Christmases.

A bedroom to come to when mom grounded me for breaking curfew or the one and only time she caught me drinking underage.

A mom who didn't work herself to the ground to make sure I had everything I could ever need. A mom who could make it to my games, instead of spending every night working to keep the lights on.

Reaching the iron gates, they open for me automatically, and I know Max has been expecting me.

I haven't been here in fourteen years, and it's barely changed. It has the same cobblestone driveway, the same large water fountain in the middle, and five sports cars parked out front.

Slamming my car door, I notice two cars following behind me up the driveway, and I recognize them right away.

Cassandra and Bea.

An audience.

Fan-fucking-tastic.

"Harley, will you just wait a second?" Cassandra pleads, Bea slamming her car door. But I can't look at either of them.

I know she isn't the bad guy, but like I said, I'm not thinking logically.

"This is just something I need to do," I tell them both, clenching my fists by my sides. I don't want to look at her, but my eyes never could look away.

"Then let us come with you. Let us be here to support you," Bea whispers, taking my hand in hers, but I shake her off.

I don't know how much Cassandra has told her, but Bea knows everything about that time in my life. She was there when the doctors came in to give me the news. She was there, waiting for me to open my eyes after each of my surgeries. She didn't leave my side until I was discharged from the hospital, and stayed with me until I could walk without aid. She and Robbie were the only two people who helped drag me out of that dark hole that I had dug myself into.

Nodding, Cassandra takes Bea's hand that she had extended out, standing side by side, leaving me to stand alone on the cobblestone steps as the door opens.

"I had a feeling I would see you here. It was just a matter of when." I hear his voice before I see his face.

Leave your aggression at the door, Harley, I force myself.

"Do you mind if I—*we*, come inside?" I ask, shoving my shaking hands in my pockets. Opening his front door completely, he gestures for the three of us to enter, and we do.

The house still has a double grand staircase with red carpet leading up to the second floor, but I'm not here to see what's changed and what's remained exactly the same. In fact, I don't want to be here at all, but I've come this far. I can't turn back now.

"I would ask why you're here," Max begins. "But I think I know."

Leading us into a main lounge room, he nods to the leather couches for us to take a seat. "Is it true?" The words tumble out of my mouth before anyone gets the chance to sit down and get comfortable.

"It depends what you're talking about, *son*."

There's that fucking word again.

Contemplating my next move, I take in his appearance for the first time since he opened that front door. I mean, really take him in and it shocks me that I never noticed it before. We share the same deep green eyes and olive complexion. His hair is dark, whereas mine is lighter like my mom's, but he and I have the same build, the same smile.

I guess I get my athletic ability from him, too.

"Why do you call me son?" I stare at him, leaning my elbows on my knees, intertwining my fingers through each other, all while the words *'stay calm'* are on a loop in my head.

"Ah, there it is." Leaning back in his chair, he draws a deep breath, staring at me, curious if I have anything else to say, but I don't, so he begins.

"Your Mom and I met right before Angela and I got married. She caught me by surprise. Small-town girl, paving her own way, and didn't care about my status. She wanted me for me and I loved that. I loved her, Harley. I did. But I loved Angela, too. We were seeing each other for a long while, but... Angela and I had gotten married in that time." He dips his head in shame, and I wonder if he ever thinks about all the people he hurt in his wake.

"When I found out your Mom was pregnant, I was hit with a wave of emotions. I was scared as hell, and excited, but I, I felt guilty, too. Guilty because I had betrayed my new, loving wife by falling in love with someone else. Guilty because I couldn't be the man I promised your Mom I wanted to be. And because I couldn't be the father to you that I hoped to someday be," he admits, shaking his head.

"I already had a wife. We were planning our lives together. Then Angela told me she was pregnant with Austin, and I knew what I had to do." He drags a hand down his face. "I couldn't live a double life, so I went to your Mom and told her. I told her I was married and had a baby on the way, but that I would be a part of her baby—our baby's life in whatever way she wanted. I told her I could be a dad to you if she wanted me to be. But she took off." He shrugs, clearing his throat.

"I had no idea where she went, or when you were born. But then I saw her in town at Katie's Diner, with a small boy sitting in the booth across from her, coloring pieces of paper while she drank her coffee. I just knew he was my son. I knew you were my son." His eyes watering, a lump forming in my throat.

"What did she do when she saw you?"

"She told me I could be a part of your life when you and I were both ready for it. Only, I hadn't told Angela about you. She found photos of you as a kid in my office drawer. Newspaper cut outs from winning games, photos of you and Austin together. My two sons together and the best of friends, too. Only, each one had no clue."

The realization is like a punch to the gut. My best friend was my brother the whole time, and I was the only one who didn't know.

I grew up with my brother right by my side.

Things could have turned out so differently if we had just known from the start. He wouldn't have hated me. He wouldn't have had it out for me. He wouldn't have dated the only girl I've ever loved. He wouldn't have destroyed everything I worked so hard to build.

"So, you watched from a distance?" I say and he nods.

"It was the only way I could be close to you without anyone getting hurt. Your Mom and I were the only ones who knew for sixteen years. But Austin overheard his Mom and I arguing and from that day onward, he deemed you enemy number one. He wouldn't listen to reason. He just wanted someone to hate." Cassandra's hand reaches over to touch mine to remind me that they're still there, but I dismiss it.

I don't want to be touched right now, not even by her.

"Who caused my injury, Max?" I ask him, point blank. There's no longer any reason to lie.

He's quiet, his jaw ticking, and I know he doesn't want to say the words out loud.

"I did what I had to do to protect my son." He rises from his seat, walking toward the bar in his dining room to pour himself a glass of whisky.

"Bullshit, Max. You did what you had to do to protect your fucking image." He nods, not disagreeing with me.

"You're right. I did. But I know he didn't mean to hurt you. He's a good person, Harley. He's a good person who did a bad thing." I don't know who he's trying to convince, but he's not convincing me.

"Do you know what the last thing he said to me was?" I ask. Three pairs of eyes honing in on me.

I've never told a soul about the last words I heard before waking up in the hospital, but there's no time like the present.

"He said, *'you deserve nothing less'* before spitting on my face and stomping on my head, knocking me unconscious." I see Bea flinch in the corner of my eye. Cassandra wipes away the tears that have fallen down her cheeks.

"You will never be able to convince me that the man who said and did those things to his *brother* is a good person. No fucking way." Max is shaking his head, attempting to close the gap between us, but I put my hand out to stop him.

"I'm sorry, Harley. Is there any way that I can fix this? How can I make this right? I've missed out on so much of your life. I don't want to miss out on more," he asks and I hate that his voice cracks.

It makes him sound sincere.

I want so badly to tell him to fuck off.

To tell him to call a press conference and admit that his son was the person behind my injury and my premature retirement.

That his son resented me so much, he ruined my life. And that it was covered up by his own father.

My own father.

But I'm not that person. I'm not that fucking person, and God, I wish I was.

I didn't come here for a father. I didn't come here to make up for lost time.

"My whole life, I wondered about you. I wondered who my father was and if he would be proud of me. If he would recognize me when I went pro and if I would finally be good enough for him to want a relationship with me. If he would come and watch my games. Teach me how to throw a ball. Teach me how to shave. Help me get over my first heartbreak." My eyes flick to Cassandra briefly as she continues to wipe tears off her cheeks.

"But now? Now, the only thing in life I want from you is to stay the hell away from me." Max's eyes close, a tear staining his cheek, his lower lip trembling, but a noise from upstairs demands my attention and Max's eyes fling open.

A noise from directly above where we're standing.

Austin's old bedroom.

Something takes over me. Like my life is flashing before my eyes and every single thing Austin ever did to me is at the forefront of my mind.

My shoulder injury being the most raw.

And that's why I allow my rage to lead the way; to will my body to move in ways it hasn't moved since the accident.

Max is hot on my heels as I bolt up the stairs toward Austin's bedroom, but it's no use. I'm younger than him, faster, too. The door is locked, an eerie silence coming from behind it.

I know he's there, hiding away like the fucking coward that he is.

The coward he always has been.

Slamming the side of my body against his door, it breaks off its hinges with the first connection, pain shooting through my arm in every direction.

I almost hesitate, but the ache is a reminder of what he did to me.

"What do you want, Wingrove?" he slurs, rolling his eyes when he sees me.

Charging toward him, my hand fits perfectly around his throat as I pin him to the wall.

His eyes are glossy, puffy and red. The smell of alcohol is leaking through his pores.

"Hey baby," he says, sending a wink over my shoulder, and I know he's talking to Cassandra, just to taunt me.

Moving my fingers toward his jaw, I squeeze tighter, forcing his gaze on mine.

"Don't you dare fucking talk to her," I spit, tightening my grip. Rage isn't the right word to describe how I feel right now. I'm well and truly past that point. "You took everything from me." He doesn't put up a fight, our spectators standing idly by. "You took everything from me and for what? Because of your daddy issues? We could have been brothers, Austin, but you took the fucking coward's way out." I loosen my grip as he brings his hand to his jaw to massage out the pain.

"Look around, Wingrove. I have nothing left. Everything I had is gone. My lies caught up with me." He chuckles as if it's the most ridiculous thing, gesturing his arms out for me to look at our surroundings. His floor is covered in empty bottles of whisky, dirty clothes, and takeout wrappers. It looks like he's been cooped up here for months, but Cassandra saw him in California last week.

"You expect me to feel *sorry* for you?" I ask.

"Alison left me. She's suing for full custody. Cassie left me. I lost my job. I have nothing left. Do your worst, Wingrove. Because I promise you, whatever you do to me right now will be no worse than what I've done to myself already."

He's right.

He's made his bed, and he is well and truly laying in it. He has no one to blame but himself.

"I didn't leave you, Austin. But I wish I did a long time ago." Cassandra's voice does something to me. Brings me back to life, forcing me to see sense. The urge I felt to destroy him, to hurt him how he hurt me, has vanished.

Now, all I feel for this man is pity.

I'm embarrassed for him and the pathetic life that he's created for himself.

"You deserve nothing less," I repeat his words back to him, leaving his room and never looking back.

Forty-One
Harley

I DON'T BOTHER CHECKING my rear-view mirror to see if Cassandra or Bea are following me. I have a feeling they both know where my next stop is, and that this is a conversation I need to have in private.

I would usually let myself into my mom's house with the key I still have, but not tonight.

Tonight, I knock.

"Harley?" She opens the door for me, tying up the front of her soft pink robe. "What's going on?"

I know she's confused about my unannounced visit.

"Max Anderson, mom?" I ask, watching all the color drain from her face, and a sob that she'd been holding for thirty years finally breaks free.

"I'm so sorry, Harley."

"He was right here. My father was right here. I idolized that man, mom. You knew it and you let me. You listened to me talk about how much I aspired to be like him, and you never said a thing. My whole fucking life, I looked up to him as some sort of...some sort of fucking *hero*. And this whole time, he was the coward who abandoned my pregnant mom. You let me look up to him after he abandoned you?"

"He didn't leave you, Harley. He left *me*." Her voice breaks as she brings her trembling hand to wipe tears away from her bloodshot eyes. "I had no idea about Angela when we met. I fell in love with him hard and fast. When I found out I was pregnant with you, I was ecstatic, but he panicked. That's when he told me about Angela. I gave him time to decide what he wanted to do, and she fell pregnant with Austin during that time. I was heartbroken, so I left town. Grangewood Creek had always been my home, so you and I moved back here when it was time for you to start school." She reaches for a tissue on the kitchen counter to blow her nose.

"He told me he wanted to be a part of my life."

"You spoke to him?" she asks, and I nod. "You stopped asking about who your father was, Harley. If you asked as you had gotten older, I would have told you. But you stopped caring." She's quick with an excuse, trying to defend her actions, failing to see that she isn't the victim in all of this.

"That's because I thought he didn't want me, Mom! Why would I ask about a man who I thought abandoned me? If I had known who he was, maybe my life would have been different. Austin wouldn't have resented me. He wouldn't have ruined my fucking career that I worked so God damn hard for." Confusion washes over her face while she tries to make sense of what I'm talking about.

"Austin didn't ruin your career, Harley. The fight did." She takes a step closer to me, but I take a step backward.

"Austin was behind it. Remember how one got away? It was him. He used Max's money, his lawyers, and his position in the NFL to make sure his name was never released. That's how the cause of my injury was never made public. Because of him and his father's connections in the game." Guilt washes over her. She feels responsible.

"If I had known he was my father, and that Austin was my brother, maybe he wouldn't have resented me. Maybe he wouldn't have hated me so much that he felt the need to break me. To take everything away from me," I say, tears falling down my cheeks.

"Who's the man in the photo I found in your bedside table?" I ask, remembering the picturing of my pregnant mom, next to a man with his hand on her bump.

"He was just a friend from school that I bumped into when I was pregnant. You assumed he was your father, and I didn't have the heart to correct you," she says, reaching her hand out for mine, but I cross my arms over my chest.

Lie after lie, after fucking lie.

"You should have told me." My voice trembles, my bottom lip quivering. I haven't cried since I was a teenager, and now the floodgates are well and truly open. After the accident, I wasn't sad. I was fucking pissed. How were there people out there with such little regard for others? How could they inflict so much pain, and not care, or have to suffer the consequences?

I never mourned my old life the way I should have. I finished physical therapy and was given the all clear to start my new normal. I paid movers to pack away my penthouse in North Carolina and had everything shipped back to Grangewood Creek.

I left behind anything that reminded me of the sport I loved and the career I longed for. I purchased the old Maxwell farm and put my business degree to work.

I was all guns blazing during the day, but once the sun went down, I drowned my sorrows in whisky and rarely left my apartment. I wouldn't be here if it weren't for my two best friends.

Robbie helped me hire a team of guys to do the renovation and construction on the winery, but we ended up doing most of the work ourselves. He convinced me we should put our heads together to create our property development business, and the rest is history.

I worked with my head down, kept myself busy, and stayed out of trouble.

It's like I've gone back seven years, the dark cloud looming over me again like it once did, and I need to stop it before it takes over completely.

"I just...I need time, Mom. I need time," I say, slamming the wire door behind me. She doesn't bother to call out my name. She just let's me go.

Quickly checking my phone, I see missed calls from Bea but nothing from Cassandra, and I feel it in my fucking chest. In the six months that she's been home, I've fallen head over fucking heels in love with this girl and I might have just ruined everything.

All she was trying to do was protect me. Trying to figure out the best way to tell me news that she felt compelled to. News that should have been told to me years ago by my mother.

But I pushed her away.

I let go of her hand when she reached for mine to comfort me.

I need advice, stat.

Me: Meet me at the football field.

Bea: On my way.

The icy chill reminds me that winter is well and truly approaching, and I'm cursing myself for not grabbing a jacket when I rushed out the door.

Waiting on the bleachers for Bea to arrive, I sit and remember all the memories attached to this place.

Good and bad.

Austin and I spent most of our time here. We trained together. Played football together. Bonded for years. He had no idea about his father's infidelity until he was a teenager.

When he found out, he acted irrationally.

I can't fault him for his actions back then.

But I will forever fault him and blame him for his actions as an adult.

"Hey, stud," Bea says. Her voice is soft, and while I was expecting to hear it, she still somehow startles me.

"Hey," I say, smiling weakly at my best friend.

"How're you holding up?" She takes a seat next to me, body facing mine while she tucks one leg under the other.

"Fucking shit," I reply, running a hand over my jaw. I desperately need a rational conversation. One that isn't controlled by rage, and Bea is exactly the person for it.

"How could I not see it?" I whisper, willing my body to face hers.

"None of us did." She sighs, reaching over to hold my hand in my lap.

"I know it happened seven years ago and I can't go back and change it. I know that the Andersons have moved on from it all, but this is so new to me. So raw. It feels like I'm back in the hospital and Dr. Lindo is giving me the news again."

"No one expects you to just get over it, Harley. Honestly, they're probably surprised you didn't just beat the shit out of Austin when you had the chance." She chuckles to herself.

"I didn't want to stoop to his level. His life is bad enough. I knew I needed to be the bigger person, but God, it would have felt good to break that mother fucker's jaw," I say, hoping it lightens the mood. "How's Herring?" I ask, hesitantly.

"She feels guilty," she confesses, squeezing my hand. I feel terrible that I made my girl feel like she's at fault. She was just the messenger.

"She berated Max and Austin when you left, though. I think she's been waiting a long time to put him in his place." She lets out an obnoxious laugh. "She told him that he was the 'scum of the earth' and that he '*didn't deserve to have a son as wonderful as Harley*'. Oh, and she slapped Austin so hard, I'm surprised she didn't break her wrist or knock out any teeth. It was pretty entertaining."

That's my girl.

"What are you going to do?" she asks, resting her head on my shoulder.

I got closure today. Closure I never expected to ever get and convinced myself I hadn't needed. But I don't want to dwell on that part of my life anymore. It consumed me for way too long, and I refuse to let it consume me any longer.

I want to move past it.

"I need time to move forward." I take a breath, drying my clammy hands on my suit pants. I can't move forward if I'm still stuck in the past, but it's not going to happen overnight.

"Will you tell Herring that I need some time?"

"Anything for you."

Forty-Two
Cassandra

"I really don't want to leave my apartment," I mutter, feeling sorry for myself. My home has felt overly empty over the last...I don't know, seven days.

Not that I'm counting.

Harley would usually be here with me, or we would be at his place together, but we haven't seen each other in seven long days, and it's been *hard*. I've hated every single second of it.

It feels like longer, though, because the last time we actually saw each other, he wouldn't even look me in the eye. So really, it's been nearly three weeks—aka, an eternity.

My sisters surprised me by knocking on my front door tonight, forcing me to get my ass off the couch and stop moping around. But I didn't want to when they asked, and I still don't want to and it's an hour later. I just want to be alone, but Lizzie can't grasp the concept of spending more than two days locked indoors, shocked that I've spent the last seven.

I hoped that if I'd stayed home, Harley would show up. I thought that maybe if I left the house, he would knock on my door, and I wouldn't be here waiting for him.

Deep down, I knew that day wouldn't come. Not this soon, anyway.

Bea told me that he needed space, and I want to respect that. His whole life was flipped entirely on its head, and he needed time to process and deal with it. To go through old trauma that feels new and raw. He needed to give himself time to heal.

He tried to spend Thanksgiving by himself. Mom told me to invite him over to my parents' place for dinner, but he'd texted back to say that he'd be spending it with Bea, Laney and Robbie. At least he wasn't alone.

"Too bad." Lizzie's voice is loud and firm. When she's determined, she always gets her way. And right now, she wants to take me out for drinks. I would love to think I have a choice in the matter, but I don't. I don't know why I ever bother to put up a fight.

"Bea said she has a booth reserved for us. Bridie's is apparently quiet tonight, so it'll be low-key. You need to get out of the house," Olive chimes in, while Lizzie is rummaging through my wardrobe. If Olive says the night is going to be chill, I believe her.

If Lizzie were to say it, I would run for the hills.

"Here. Wear these jeans with this red leotard, these heels, and...here, take this jacket. It's cold out."

Yes, Mom.

I reluctantly take the clothes from her, but not without rolling my eyes and muttering gibberish under my breath. She needs to know that I'm doing this against my will.

"Happy?" I ask, as I walk out of my bathroom, wearing every piece of clothing I was handed. I've added my signature red lip, put some concealer under my eyes to hide the dark circles (thanks, insomnia), and taken my hair out of its ponytail, letting it fall around my shoulders.

"It'll do." She huffs, a mischievous smirk slapped across her face. Dragging me by the arm, the three of us head out the door.

"How are you doing?" Bea asks as I slump myself down on a barstool, resting my elbow on the bar top, my cheek heavy in the palm of my hand.

"I'm okay." I smile softly at her and she smiles back. "How is he doing?" I hold my breath while waiting for a reply, but she just shakes her head in response. I don't know if she just doesn't want to talk about it because she doesn't want to hurt my feelings, or he's asked her to not talk about it with me. Or, she just doesn't know because he hasn't spoken to her about it either.

Regardless of the reasoning, I don't pry.

"What drinks are you after?" she asks, changing the subject, and I'm grateful for the distraction.

"Two margaritas and a coke, please."

"You got it."

Handing over the money, I watch as she makes our drinks, and a loud commotion comes from the door, telling me the Bridie's just went from chill to rowdy in a matter of seconds.

One guy is wearing a t-shirt with thumbs pointing at his face and writing that says '*this guy's getting married*' and I can't stop the laugh that rumbles in my chest.

"Here you go," Bea says, and I focus my attention back to her to thank her for the drinks. "Enjoy those. And hey, Cass? Don't take it too personally, okay? He's going through a lot. He just needs time to process," she reassures me, and I give my thanks in a nod before heading back toward the booth, where my sisters are waiting patiently for their first drink of the night.

It doesn't take long before one drink has turned into four, then five, then six, and I can hear my words slurring no matter how hard I concentrate.

"The next round is on me," a voice calls from over my shoulder, coming from a man I don't recognize.

"No thanks," Lizzie replies for me and I turn away from him before he can ask again. Apparently the words '*no thanks*' actually mean '*here, come and sit next to me*' because that's exactly what he does.

"Come on, let me buy you three beautiful girls a drink," he insists, but the three of us shake our heads in unison.

"Hard pass on that one. You can go now." Lizzie speaks again, waving him away, her voice having a frustrated tone while Olive stands, ready to approach security if we need to. That's the thing about Olive. She might be quiet and reserved, but she's never afraid to give you a piece of her mind or back you up in an argument if needed.

"Listen, guy." I poke my finger so hard into his chest that I'm almost convinced I've broken my nail. That doesn't stop me from continuing to say what I want to say.

"Firstly, you are not my type." I make a point of trailing my eyes down his body, with a look of disgust splashed on my face before I continue. "And second, even if you were, I wouldn't be interested in you. I have a boyfriend and I'm very happy," I say, and even though I'm drunk, I know I didn't slur my words, because I mean them.

"If you have a boyfriend, then where is he?" That's a good question, and one I would very much like to know the answer to, too. I don't say that out loud, though.

I roll my eyes, taking a sip of my seventh margarita, trying to ignore the ever-growing jerk who sits beside me.

"Let me show you how a real man can treat you," he whispers in my ear, taking my wrist in his hand, attempting to force me to stand.

"Let go of me," I warn. Struggling to rip my wrist free, he chuckles.

"I don't see a boyfriend here or a ring on your pretty finger, so as far as I'm concerned, you're up for grabs."

"Do you want to try that again, dickhead? Or would you rather a broken fucking nose? My girl told you she isn't interested, so I suggest you back the fuck up before I make you." My whole body tingles when I hear his voice, feeling all my blood rush to my cheeks. Everything in me erupts, coming to life for the first time in weeks, and I haven't even laid eyes on him yet.

"Oh, come on, man. I was just messing around. All in the name of fun, right?" the jerk says with a sickening laugh as he reaches for my hand again, apparently not getting the hint.

"Touch her again, and your nose won't be the only thing I break. I fucking dare you," Harley threatens, and the creep's eyes dart between mine and Harley's.

"I didn't mean any trouble, Wingrove. I just want to show the girl a good time. She looks a little...uptight, if you know what I mean."

His hand flies up, wrapping firmly around the man's throat, eyes glued to the man in front of him. He says, "You three, outside. Now. My car is there. Wait in it for me." Throwing me the keys, he nods his head toward the exit for my sisters and me to leave.

"You don't want your girl to watch you get your ass beat, Wingrove?" The guy's voice is rocky, breathing inconsistent, and I know that Harley has a good grip around his windpipe.

"*No*. I don't want my girl to see me be violent. She's seen enough of that lately." Harley smirks at me, and for a moment, I think my Harley could be back. But the smirk fades when he rips his attention away from me, and the three of us run out the door.

My sisters and me are sitting in the car for what feels like forever before Bridie's doors swing open, and Harley all but throws the guy out by his collar before he approaches the car door and slams it shut.

The car ride home is silent. He's barely looked at me, but he hasn't let go of my hand. Eyes kept firmly on the road. Lizzie tried to break the uncomfortable silence, but it didn't work. No one said a thing since.

He dropped my sisters off at their apartment building, where Lizzie slurred her 'thank you' and Olive sent a smile his way. Then we headed toward my apartment. The last place I wanted to be if he wasn't going to be with me.

"Will you come inside?" I ask, reaching for my seatbelt.

"Not tonight," is all he says before placing a quick, soft kiss on my cheek, dragging his gaze back to the deserted parking lot at the bottom of my apartment building.

"You said I was it for you," I whisper, wiping away the tear that's fallen down my cheek.

"You are, Herring."

Herring.

He didn't call me Cassandra.

That's all the hope I need.

Forty-Three

Cassandra

I'VE TEXTED HARLEY A few times since seeing him at Bridie's last week, but the responses I've received have been minimal, if anything at all. He hasn't been at Wingrove Estates at all, either. I have a good view of his office from mine, and his door remained shut and locked every single day.

When he dropped me back off at my apartment, I packed a bag, called my mom crying, and she came to pick me up. I've been at my parents' place since.

I needed a distraction, so my sisters and I have bunkered down in my old bedroom, with two of us on my bed and one on a mattress on the ground.

Alternating, of course.

My mom has spent hours cooking delicious, home-cooked meals for us to devour each night, while my Dad has spent his time swearing under his breath, muttering the name 'Max Anderson' every so often.

He and my Dad were chummy while Austin and I dated. Same with my mom and Angela. But the moment they found out that Austin's family knew he was cheating on me, they burned all bridges with the Anderson family almost instantly.

Cross one Herring, you cross us all.

They only found out about Harley and me recently, too, and were mortified when I told them what Austin had done to him. Turns out, my Dad followed Harley's career closely and felt so terrible for him when he had to retire so young.

"Of course, I supported the young boy from Grangewood. We needed a new champion in this town," Dad had said, making his distaste for Max very clear.

"What movie should we watch tonight?" Lizzie asks, scrolling mindlessly on her phone, hair in a braid, hanging over her shoulder.

"A Walk to Remember," Olive replies quickly. "I'm a finalist for that song contest I applied for. I need to do some research on sad movies with sad songs on the soundtrack. I don't have anything sad happening to me, and I need some inspo. Plus, I feel like a good cry sesh," she says like it's no big deal, shovelling a mountain of popcorn into her mouth.

Who willingly feels like a good cry session? After all the crying I've done over the last few weeks, I think I'm fresh out of tears to shed. My eyes feel like the Sahara Desert.

Permanently dry and red.

"You're a finalist?" Lizzie and I shout in unison, her phone falling to her lap.

"It's not a big deal, chill." She's so calm about it. Does she not realize her songs could be in an actual movie? Like a movie with real actors and real directors? I would ask why she isn't more excited, but it's Olive. I shouldn't expect anything more than a casual reaction with the occasional hint of sarcasm. She could be selling out stadiums and she'd still shrug it off.

"When do you find out?" I ask calmly, trying to not overreact.

"Not until the end of next year. They have to get all production and shooting done, then they'll decide on the soundtrack," she says while reaching for the control to put the movie on. "It has some actor guy in it that's new to the acting world, but has a huge fanbase of young girls thanks to his modelling career." She shrugs, scooping another handful of popcorn into her mouth.

Typical Olive.

"The end of *next* year?" My mouth hangs wide open.

"But that's so far away!" Lizzie whines, voicing my outrage, because my mouth refuses to do so.

"Exactly, so let's get through Christmas first. I'll keep you guys updated if I hear back."

Christmas.

I forgot that was so soon. Like, this month, soon.

It used to be my favorite time of the year. Until it became tainted with the memory of Austin proposing to me, and that his love child was due to be born on Christmas Day, if he's not here already.

Whenever the baby enters the world, I hope Austin steps up and is there for Alison and his son. I hope he's a good Dad to the innocent little boy. Though, going by what he said to Harley, I think the chances of that are slim. I still shudder when I think about it.

I know Alison will be a kickass Mom, though. She's the only parent that baby will ever need.

"I have a feeling this Christmas is going to be better than last." Lizzie squeezes my hand and I squeeze hers back, the three of us curling up on my bed in our pajamas.

We wipe our eyes as Jamie Sullivan tells Landon Carter that she's sick, crying tears of her own, and by the end of the movie, the three of us are blubbering messes, knowing Landon Carter lost the love of his life way too soon.

So much for the Sahara Desert.

***

My mom has always gone big for Christmas. She's always been known for it by the entire town.

This is the first Christmas in years where we haven't been joined by the Anderson family, and while it's quieter, my heart feels fuller. I've been tasked with organizing and decorating this year. I chose white, red, and gold (obviously) as the color scheme. I like the simplicity of it.

The snow hasn't let up at all since it started at the beginning of December, and forecasts predict it's going to be a long, ice-cold winter.

I haven't owned proper winter clothes in over a decade because winters in California barely made me shiver, so I'd completed a giant online order two weeks ago to fill my wardrobe, and everything arrived today, just in time.

I set the table with Christmas themed paper plates, paper cups, and bamboo cutlery, because mom refuses to do dishes on the holidays and quite frankly, so do I. Even some decorations are paper, so everything can go straight into the trash once the year is over.

I still haven't spoken to Harley, but I knew he needed more time and I realize that it's okay. While I know in my heart that Harley Wingrove is the person I'll end up with, this month apart has been good for me. Hard, but good.

He needs to figure it all out on his own and will come back to me when he's ready. Though, my Christmas wish this year is to see him. Even if only for a moment, but I know my chances are slim. I hope once the year is out, he and I can start again, but tonight I'm focusing on spending Christmas with my family.

Doing traditions we've done since we were kids, waking up knowing that 'Santa' came to visit. My sisters and I buy gifts for our parents every year, and label them 'from Santa' so they feel included, too.

Once we're all finally seated at the table, Dad stands to make a toast. He's sporting his own, red, ugly Christmas sweater, with a giant red reindeer nose, and a pair of 'Dad jeans', as my sisters and I call them, along with a sparkly pink Santa hat.

"To our girls. We're immensely proud of you all." We all raise our glasses in preparation to cheers.

"To family," my mom finishes as we all echo her words.

"To family."

Digging in, I go straight for the maple glazed ham, mashed potatoes, green beans, and turkey. Each portion of food hitting the spot exactly, and I struggle to breathe while undoing the top button on my jeans.

This is how Christmas should be.

"I'm so full." I slouch back in my chair, wiping my mouth with my napkin.

"I'll clean up," Olive says, pushing her chair out, collecting our paper plates and utensils before putting them in the trash.

"Go freshen up, girls. I've laid out your pajamas on your beds. It's time for hot coco and *Elf* before we play charades," mom teases.

She started doing this for us every year when we were kids and just kept doing it. It became our little tradition. A knock on the door sounds as the three of us head up the stairs, but none of us are eager to check who it is. We're too busy arguing about who gets to be the judge in charades and who gets mom or Dad on their team.

None of us want Dad; he gets too grumpy and is a terrible drawer.

"Guess I'll get the door," he huffs, knowing full well none of us were even going to bother.

Closing my bedroom door behind me, I lean against it, shutting my eyes, allowing myself to *feel*.

To feel happy.

To feel sad.

To feel confused.

But mostly, to feel grateful for the love that's radiating within the walls of this home.

The place I'd probably always call home, no matter where I live.

When I finally open my eyes, I expect to see colorful Christmas pajamas as promised, but I don't. I see something else entirely.

A ball gown.

"What the hell?" I whisper to myself, staring at the deep emerald dress, laid out neatly on my bed. A dress that's eerily similar to the one I wore to prom, only slightly different.

Slowly approaching my bed, I see a folded piece of paper sitting on top of a white orchid corsage in a box.

Put this dress on & meet me downstairs.
-H

Picking up the dress, I hold it in front of my body, staring at myself in the mirror, admiring the feel of soft satin under my fingertips. It has a sweetheart neckline with a subtle v, and I know my breasts are going to be mildly on display.

"What's going on?" I ask myself out loud, slipping mindlessly out of my jeans and ugly sweater to step into the gorgeous gown.

I let my hair down, add a nude lip, some strappy, black heels and look myself over in the mirror one last time before I make my way down the stairs, feeling grateful that the dress isn't tight fitted, and flows loosely all the way down to my feet.

While I have absolutely no regrets about the mountain of food I just consumed, I know I would struggle to breathe even more if the dress hugged my body.

Standing at the bottom of the staircase is the most beautiful man my eyes have ever seen. My heart goes wild while butterflies swarm my stomach, like they always do when he's in the vicinity.

He's wearing a black fitted suit, a white shirt and a black bow tie. His wavy, golden hair is combed over to the left, the sides having the perfect fade. His deep green eyes are hooded, his clenched and chiseled jaw ticking as he watches me carefully, slowly approaching him with caution.

"What are you up to, Wingrove?" I say as I take the hand that he holds out for me.

"I'm doing what I should have done fourteen years ago," he says, smiling at me as he leans in to place a kiss on my cheek, and my hand rushes to feel the space his lips touched.

"Have her home before curfew," Cranky Hank pipes up, my mom smacking his chest as she watches the two of us with tears in her eyes.

"Will do, Mr. Herring," Harley replies, but his eyes don't leave mine.

Not even for a second.

Closing the front door to my parents' home, he holds my hand down the front porch steps, leading me to a limo parked out front. My skin crawling with goosebumps and teeny tiny snowflakes, but I'm too full of adrenaline to feel the cold.

"Harley, what are you doing?" I ask again, as he opens the door for me to get inside the well-heated limo, partition raised.

"Patience, Herring." He smirks, sliding into the seat next to me.

Taking my hand in his lap, we sit the rest of the drive in silence.

Forty-Four
Cassandra

PULLING UP AT THE high school gymnasium, he steps out of the limo first, offering his now black gloved hand for me to take. Helping me step out, his palm rests firmly on my lower back, and I feel a sense of comfort and protection wash over me. A feeling I've missed.

It's dark out. The parking lot is covered in a thick layer of snow, but there's a clear trail leading up to the doors for us to walk along. White fog leaves Harley's mouth with every breath he takes. I should be cold, too, but I'm too overrun by anxiety, my nerve endings on fire.

"Are you going to explain yet?" I raise a brow, trying not to let my eagerness take over as he places his coat jacket over my shoulders.

"This is the night everything was supposed to change for us." He smiles, squeezing my hand, leading the way. He doesn't turn to face me, though. It's like he's trying his best to keep his composure and he knows that if he looks at me, it's game over.

Once we reach the double doors to the gym, my mouth gapes open, getting a strong sense of déjà vu. It's decorated exactly how it was at our prom, fourteen years ago. Navy and gold balloons hang from all over the ceiling with a large disco ball hanging in the center. Large lights flash, illuminating the dance floor. There's a DJ booth in the corner, occupied by Bea, as she stands behind it wearing giant headphones, smiling at us.

Harley hasn't let go of my hand.

He leads me into the middle of the dance floor when *Make You Feel My Love* by *Adele* begins to play. Gently, he pulls my body into his when he finally locks eyes with mine. My heart thunders in my chest, calmness coursing from my head to my toes.

I hadn't even realized how tense I'd been for the last few weeks and yet, suddenly, I feel like I'm floating above us, watching myself live out a lifelong fantasy.

"I love this song," I whisper, resting my cheek on his chest. Both of his hands sit comfortably on my lower back, his chin resting on top of my head.

"I know," he replies. I can hear his smile through his voice. "I don't know if you remember, but you promised me a dance at prom," he says halfway through the song.

"I remember." Closing my eyes, I focus on the sound of his heart beating perfectly in time with the song, not letting my mind wander to what happened that night instead.

"I remember this song playing, so I went to find you. Have a secret dance. But then I watched you leave." I don't think I've ever admitted that to anyone before. I ended up dancing with Austin, even though I told him I didn't want to. We danced, and I buried my face in his chest, closing my eyes so no one could tell that I was crying.

Harley was who I wanted to be there with, but I had accepted that we would never be. It was after prom that I told myself I would give Austin a real chance.

At sixteen, I wanted to be in this exact position with Harley. But getting to live this moment at thirty feels like a dream come true.

He feels like home to me.

"I left to call my mom. I wanted to tell her I was going to have one last dance before coming home, because she was expecting me. But when I came back, I saw you dancing with Austin and I knew that if I interrupted, he would cause a scene. So, I left." He shrugs. "All these things that happened over the last fourteen years led us right here," he says, taking my hand in his, leading us to a nearby table. Both of us taking a seat.

"I'm so sorry, Harley," I say as he pulls me from my chair onto his lap.

"You have nothing to apologize for."

"I thought you hated me."

"Why would you think that?" he asks, tucking a loose strand of hair behind my ear.

"Uh, maybe because I haven't seen or heard from you since you got into a fight at Bridie's. And when I did hear from you, I only got one-word responses," I say sarcastically.

"That guy had it coming," he spits, defending his actions.

"How did you even know I was there?"

"Bea texted an S.O.S," he says, placing a kiss on the back of my hand. "Plus, tonight has been in the works for weeks. Since the night at the Anderson house, actually." He says the name Anderson like its venom on his lips, and I can't say I blame him. But he shrugs it off and carries on like he's forgotten all about it and moved on.

"Organizing all of this took time. I enlisted the help of your family and Bea. Even Jenna had an input all the way from California." He laughs. "I couldn't risk seeing you, Herring. I'm so bad at keeping secrets. I would have ruined my entire plan. But when Bea texted that you were in trouble at Bridies's, I got straight in my car without thinking twice. I couldn't risk you getting hurt just because I didn't want to spill the beans on this." He gestures around the gym, puffing out his chest.

"I know Christmas is your favorite holiday, but I also know that it's been tainted for you. I wanted to give you a fresh memory that you could look back on instead. To reignite your love for the holiday." The air crackles around us, even with the music still playing. His face looks so genuine, eyes so sincere. I know the last few weeks must have been as hard for him as it was for me.

"I love you, Harley. I think part of me always has and I know you might think it's soon, but I—"

"I love you too, Herring."

I've never been happier for my words to be cut short, with the most beautiful man staring back at me, telling me he loves me, too. He kisses me softly, but I feel the need, the *want* behind it.

"Come with me. I have something to show you."

Forty-Five
Harley

RIDDLED WITH NERVES, THE limo comes to a complete stop, my stomach dropping at what's about to happen. Even though I've planned for tonight to go exactly like this, it doesn't make it easier.

Grangewood Creek is known for its snowy winters, and I can tell Cassandra isn't eager to get out of the car. Especially considering all she has on is strappy heels and a thin, deep green dress that looks like it was made for her.

Correction, it was made for her.

Her sisters and Jenna arranged it all, making sure it would fit her perfectly. She looks fucking breathtaking, and if I didn't have plans to show her what I was about to, I'd be taking her home right now, peeling off her dress gently, careful not to ruin it.

But I can't, so I'll save that plan for later.

"Put these boots on," I say before I open the limo door. Her shoes are open at the toe and she's about to step directly into a foot of snow. I wasn't going to be the reason she developed frostbite.

I met up with Lizzie earlier in the week to collect her combat boots and a pair of thick socks, so her feet wouldn't feel the cold.

She eyes off the shoes suspiciously, unable to see our whereabouts through the dark tinted windows. Slowly, she takes them off me.

"Do you trust me?" I ask, watching as she slips on one sock and boot at a time, placing my suit jacket back over her shoulders.

"Yes," she replies through a heavy, steady breath.

I open the limo door, stepping out before extending my hand for her to take. As she steps through, I watch as her eyes skate around, wheels turning in her head, but can't quite figure it out.

"Where are we?" She shivers, taking in our surroundings, lit up by the single streetlight we just had installed for tonight.

"This lot of land backs onto Wingrove Estates, and I now own it. It's where I'm planning to build my future home. *Our* future home, if you want it to be." I smile, taking her hand in mine, walking her onto the lot. It may be completely empty, but that doesn't stop me from explaining my vision to her.

"Right here will be the kitchen, fully equipped with a butler's pantry, a giant marble island and so much storage we won't know what to do with it." I walk over to the other side. "And over here will be our bedroom, where we'll have a California king bed, a huge TV to watch whatever rom-com you want, and a fully fitted black stone ensuite," I joke and she brings her hand up to hide her giggle, but she doesn't interrupt me.

"Next door to our room, you ask? Well, that's going to be for the triplets, of course."

"Triplets?" She snorts, as if it's the most shocking thing she's ever heard.

"Oh, I plan on filling this house up with so many kids. When we're ready, of course." I laugh, hoping she knows I'm not trying to pressure her into anything she's not ready for. And if we decide to not have any kids, that'll be okay too. I'll be happy living my life by her side, no matter where it takes us.

"The reason I brought you here, Herring, is because I want you in my life. I don't see a future without you in it. I never have. I want to spend my days and nights with you. I want to go to sleep next to you and wake up next to you. I want our future children to be embarrassed by our relationship because we can't keep our hands off one another." She rolls her eyes, laughing at the same time as I close the gap between us, taking her into my arms.

"I told you before our first time that there was no going back, and I meant it. I'm in this for the long haul, if you'll have me."

"Well, it looks like I'll have to sell my apartment. Or my sisters could rent it from me. Maybe the old owner wants it back. Do you think you could contact him?" she asks, her expression dead serious, and I bark out a laugh.

"About that," I say reluctantly. "I...am the old owner." Her eyes widen in disbelief as she smacks me across the chest.

"I'm sorry. I knew you wanted to stay here in Grangewood, and I wanted to help. I own the entire building, actually, and that apartment wasn't occupied." I shrug casually because it really was no big deal.

"How will I ever thank you?"

"Move in with me." It's not a question, but a request.

"I can't move in with you if there's no house built yet, Harley."

"No. Move into my apartment with me. Like, tomorrow. Or tonight. Whenever you want. Just move in with me, Herring."

"What?"

"Move in with me. You're at my place all the time, anyway. Rent your apartment out to your sisters and move in with me."

"Okay, I'll do it. I'll move in with you. I don't want to be apart from you anymore, Harley. I spent too long doing that."

"I don't want that, either. I love you, Cassandra Herring."

"I love you too."

Pulling out my phone, I create a text thread to get the wheels turning on probably the biggest surprise I'll ever pull off, without the help of the best event planner I know.

> **Me**: I'm going to need your help to pull off the impossible.

Forty-Six
Cassandra

IF YOU HAD TOLD me seven months ago that I'd be where I am now, I wouldn't have believed you.

Seven months ago, I was curled up on my couch eating choc-fudge brownie ice cream straight from the tub. Mourning a relationship while watching way too much tv.

I thought my life was over.

I mourned a relationship that didn't even deserve a drop of my tears. I spent so much time obsessing over things I thought I could change, constantly replaying everything that went wrong. On a loop in my head, every single day. I thought I would never have the future I always dreamed of.

But the truth is, everything needed to happen the way that it did. If it didn't, I wouldn't have moved back home to Grangewood Creek. I wouldn't be close to my family. I wouldn't have rekindled my friendship with Bea, and I certainly wouldn't be waking up in bed next to the most incredible man I've ever known.

I wouldn't have learned to be by myself. To love and respect myself. To make decisions for myself. To focus on myself and put me first.

If you had told me seven months ago that I would be *glad* my relationship with my fiancé ended, I would have called you insane. But I've never been happier to lose someone in my life. Because by losing him, I gained my whole world.

As I stand in my almost empty apartment with boxes stacked on top of each other, it's all too familiar. Only this time, I'm eager to start my new life and not cling to the past.

"What are you thinking about?" I hear his sexy, deep voice rumbling from behind me before feeling his arms loop around my waist.

"Only good things."

Turning to face him, I wrap my arms around his neck, staring into the emerald eyes I've subconsciously thought about since I was sixteen years old. He's dressed for comfort today as we prepare to move the last of my things to his apartment.

Our apartment.

He opted for a white t-shirt that clings to his biceps and chest with grey sweatpants, and every part of me wants to rip his clothes off and let him have his way with me for one last time in this apartment, bid farewell to each room with a *bang*. But I know we have all the time in the world to do that. All the time in the world to explore each other.

Get to know each other.

Grow with each other.

Also, we run a very high risk of being bombarded by family or Bea and Laney, and I would rather not scar them for life.

"We should get going," I say, reluctantly pulling away from his grasp, sliding on a pair of black leggings while throwing my hair into a messy bun on top of my head.

"What's the rush?" He groans, yanking my body back to his while gripping my hips firmer.

"The sooner we're home, the sooner you can do what you want to me." I wink as I giggle and shimmy out of his grip.

"Mmm, I like the sound of that. Our home." He smiles, placing a soft kiss on my lips, butterflies instantly swarming my stomach.

A feeling that I hope will never end.

There's the knock at my door I predicted, and I know whoever it is, they're here to help load some of the last remaining boxes onto the truck. "Saved by the bell." I smirk.

"You're lucky, Herring. I wasn't going to go gentle on you."

"I never want you to go gentle on me, Wingrove."

"I can hear you guys, you know," Bea's voice sounds from behind my front door.

"Sorry, I'm coming," I shout in response.

"La la la la, I didn't need to know that."

Opening the door, I find Bea and Laney dressed and ready to help, and contentment rushes over me.

This really is my home.

***

"We're about the same size, right? Can I borrow this dress?" Lizzie asks as she rummages through my wardrobe, clearly feeling comfortable and right at home in my new apartment.

"Sure. As long as you bring it back in one piece," I say to her, warning in my tone. If I know one thing about being an older sister, it's that once your little sisters borrow your clothes, it's game over. You either never see them again or they're returned in worse condition than when they first borrowed it.

I can't count the number of times I've lent clothes to Lizzie and Olive, only to never be able to wear them again.

"I always bring things back in one piece." Lizzie gasps as if I've just said the most outrageous thing in the world.

"Sorry, let me rephrase. As long as it comes back in the same condition as it is right now, then yes, you can borrow it." I raise an eyebrow at my younger sister, but she doesn't fight me on it.

"I promise I'll have it back to you in a couple of days, in this exact condition." Repeating my words, she's being sarcastic, but I'm too tired to care. I just want to curl up next to my boyfriend on the couch, watch a rom com, eat some popcorn, and settle into our home.

"Whatever you say. Now, I mean this in the nicest way possible. Please get out of my apartment."

"Okay, okay, I'm going. But wait, I need shoes too."

"Take what you need, Liz, then get the hell out." I hear her manic laughter erupt from my bedroom while she loads her arms with whatever she can carry before hurrying out, slamming the door behind her.

Sighing, I make my way to the couch, where Harley is waiting with two freshly poured glasses of Wingrove Estate's newest wine sample, popcorn, chocolate, and ice cream.

"What are we watching?" I ask as I nuzzle my head in the crook of his neck.

"I'll let you pick."

His thumb rests under my chin, lifting my lips to meet his and I've briefly lost all train of thought.

"You're going to regret letting me pick. My favorite romance book just got turned into a movie." I chuckle as I reach for the remote.

"What's it about?" he asks, trying to sound interested, even though romance movies are not his thing. He would much rather be watching John Wick or something.

"A super hot hockey player." I wiggle my brows and he nudges me with his shoulder before wrapping his arms around me. "What? Hockey is my favorite sport to read about, after all. The romance, the spice, the sexy men." Groaning loudly, I know the more I go on about it, the more frustrated he's going to get, but I can't help myself. "Hockey players are hot." I squirm out of his arms to lunge for the remote, but he's quicker, turning it off before crashing his lips down on mine, shutting me up.

"Fuck hockey," he grunts at me, and I happily give in to the temptation that is Harley Wingrove.

Epilogue

Me: Is everything ready to go?

Olive: yep, all set.

Lizzie: we're here waiting for you both.

Jenna: I'm so fucking excited

Bea: Me. Too!

Lizzie: I can't wait to see her!

Jenna: she's going to look so beautiful

Lizzie: I hope everything fits properly

Bea: I'm sure it will!

Me: Thanks, Olive.

Jenna: Did he just ignore the rest of us orrrr?

Lizzie: Rude!

Me: Olive was the only one who answered my question. Aren't you girls all in another group chat you can talk in or something?

Tucking my phone away into my pocket, I take in the beautiful girl who stands in front of me, and I can't help but stare in disbelief that she's my reality. Her long, brown hair hangs down her back in waves, with her face bare, showing the soft freckles across her nose that I love, her eyes covered by a white blindfold. "Where are we going?" she repeats for the fourth time, her voice getting more and more agitated with each ask.

I can't say I blame her, though. My response has always been, "Patience, Herring", which frustrates her more.

It's been exactly one year since I decided that there would be no going back. And I meant it. Exactly one year since I told her she was it for me and that I was all in. The last year has been a chaotic downpour of emotions, taking the good with the bad, and I don't think I would change any of it.

Do I have a relationship with Max Anderson? No. He has attempted to connect with me, but he's no longer someone I admire or look up to. Austin hasn't bothered to reach out, either. Not even to apologize after our confrontation.

His son, Milo, was born just after Christmas, but I don't know if they have any sort of relationship. I heard through the rumor mill (thanks, Mrs. Bishop), that he's been to rehab and therapy for his anger issues, though, so I guess that's better than nothing.

My mom wanted me to press charges, and I'd considered it, but I realized there was no point. The damage was already done. I didn't want to go through months of court over something that would be my word against his. There's not a chance in hell that he would ever verbally admit to anyone what he did.

It took my mom and I a little while to get back to where we used to be, too. Our relationship is almost back to where it was, albeit a little strained. I don't know if I'll ever understand why she went about it the way she did, but she did the best she could. She was all that I had for a long time, and I couldn't lose her.

All the fucked up shit in my life lead me right to this moment, with this girl in front of me. I may be about to do something in the most unconventional way, I just hope she loves it all the same.

"Now can you tell me where we're going?" she asks one last time, and finally, I take off her blindfold as we stand in the kitchen of our brand new home, together, for the first time. "Harley. Wow—" she says as she glides her hands over one of the marble countertops. "This is beautiful." Her voice is low, and I nod in agreement, smiling at her while she takes in the beauty of our home, and I take in the beauty of all that she is.

"I thought we could celebrate tonight. Maybe have a party with all of our closest friends and family," I say with a shrug, keeping my voice casual.

"But I don't have time to plan anything, Harley." She drops her purse to the ground at her feet, pulling her phone out of the back pocket of her dark jeans frantically, hoping to contact local suppliers for rush orders.

Everything has already been taken care of, but she doesn't know that.

"Herring." I chuckle, hoping to get her attention, but she ignores, pacing the room, phone to her ear, waiting for the person on the other end of the line to answer her call.

"Come on, come on, pick up."

"Herring," I repeat, my words going straight over her head as she hangs up and attempts to call someone else.

"I can't believe you would spring this on me at the last minute, Harley. I am *the* party planner in Grangewood. If people are attending my party, everything has to be perfect. Come on, pick up the damn phone!"

"Cassandra!" I first name her to get her attention, and it worked.

"Hang up the phone."

"Why?"

"Just, hang up. Please." Finally, she closes her eyes, deep breaths through her nose and out of her mouth. Greeting me with a soft smile, she places her phone down on the counter top. "No one is going to answer your calls today, Cassandra," I say, confusion wiping her frustrated expression clean off her face. I only call her by her first name when conversation is important, and this is about to be the most important one we've ever had.

Bridging the gap between us, I take her hand in mine as she stares at me, wide-eyed. "What are you doing?" she whispers, her bottom lip trembles.

"I know you never want to be engaged again," I begin, but my impatient girl cuts me off.

"No, I would happily be—"

"Let me finish, Herring," I urge her, raising my eyebrow as I place a kiss on the back of her hand. "I know you never want to be engaged again, which really fucking sucks, because I want to marry you." I pause, waiting for some kind of interjection, but she doesn't say a word. I can tell it's taking everything in her power to be silent. "I want nothing more than to marry you, but when you kept telling *everyone* you never wanted to be engaged again, I had to think of a...loophole."

Silence, still.

"In our room upstairs is a box that has a ring in it, made to live on your left ring finger, but the issue is that it's an engagement ring." I give a lopsided smile, watching as she throws her head back, rapidly blinking her tears away, throat bobbing from the lump she's swallowed. Slowly bringing her hazel eyes back to mine, I continue. "Next to the engagement ring sits it's matching wedding band. Because I don't just want you to wear the engagement ring, I want you to wear both. I don't just want you to be my fiancé, I want you to be my *wife*, and I would love nothing more than to be your husband." Wiping the tears away from her cheeks, she nods frantically, but I'm still not finished.

"I'm not asking you to marry me so we can be engaged and get married eventually, because while I do want to marry you, I want to do it today. I want to be able to tell everybody that you're my wife and

I want that to start today. So, if it's okay with you, Jenna is waiting upstairs in our new bedroom. She has her team with her to do your hair and makeup exactly how you want it." I take a deep, steady breath, watching her tears as they freely fall.

"After that, she'll help you put on your custom-made wedding dress that we've had tailored to fit you perfectly. Once you're ready, Hank will be waiting at the bottom of the stairs to walk you down the aisle to meet me. Does that sound like something you might want to do?" She's silent for a beat, so I quickly interject with a second option.

"Or we can be engaged for as long as you want if you're not ready to get married today, and we can use today as an engagement party. There's a dress upstairs for both options."

"I've never wanted to do anything more in my life," she finally says, leaning in for a soft kiss before turning on her heels to head for the stairs.

"How did you pull this off?" she asks over her shoulder.

"I had a lot of help. Oh, maybe try to write some vows while you're getting ready." I wink before heading to our backyard, where everything is set up and ready to go.

She told her sisters when she first moved back home that she wanted to get married at Wingrove Estates, but the venue is the only thing I decided to change according to her actual plans. Our home got built just in time. I thought she would love it if we got married here instead. And technically, it is a part of Wingrove Estate, it's just at the very back.

We arranged a giant marquee to be set up in the backyard for the reception, with an enormous dance floor for our guests to enjoy and dance all night. Round tables with white tablecloths, gold chairs, and candles with white orchids for the centerpieces, all scattered around the outskirts of the dance floor for when our guests are seated.

For the ceremony, there's a white carpet down the aisle for her to walk down to meet me with the same chairs sitting on either side. A rustic, wooden arch with a handful of white flowers in the corner stands tall at the end of the altar, for us to say our vows and commit forever to each other.

I was determined to pull this off, but couldn't have done it without everyone's help.

"How're you feeing, Stud? Are you ready for this?" Bea asks, sipping on her glass of champagne.

"I'm so ready," I reply, taking the glass of champagne from her hands, chugging it before she gets the chance to take it back. Maybe I'm more nervous than I thought. "I just hope she shows up," I joke, but on the inside, part of me is genuinely worried. This is a lot to ask of someone, especially at the last minute.

"I mean this in the nicest way possible. Shut the fuck up. Let's go suit up."

Cassandra

I take the stairs two at a time until I'm staring at our closed bedroom door in shock.

I would have said yes to marrying this man and stayed engaged to him for as long as he needed, but the fact that he wanted to make me his wife above anything made my heart feel weightless, floating way above the clouds. He paid attention to the things I wanted in ways no one bothered to do before, and with that alone, I knew today was going to be perfect. As though I were the one to plan it myself.

I trust my best friends. I trust my sisters. And I trust my almost husband to have planned this day exactly as I pictured it twelve months ago. Only now, my groom isn't faceless. He's very real, very perfect for me, and will be waiting for me at the end of the aisle to commit to me and commit to us, forever.

"Here she is," Jenna says, a smile on her face and tears in her eyes. Her hair and makeup are both done, while three gold satin dresses hang on clothes hangers beneath the arch window, my dress remaining hidden in a garment bag, hanging above theirs.

"How did you guys do all of this?" I ask, taking a seat on the chair labeled Future Mrs. Wingrove.

"He was very determined." She smirks as she parts my hair, ready to turn me into a bride.

"How did you know my dress measurements?" I ask, mind going a million miles a minute, a thousand questions on the tip of my tongue.

"Lizzie borrowed clothes from your wardrobe, remember?" She laughs as we wait for her curling iron to heat up completely.

"And my shoes." I gasp, remembering the exact moment. "That was five months ago! You sneaky bitches."

Staring at myself in the lit-up vanity, it hasn't hit me yet that today is my wedding day. I'm getting married to my soulmate.

"Oh, before I forget. Here," my best friend says, handing me a white velvet box.

I hesitate to open it at first. Not because I'm second guessing everything. The complete opposite, actually.

"It's beautiful," she insists, encouraging me as I feel my heart hammering in my throat, hands trembling. Forcing myself to take a breath, I shimmy the nerves away before they wash over me entirely. Opening the white box, my stomach flutters, eyes well with tears, bottom lip quivering, when I see the ring he's designed for me.

A beautiful, emerald stone, oval in shape, set on a dainty, plain gold band. Beside it lay two thin gold bands with smaller diamonds wrapped all the way round.

"They're to complete the set," Jenna says, answering the question I hadn't yet voiced.

Why are there two?

"One is for your wedding band, and the second has two potential uses. Either for your first wedding anniversary, or for the birth of your first child. Whichever one comes first." She smiles softly at me in the mirror, continuing to do my hair.

Fanning my face with my hands to keep the tears at bay, I slide the engagement ring on my finger and leave the other two in the box, even though I intend to have one of them on my finger in a matter of hours. The other will stay in the white velvet box until this time next year.

I'm not in a hurry for kids. I want to be selfish and spend as much time alone with my future husband as I can before our lives flip completely.

"Are you excited to be living near me again soon?" I ask Jenna. She's about to work on her very first film set, and the movie is shooting in Grangewood Creek. At Wingrove Estates, actually.

"You have no idea how happy I am to have you be a three song drive away rather than two and a half movie lengths by *plane*." She beams, spraying my hair to keep it in place. The cast and crew will be living in the old Mercury Hotel that Harley and Robbie have completely redone and turned into apartments.

"Do you think you'll see much of Cole Green?" I ask with a smirk, watching my best friend shift uncomfortably on the spot.

"Ha ha, very funny. He's the main character and I'm the lead hair stylist. He'll be in my chair every day, I assume," she says, refusing to make eye contact. She's hiding something from me, and I'm determined to get it out of her.

"Why are you staring at me like that? I can feel your eyes burning a hole in the side of my face, deep into my soul." She shudders.

"What are you not telling me?" I raise a brow as she releases my hair, taking a step back.

"What do you think?" she asks, changing the subject.

She's used three diamond hair pins to pin up the side as the rest of it falls in large brown waves down my back. I never doubted my best friend's ability to do my hair on my wedding day. Having her here as my maid of honor just feels...right. I couldn't get through today if she wasn't by my side.

"I love it, but stop trying to change the subject."

"Fine. I sort of think I...met someone."

"Who?"

"Last night, actually. I was invited to the Film and Television awards as a guest. He came back to my hotel room and we just...yeah." She shrugs. "Something about him just, set me off, in a way. I've never felt anything like it." She groans.

"What's his name?"

"We didn't tell each other our names. We slept together. He spent the night. The next morning, we both had flights to catch. He was gone before I woke up."

"How was the sex?"

"I don't even think the word 'phenomenal' is strong enough to describe how good it was. But I have the next three months to completely forget about him."

"Maybe Cole Green will be a nice distraction for you." I wink in the mirror as she rolls her eyes.

"Doubtful."

As we move onto my face, we opt for a soft glam, with my lips the key feature to make a statement.

Crimson red.

"Can I see my dress now?" I ask impatiently. It's been staring back at me, still in the garment bag. All I need is my best friend to give me the ok, and she does.

Leaping off my seat, I grip the bag by the hanger, unclipping it from the ledge it's been hooked on. Finally able to unzip it, an audible gasp leaves my mouth while I stare at the gown in front of me.

It's ivory in color, made from a Nouvelle satin material, spaghetti straps, and a soft, scooped neckline. Accompanied by a ruched bodice and a waist-high slit in the flowy, yet slightly puffy skirt.

Shimmying out of my jeans and singlet, I slip the gown over my body, and it fits like a dream.

"Pockets?" I ask, sliding my hands into them, raising a brow at my best friend.

"That was my addition." She chuckles.

Of course it was.

Twirling in the mirror, I notice the deep V back with satin buttons trailing down the hem.

The dress is immaculate.

"Your dress is the only thing Harley hasn't seen. It looks perfect on you," my Mom's voice comes from behind me, trembling slightly. She stands in the door way, wearing a soft pink dress that screams *mother of the bride*.

"Knock knock, we need to put on our dresses." Lizzie's voice is next from behind my mom's shoulder.

"You look incredible," Olive says to me while Lizzie eyes off my dress like it's the first time she's seen it.

"Enough sappy shit, let's get our dresses on and get this show on the road," Lizzie orders, clapping her hands together, getting everyone organized.

Once we're all ready, my sisters and Jenna make their way down the staircase, and I follow slowly behind them, where my father stands, face as stoic as ever, but his hand is shaky as he reaches it out for me, eyes glazing over, looking me up and down.

"Is old man Hank feeling nervous?" I smile as I take it, letting him guide me down the last few steps.

"Just something in my eye, honey. You need to have someone come and dust your house."

"My house is brand new, dad." I smile, hugging him tight. His deep breath quivers in my ear.

"Are you ready for this, pumpkin? I know you didn't have time to prepare like most brides."

"I didn't need to prepare, dad. Not this time."

Make you feel my love by *Adele* plays, and the guests all rise.

Linking my arm through my father's, he takes one last look at me before we begin to walk, and Harley turns to face me.

Harley.

Wearing a black fitted suit, a white shirt underneath with black buttons, a black, skinny tie and black shoes to complete the look. He oozes sex appeal and God, I'm lucky.

"Hi." He smiles as we make it to the end of the aisle.

"Hi."

He breaks eye contact with me to quickly shake my father's hand and give him a hug as my father whispers in his ear before letting him go.

"You look perfect." He gives me a soft kiss on the cheek, holding my hands in his.

Standing in front of the celebrant, our friends, our families. "So do you," is all I say. Because I know if I keep talking, I'll burst into tears.

Happy ones, of course.

Looking over his shoulder, I spot a very emotional Bea as she stands as his best maid (as promised), and Robbie is behind her as a groomsman.

"Now for the vows," the celebrant says after going through all introductions and formalities.

Harley pulls his piece of paper out of his pocket. Taking a deep breath, he holds one of my hands in his while the other shakily holds his hand written vows.

"Cassandra Herring," he pauses, releasing a deep breath. "If you had told me at sixteen that I would be standing here in front of you, ready to commit for the rest of my life, I would have wholeheartedly believed you." He smirks at me, emerald eyes sparkling when he looks into mine, and the crowd laughs.

"For those of you who don't know, I've had a crush on Cassandra since pre-k and while there were minor setbacks, I always hoped we would find our way back to each other." His voice shakes, but he pushes through it. "The moment she wandered into Wingrove Estates, looking for a job, was the moment I knew the universe had my back and was giving me a second chance at the life I'd always dreamed of. Herring, I vow to love you, honor you, and protect you for the rest of my life. I promise to have a fresh pot of coffee waiting for you when you wake up in the morning, and make sure your bookshelf is filled with all the romance books you could imagine. I promise to fold and put away all the laundry. And most of all, I promise to give you the life you always wished for." Looking up from his piece of paper, he winks at me, puffing air into his cheeks while folding his piece of paper to place back in his pocket.

How am I supposed to compete with that?

"My Mom once told me 'you don't know how much love you have to give until you meet the person you're meant to give all of your love to'. I thought I knew what love was, but nothing could ever have prepared me for this. Nothing could ever have prepared me for what it felt like to love and *be loved* by you. You help me face my fears, and while I will never jump into that damn creek again, you support that. You support all of my dreams and want all the same things in life that I want." I pat the tears in my inner corners so they don't fall and ruin my make-up.

"There was something you said to me exactly one year ago today that I always wished I'd said back to you but never got the chance. Until now. I'm going to say it in my own words. I'm all in, Harley. There's no one else. There's no doubt in my mind that you're the person who was made for me. There's no going back. *Not for me.*"

The End

What's Next?

Curious to find out about Jenna and the mystery man who she can't
stop thinking about?
Truthfully...me too.
Their book is next!

In the mean time, follow me on social media to stay up to date!
Tiktok: jadeyoung.author
Instagram: jadeyoungauthor
Threads: jadeyoungauthor

Acknowledgements

My incredible husband.

Thank-you for encouraging my silly little pipe dream, and helping me turn it into something so much bigger than I ever imagined possible.

I love & appreciate you and our little family more than I could ever put into words.

Printed in Great Britain
by Amazon